MW01489038

LADY PRESIDENT

ISBN 0-9654507-0-8

Library of Congress Catalog Number 97-92604

Carbajal, Xavier Joseph   Jodway, Sherry Lynn

Lady President / Xavier Joseph Carbajal and
Sherry Lynn Jodway-1st ed.

1. Title

For more information contact: New Future Publishing, Inc., 2222 Fuller Court Suite 505A, Ann Arbor, Michigan 48105

Printed and bound in the United States of America

Typeset at Beljan, Ltd. of Dexter, Michigan

This book is dedicated to the men and women who serve and have served in the United States Military to protect our country and our Constitution so that we have the freedom to live, choose, think and learn.

A special thank you to Alex, Bert, Uncle Ben, Uncle John, John and Mr. Lesinski, Uncle Eddie, Uncle George, 'Big' Uncle John, Uncle Chuck, Uncle Dave and all our other family and friends who served this country.

In memory of my father

Staff Sergeant Henry Carbajal
U.S. Marine Corps

and my grandfather

Private Santiago Tafoya
U.S. Army

This book is dedicated to Princess Diana
who campaigned for human rights to ban the use of land mines
and tried to help bring peace to Bosnia and the world.

LADY PRESIDENT

PART ONE

ONE

VICE-PRESIDENT MARIE ARCOLA adjusted her chair, squinted her tired eyes and finally closed the Central Intelligence Agency's report on the Iranian Disaster. She straightened the pages into the files and placed them in front of her, on the edge of the desk. A pair of strong, dark fingers began to slowly crawl over and under her silky blond hair. The fingers took a journey, tantalizing the skin on her neck and temples; warm, tickling now, down the back of her neck, always playing with the ties on her sheer pink nightgown. Softly she sighed, her head tipping back to feel his kisses against her forehead.

"Umm. Darling, before you start driving me crazy. Did you write all the checks for the bills? And are the kids getting ready for bed?" Marie asked, welcoming the wonderful hands, massaging her shoulders.

"Everything is under control, my love." David said, causing his wife to giggle with his attempted impersonation of Cary Grant. The streetlights on the subdivision off of Bradley Avenue near Chevy Chase Circle were relaxing and hypnotic to watch. Drizzle on the December evening waved in gentle sheets, slightly bending the reflection of the streetlights, looking almost like snow. Two houses were already decorated with Christmas lights of blue, red, green and yellow. A set of white lights streamed up the second story of one of the cobblestone houses, flashing a long trail up to the brightly lit star at the top of the chimney.

"What are you thinking about, my Marie?" The tall Latin man smiled, running his hands over his beautiful wife's belly as he kissed and nibbled her ear.

"I'm just looking at the Christmas lights." She purred resting her head against his arm, running her fingers up and down his forearms, slowly moving to the jazz music, playing on the radio.

"Every year Pete and Tim always try to out-do each other with the decorations. Look at those flashing lights on Pete's roof. You could land airplanes with that many lights." David chuckled.

"What's wrong, honey?" He asked, when she didn't smile.

"I'm just worried because of the military reports about that explosion in Iran. And those bombings in Cairo last week at the airports. I don't know why you have to fly out to Tokyo right now. Maybe you should wait a while. I just don't know why you have to go." She said, holding his arms tightly, her deep blue eyes pouting up at him.

"Marie. I have to go because I own the company. It's good politics. It'll mean by this time next year, I'll be selling the new line of cellular communications equipment to China, Japan, and most of Asia. I've been flying for twenty-nine years. Now let's talk about important stuff. Did you call the decorator?" David said with a hug.

"Yes, I did. They'll be here on Friday. I don't know why you don't put the decorations around the front of the house with the kids like you used to."

"What? Remember what happened at our old house. Our families spent the holidays with a lovely view of plywood boards in the living room. Right there, next to the Christmas tree. Your brother still gives me boxes of nails and tools on Christmas, just to make certain I don't live that one down." She smiled and pulled him closer, both of them breathing harder; David's nibbling turning into bites and kisses.

"Do you realize, Madame Vice-President, that this is the first time I've been able to kiss you all week without a secret service agent watching me or a page saying 'Oh. Mr. Arcola, it's you. I'm sorry, but do you have an appointment?'"

"Mmm. Please don't stop kissing me." Marie giggled, feeling his nibbles tingling her neck. He slowly played with the straps on her gown with little bites.

"Oh, David. Everything just feels so right in our lives. I've already had offers for three of my children's books. I can finally slow down. David, that tickles. Now pay attention and wait until

4

the children go to bed." Marie laughed, pulling her husband closer.

"What happened to that dream about becoming the first lady President?" David asked in one of his playful impersonations.

"That was before Shelley and Francis. Besides, the poles show that Senator Thomas is almost eighty percent certain to win against President Johnson. We can move back to Connecticut and live happily ever after. You even said you wanted the children to go to Quinnipiac for law school. Remember?" Marie tilted her head to give him an intimidating smile.

"Oh yeah. I did say that."

"And you did say once Arcola Electronics topped a hundred million we'd finally have that second honeymoon."

"I thought we already had our second honeymoon?" David said, winking his big dark eyes, making a funny face, attempting to avoid the question.

"Okay. You don't have to be President." He looked into her dark blue eyes and ran his hands up and down her body. "You are such a beautiful woman, Marie. All the bad times we've gone through. You've made me such a lucky man." David pressed his lips to his wife's. Their embraces became so strong, so magical. Marie took David's face in her hands and looked deep into his dark brown eyes. Their mouths nibbling and tasting each others lips and necks. Their bodies rubbing against each other with every kiss and every touch.

The dark walnut door opened slightly. David and Marie slow their lovemaking and grin as they glanced across the room at the sound. The door opened another few inches and stopped with a shrill creak. The little blond haired girl struggled to peak into the bedroom at her mother and father. Her younger brother, Francis, squeezed underneath her, widening the opening of the bedroom door with an irritating screech.

"Mommy." The little blonde, blue eyed girl whispered loud, pulling up at her pajamas.

"Yes, Shelley dear?" Marie sighed and checked her gown. Francis rushed into the bedroom and plopped his toy airplane and football on top of the bed.

"Mommy." Shelley glared with her little hands on her hips.

"Dad. Can we please have some privacy?" David chuckled and checked to make sure his pajamas were buttoned properly.

"Privacy? Oh, yes. I guess this means I better let you ladies have your little conference. I'll just go brush my teeth." David said, grinning at his wife. Shelley leaned over to peer around the corner as her father walked down the hallway. She rushed to her mothers arms, pulling her over to the bed.

"Francis and I have to talk to you. It's about daddy's Christmas present. Francis and I don't think it's a good idea to give him a tie. We always give him ties." Shelley said folding her arms across her chest, using her mother's pout. Marie smiled with relief, thinking there was a more serious crisis.

"Well. Let's see. A Christmas gift for daddy." Marie said, with Shelley and Francis snuggling closer on the quilts, next to their mother.

"How about a wallet?" Marie suggested, running her fingers in circles through Shelley's shiny blond hair. Francis held out his favorite football. He struggled with the words, in his five year old voice. "This would be nice." Francis said.

"Honey, that's a wonderful idea. Daddy loves sports."

Shelley turned and looked up at her mother. "How about something for his golf bag. Like those cartoon mittens that go on top of the golf clubs?" Shelley asked with a yawn.

"Of course. Francis and Shelley, you two are so smart. What a good idea. But. Shhh, this is just our secret." Marie pulled her babies close to her then scooted them off the bed.

"Ok, it's sleepy time. Are your suitcases packed for your trip to China with daddy tomorrow?" Marie asked. Francis nodded and yawned, holding tight to his football and toys.

"Yes, mommy. We're all packed."

Marie gave them both a quick pat on the behind, scattering them, giggling towards the hallway door. Shelley stopped at the doorway. "Mommy. Will you become President someday?" Shelley said rubbing her tired eyes with a stretch and a yawn.

"We'll see honey." Marie said with a smile.

"Even if you don't become President, I'll still love you. Cross my heart. I just love you being my mommy."

Francis emerged from the dark hallway with a slap to his

sisters shoulder. "Tag. You're it." Francis chuckled with a hoarse laugh.

"Mom. See what I have to put up with? Frankie is such a child." Shelley rushed to give her mother a quick hug and kiss.

"Sweet dreams, mom. I'll see you when we get back from our trip. I love you." Shelley turned and charged out the door into the hallway after her screeching little brother. The little girl's body faded into the darkness of the corridor and the glowing night lights. Shelley cautiously opened doors, trying to find Francis.

"I love you too, angel." Marie said. David tip-toed in from the master bathroom and slid his hands up and down Marie's body. Their warm kisses played, both of them trying to breathe. Their fingers hungry to touch. David rolled his tongue down her neck to her breast.

"Oh, David. How did we get so lucky?" Marie sighed.

"We worked hard and worked together. Even through the rough spots." David said, loosening the ties on Marie's gown. "Besides, we did get lucky. Hey look. I'm wearing my lucky pajamas. Nyuk, nyuk." David said with one of his Three Stooges impersonations of Curly. Marie gave David a scolding look, shaking her finger.

"Do you know I got a phone call from one of Frankie's kindergarten teachers. He keeps going around to them saying 'Hey, what's up toots.' Now I know he got that from the two of you watching your Three Stooges videos." David moved away, picking up his pillow, heading for the door. "Where do you think you're going?" Marie giggled.

"Why. I'm going to sleep in the living room." David tilted his head with a sad face.

"You come back here. I'm not finished with you. Remember, you're wearing your lucky pajamas." Marie cooed, pulling the sheets to her breast, tossing her nightgown to the floor.

David's eyes widened and he crept back to the bed. "Yes. As you can see. I have on my lucky pajamas. You gave these to me on our seventh wedding anniversary, in Seattle." David said mimicking Peter Lorre, lifting up the sheets to take a peek at his naked wife.

"No. It was our fifth anniversary. Boy are you getting old." Marie giggled and rubbed her legs, warming his thighs, slowly nibbling his ear.

"Yes. Old like a fine wine." He said, kissing her naked shoulders.

"More like an old dog." Marie teased. A chill made her shiver and she pulled David closer, wrapping her arms and legs around his body. David nuzzled his chin, placing wet kisses around his wife's breast, his hands slowly stroking the small of her back. She willingly responded by opening her legs and slid her feet up and down his thighs.

"I always think you'll forget me." Marie sighed, feeling her husband's hands warming her belly, slowly moving down her thighs. "You won't forget me, will you David?"

His breath was hot against her skin with every kiss. "I love you more and more each day, my Marie. I will love you forever and beyond."

She clasped her arms around his neck, running her hands wildly up and down to the small of his back; their tongues hungry with each wet kiss. Cautiously, like a mother, she listened for Shelley and Francis; softly moaning, her eyes rolling back, closing. Holding hands, their fingers locked with the heat of their bodies flowing in warm waves, to the jazz music, that was quietly playing on the radio.

TWO

NGELIC SHADOWS ETCHED up the climbing, marble
white pillars of the National Cathedral, dancing colors
from the stain glass windows, down across the barrel of
the rifle, aimed down at the President of the United States of
America. The Hammond organ groaned out low, vibrating the
walls, drowning out the sound of the bullets being clicked into the
chambers of the guns. One by one. Joey glanced down at his wrist
monitor, waiting for updated information from Dewey.

"Dewey? Where is it?" Joey whispered hard into the microphone on his headset. The screen on his monitor was still a blank
blue. Below, the mass continued while the priest continued through
his homily. Joey half-listened, something about two brothers named
James and Jude.

"The danger of false teachers, was the concern, that Jude tried
to emphasize to the people. While James, his brother, emphasized
the importance of faith. That no matter what. Faith in God was
the true, ultimate power of the spirit." The priest paced as he
talked, moving back and forth in front of the altar, swaying his
green, purple and white silk robe. The scope of the rifle stayed
focused on the head of the President.

"At times, we may wonder how these two brothers might have
been, in a time of religious discord. In a time of great troubles.
With war. Slavery. Starvation and disease. James and Jude, and
their works are an example of our own modern world. With it's
conflict's in our beliefs, and the need to have faith to conquer
evil." The priest stopped. Joey rolled over and noticed his brother,
Jason, crouching down at the end of the railing. Jason gave a
'thumbs up'.

"Ok. Look alive, bro. Dewey's having a problem with his electronics. One of those guys down there is going to try to kill the President." Jason whispered into the headset. Joey pushed backward against the overhang, anxiously breathing, peering over the side. The congregation stood to the upraised hands of the priest. The organ followed the voices of the choir as the song began. The people began to sing.

"Angels we have heard on high . . . Gloria. In excelius deo . . . Gloria . . ." Joey quietly sang. A voice interrupted over his headset.

"Joey stop singing until you can learn the words. You're messing up the communications. Can you see the President?" Dewey said in a panic. The altar boys passed the wine, water and hosts to the priest. Ushers stepped to the front of the church and passed the baskets for offerings into the pews. Secret service agents adjusted their positions; three to the left of the President, three to the right and two behind the President. All of them shuffling cautiously in the pews.

"Joey, can you see the President?" Dewey whispered into the microphone; panic in the tone of his voice.

"I got the President. Anyone one around him is a piece of cake. One. Two. Bang."

Joey squinted his eyes and tapped the side of his monitor screen. The blue screen faded to black. "Dewey. My monitor just went down." Joey anxiously twisted, gazing up over the top of the railing. A series of clicks were heard through the headsets.

"Hold on. Jason? Jason? Did you get the digital make? Trench? Fielding? What about the doors?" Dewey called out, trying to adjust the transmission on his computer display. A man in a dark silk suit smiled and pulled his church program close to his face.

"Amen, brothers." Fielding talked softly into his wire.

"Amen, amen." Trench chuckled, whispering as he checked his wool suit for white specks of lint. Another man raised a rifle to the top stairway rail. Slowly he shifted his body, blending back into the shadows, always keeping his eye on the scope, resting calm, aimed at the President. Joey turned his monitor upside down and gave it a shake. The monitor still showed a blank blue screen.

"Dewey, who the hell am I looking for? And how many are down there?" Joey adjusted his Ruger.

Jason scooted across the floor. "Easy bro. We'll both get the target. Remember, one, two." Jason smiled crinkling the scars on his face.

The priest cleared his throat and raised out his hands to the congregation. ". . . Peace be with you." "And also with you!" The church echoed in response, with the congregation standing. "Let us now offer the sign of peace."

Handshakes were exchanged with smiles and hugs. A man patted the President on the shoulder. A woman turned in her pew and gave him a quick kiss on the cheek. Trench glanced through the crowd, trying to keep his eye on the President. He stepped a few pews closer, in the aisle, towards the President.

"Sorry, gentlemen. Improv time. One of those guys down there is the bad guy. And he's going to kill the President." Dewey said, reaching for his Glock, rushing toward the stairs. A gunshot rang, echoing throughout the cathedral. One of the secret service agents shielded the President, but collapsed against the pew, holding his chest from the bullet wound. Two more agents pulled at the President, struggling to free him of the pew while the church went into a frenzy. Another bullet exploded and echoed out. The congregation shuffled and reeled to get down in the pews, screaming in panic. A woman agent grabbed at the assassin and was downed by his bullet. The assassin slapped a velcro strap and wires around the President's neck and screamed out. "You will pay! You will all pay! Your country will pay!" The assassin yelled, revealing a detonator in his hand; the blinking red light, drew Jason's attention. "I have a bomb! I will kill us all!"

The secret service agents backed away. The terrified men, women and children pushed away, against the backs of the kneelers. A little girl fainted and was dragged by her mother, down to the floor. Jason calmly stood up with his rifle aimed and whispered into his headset. "I've got the right arm and the trigger. One. Two."

Joey smiled and rested his rifle on the railing, aiming down into the crowd. The assassin started swearing and pushing at the President. He kicked a woman on the floor out of the way. The scope was sighted at the President and then back at the assassin.

Trench slid himself across the pew, up under the bench, slowly lifting the kneelers.

The assassin began kicking the President with his leg, frantically studying the secret service agents with their guns held out, aimed at his face, head and chest. "I've got a bomb! Lower those guns!" The assassin yelled, smiling as the agents obeyed.

"Set the detonator down!" Fielding said; his eyes squinted cold, his head tilted a degree to focus his gun sight, with the barrel of his 649 touching the assassins hair. The assassin grinned and laughed, raising the detonator to remind the secret service agent.

"Fuck you, you pig!" The assassin cursed, spitting and pushing the President almost into the aisle. The President shook, his hands held in the air, as he stumbled on the kneelers. Jason, Joey and Fielding studied the detonator held in the assassin's hand. The button glowed, recessed an inch or two away from the assassin's thumb. The triggers were pulled. The bullets whistled from the barrels.

"One. Two, bro!" Jason smiled, satisfied as his bullets hit their targets. A bullet hit the assassin's wrist, another bullet hit the assassin's chest. Within a fraction of the same second, Joey hit the target; a splat blistered the assassin's head, forcing him to blink his eyes, spastically. In his dizziness, the President was released into Fielding's direction, the bomb light still glowing. Trench reached up from the back of the pew, forcing his foot into the ribs of a woman underneath him, grabbing the detonator. The assassin fell backwards against the pew. A female secret service agent pulled his body further down, onto the bench, checking the body for weapons, distancing him from the President; her revolver aimed at the man's collapsed body.

"Whoa! All clear!" Trench called out in relief, shaking from the rush of adrenalin, and removed the bomb from the President's neck. The light went off and began to beep.

"What? You mean the bomb went off? We're all dead?" Trench said, glaring up from the church pew. The congregation and the priest stood up and stretched. The assassin opened his eyes and looked around, wiping paint off the top of his forehead and out of his hair. Men and women dressed in their Sunday best, stepped forward with clipboards, looking at their watches and jotting down notes. Jason and Joey checked to make certain their rifles were safe and positioned them to their shoulders.

"Alright, little brother. We did the best we could." Jason said with a smile, smacking his brother, Joey, on the back. Dewey rushed out from the stairway, shaking his head in disbelief, pointing his finger in anger.

"Oh no! Unacceptable! Unacceptable, gentlemen! What the hell kind of scenario is this supposed to be, Howie!? How the hell am I supposed to save the President with you and your technicians interfering with my equipment!?" Dewey yelled, butting his chest up against one of the technician's back, knocking him down to sit on the wooden pew.

"You better chill, Dewey or I will have you walking the grounds of the White House for the next two years!" Howard, the technician said, smacking the enraged soldier in the chest with the clipboard.

"Where the hell do you FBI college boys get this power-trip shit!? What happened to all that talk about 'a team effort'? Well, give me an answer, boy!? What happened to the original scenario we were supposed to practice!? How are we supposed to get a goddamn bomb off the President with the damn bomber right next to him with the trigger in his hand!? Can you answer that!?" Dewey was pumped full of adrenalin leaning over the FBI technician. Jason wedged himself between Dewey and the FBI technician, putting his arm around the soldier.

"Easy, champ. We did great. We did the best we could with this scenario. We're still the best team in the secret service. Ain't that right, Howie?" Jason asked with a smirk, patting Howard on the cheek. Fielding had to be a smartass.

"Here ladies. Here's one of your toys." Trench smiled, dangling the practice bomb into one of the technicians hands. "Now remember to put down in your notes that a bunch of decorated soldiers died trying to save the President because you assholes decided to go hot-dogging. You techs, always in the shadows, writing your textbooks while the real soldiers die."

"That's it fellas. It's 8 pm. Time for beer and pizza. Let them go back to their little office and compare their results. We all know we are the number ones in D.C." Joey said stretching his back. Dewey kept eying Howard with a revengeful glare, while Fielding laughed and pulled him backwards, down the aisle of the cathedral.

"Now come on. We'll all be heading down to Virginia beach on Thursday. We'll grab some honeys and hey, we'll make Trench pay for the hotel rooms and the drinks. We'll get a little crazy and maybe rough up some sailors." Fielding said, grabbing onto Dewey's shoulder.

"Damn it, Fielding. When I was in the Navy, we got treated with respect. Don't make me even madder than I am by making fun of me. I'm tired of these little FBI suit-n-ties going around like Big Brass." Dewey said slapping his partner's arm away. Trench walked behind Jason, Joey, Dewey and Fielding, out towards the front entrance.

"So, why do I have to pay for this weekend extravaganza?" Trench asked.

"Well, you're Mr.Lotto winner. That's why you shouldn't go around bragging when you win some money on the D.C. Lottery. People will start bumming money off you." Joey laughed.

Trench raised his eyebrows and gave a half-smile from under his fuzzy mustache. "Guys. I only won two grand."

The group of secret service agents teased and slapped each other around. "Two grand!? Damn, Trench. That won't even cover the cost of bail." Jason laughed, dragging the fuming Dewey by his flap-jacket, toward the door, surrounded by his secret service team.

THREE

THE SECURITY GUARDS and porters cursed at the drivers trying to block the front drive to Dulles Airport while they hurried to drop their luggage onto the carts. A group of taxis inched forward, blocking out a mini van with a woman yelling that her mother was almost run over, trying to reach the passenger door. A hectic crowd rolled their luggage carts, kicking at the doors, struggling to get into the main lobby. The President's black limousine rounded the corner with Shelley and Francis, their faces pressed up against the windows, watching the gigantic airplanes fly overhead to land, on the other side of the terminal.

"David. I heard the latest figures about your new cellular phone batteries. It's wild that something so simple could take-over a market."

"It's always been an obsession of mine and once Platinum Technology and Arcola Electronics merge next year, I'm going to be internationally unstoppable. I've already had two major long distance telephone companies offer special incentives if they can put their logos on my company's new cell phone line."

"Your timing was brilliant. Especially with the upcoming anniversary of Hong Kong's independence from Britain."

"I guess I just got lucky. Already shares are selling like hotcakes on the NASDAQ. The last reports were faxed to me from my partners in Hong Kong and Japan. The stocks on the Hang Seng and the Nikkei went through the roof. After my meetings in China and Taiwan, I've got meetings lined up with Telefon Argentina and Brazil Electronics next month. I've had an offer from Siemens to bring Marie and the kids to Germany to meet with the top executives, to discuss the sale of my new micro-battery design to be used in the medical field to treat stroke and Parkinson's disease patients."

"Well, remember. I still need your wife to help me with my campaign. It's gonna be a roller coaster of a year." President Johnson said.

"Dad. Do you always have to talk business?" Francis said in his hoarse, little voice. David and the President looked at each other and tried to hold back their laughter.

"So, Frankie. Have you ever been on an airplane before?" President Johnson asked the little boy.

"Uh,huh. Three times." Francis said holding up three fingers.

"Francis Andrew Arcola. You've been on airplanes dozens of time. Do you see how children are nowadays, Mr. President? I know I've been on an airplane at least twenty times. How about you, Mr. President?" Shelley tilted her head and asked, with a confident tone in her voice, trying to act like an adult. President George Johnson crinkled his brow in thought, giving David Arcola a quizzical look. David just smiled and reached for his beeping cell phone.

"Well, Shelley. I flew an F-16 and a Stealth fighter when I was in the Air Force. And as a senator and Vice-President, I traveled all over the world. I guess I've been on planes a couple of hundred times." The President chuckled. David kept smiling as he talked on his cellular phone. The limousine rolled underneath a boarding tunnel, down to an entrance near the tarmac.

"Yes, dear. We'll be careful. I won't let the kids out of my sight. Even when we're with Brighid in Tokyo." David said to his wife, Marie, over the phone.

"Daddy." Shelley asked, with a pat to her father's knee. "Tell mommy we'll send her a postcard everyday."

"Okay, honey. Dear. Shelley says we'll send you a postcard everyday. Okay. Okay. I love you, too, dear. Goodbye." David was still smiling as he hung up and clicked the phone shut. "Mommy said to make sure Frankie sends her a postcard, too."

"Why didn't mommy want to talk to me?" Frankie asked with a pout. David reached out and pulled his son onto his lap. "Mommy had to go meet in the Capitol with a bunch of senators to talk about all sorts of important stuff like laws and proposals. See your watch? Mommy has to meet with the Senate at eleven o'clock. Can you look at your watch and tell me what time it is?" David asked.

Francis glances down at his orange and blue neon colored watch. "Yes. It's after ten. See, the big hand is on the ten and the little hand is on the five." Francis smiled with a missing front baby tooth. President Johnson and Shelley checked their watches.

"That's right. It's ten twenty-five. That's pretty good, Frankie." David replied.President Johnson tapped the face of his Rolex, wondering why the time was off by five minutes. "Well. The governors will be here pretty soon." President Johnson peeked out the window across the runway. "In fact. I think that's their plane over there."

A gleaming 777 called the landing crew to attention, scurrying onto the runway . A tunnel was extended out to the side of the plane. A small maintenance truck positioned itself under the belly of the plane, while attendants pulled large,long hoses from a tanker. A mechanic knelt down to begin inspecting the wheels and the hydraulics on the landing gear. A guard checked his watch and approached a catering truck stopped next to a work shed. He checked the license plate and talked into his walkie-talkie. Wonderful, full round clouds played with the sunshine, casting shadows onto the tunnel and the 777. A bomb sniffing golden retriever gave a bark and tugged at her leash, making one of the secret service agents abruptly stop in the middle of his yawn. The agent scratched the back of his neck and made certain he knew where the airport cameras were facing. President Johnson extended his hand out to greet one of the governors, as the passengers exited the tunnel. Chauffeurs stepped up holding signs, greeting some of the governors, making the secret service agents anxious.

"Hello, Norman. How was the flight?" President Johnson said with a smile, as the remaining governors squeezed by, heading for the pay phones and the restrooms.

"I don't know, George. Two weeks of airplane food. It's starting to get to me." Governor Norman O'Conner said, tapping his pot belly, shaking his head.

"A few days on the treadmill at the White House gym and you'll feel great. Oh. And my chef has a special corned beef and cabbage recipe that will melt in your mouth." President Johnson said, patting the governor's shoulder as they exited the tunnel.

"Okay, Georgie. And you owe me a rematch at backgammon too. I want to win some of my money back." Governor O'Conner chuckled.

"Oh, good. I've got a thirty year old bottle of Bushmills for us. We can talk about those old football days when we were back at Northwestern. My wife is out of town for the week so we can get some of the old timers over for a little reunion." President Johnson said.

"Trying to get me drunk, are ya. That's how you stole my money last time." Governor O'Connor smiled and tugged at his white walrus mustache, giving the President a friendly grab of the arm.

Francis ran by huffing, his football under his arm, down the tunnel onto the airplane, laughing and calling out. "Uncle George! Uncle George! I'm going to touchdown! Try and get me!"

"Give me a call once you get settled in, Norm. I gotta go win this game. Like the good old days. Here I come Frankie!" President Johnson yelled out as he lowered his hands, running after the five year old hellion. A secret service agent adjusted a small video monitor and moved to delay a group of photographers. A third agent stepped to the end of the row of glass windows, curious about a security guard standing down by the maintenance shed doorway. David's pant leg was tugged on by his daughter Shelley. She pointed down the tunnel.

"I'm going after Frankie."

One of the female agents took a quick glance down the tunnel. A fourth agent waved his hand at one of the agents who nodded his head. He rushed to follow the governors as they left the pay phones, down the terminal towards the entrance. Shelley pushed some business women out of the way, as they placed their laptop computers under their arms. They were hurrying off the plane, talking about a golf game at the Kenwood Club. The clouds bent the light of the sun invading the tunnel. David walked by and smiled at a secret service agent, standing vigilant, dressed in a brown suit. She nodded, but didn't return a smile. David checked his digital watch. The display showed: 10:45 AM. President Johnson and Frankie laughed, while Shelley bounced up to try to look at a light reflecting up and on top of the inside of the tunnel.

"Daddy. What is that light?" Shelley asked, squinting her eyes. David stepped up to the windows and studied the vehicles on Dulles Airport runway.

"It looks like a reflection off of that catering truck. Doesn't It kinda look like the star on Mr. Tim's roof?" Loud laughter drew David's attention as little Frankie rushed into the off ramp tunnel with his football, chased by a hilarious President Johnson. David's cell phone rang and he clicked it open. "Hello?"

A bright white flash caught the inside of the airport terminal. David's legs went weak and he felt a powerful heat as he inhaled into his lungs his next breath. The smell of clean chemicals and flame knock a stewardess back onto the airplane. Frankie collapsed to the floor. President Johnson's pupils burnt gray, his black silk suit on fire as he screamed out from the pain. David's skin bubbled like burning sugar, his back slapped into the wall of the tunnel, his hands spasming to put out his burning hair. The woman secret service agent covered Shelley and dragged her out of the tunnel, across the floor; collapsing motionless to the side of a row of empty seats. The smell of burning hair and skin was replaced by the cold winter breezes, extinguishing the fire at the top of the tunnel canopy. A cloud moved away from the sun and David closed his eyes. A whistling of the December wind cleansed the tunnel, taking the souls and ashes, up into the sky, into heaven.

FOUR

T HE CLOCK SHOWED: 10:55 a.m. Senator Trevor
Thomas shoved his way into the hall holding his hand
out to one of his campaign managers, waiting for her to
open the door for him. "Very good, Lauren. I've trained you well."
The senator smiled a devilish, little boy grin.

"If you take me home tonight, you can train me better." Lauren
replied with glittering green eyes.

The big wooden doors opened and Senator Thomas stepped
into the Senate. His baby face still pleasingly attractive for his age.
His menacing six foot-five frame drew the attention from most of
the females present. "Good morning, ladies," he said, in a commanding yet discreet, bassy voice, looking to the podium, and
imagining himself as President someday.

"Hello, Trevor." The silver haired woman purred with music in
her voice, brushing up against his arm.

"Hello, Tina. I like that dress." He quipped, flirting back.

Fifty senators, secretaries and pages entered the great hall.
CNN and CNBC were adjusting their cameras, focusing and taking light readings; while the Quorum Call ended. The Sergeant at
Arms stepped over to the camera crews and reminded them that
their cameras were to remain off during this emergency meeting.
A pair of senators discussed the incident in Iran. One of them
stated that it may be worse than the Chernobyl or the Bhopal
incident.

Senator Thomas handed his fedora to a young man and listened in on the two senators conversation. He petted the sides of
his wrap coat, just because he liked to feel the richness of the
cashmere and camel hair. Trevor was statuesque; very beautiful

for a man who fought in Desert Storm and Bosnia. His dark brown eyes gleamed, prowling the Senate chamber, waiting for her.

She entered the room. Her eyes and hair wonderful. Her every move, unplanned, very natural. Never vain about her looks. Always confident. She thanked pages and advisors, confirming international reports. Always that magical smile. Her frame magnificent and intimidating, making most men stutter; and forget what they wanted to say to her. A mother and a winner of awards for literature; even with her struggle from humble beginnings, raised in a trailer park outside of Syracuse: she made her way through the army and law school. She glanced at the teleprompter. Her press secretary, Benny, pulled a coaxial cable out from under her heel.

"It's alright. Think of it as just practice." Benny smiled up, adjusting the cables underneath the carpet, so the Vice-President wouldn't trip.

"Good morning ladies and gentlemen." Vice-President Marie Arcola began. "Let's get right to the matter. The explosion at the biological and chemical weapons factory near Esfahan, in Iran, is becoming a grave concern for our allies in the Persian Gulf region."

"From what I understand!" Senator Trevor Thomas called out. "Terrorists near Esfahan were creating biological and chemical weapons! Maybe to kill us! If an accident is going to kill off a hundred of them, I think that's their business!" Senator Thomas marveled at the applause and praise for his gutsy choice of words. Laughter and whispers drew the Vice-President's attention. A page rushed down from the back doors with a portable radio. The CNN camera crew shuffled with incoming reports over their headsets. The page placed the radio on a podium in front of a microphone and turned up the volume.

"Reports are still coming in from Dulles Airport security. The fire is under control and there are still, two passengers from the plane reported missing. It has been confirmed: President George Johnson has been killed. Of the remaining fifteen killed in this bomb attack, David Arcola of Arcola Electronics and his two children have been positively identified and were declared dead at the scene. David Arcola is the husband of Vice-President Marie Arcola."

The room seemed dull. It was difficult to remember. It was hard to focus on all the bright lights, turning gray and black at the sides. Her hands tingled and went numb. Her eyes rolled back and her jaw dropped with her head falling limp. Vice-President Arcola collapsed against the podium. Benny and two secret service agents rushed to grab her, calling out for the agents to help. The room was light. Marie looked at her hand; she began to breathe hard.

"I'm right here for you." Benny whispered and helped carry her from the room. Senators and pages began huddling up to the radio, as the Senate built into hysteria. Secret service agents stepped forward, mumbling into their microphones. A secretary and Benny helped Mrs. Arcola walk back to the ready room. The Senate Chamber roared with the shouts of senators, representatives and staff, rushing out, down the hall where a television set was wheeled on a cart out of the lounge.

"Jesus Christ. It's true." One of the senators said, trembling with a deep breath. He began switching channels, hoping this is a practical joke.

"At eleven a.m. at Dulles Airport. President George William Johnson was declared dead at the scene of a massive explosion that is now under investigation by the FBI, the National Transportation Safety Board, the Secret Service and several government agencies. I was one of the first reporters on the scene; reporting a story on the governors of ten states visiting Washington, D.C. for the holidays and their new trade agreements from several international businesses. I saw the bodies of Mr. David Arcola and his daughter, Shelley, as the paramedics . . ." The woman reporter lost her train of thought and composure. She broke down in tears and turned away from the cameras. One of the pages changed the channel.

"Reports have not been confirmed as to whether or not this bombing is in retaliation by Iran for a suspected bombing by U.S. troops at a factory outside of Esfahan. A factory that Iranian officials claim produces cleaners such as sodium hydroxide, sulfuric acid and other solvents. Chemicals that Iran claims, they use for cleaning machine parts. While U.S. officials claim there was no attack on the factory. The United States has also offered assistance in gathering evidence and also has offered to send medical teams to help the people of Iran. So far, an estimated twenty thousand people have died from what the Pentagon calls one of the deadliest biological and chemical weapons disasters in history." Senator Thomas changed the station.

"I'm standing here outside the terminal of Dulles Airport where it is believed a terrorist bomb was detonated less than twenty minutes ago. A terrorist bomb that killed President Johnson and sixteen other people. As you can see behind me, the ATF and the FBI, are working closely to preserve and gather evidence. The wind is starting to build near the tunnel of a 777 which landed earlier, bringing governors from various states. The governors exited the plane, just moments before the bomb went off. The boarding tunnel above me, about three hundred feet away, is where investigators believe the explosion took place. You can see, that only the shell of the tunnel remains. The interior layers are quite thick for safety reasons and to also reduce noise, now shredded away from the blast. You can see agents, up in the terminal, examining the body of a female secret service agent who died moments after the blast. Investigators say she gave them some information as to what happened when the bomb went off. Information the FBI will not release at this time. We were also told, that the agent was commended for using her body as a shield to try to save Shelley Arcola's life. Shelley Arcola is the daughter of Vice-President Marie Arcola and David Arcola; the electronics mogul. He was also killed in this vicious attack on American soil." One of the senators changed the station.

"The country is in a state of shock and grief. The death of President George Johnson has already reached the airwaves in forty countries and continues to shock the world. Other Presidents and ambassadors have been warned not to travel through any international airports at this time because of the recent bombings in several airports around the world."

"Holy shit! Where did all these reporters come from?" A woman senator said, staring out the window at hordes of secret service agents, detaining the crowd while Vice-President Arcola was rushed away to the Presidential helicopter. Reporters shouted, shoved and tripped over each other, trying to make their way into the front lobby. Cameras began flashing at any and all, huddled by the television. Senator Trevor Thomas examined his dress shirt, to make certain his pleats were even.

"Well. Santa Claus got us an early Christmas present, Lauren?" Senator Thomas laughed and cupped his hands. "Check my back for any lint. We don't want me to look bad on the cover of USA Today. Now do we?"

"Yes, sir." Lauren replied, obedient with enthusiasm, brushing her long blond hair back, brushing and adjusting the senator's suit coat.

"Lauren. I want you to get out of here and alert our campaign team. I think we can use this to help us out towards winning the elections. Just say 'yes' Lauren, and be on your way." Senator Thomas adjusted his tie and eased forward into the mayhem of reporters and senators. Lauren said 'yes' and scurried away to the exit at the end of the corridor.

"Senator Thomas. Is this the beginning of major terrorism in our country? Can we expect more bombings until this situation in Iran is resolved?" The slim, brown haired woman reporter asked, catching the senator's eye. He studied the woman and carefully chose his words.

"I can only say we are doing our best to reassure the people that this explosion may not have been from a terrorist bomb. Most of you know the FBI and the FAA have not released any official statements." Senator Thomas began, then was abruptly interrupted by another reporter.

"Senator. Reports say that Vice-President Arcola had a nervous breakdown when she heard the news her husband and children were killed in this assassination . . .".

"Now there you go. No one has said this was an assassination. You reporters have to stop misleading the public. How do you know this wasn't just an accident? Wait until the investigators do their jobs and gather the evidence." The large crowd of staff and senators turned away from the television to listen in on Senator Thomas's remarks to the press.

"Senator Thomas. Who's going to run the country now?" A

reporter yelled out. Senator Thomas rubbed his neck and focused away from the cameras, hesitant to answer the question. "I think you all know the answer to that. Vice-President Arcola is the best qualified." Senator Thomas replied in a sad tone of voice.

"Senator Thomas. Many people know that you lost the last election. Will this terrorist bombing help or hurt?"

"Now look. Please, everyone. Just calm down with this terrorist talk. We have our best teams checking the plane for a bomb. I realize all of you want a great story, but you have to understand the extent of this tragedy. So, please. Do not start spreading rumors of terrorists attacks or bombings." Senator Thomas huffed.

"So the possibility of Iranian terrorists hasn't been ruled out?" A man said, sticking a microphone into the senator's face. Senator Thomas took a deep breath, trying to cool himself down, standing in a boxer stance; tall and lethal, with a glass cutting stare.

"Son. There is no proof that Iran or any other foreign country is responsible for this. So, if you ever want to set foot on any government property again, you best learn to be respectful. Do you understand that?" The senator said with fiery eyes. Secret service agents studied the man's identification badge and began to escort other reporters away from the senators and the staff. Senator Thomas adjusted his Rolex, rushing away, to try and find a telephone.

FIVE

VICE-PRESIDENT MARIE ARCOLA sat silently, staring out the window at the crabapple trees and the flowerless tulips; from the big chair behind the President's desk. Crowds of supporters and well-wishers by the hundreds were huddled away back to the large circle drive, while reporters were turned away from the east wing entrance. Secret service men and women stood watching a small group of press agents in the lobby.

Benny took a deep breath and walked up the stairs, past the white pillars on the terrace, and through the French doors. The Chiefs of Staff left the rose garden, close behind the advisor. Slowly, Benny opened the door to the Oval Office to see his lady President trembling, her eyes red and swollen from tears. Pictures of David, Shelley and Francis, silently sat in a frame, next to the bust of Abraham Lincoln. Benny held out his hand for one of the secretaries not to enter the office. Marie Arcola gazed at the flag of the United States of America and swiveled her chair to look across the top of the oak timber desk. The sunlight added a light glow to the gold damask drapery; on and off with each passing cloud. Benny moved forward and stopped, checking to make certain he was standing up straight; just outside of the Coat of Arms, woven into the Oval Office carpet. A small radio broadcasted on and on, about the bombing at Dulles Airport. The news commentator announced Vice-President Marie Joanna Arcola was about to become the first woman President of the United States of America.

"Yes, Benny?" Marie spoke quietly. "Marie. The Chiefs of Staff are here. And Judge Watson from the Federal Court. Are you ready to be sworn in?" Benny asked, almost in a whisper.

Marie touched her palms to the desk, caressing President Johnson's desk pad and monthly planner with every fingertip, looking up at his families pictures. Feeling every ghost of a President before her. She looked up with that confident, perfect smile. "Of course I'm ready, Benny. Let's get to work." She replied.

The door opened wide and a parade of generals entered the office. A tall, thick man reached his large hand out to shake Vice-President Arcola's hand, his dark brown face comforted her when he gave her a big smile. He looked very informal in his gray, cotton suit. Aides stood, huddled: curious at the Oval Office entrance, out in the corridor. Marie stood in the center of the room. General Stanton and General Millings to her left; General Tyler a few steps behind her with Benny, her press secretary, eagerly writing down the moments of this remarkable, historical event.

"Place your hand on the Bible." Judge Watson commanded softly, with his deep, bassy voice and that fatherly smile. Cameras flashed, taking pictures of this fabulously, strong woman, standing tall. All of them knowing she had just lost her family, only hours ago; and now she must prevent the United States from going to war.

"Are you ready to take the oath, Vice-President Marie Arcola?" Judge Watson asked.

"Yes." Marie replied with a nervous, deep breath.

"Please raise your right hand and repeat after me." Judge Watson said, raising his right hand, while the Vice-President did the same.

"I, Marie Joanna Arcola, do solemnly swear."

"I, Marie Joanna Arcola, do solemnly swear." "That I will faithfully execute the office of the President of the United States."

"That I will faithfully execute the office of the President of the United States." Marie repeated.

"And will do to the best of my ability." Judge Watson said.

"And will do to the best of my ability."

"To preserve, protect and defend the constitution of the United States."

"To preserve, protect and defend the constitution of the United States."

"So help me God." Judge Watson finished.

"So help me God." Marie replied, her eyes glassy, as she sighed.

Judge Watson reached out and shook Marie's hand. "Congratulations, President Marie Joanna Arcola. You have just become this country's first woman President." Marie cleared her throat and took a deep breath.

"Thank you, your honor." President Arcola said with a tearful smile. The generals and aides began to applaud. Cheers and clapping rang out from the halls.

The phones were hung up and secretaries were quick to answer after the swearing in. "President Marie Arcola's office, may I help you?" President Arcola's secretary, Jeri sang out. People filtered into the Oval Office, many of them were detained by the White House Guards, others congratulated the President with handshakes and hugs. Benny cleared his throat and sniffled watching Marie sign the contract.

"Well, Madame President. Now comes the hard part. The media." Benny said.

"Okay. Only a few questions for now. I have to meet with Agent Naughton at the hospital. Set it up so that I can address the nation at 8:30 tonight. General Stanton, I need to speak with you and the Chiefs of Staff in two hours about this situation in Iran. You know as well as I do, the media is going to blow this thing out of proportion." President Arcola said.

"Yes, ma'am. We'll set up in the Cabinet room and be ready when you return." General Stanton replied putting on his hat and checking his watch for the time. The aides and the secretaries parted to each side of the corridor. President Arcola strutted by, brushing the wrinkles out of her burgundy suit, escorted by a small army of secret service agents. The Presidential helicopter sat ready as the reporters and the camera personnel swooped across the south lawn. FBI sharp shooters aimed their rifles from the balconies and the rooftop. Microphones were shoved over the shoulders of the agents as the questions were yelled out.

A shouting match between a large group of Pro-Choice and Pro-Life supporters began. One woman grabbed another woman by the collar of her shirt and shook her, while a small gang of women began clawing and swatting with rolled up protest signs.

"Pro-choice! Pro-choice! Keep your hands off my body!"

"Stop murdering babies! Life! Life! Life!" The screaming and chanting echoed to the flash of cameras as President Arcola was helped through the herd of people, shielded by White House guards and the secret service.

"Have they identified the terrorist!" A male reporter screamed, his arms being secured by a White House guard. President Arcola stopped, to the surprise of agents and security officers, shielding her from the frenzied crowd.

"Let me talk." President Arcola said to Benny, who paused the caravan of security just a few hundred feet from the President's helicopter.

"Will there be retaliation against Iran for this bombing?" The reporter asked.

"We have no evidence that the explosion at Dulles Airport was caused by anyone from Iran." President Arcola answered.

"What about the chemical and biological weapons factory that Iran said the United States bombed?" Another reporter said, holding out a microphone.

"I'm sorry. The Pentagon and the Chiefs of Staff tell me that the United States would have no reason to do such a thing. We have reason to believe there was an accident in the factory. We're hoping Iran will cooperate with an investigation."

A woman reporter butted in. "Now that you're President, will you be for or against abortion rights in our country?"

"Please. There are more important issues that need to be dealt with right now. I think even you would agree if you were in my position." The President snapped back. "Yes. You. One last question." President Arcola said, pointing to a woman waving her hand.

"How does it feel to be the first female President?"

President Arcola looked around the south lawn at the chaos between the protesters and the clash of security with photographers; she had to smile. "It feels good. It feels real good. But, you have to understand. I have work to do. Thank you." Madame President waved and continued walking toward the helicopter to the screams and calls of questions by the reporters.

"What about the environment!?"

"The owls!?"

"What are you going to do about our taxes!?"

"Unemployment!?"

"Gun control!"

"The homeless! What about the homeless!?"

President Arcola continued to wave as the the rotors and the blades of the helicopter blew at her and the security guards. She still smiled, even as she boarded the helicopter, and an agent slid the bay door shut.

SIX

THE WALLS OF THE building were clean and tall, shiny white, echoing the hum of the air-conditioner and shoes squeaking on the well-buffed ceramic tiled floor. A husky, man with broad shoulders pushed his dark rimmed glasses up his nose and reached his hand out to President Arcola; his suit coat a size to small, his arms bulging at the sleeves.

"Madame President." He introduced himself with a firm handshake. "I'm Agent Scott Naughton of the FBI. Are you sure you want to do this?" The agent asked, lightly touching her arm as she nodded her head.

"Yes. I have to do this. You understand, don't you?" She asked slowly walking down the corridor with Agent Naughton.

Around the corner, tall, thick tinted windows covered one wall of the corridor. Through the windows, a room filled with white robed men and women swarmed around a dozen bodies, lying on gurneys, underneath lights and video cameras. White sheets were draped over all but two bodies. A lab technician caught a glimpse of the lady president and turned her head to look away. A sad expression could be seen in the examiner's eyes, even through the mask and safety glasses.

"The bodies are all severely burned. The technicians are searching for any foreign objects that may have been burned onto the victims at the time of the explosion."

"Can I go in there to see my family?" Marie asked.

"No. I'm sorry." Agent Naughton bowed his head. " We can't take a chance of any evidence being contaminated. The prosecuter's office has already advised us to detain all family members. We can't let whoever did this get away."

"Yes. That's true. That makes sense." Her voice was small and lonely.

"The ceremonies for President Johnson and for my family will be separate. Closed casket."

"Yes, ma'am." Agent Naughton replied, his tone respectful.

"I understand one of your agents shielded my daughter Shelley and tried to save her from the explosion."

"Yes, ma'am. Agent Rajavi was one of our finest. She graduated from the University of Baghdad with a masters in history. She also used to be part of the National Liberation Army and part of the National Council of Resistance of Iran. She and her family fled Iraq in 1997. A year after that, we asked her to work for us. Somayeh was with the FBI anti-terrorism team for eight years."

"I'd like to contact her family personally about this incident."

"I'm sorry, Madame President. Her only family was killed in a raid in Israel two years ago. She also signed a vow not to marry or have children, as long as she was in the anti-terrorism division of the FBI."

One of the lab technicians touched the exposed teeth of one of the adult bodies with a stainless steel pick. The blood-blackened face lay stiff. The lips had burned away. The skin was blistered up to the top of the head. The skull was small and all the hair was burned away. The eyebrows and eyelashes were gone and the eyelids were closed, in a peaceful, forever sleep.

"Was Agent Rajavi pretty?" President Arcola asked.

"Yes. Yes, she was very attractive. Dark brown eyes. Black hair. She loved to play basketball. In fact, three of my agents were warned by me personally when they made some comments to her which she felt were questionable."

President Arcola caught a glimpse of a small body, being examined in the back of the room. The face was blackened and burned with half a head of singed, blond hair. Part of the face was glossy red. Only a small area from the chin to the temple looked baby soft, with a tiny swollen eye; one that Marie wished would open. A lab technician jotted some notes on a clipboard, and pulled the white sheet over Shelley's body.

President Marie Arcola took a scalding deep breath and balled her hands into fist, wanting to pound at the windows. The adrenalin flowed through her the anger she held back. She took another deep breath, trying to keep her thoughts clear; trying to focus on the other people that were killed in the explosion. "If Iran is responsible for this, Agent Naughton. I expect them to suffer. I will not tolerate any mishaps in this investigation. Is that clear, Agent Naughton? I want whoever did this to pay with their lives." President Arcola took one last look at her family.

"Now. I have a meeting with the Chiefs of Staff in thirty minutes. Please feel free to contact me as soon as you have an answer to this. I don't want any mistrials or acquittals. Am I clear, Agent Naughton?"

"Yes, Madame President." Agent Naughton replied. President Arcola stepped quickly back down the corridor, leaving her family and her feelings behind.

SEVEN

GENERAL STANTON SNUCK another quarter of a ham and swiss cheese sandwich from the silver tray. General Millings took a sip of whiskey and poked at a reluctant olive rolling on the relish plate. President Arcola entered the Cabinet room, pausing to take a few sandwiches and some fresh fruit. A page rushed in with four boxes of pizzas. General Tyler's face lit up, when a pepperoni pizza was set down in front of him.

"The satellite reconnaissance shows almost half the countryside near the factory littered with bodies. Maybe forty thousand dead. We really needed the evidence from that SEAL team."

"CIA sources have confirmed the chemical collected from water samples in Saudi Arabia and Kuwait. It's anthrax, alright. Tehran is reporting that a group of unknown American soldiers were captured ten miles south of the target. Iranian officials say the SEAL team has confessed to bombing the factory." General Tyler finished his comments and began passing out folders around the table to the President and the staff members.

A tall, lurching, vulture of a man twirled the unopened folder in front of him, on the large wooden table. General Millings watched the man and cleared his throat, to begin with his introduction.

"You all know Professor Matthew Berger, the distinguished gentlemen from the American University. Professor Berger is what the Pentagon labels, an expert on statistics dealing with any and all foreign probabilities, especially the history of terrorism." The general said, in his charming Georgia accent.

The professor placed his gold rimmed glasses atop his prominent, wide nose. His wrinkled eyes squinted to view the contents of the folder. And then he went off on his own, arrogant way.

34

"Yes. Good aerial shots from your people, General Millings. What I like to call, 'state of the art'. Your spy satellites are very much in focus." Professor Berger took a drink of the Bushmills and swished the flavor over his gums.

"I won't kid you, Madame President. I hope I have been asked here to assist you with the possibilities of unforeseen and outrageous variables that could never be concocted by even the most brilliant of military mind; excluding those present. Of course." The professor tucked his arm to his chest and bowed to the generals, as if he were the master of ceremonies in the center ring of a circus.

"Yes, Professor Berger. We have all heard very much about you. In fact, you've earned some colorful titles along the way with your career. The Grim Reaper. Doomsayer." President Arcola said.

Professor Berger held out his hands, palms out in surrender. "Yes. Satan. Nostradamus. I've even been called the Anti-Christ. And although I have been honored with all those well deserved metaphors, I assure you my intentions are for bettering the world and universe for all humankind. You notice I said 'humankind'. I work very hard to earn all the descriptions of my ideas. Did you know, I've sold close to twelve million copies of my books? But let's continue. So Iran made a boo-boo and one of their chemical weapons factory workers spilt some anthrax."

"Some anthrax!?" General Tyler shouted. "That anthrax was strong enough to make it down south into Kuwait and Saudi Arabia and kill people! That's nearly four hundred and fifty miles away from the factory. And there were even traces of sarin in some of the victims' bodies."

Professor Berger's eyes rolled at General Tyler's excitement. "Thank you for that much needed information, general. So Iran spilt a lot of anthrax. The Iranians also say they captured the SEAL team that went in weeks ago. From the stories printed in the Tehran Times and the Iran Times, it is obvious Iran is attempting to use this accident to gain world sympathy. They have already requested that all unilateral and secondary sanctions be lifted. That if the sanctions are not lifted, the world will be held responsible for whatever consequences unfold."

"Yes. Sympathy for Iran might force many countries to have

sanctions lifted temporarily. What if another country set off that explosion? Or maybe it was one of Iran's own?" General Stanton said.

"Yes. Sabotage can't be ruled out." General Millings added, hardly looking up from his laptop computer. Most of the Chiefs of Staff shook their heads in agreement, now pondering the thought.

"Oh, oh. Another problem." Professor Berger stated, using a magnifying glass to study one of the satellite photographs.

"Another problem, professor?" President Arcola replied, taking notes while drinking her orange juice, as she studied the debate between the professor and the generals.

"Yes. Photograph C408 and C696 were taken twenty-four hours apart. If you look at your copies you'll notice the build up of troops on the Iraqi border near Al Amareh. And look over in Pakistan near Mirjaveh. And in Afghanistan, outside of Shindand." Professor Berger grumbled.

"Tanks and anti-aircraft cannons. What about that semi truck and trailer?" President Arcola asked, tipping her reading glasses, getting a closer look at the copies of photographs from her folder.

"It could be military equipment to help them secure the region." Benny said.

"What if it's cruise missiles? Iran has been working on missiles similar to our Tomahawks for years. They could hit one of our aircraft carriers." General Millings said.

"It might be something with nuclear capabilities. Could you imagine if the Afghans moved a nuclear bomb into that factory. They could hold the entire Middle East hostage." General Stanton said.

"Or they could intentionally or accidentally, blow up that factory and kill off one tenth of the population in that region. Depending on how the wind blows, an explosion in that factory could send an anthrax storm raining down from Iraq to Israel. Or it could head over into India, or even north into Russia." General Tyler said, studying his world atlas, drawing a big red circle, hundreds of miles away from Esfahan.

"Do you think those troops are moving in to help Iran launch an offensive in retaliation to the explosion? The Tehran Times has been printing stories that the U.S. set off the bomb, hoping to cripple Afghanistan and Pakistan, as well as Iran." Benny said. President Arcola sat back in her chair, twirling her pen around in her fingers, studying how these generals thought.

"Well, who the hell would have the strength to side with Iran against the rest of the world? Especially since biological weapons were involved. According to International Law, under the Chemical Weapons Treaty, we would be allowed to retaliate against any country that would aid Iran." General Millings commented in anger.

"Bin Lodin." General Stanton suggested, examining another set of satellite photographs.

"Bin Lodin? Yes. The billionaire who supported and trained the Muja Hudean and Hezbullah the beauty of terrorism. What about the followers of Ramzi Yousef?" General Stanton huffed, his face turning red with his disgust for the terrorists. He turned away at the mention of the airport bombing; in sympathy for President Arcola.

"Yes. All those groups are being investigated. Even the IRA and the Sinn Fein. The FBI Anti-Terrorist Division is comparing this U.S. bombing to the one this past September in Adana; the one that killed sixty-two people. Of those dead, ten were American soldiers." Professor Berger said, leaning over the big wooden table, looking with those big dark eyes, as if he was ready to pounce. The generals began to read FBI notes about each of the bombings.

"Yes." Professor Berger started again, with that funny way of saying 'yesssz . . .'; his finger pointed up in the air, to emphasize his new idea, as he began to pace around the Cabinet Room.

"We shouldn't be so concerned about Iran gaining allies. No. Not allies. In fact. We should be more concerned with the other scenario. Iran being weakened to the point that any of Iran's, feuding neighbors could walk right over those borders and take control of that factory. The way China has been building it's military ever since they took over Hong Kong, I wouldn't be surprised if they weren't the next country we hear of heading into Iran."

"Could that be possible?" President Arcola asked, calmly eating a sandwich and jotting down notes. Professor Berger began to pace around the table holding his chin as if he were deep in thought. His tall, dark frame flowed around the table; those glittering black eyes, gazed up, as he began to play out his vision of Armageddon.

"Is it possible? Yes. Possible and probable. Have you studied Iran's borders? The tension in that region, since the beginning of the twenty-first century, has quadrupled. The random attacks over the last eight years are mind boggling. The bombings of mosques in Afghanistan, Pakistan and Iran last year. Three hundred people killed. And the plutonium that was sold to Turkmenistan, still could be linked to Russia. All these countries desperate from unemployment, over-population and starvation; all on the brink of civil wars. Imagine them using this incident to combine their forces against Iran." Professor Berger smiled, his hand raised over his audience; feeding off their sense of uncertainty and hopelessness.

"So what you're saying, professor. Is that these great armies of biblical proportions are going to march into Iran, rig a nuclear bomb up in that factory and hold the world hostage. And that the U.S. might have to go in an take over that part of Iran." President Arcola said.

"Madame President. I am saying we might have to send thousands of troops and heavy artillery into Iran and defend that country from being overthrown." Professor Berger picked up a photograph showing the bodies scattered along the roads and hills near the factory in Esfahan.

"That's insane. We can't send troops into the middle of a foreign country contaminated with anthrax. The air's poisoned. Most of the central water wells and ghanats are poisoned. All our troops would eventually die." Benny said in protest.

"Yes, son. That's correct. But if we do not get in there now, and those other countries take over Iran; we may be looking at the beginning of World War Three." Professor Berger studied the unsettling affect of his words, by the shuffling of the nervous generals.

"Madame President. We have a CVN 80 sitting in the middle of the Arabian Sea. We can have another Nimitz in the Oman in four days." General Millings gasped in panic.

"No. Any build up of naval activity in the Persian Gulf may confirm that Iran does have a serious problem. I say everything should look as if nothing is wrong and the Esfahan incident is not a major concern. Nothing drastic. What I do suggest, is that we send in another SEAL team to try and gather that evidence. We really need to know how much biological and chemical weapons are still in that factory. And we need to use that evidence for allied support, in case this problem does escalate. We need proof that those SEALs, Iran captured were not responsible for this. Evidence would give us a great advantage." President Arcola said.

"What was the first SEAL team supposed to do?" Benny asked.

"Collect air and water samples from in and around the factory. Take blood samples from some of the victims. Take photographs. Make videodiscs. Hopefully find something in that factory to hold against Iran." General Tyler answered.

"Yes. It would put us at a great advantage if we had hard evidence to show who was making or purchasing these biological weapons." General Stanton said.

"Boy. Evidence like that would stop the Majlis and the Council of Guardians from their blackmail campaign." General Tyler laughed, rubbing his bald head.

"General Millings. How long would it take to get another SEAL team over into Iran?" President Arcola asked. General Millings picked up the receiver of his telephone. "I'll check for you now, Madame President." General Tyler brings up a list of possibilities on his laptop computer.

"Well. We have seventy candidates. Let's see. Only ten are immediately available. All ten are on the secret service special teams. Six ex-Marines, two ex-Army and two ex-Navy SEALs. Of those agents, two are one hundred percent shooters. They're brothers. Sergeant Joseph Adair and Lieutenant Jason Adair. Good eyes must run in the family, their father used to train FBI shooters at Langley. Until the father became sick and died. The whole team has outstanding records. They've practiced scenarios against terrorism, assassination attempts and hostage situations." General Millings continued checking his computer data.

"Where are they now, general?" President Arcola asked.

"Well. They're away in Virginia Beach, doing some R and R. It looks like they're at some topless bar. Oh. I'm sorry, Madame President." General Millings apologized.

"Gentlemen. Remember? I was in the army. When it's just us, like this, I can understand how me being a woman could be a concern. I expect all of you to act the way you always have. But don't quote me on that." The President lightly chuckled along with the generals. "Remember. I used to fly an Apache helicopter and I was very upset when I couldn't fight with my squadron in Desert Storm, to defend Kuwait. Just because I'm a woman. I understand the different rules for different soldiers." President Arcola's words were stoical and cold, yet sincere. She changed the subject, returning to the point. "But I was appreciative of the benefits that paid my way through law school."

"The first SEAL team that was sent to Iran was made up of an explosives expert, a tactics officer, a sniper and a cryptanalyst, fluent in Iranian languages. We could use the secret service agents, but I suggest we should only send in one of the shooters. In case we need to slap together a third team."

"So, that's what we do? Keep sending soldiers into Iran with poisoned air and poisoned water. To be captured and tortured to death?" Benny said, disturbed at the nonchalantness of the decision being made.

"Well, son. It's a lot better than sending in a thousand troops to die in the middle of Iran, to a factory that might be rigged with a nuclear bomb with biological and chemical weapons!" Professor Berger leaned over the table, to make certain his words were intimidating.

"So we keep sending SEAL teams into that factory to be wasted? What if the media gets a hold of this information? They'll twist this around." Benny said looking up from his notes.

"I don't think the media has to know anything." General Millings said.

"It seems like this is the only way to go at this point. The House and Senate are going to have to make a decision soon. We might have to deploy a full scale escalation of troops . . ."

"Professor Berger!" President Arcola stood and interrupted. "I will make that decision when the time comes. Please understand,

I and we do appreciate your input and your opinions in these types of matters." President Arcola stared with flaring nostrils, holding back her urge to lunge, leaning with her fist mashed into the wood top of the table, causing her knuckles to turn white.

She sensed some of the Chiefs of Staff might try to make decisions without her; because she was a woman. She noticed that two of the generals avoided eye contact with her. The old professor blinked, twitching, rolling his chair softly under the table, slowly gathering his folders together.

"Please, Madame President. Gentlemen. I apologize. I always get wound up and, well, I end up stepping over the line. You have to understand, I'm a very deeply disturbed, cynical old man." Professor Berger said, curling his lower lip. Benny's wrist watch beeped.

"Madame President. You have thirty minutes to get ready for your Address to the Nation." Benny said.

General Stanton reached out to shake the Presidents hand. "Thank you, Madame President. Agent Naughton will be by tomorrow. He should have the final reports of all the physical evidence from the explosion at Dulles. We also have requested a video-conference with Iran in two days. If they'll talk to us."

President Marie Arcola gave General Stanton a cold stare.

"Why wouldn't they talk to us, general? Because I'm a woman?" President Arcola snapped.

"These gentlemen from Iran will make it difficult for you. Especially with those troops building up on their borders. We just don't need another Vietnam." General Stanton stated, fumbling with his hat and straightening out his jacket.

"Believe me, general. I will handle this situation." The President said.

The generals rose from the Cabinet Room table to stretch, scooting away their notes and photographs into their files. Professor Berger cleared his throat, to gain his audience's attention, before the meeting retired. He caressed his abused, black leather briefcase as if it were a child. The Chiefs of Staff paused, almost bowing to the lady president as they stood.

"Oh, one more thought before we adjourn." The professor began, as the President and the generals shuffled their notes into their files.

"Do you have another vision, Professor?" General Millings chuckled.

"Yes, general. I do. Those latest satellite photographs with the truck heading toward that factory near Esfahan. Study those photographs again tonight. If there are cruise missiles or even some type of bomb in that truck, it won't stop at that factory. The better place to hold hostage is further south, in those oil fields near Shiraz. Cruise missiles launched from the center of one of the Middle East's largest oil fields would make a more effective bargaining chip. Have a good evening." Professor Berger finished, itching his eyebrows, with that nasty little smile, glaring at the Chiefs of Staff; their expressions frozen with fear.

EIGHT

A GROUP OF SHOPPERS STOPPED in front of the televisions at the Sears department store. A saleswoman noticed the crowd and picked up a remote control, increasing the volume. There was a crowd of almost a hundred, standing, mesmerized as President Marie Arcola stepped up to the podium in the East Room and stared out at the press, adjusting their chairs as they gathered for her Address to the Nation. Her eyes were dark blue. Her hair blonde with a slight hint of gray. She stood tall and straight, in her burgundy wool suit. With her head held high, she placed her palms to the podium. The world stopped breathing.

"Good evening ladies and gentlemen. As all of you know, President George William Johnson was killed in an explosion at Dulles International Airport this morning at approximately eleven a.m. During this explosion, my husband David Arcola, my daughter Shelley and my son Francis, were also killed. This is a terrifying time for all of us. To feel threatened and trapped in our own country. It disturbs all of us, that even our own President, with the greatest security forces America can provide, was killed. The reports have been confirmed by the FAA and the FBI that the explosion at Dulles Airport was caused by a terrorist bomb. At this time, there are rumors in the news, attempting to suggest this attack on U.S. soil is in retaliation for the accidental explosion at an Iranian factory two weeks ago. A factory that has been confirmed to have been manufacturing chemical and biological weapons. At this point there is no evidence one way or the other that this bomb incident is from the same terrorists responsible for the September bombing in Adana or the bomb that killed twenty-one people in Turbat, Pakistan. Because of the magnitude of this explosion; the FBI is working as hard and as fast as humanly possible, to gather evidence, examine the scene and bring to justice, the person or persons responsible for this horrendous act of cowardly behavior, unlike anything this nation and it's people have ever seen. Because of the death of President Johnson, I will be serving as your President until, you the people, elect another in next year's elections. At this time, I ask all of you not to prejudice our friends and neighbors with roots in the Middle East or their families. None off us should be quick to blame responsible, U.S. citizens. We are Americans.

We have lived through worse times before. We must pull ourselves together. The wounds of this tragedy will take time to heal. Please don't let the life of President Johnson or the lives of my husband or children . . ."

President Arcola paused at the thought of her lost family, and bowed her head, clearing her throat; regaining her composure.

". . . be wasted to prejudice, rumors and false allegations made by over-eager, news reporters and their need to sensationalize this tragic incident. Now. I will take a few questions and then you have to understand, I have funerals to attend to."

The reporters began screaming over each other to ask questions. "Yes." She said, pointing to a woman reporter.

"You mentioned punishment for the person or persons responsible for this bombing. Will that include the death penalty?"

"That decision would be up to the judge and jury, when, whoever did this is arrested and tried. Yes. You sir."

"Now that you're a woman with the highest title in our country, as commander and chief, will you change the appearance of the White House? Maybe have more luncheons?"

"I think there are more urgent matters to deal with other than the colors of drapes or having tea with the girls." President Arcola snapped back, biting her tongue before she started to swear at the man; getting thankful, light applause from some reporters who thought the man was out of line. She pointed to another reporter.

"Is it true Kuwait and Saudi Arabia are reporting that rain falling in their cities has been causing burns, breathing problems and death among their people?"

"Yes. There are reports. But experts from the Pentagon agree that the chemicals from the explosion a few weeks ago, have weakened considerably. One more question. Yes?"

"If the bomb that killed President Johnson, is linked to Iran, will the United States retaliate with troops and allied forces?"

"The person or persons that detonated, built or in anyway, aided in delivering that bomb, will be held responsible to the fullest extent of our country's laws. As for the accident at the chemical and biological weapons factory near Esfahan; I hope Iran will set aside our differences and let us help them, before thousands more of their people die from contaminated water and air. That's all for now. Thank you, all. Have a good night."

Cameras flashed and reporters started calling out for the President to stop and answer more questions. The videotape clicked, President Arcola eased back onto the couch, setting down the remote control, only taking a sip of wine. She glanced around the President's bedroom. Boxes filled with books, clothes and belongings were set in one corner; dropped off by the Secret Service. She glanced at the football and the pile of toys, on the floor where the children used to play, with their Uncle George. Benny noticed the lady president's sad stare and tried to get her to talk. He sat up in the love seat across from her and smiled, taking a sip of his Bushmills.

"Well, Benny. The whole world is watching my every move now. How did I look out there?" Marie said sighing and covering up her yawn. He adjusted his tie and realized he was sitting on top of his suit coat. He tried to brush out some of the wrinkles.

"Oh. Well, your hair looked great. But that burgundy outfit was hideous. Honey. You gotta go out and do some serious shopping." Benny said, positioning his hands in front of his eyes, as if he were a photographer about to take her picture. Marie's eyes went wide with laughter. She dripped a little of her wine down her chin.

"Shut up, Benny. You know what I mean. Did I look like I was scared? Did I speak clearly? I was ready to jump on that one reporter for talking down to me like that. Doesn't he know my family was just killed? Where's the respect?" Marie huffed in anger. Benny rubbed his dark brown eyebrows and yawned.

"Now. You've hung around this Boys Club since you were senator. You're the new kid on the block. And yes, you happen to be in an interesting situation. You just happen to be the first female President of the United States of America. Wait until tomorrows headlines. We've already received calls for interviews from Turner and Murdock's cable networks. All I can say is you are the hot news right now. You're a woman. A very pretty woman. You intimidate men. And women. And now you are the President. It's gonna be a zoo everyday, until next years election."

Marie turned her eyes to the shadows of the portraits of Churchill and Franklin. On top of a moving box sat matted finger paintings made by Francis and Shelley. "How will I know when I've screwed up?" She asked.

"Just keep an eye on the stock market tomorrow. If the stocks go bad, it's your fault. Everyone is taking all their money and moving to another country." Benny said taking a sip of his drink. Marie gave him a shocked look and then smiled, realizing that he was joking.

"So what's that supposed to mean? Now everything is going to be my fault?"

"Yeah. It's part of being President." Benny chuckled.

Marie sighed and laid her head back against the pile of pillows. Benny sat in the silence, admiring her beauty. Her face and skin, China doll soft; calling a man's touch. Those beautiful blue eyes closed from exhaustion. Her feet slide underneath a thick, comforter at the end of the sofa. She appeared small in this big room; a beautiful gift painted into the background of the house, by God.

Benny sighed checking the bottle of pills the doctor gave her, to help her sleep. He picked the almost full glass of wine from the floor and finished her drink; tasting her lipstick, laughing at the absurdity of his feelings for Marie.

He switched off the Tiffany lamp on the end table. Little colored lights twinkled on a small Christmas tree by the window. A Big Bird night light lit up the bathroom. Quietly, he studied the bathroom. Boxes with David's colognes and Frankie's toy boats and submarines sat in the corner. Benny tilted his head, with his personal thoughts. Memories of his friend, Marie, from their years in law school. His wrist watch beeped: 11 p.m. He took another sip of his drink and thought to himself; twelve hours ago, the world changed. Benny wondered if the good times in life were over. Her warm, lively hugs and kisses every time they met. Now there was the roar of silence; the sounds of the missing children, always playing their practical jokes on their Uncle Ben. It was only now, that he realized the emptiness. His friends were gone now; gone forever, never to be replaced.

A pile of Frankie's toy soldiers sat in a basket next to the bathtub. All the nights they used to spend launching amphibious strikes against the super-powered submarines under the bubble bath water with pilots maneuvering their little plastic jets through the halls of the house. And Shelley, commanding the walkie-talkies calling in the information to General Frankie and General Uncle Ben. Frankie would spit out the sounds of explosions with drool as he navigated the olive-green jets across the hallway floor. Shelley always talking over the walkie-talkies, wanting to have the planes talked down, while commanding the mission. Benny put his shoes on and yawned, as he tugged on his wrinkled suit jacket. He finished his Bushmills and noticed the ghosts the Christmas tree cast across the ceiling and walls of the bedroom. Benny took one last look at his friend, and whispered before he left for the evening.

"I love you President Marie Joanna Arcola."

NINE

THE WHITE HOUSE GUARD slowly marched down the corridor, opening each door, inspecting each room, checking each window. A strange howling, like wind, drew the guard to the base of the stairway to listen closely to the noises. A woman could be heard, sobbing and crying. He pulled his revolver from it's holster and whispered into his headset microphone for additional guards to position themselves at the bottom of the staircase.

At the top of the stairs, shadows crossed the walls within the dim light of the fading wallpaper, across the antique bookcases, down the hallway. The guard held his hand out and whispered into his microphone for the guards to stand by, downstairs. President Arcola paced back and forth, up and down the hallway in her white cotton robe, holding her face as she cried.

"Madame President." The guard whispered out, lowering his gun down to his side, back into the holster. Cautiously, he stepped up into the second floor corridor watching her disappear into the sitting room. A voice responded over the guards headset. "Is everything okay up there?" One of the guards said.

"Yes. Everything's fine up here. The President is having a problem sleeping. Keep an eye on the east entrance. I'll be down in a few minutes." The guard replied to the pair of secret service agents rushing to the bottom of the staircase. She sat alone on the oak rocking chair; her hands clasped tightly across her lap.

"I just needed to cry. My heart hurts so bad. Part of me is missing. Oh, please, God. Please make this pain stop." President Arcola gasped for air, her chest heaving with every breath.

"Madame President. Are you alright?" The guard said, tipping his flashlight away from her face, aiming at the floor.

"I used to rock my babies in this chair whenever they couldn't sleep or when they had nightmares. It took them a while to get used to the dark. I was always there for them. Why wasn't I there? I'm sorry. I just got lost. I'm not used to being here yet." President Arcola said, wiping her nose and tear-filled eyes on the sleeve of her cotton robe. The guard leaned over to her.

"Here, ma'am." The guard held out a white handkerchief.

"Oh. Thank you." She smiled at the thoughtful gift. "What's your name?"

"Private Jeffrey Novak, ma'am." The tall, dark guard stood at attention, out of habit. President Arcola smiled at the young guard.

"Well, thank you for the handkerchief, Jeffrey. I'll make sure my secretary delivers a new one to you."

"If you wish, ma'am." Private Jeffrey Novak replied. "Will you be needing anything else?"

"No, thank you, Jeffrey. I just need to sit here for a while. I'll be fine." President Arcola said, patting the White House guard softly on the arm. The guard nodded his head and stepped slightly backward, watching President Arcola's shadow in the dark, slowly rocking in her chair, holding a pair of baby blankets.

TEN

THE CLOUDS AND SKY reflected back against the tinted black windows. People stopped and stared, curiously wondering, sad and confused; feeling the loss that she felt. The world seemed closed out, as she glanced at her secluded reflection on the bulletproof window, hopelessly gray; weakening her soul; making it hard to breath and concentrate. Her eyes were swollen and she shook from being so very tired, and very alone.

The secret service agents rose out of the sedans, buttoning their jackets and checking their weapons as they surround President Marie Arcola's limousine. Joey held out his hand to help the lady President out of the vehicle. She took a deep breath of the warm, December air. Some of the buildings displayed Christmas decorations with jingle bells ringing from the ivy, swaying in the breeze. Marie remembered the evenings she would spend with David and her children, driving through the streets of Georgetown. She noticed most of the trees had lost their leaves, making the streets seem darker.

Police blocked the far end of the street, keeping away the crowds of on-lookers and photographers. President Arcola moved slowly up the stairs to the funeral home doors, escorted by Joey and two secret service agents. Joey glanced at the lady President, her face covered by a black veil. Only the passing of the clouds allowed the sun to sparkle her eyes.

As she entered the room, the stain glass windows bathe the walls next to the closed caskets. The flag of the United States was draped across the top of David's coffin. Marie raised her veil, back over her head; she struggled to keep her balance. Her eyes lowered and her lips began to tremble. The secret service agents inched forward and then paused, to look discreetly away.

Then she noticed her babies' caskets. She let out a small gasp, now her eyes welled with tears as she clutched a handkerchief to her face. Her head slightly shook as she began to cry at the sight of the two small black caskets. From twenty feet away, to each side of the caskets, thousands of stuffed animals, toys, little gift boxes, dolls, roses, books, Christmas ornaments, blankets, cards and flowers were laid at the bases of the kneelers across the floor. She stepped slowly to the caskets, her body weak from the sight of the gifts. The light was somber with the colors of the stained glass windows, reflecting on top of the shiny black caskets. The smell was relaxing, the soft music, playing solemnly in the background.

"I know now that you can see everything clearly." She tripped on a stuffed animal and touched one of the caskets. And then, the other. She bowed her head and caught her words as she cried. "Sleep in your long dreams, my angels. Nothing can hurt you now. Not the cold. No disease. Come visit me in my dreams anytime. Just please don't forget me." Marie slid her hands, caressing one coffin and then the other. She fell to her knees, from pain, from exhaustion, and from sorrow. A part of her is gone. Her chest hurt from the deep, heaving gasps for air, and the endless hours of crying. Marie fell to her knees and folded her hands to pray. "Please help me. Please my babies. Let me forgive them."

ELEVEN

SENATOR TREVOR THOMAS tapped the face of his Rolex, wondering why it stopped; making a secret service agent very nervous at the end of the Rotunda. The senator gave the agent a mischievous grin and raised his eyebrows. He removed the watch and handed it to a tall, thin pimple-faced man dressed in a thick, blue sweater and dark brown slacks. "Here, my loyal assistant. Be a nice young man and go have this checked out. I need it back by three p.m. sharp. If not. Charge a new one to my account." Senator Thomas said while pointing his finger with a playful wave of his hand.

Two former Presidents walked up to the casket of President George Johnson and set down a pair of wreathes made of red roses. The ambassador of France stepped up and greeted them while the Prince of Kuwait joyously shook their hands. Senator Thomas quickly knelt in front of the coffin and gave a curious, sympathetic look. He studied the flag of the United States, draped over the casket, in the center of the flowers and wreaths, and wondered what it would be like to be dead. And he wondered what the burned President looked like. He made the sign of the cross and rushed to catch another man walking through the Rotunda entrance.

"Arthur. Did you make the arrangements for the children?" Senator Thomas whispered loud, grabbing the white haired man by the arm.

"Yes, Trevor. The first lady gave us all a call. She told us you had a good, long talk with her about the importance of President Arcola's children being allowed to be buried in Arlington Cemetery with their father. What makes you think you're always going to get your way, Trevor?" Senator Arthur Graebul asked.

"Because I'm charming and rich. And next election, I'm going to be the first Republican President in twenty years." Senator Thomas patted Senator Graebul on the shoulder and gave him a classic smile.

"The first lady also said you put up all the money to make sure President Arcola's children could be buried in Arlington. She's a Democrat." Senator Graebul said with a puzzled expression on his face, walking with Senator Thomas outside, to the stairs.

"Yeah, well. Don't worry, Art. I already had the press notified about my donation. I also told them that the money came out of my own pocket, so that there wouldn't be any political uproar about the use of taxpayers money." Senator Graebul shook his head in disbelief.

"Come on, Art. It's gonna be great for votes. When President Arcola starts to throw in the towel and realizes it's 'a mans world after all', it'll be a landslide in my favor." Senator Thomas gazed off of the steps of the Capitol, across the reflecting pool, out over the mall. "But, I also did it because I'm a nice guy." Senator Thomas grabbed Senator Graebul's arm to check his watch, for the time.

"Gotta go, Art. See you at the funeral." Senator Thomas said with a wave, scampering away, down the stairs to a woman waving from a beige Mercedes.

TWELVE

"RACHEL, CAN I OFFER you something to drink?" Senator Trevor Thomas said reaching over and opening his little refrigerator on top of the rows of black and gray three drawer filing cabinets. The attractive newspaper reporter leaned against his desk, as she tried to look at the selection of drinks.

"Yes. I'll take one of those bottles of ice tea." She said with a smile that crinkled her eyes and curved her cream-colored lips. She pulled her long brown hair, tossing the mane behind her shoulder. Senator Thomas took a long, shopping look at her firm legs as she crosses them, placing her note pad on top of her knee.

"Thank you." Rachel said, batting her eyes at Trevor, taking a drink of her tea, starting the tape recorder and setting it on the senator's desk.

"I'm sorry I forgot about this meeting. It's been a little crazy around here since President Johnson was killed."

Rachel slid her violet jacket off, letting it fall to the love seat, unbuttoning the top button on her silky beige blouse, to get the senator's attention. She stood to look at the plaques and awards hung on the walls of the senator's office. She ran her fingers with their perfectly maintained pink nails around a trophy and held it up for her to read the engraved words. "You took second place in fencing at Indiana University? I thought you just played basketball?" Rachel turned to smile at the senator.

"Fencing helped me appreciate conflict and gave me a way to understand an opponent 'one on one'. It also gave me more composure and balance. Besides, I didn't want the guys teasing me in the locker room because I was taking ballet."

"Oh. I took ballet. It's not that bad. It's also very relaxing. Like meditation."

"Well. I would have taken ballet if there would have been women like you in the class."

Rachel gave a squeaky, little girl giggle and flashed a smile at Trevor. She continued to study a sheet of thirty-two cent, postage stamps, hanging on the wall, matted in a glass frame. The stamps were rectangular, with a silhouette of a woman looking over her right shoulder, at a pink ribbon. "These are original stamps for Breast Cancer Awareness from 1997. I see you received a gold plaque for your contributions. I also know that you influenced the vote in the Senate to help pass special case laws for women."

"I don't like to use the word 'influenced'. I prefer the word 'persuaded'. One of the smaller companies I own also specializes in medical equipment that helps with early detection of breast cancer."

"You know, you're known in the media world as a womanizing manipulator." Rachel said, teasing with that squeaky laugh.

"Of course I am. Women's votes are very important to me. And so are their campaign contributions." Senator Thomas stepped to the front of his walnut desk and leaned back, popping open his Diet Coke, staring at Rachel's ballerina legs. "I also supported the Breast Cancer Foundation because my ex-wife had a scare and was facing a mastectomy. I've been in two small military operations and was very close to having my left arm amputated. I still have a bullet in my shoulder. I know how terrifying the thought of having a part of your body cut off can be."

Rachel counted the medals and bars in one of the glass cases, sitting on top of a bookshelf. "You received three Purple Hearts and two Medals of Honor. I'm impressed." Her long thin fingers stroked the walnut case. She smiled at the senator. "You seem to be in wonderful shape for someone who was wounded in those wars."

Senator Thomas glanced down at the tape recorder and chose his words carefully. "I assure you. Everything works fine. Just a few bullet wounds. Just a few scars and some bad memories. And they weren't really wars. They were battles. Didn't you learn about Operation Desert Storm or Operation Joint Endeavor? Or even Operation Joint Guard?"

"No." Rachel replied.

"What did you say you studied up at Michigan State University?"

"I received my bachelors degree in International Studies. I just don't think those battles were that important. The United States fighting someone else's civil disputes for someone else's country. I think wars are for idiots. All those people dying for no reason at all."

"I see your point. While you were riding your tricycle up and down your mommy and daddy's driveway, I was in a foxhole outside of Butmia, bleeding and holding my sergeant's dead body over me, while fourteen and fifteen year old boys marched by, lobbing hand grenades into farmhouses."

"If you were hiding, how could you tell they were teenage boys?"

"Because, after they passed by. I killed three of them."

"Well. You could have let them go."

"Later on, two of the boys were identified by the local army. It seems these boys attacked a woman, raped her and cut her throat, while her two children watched. That 'civil dispute' went on for four years and took the lives of two hundred and eighty thousand people. Mostly women and children." Trevor's dark eyes sparkled with heated disgust. "International Studies? Is that some new kind of program in a community college?"

"Michigan State is not a community college."

"Maybe you're right. I just remember every time I played basketball against the Spartan's, the Hoosiers always won."

"And playing basketball in college made you educated in politics?"

"Yes. There is politics in basketball. There are rules and teamwork. But my degree in Liberal Arts, my two years in law school and my seven years in the army also helped. It's good to learn to get along with people. You probably never had any family members in the armed forces?"

"No. All the people in my family had real jobs. So why would they want to put their lives in jeopardy? War is for idiots."

"Oh. I see. All those men and women giving their lives for this country to guarantee you and your family freedom, so someone like you can graduate from college to become ignorant and disrespectful."

"What's that supposed to mean?" Rachel responded, with a blank, Barbie-doll expression on her face.

"Never mind." Senator Thomas said, wondering how this female ever got through college. He glanced down to check the time on his desk clock. "You've got five minutes. Ask me some questions."

Rachel rushed to sit down on the sofa with her pen and note pad. "Are you going to vote for the United States to send troops into Iran?"

"That vote is going to be up to the Senate. And then, eventually, the decision of the President. At this time, I don't see why we should be involved with Iran."

"Even though Iran stated that they captured the four American soldiers who blew-up a bomb in that paint factory?"

"Paint factory!? Where do you get your information? Those chemicals have already killed people hundreds of miles away in other countries! What kind of paint is that? Iran and three other countries, including Russia, have created new weapons through loopholes in the Chemical Weapons Convention, ignoring Article 10 and Article 11 since 1997."

Rachel jotted some of the senators words down on her note pad and nervously went on to the next questions. "You have the money and the votes and were planning to run against President George Johnson in next years election, now that Marie Arcola is President, will your plans change for the better or the worse?"

"Better and worse. Better for me, because I have earned the faith and represented several large domestic and international businesses that have interest in the Middle East, China and Taiwan. Their confidence in my decision making and my loyalty to them is beyond money and votes. It is the true essence of the security of our country and the preservation of our rights, guaranteed under the Constitution. Worse for the Johnson/Arcola Administration, because her ability to deal with this situation in Iran will probably escalate into a bad international panic. And that panic could lead to the end of her political career."

"Is that because of her being a woman President?"

Senator Trevor Thomas set down the empty can of soda pop. "I happen to have worked with some of the most brilliant women in

Congress, the Senate, the field of Law and the Armed Forces. I have always respected the integrity of anyone choosing a career in politics. Men and Women. Their sacrifices for this country are endless. I happen to think it's timely that a woman became President of the United States. I just wish the situation that made her President was different."

"What about the recent riots that began after the Dulles Airport explosion? Do you feel the riots and the demonstrations will continue?"

"The concern about the riots is one of the reasons why the governors stopped over in Washington. I don't know if the riots will continue. There is a lot of tension in the world now. A lot of racism on our college and university campuses, especially since China lied about Hong Kong and now is threatening Taiwan. China has pilfered close to two hundred billion dollars from Hong Kong banks and businesses since August of 1997. There's a lot of distrust toward the Chinese military right now."

"Will the Senate pass a bill to deny visas for students from China?"

"There is talk. China's military has taken most of the money from Hong Kong and built up it's armies while imprisoning more of Lee's democratic leaders. The people of Hong Kong are confused and being terrorized. There are an awful lot of human rights issues that need to be addressed."

"Do you think the riots are the reason President Johnson was assassinated?"

Senator Trevor Thomas became silent, pausing deep in thought as he rubbed his chin. The idea of the riots being the reason for the explosion at Dulles Airport never crossed his mind. "The FBI is investigating all the possibilities."

"Do you have anything you'd like to say to the average person on how to protect themselves during these riots?"

"I just wish more American's would preserve their second amendment rights so they can protect their families and their homes. The last I heard, twenty-nine people were murdered in their own homes in Detroit, San Diego and Des Moines. Now I bet a lot of those whining liberals wish they had a gun in the house to protect themselves. If people don't have guns to protect themselves and their property, that's their fault. My job is to make certain they are allowed that right under the second amendment. These riots are under investigation by my administration, the Thomas Administration, and I have made it clear to President Arcola, that I am totally dedicated to preserving the rights of our citizens. The criminals and gangs starting all these fires and looting all these businesses will be held accountable and will be punished."

Rachel scrambled through the pages in her note pad, giving Trevor the opportunity to re-inventory her figure and her soft, pretty face.

"I must have left my other questions back in my apartment. My place is only a few minutes away, on Bryant Street. I can be back soon."

"Bryant Street? Why would you want to live in D.C.? Everything's crazy and expensive."

"I'm hoping to meet the right people. You know. Make connections. Besides, someday I'm going to get a job that makes six figures." She stood, setting her sparkling gold pen and note pad into her shiny new, black leather briefcase. She purposely opened the slit in her skirt while she smoothed out the creases, showing Trevor her leg.

"Of course you are. Your background in International Studies is an important asset to Washington." Senator Thomas glanced at the clock and began putting on his jacket. Rachel handed him a business card with her name, address and phone number written on the back. Trevor smirked and reached down, clicking the tape recorder off.

"I'd like it if you'd give me a call sometime." Rachel said with a smile. "I'd love to be your exclusive writer on your campaign trail."

"Well, Rachel. One thing at a time. You can give me a ride to the White House and I'll answer some more questions on the way."

"You're going to see her, aren't you?"

"Her? President Arcola? Of course. That's my job. And while I'm there. I can see if my practice putting green will fit in the Office."

Rachel picked up her coat and briefcase, with that same blank look on her face.

THIRTEEN

BENNY SET A LUNCH TRAY down on President Arcola's desk in the Oval Office. The President slowly paced the room, while a press agent and a speech writer frantically scribbled down notes. Benny's digital watch beeped and he looked to check the time, and waved it off whispering 'never mind'. There was a light knock at the door.

"Madame President. It's Senator Thomas. He's here and he says it's urgent." The secretary said, poking her face through the opening.

"Oh. It's always urgent with that asshole." President Arcola huffed in a perturbed voice.

Senator Thomas pushed his way into the office. "Excuse me, miss. I heard what you called me, Madame President. You won't be winning many votes with that kind of talk. Maybe we can be alone for a few minutes. I think everyone here can leave, except for this man."

Senator Thomas pointed to a black haired man in a faded, dark gray suit, sitting in the easy chair. "Agent Naughton. Am I right? I'm Senator Trevor Thomas. I think I served with your dad in Bosnia. That was quite a picnic." The senator held his hand out to the reluctant agent.

"Senator, what the hell do you think you're doing?" President Arcola asked, watching the press agent and the speech writer, stop with puzzled looks on their faces.

"It's okay, Madame President. We're gonna break for some lunch. Is fifteen minutes good?" Benny said stretching his arms to his sides.

"Sure Benny. Thanks." President Arcola gave the senator a cold glare, as her aides left the Oval office and closed the door.

"What do you mean 'what the hell do I think I'm doing?' I'm trying to be your friend. Especially in these troubled times." Senator Thomas stated, sitting on the desk, helping himself to a handful of mixed peanuts.

"Your seedy reputation makes it difficult for anyone to work with you." The President said eating her chicken sandwich.

"What? That I treat women like trash and workers like slaves? That's just talk. It's just part of politics. So, Agent Naughton. How does it look in Iran?" The senator smirked, changing the subject.

"The situation in Iran is very much under control, Senator Thomas. Reports are being monitored carefully. Even the radio communications on Radio Free Iran report that everything is under control." Agent Naughton answered, barely looking up from his laptop computer.

"Come on, Eugene. Don't bullshit a bullshitter. You've had a four man SEAL team captured and puppeted on television stations coming out of Iran for all the world to see. Half the Middle East is starting to believe the stories that those soldiers blew up that chemical weapons factory and the last reports say almost a hundred thousand people are dead in Iran because of this incident. Reports are still coming in from Kuwait that rain is falling in Mina Suud and people are getting sick. There are also reports that the same rain from Ras al Khafji to Bahrain has contaminated the drinking water." The senator said, shaking his head in disbelief.

"Most of that information has not been confirmed." Agent Naughton replied, glancing calmly back and forth from his laptop to Senator Thomas.

"I happen to know that information has been confirmed. It's going to make you slide in the polls, Madame President." The senator chuckled.

"Is that all you care about, Senator? Being elected to become the next President of the United States?" President Arcola huffed.

"Hell yes! That's my only goal in life. To knock you and your liberal bull out of the arena. You Democrats mess with gun laws, screw up international trade policies and fleece all the taxpayers money on unnecessary programs. If it wasn't for the Balanced Budget Amendment passing years ago. We'd all be speaking Mexican or Chinese. You're going to need some of those senators votes when this thing goes down with Iran. And I've got most of those votes right here in my pocket." Senator Thomas helped himself to a Diet Coke on the Presidents desk.

"So you know the explosion in Iran and the bomb from Dulles Airport may be linked?" President Arcola said, her eyes studying the senators every move and expression.

"What? That the detonators were similar? That it was a standard Taliban scenario? That the airport cameras have pictures of three individuals that may be the suspects? I know many things, Madame President. Even secrets about you. I know you're weak and I can help you. Iran is going to kill those soldiers from the SEAL team. You have to think like a soldier always. I served with the shittiest parts of Desert Storm and Bosnia. One time we parachuted into the middle of a goddamn mine field. We had to crawl on our bellies in the blinding rain. The worst shit I had to endure was hearing my buddy, Todd, blown to pieces in a pasture outside of Sarajevo. Snipers shooting all around us. I'm sitting there for hours hoping and praying that this poor bastard, with no arms; trying to hold his guts in with his knees, would just stop screaming and would just die." Senator Thomas noticed Agent Naughton trembling. "I told you that story to let you know how much I fought for this country and earned and deserved everything I accomplished."

"Are you suggesting I didn't 'earn' this presidency?" President Arcola said.

Senator Thomas raised his eyebrows at that notion as he paced the room. "I don't think I need to suggest anything. I'm just saying you should open your door to the real people that can solve these problems, instead of hiding behind your administration. I want these pieces-of-fucking crap that killed President Johnson, just as bad as you. So, how are you going to convince this nation and it's people these terrorist bombs won't kill again? How are you going to reassure the people of this country, Madame President?" Senator Trevor Thomas's eyes glowed red with rage. President Arcola poured herself a cup of hot tea and stirred in a spoonful of honey.

"You seem to have forgotten my husband and children were

killed in that explosion. And I also was a soldier who served this country in Desert Storm." Senator Thomas gave the lady president a grimacing look.

"We're sending a former SEAL team in from the President's secret service special forces." Agent Naughton added.

"What? A bunch of old guys who haven't seen real action in almost ten years?" Senator Thomas forced a snide laugh.

"We need more accurate evidence. We have to be able to disprove the propaganda Iran is using to saturate the media. The next team will go in and gather samples of the chemicals. They'll have equipment to transfer information immediately from the factory to one of our aircraft carriers in the Persian Gulf. DVD's can transmit digital photographs right to the Pentagon." Agent Naughton said.

"So you think Iran is going to let those soldiers walk right on in there and do all this wonderful stuff without a fight?" Senator Thomas questioned, folding his arms, leaning back on the President's desk.

"If we move in within the next two days, I don't think we'll have any problems. Our satellites show no immediate activity that would endanger the mission. Reports from Iran tell us their military forces plan to stay almost fifty miles away from the factory, probably until the air clears up. But once the factory is back in the hands of the Iranian government, we might never know what really happened. And then Iran will carry out their execution of that SEAL team." The FBI agent said.

"We can't allow Iran to convince other countries we are responsible for this incident. I can't allow them to dismiss the fact that those are biological and chemical weapons in that factory. They are already convincing other countries to free-up sanctions by using this incident." President Arcola said.

"China and North Korea have already suggested they'll supply Iran with modern weaponry to protect their country in exchange for oil." Agent Naughton stated.

"That's crazy. We wont allow that to happen." The senator remarked.

"It's an opportunity for everyone, Senator Thomas. That's why we need more evidence." President Arcola was stoic, glaring back at the senator with those blue eyes of ice. Senator Thomas tried to read her thoughts.

"Oh my God. You want this 'slapped together' SEAL team of yours to go into that factory, hoping to prove Iranian terrorists killed your husband. You'd actually put our country at risk of going to war, for a few lives? You, of all people should know the kind of danger this could place on the security of America." Senator Thomas paced about in anger.

"Evidence could also prove Iran didn't kill President Johnson." Agent Naughton said, defending the President's decision and trying to take control of the situation.

"So what are you going to do? Just keep sending improvised SEAL teams into Iran, having them die from exposure to these chemicals? Or to be executed? What's next? Send in the Boy Scouts?" The senator said.

"With medical teams from the U.S. Navy and the Red Cross, we could help these people out before half their country is destroyed. I have people from my administration trying to work out a deal with the Mullahs and the Red Crescent." President Arcola opened the Oval Office door and motioned her hand for Benny and the aides to return.

"What a bunch of liberal crap. So now you think you're going to play mommy to the world? Look, Madame President. One day you'll wake up and see these other countries do not recognize us as being human beings. That's why they're so bent on destroying and bombing, and murdering us. Right now, in Northern Iran, little boys are being trained to fire rifles and make bombs. They are out there shouting 'death to all Americans.' Those boys will be the first to ram their bayonets into those soldiers that were captured. And they are coming after you and me!"

"What about our integrity as leaders in the eyes of other countries!? Everyone's watching us during this crisis, senator. What about God and country!? What do you care about?" President Arcola demanded.

"What do I care about? I care about the continuation of our species. The American species. It is our design to become the superior race. It is necessary for us to be the strongest, economically, educationally, militarily and everything humanly possible.

We must become the most superior race in the world. Period." Senator Thomas replied.

"You sound as cold and depraved as the terrorists." President Arcola snapped back, signing a letter Benny set on her desk.

"Depraved!? May I remind you, again, Madame President. It was their chemical and biological weapons factory that caused this massive plague. In their country! They did this to themselves. Not us. Maybe it's Allah that did this? Maybe it's just plain evolution of mankind. I don't believe we should keep sending our finest soldiers in harms way. Into the middle of Iran and anthrax." Senator Thomas slammed his empty soda can to the desk.

Agent Naughton's cell phone rang. He only responded with a few 'affirmatives' and nods. "The second team has been assembled, Madame President. Defense Secretary Rawlings approved the action and said he'll contact you when he gets back from London tomorrow." Agent Naughton said, setting files on the President's desk, giving the senator a smug look.

"Do you realize you could take us into a long, drawn out war?" The senator huffed.

"The Joint Chiefs of Staff don't agree with you, Senator Thomas. These SEAL teams are going in on a humanitarian mission."

"Madame President? A humanitarian mission? This is a stupid clown act that's going to increase Iran's propaganda against the United States and escalate more terrorist attacks. I hope you plan on losing the taxpayers votes." Senator Thomas said with a smile, checking the time on the grandfather clock.

"The taxpayers pay damn good money for these soldiers to defend this country. And if a few small SEAL teams die to prevent this country from being the pawn in a Third World War. Well, I plan to take full responsibility for my decisions and the deaths of any and all soldiers. So what do you think of mommy now, Senator Thomas?" President Arcola glared down her nose at Senator Thomas. He shuffled in place, giving her a quizzical, disgusted stare, then stormed out of the Oval office.

FOURTEEN

THE SECOND CEREMONY was in St. Matthews for President George Johnson. The casket was closed and barely visible. Draped over the casket was the flag of the United States of America: red, white and blue, in all it's glory, for the world to see. President Marie Arcola walked down the aisle with Benny and knelt before the casket. From underneath her black veil, she turned and noticed the congregation gathered to say goodbye to President Johnson. From all over the world, over eighty nations, ambassadors, diplomats, dignitaries, politicians, business leaders and reporters; were all here to pay their respects.

Jason held steady with his Remington, in the shadows of the balcony. The organ played softly while the choir sang the closing hymn. President Arcola whispered to Benny that she felt light-headed and held tight to his arm. Trench and Fielding walk side by side with the President and her advisor while two additional secret service agents were within arms' reach. The agents were vigilant, as she hugged and shook hands with ambassadors at the church entrance. Joey positioned himself on the front of the roof. President Johnson's casket was rolled through the church, to the doors leading out to Rhode Island Avenue. One of the agents opened the door of the limousine waiting at the bottom of the church stairs. The Prince of Kuwait held President Arcola's hand as he walked her to the vehicle. The Sharp Shooters and Secret Service became especially uneasy as the Prince crawled into the limo at her request.

The blue skies and sunshine beamed down on the streets of Washington, D.C., out of place, for this saddest of days. The riderless horse moved at a slow gait as the procession began. The horse was saddled with the boots of a missing soldier, facing backwards in the stirrups. A group of secret service agents marched through the rows of police officers and security guards.Three dozen soldiers from the 3rd U.S. Infantry Regiment, magnificently dressed in caps and uniforms moved in rhythm; the unison of their well-shined shoes, clicking on the street. Seven drummers slowly beat their drums to the low mournful call of the bagpipes. The sentinels stepped in formation as the casket of President Johnson rolled on a caisson, down the middle of the road to the astonished stares of the crowd. A single sailor of the United States Navy, marched in short steps proudly carrying the Presidential Flag.

The haunting silence of the thousands of people who lined the streets, slowly plucked at roses, letting the pink, white, red and yellow petals slowly blow on Rhode Island Avenue, as the caskets of David, Shelley and Francis Arcola appeared behind the riderless horse. Police motorcycles escorted President Arcola's limousine, slowly riding by her side. She watched and waved from the window, at all who had showed up to express their condolences. Men, women and children dropped roses to the street, waving American flags. Marie whispered out 'thank you' to all the people as the cortege passed.

Home-made signs were held by supporters. Signs that read 'We love you', 'Be strong', 'I lost my baby too', 'We're here for you', 'Everything will be fine', 'Be strong Lady President'. President Marie Arcola bowed her head, overwhelmed with sorrow.

Sharp shooters patrolled the Potomac River in powerboats, trolling to the north and south under the Arlington Memorial Bridge. At the crossroads of Schley and Eisenhower Drives, President Johnson and the Arcola procession were met by a hundred Marines, Air Force Pilots, U.S.Naval Officers and Infantry from the U.S. Army. Each of them stood at attention as the riderless horse slowly cantered by, with the caskets following slowly behind.

The limousine door opened and she stepped out into the afternoon sun. Shadows from the Arlington Memorial Gateway stretched out, shading the three Arcola coffins as they are moved by the pallbearers moved President Johnson's casket to the front of the tent, near the grave, where he was to be laid to rest.

Two Air Force Captains slowly removed the American flag, folding it into perfect angles as they passed it back and forth until it was folded into a tight, neat triangle. First Lady Johnson tried to hold back her tears as the young captain handed her the American flag from her husband's coffin and stood at attention, giving her a salute. He stepped backward three paces and remained at attention. There was a long pause of silence and all present bowed their heads in a quiet prayer. The Senior Master Sergeant called out and the seven smartly dressed and decorated Airmen raised their rifles into the afternoon sky. The first round of the twenty-one gun salute crackled, making the congregation flinch. President Arcola prepared herself for the second round; and then the third. The lone bugler softly began to play taps, standing tall against the backdrop of the clouds moving to allow the blue skies and sunshine to bathe Arlington Cemetery.There was a high pitched shrill, up in the Washington, D.C. afternoon sky, drawing the attention of the congregation. They looked upward as the jets roared by in formation.There were four F-16Ns and an empty space where there should have been a fifth; symbolizing and honoring President George Johnson.

President Arcola realized the alteration of her destiny, the power and the obligation her life had taken, as she gazed across the rolling hills with the white crosses and headstones of Arlington National Cemetery. She squeezed Benny's hand and stood straight and tall while she peered through her dark sunglasses, covering red, swollen eyes, while tears streaked down her cheeks. The bagpipes began to slowly and softly play 'Amazing Grace'. She sighed, taking a deep breath of the warm December day, and whispered. "I'm the President."

FIFTEEN

"MARLA! MARLA, MY LOVE!" Trench yelled out, over the music blasting from the jukebox at the other end of the dance floor, with it's flashing, multi-colored lights. Some drunks threw dollar bills to a dancer on the stage in the corner. He grabbed the waitress in the revealing yellow midriff and tight blue jeans by the waist. Jason and Joey shook their heads and laughed at Trench's antics, as he pulled out a stack of fifty and hundred dollar bills. He plucked out a fifty dollar bill by the ends with his middle and pointing fingers.

"Here. My favorite President would like you to bring us a round of Cuervo and another pitcher of Bud Light. Bud Light, because we must stay trim and fit, as defenders of our country, we must always be ready to do battle." Trench smiled and raised his glass to his team. Jason and Joey joined the toast, while Dewey and Fielding seated themselves on bar stools underneath a television set, preoccupied by the news coverage from President Johnson's funeral. The pretty brunette waitress teased the fifty dollar bill away from the doting lieutenant.

"Now. It's going to take more than money to get me, Trench. I'm looking for a man who's ready to make a commitment." Marla flirted, tugging at the soldiers thick mustache. Jason laughed and guzzled the rest of his beer, staring up at the television.

"But I love you. I've always loved you." Trench pouted with a playful, sad smile.

"Sure you love me. As long as I'm fetching you beers or handing you the remote control. So how's it gonna feel, working for a female President?" Marla smiled, popping her gum, looking around at a couple sitting down in a booth.

"Hell. As long as I keep getting my paycheck. One year more of service and I retire with benefits, a bonus and a full pension anyhow."

"You'll see. In a few weeks, you'll be going crazy like any other man would that works for a woman." Marla said, stepping away to set down napkins and menus for a group of college students seating themselves at another table.

"Damn, Trench. Don't go flashing a wad of cash around here. We're on the Strip. You'll get us all in another fight and get us kicked out of this fine establishment for good." Jason said, sarcastically, staring at two blondes, one dressed in a black leather mini-skirt and the other in a blue neon jumpsuit, sitting at the next table; playfully waving 'hello'. "Hi, ladies." Jason said, giggling, waving back at the two women, smoothing out their clothes, as they sat.

"Look at this shit, will ya! They're parading Squid's SEAL team around the streets of Tehran like they're pieces of meat. Poking them and sticking them with sticks." Dewey remarked in cold disgust making a face until the veins swelled from his forehead. He poured himself another beer, watching the CNN reports on the television above the bar.

"At least they're still alive." Fielding commented, itching his tattoo through his blond buzz-cut hair.

"Whatcha got there, Fielding, the barber cut your big fat head again?" Dewey said with a chuckle.

Fielding turned his head showing the other soldier the back of his neck. "No. It's my new tattoo. See. It cost me seventy-nine bucks. Ain't she a pretty one?"

"'In God We Trust'. A very profound statement, Brother Fielding." Dewey said turning back to curse at the news on the television. "Look at these stupid professors and specialist, saying that those SEALs are trained to be punished and tortured like that! Right! So what the fuck are their minds gonna be like if they get out!? Being slapped and shook around with their brains being scrambled in the inside of their skulls. Blindfolded and kicked by all those fuckin' bastards. This is nuts for this to go on. We still have soldiers that aren't themselves from 'Nam. Something changes in a man's mind, you know. The United States should get in there and start kickin' some ass." Dewey said, showing his teeth, rubbing his nubby reddish-brown hair, flashing those spastic, bloodshot eyes while that vein bulged from the left side of his head.

"You know they're goin' to send us in next. The FBI and CIA are saying the hills and roads are littered with bodies. Hell, even the flies and maggots are dying. People's eyes hanging out of their sockets by the optic nerves, laying in piles of their own intestines and organs." Fielding mumbled, pulling out his Leatherman, clicking open the pliers, so that he could pluck a long, black nasal hair.

"Yeah. I heard even the rats and buzzards were puking up blood from eating the bodies." Joey said, pouring another glass of beer.

"Jeez, brother. What kinda talk is that in front of the ladies? You know, I wouldn't mind scoring something tonight." Jason said with a wink, slapping his arms around his brother, giving him a hug and a kiss.

Fielding observed his catch at the end of the pliers, with tear-filled eyes; wiping the hair off onto his jeans. "Goddamn. That almost hurt worse than my cystoscopy last May. That hair was about a half-a-foot long. Always sticking me in the eye." Fielding laughed, boldly drinking right out of the pitcher of beer, playing with a stack of two dollar bills. He reached into his top pocket and flicked open a pig-sticker. The soldier laid out five of the bills on the bar and began meticulously sculpting away with the nine inch blade.

"Well. Iran can't be any worse than tomorrows hangover or Fielding's 'Hell,Fire and Damnation' Chili." Jason laughed, half-watching one of the strippers on the lighted stage in the corner while helping Marla with the shots of tequila. Marla set Trench's change down by the shots of tequila with two more pitchers of beer.

Fielding cut around the face of Thomas Jefferson, just below his name, careful to stay within the black border above the word 'the'. He pulled out a glue stick and flipped off the blue cap. With a twist, the waxy glue appeared. Dewey and the bartender took notice when Fielding set a pile of twenty dollar bills out in front of him. He slid a crisp, new twenty across the bar, from the pile of bills, turning it over and over again, raising it to his nose to smell the new ink.

"Now, you know I'm keeping track of how much you fellas are drinking. I will take your car keys away and make you walk home." Marla said smiling, shaking her finger at Joey, Jason, Dewey, Fielding and Trench. Joey crossed his eyes and with a deer-in-the-headlights-stare, purposely drooled beer and blew bubbles until the waitress scolded him. "Now, Joey. I expect that kind of behavior from these hooligans but not from you. See what you boys did? You corrupted my little Joey." Jason and Fielding look down at Joey's lap.

"Oh, now Marla. The way Jason's working the room, these lovely young ladies will be driving us home." Trench said, handing the change and another fifty dollar bill to Marla. "And if that don't work. We've got a chauffeur waiting out front. A pretty young redhead out there with our Abrahms tank."

"Now if you keep giving me all your money like there's no tomorrow, I won't be able to marry you. You'll be poor." Marla said, taking the money.

The secret service team gave each other a cool, undaunted glare, with each one of them sporting a sinister squint of their eyes. They all reached into their shirt pockets and pulled out Cuban cigars. They raised their shots of Cuervo in toast.

"To the next SEAL team to go save the fuckin' world. To the Eagle team and to no tomorrow." Jason said tapping his shot glass against the glasses of his buddies. Marla lowered her eyes and scooted away, realizing these men would soon be sent to their possible deaths. A bartender held up a remote control and switched one of the TV channels. Fielding took a drink of his beer to chase down the tequila and turned to watch the continuing news footage about the explosion at Dulles Airport that killed President Johnson. He passed some twenty dollar bills over to Joey.

"Now, see. This is the way Thomas Jefferson should be displayed, on the twenty dollar bill. Jefferson did more for our individual rights and freedom, than Jackson. I think it's a disgrace."

"Real good work." Joey said, looking at the twenty dollar bill Fielding passed with the cut-out of Thomas Jefferson over the face of Andrew Jackson.

"So why do you believe Jefferson belongs on the twenty dollar bill?" Joey asked.

"Because twenty dollar bills are used more often than two dollar bills. Besides, if you look at the back of the two dollar bill, there's a picture of the signing of the Declaration of Independence. Young punks now-a-days don't even know the importance of that moment in our history. The preservation of our rights and freedom. This picture is definitely more important than the picture of the goddamn White House." Fielding handed a fresh two dollar bill to Joey.

"Guess which gentlemen in the signing of the Declaration is carrying a gun?" Joey took the bill and turned it sideways, trying to examine the picture closely, in the dim light of the bar. The news showed a video clip of President Marie Arcola.

"Wow. I didn't realize that the lady president was so good looking. Blonde hair and blue eyes. Man, what a figure. She's even got some nice looking legs." Trench said taking a deep breath and sighing.

"So, Trench. What're you gonna do, ask her out on a date?" Joey laughed, taking a puff of his cigar, blowing out smoke rings.

"Well. She is kinda single. I wouldn't want her to be lonely." Trench said smacking Joey on the shoulder.

"Man, you are one twisted puppy, Trench." Jason said, shaking his head and pouring himself another beer. Dewey nibbled slowly on a curly pretzel, staring cold at the news reports about the bombings. Each bite was little, always careful and methodical, breaking away one section of the pretzel at a time.

"She might look good. But she's gonna fuck up this country. Just like President Johnson did with all those new gun control laws and those new search and seizure laws. Too many laws like that piss people off. That's probably why he's dead." Dewey took another drink of beer and burped. "Just like those FBI punks and the Big Brass."

A heavy metal song began to play on the jukebox. Dewey tapped his fingernails on the shellacked round wood table; nibbling at his pretzel. Jason and Fielding swaggered arm and arm, joking and hugging as they crossed the dance floor, shuffling a little dance on the way to the men's room.

"The CIA still thinks Iran is responsible for the bomb at Dulles. Those Iranians blow up everything. Could you imagine our country with citizens that couldn't buy guns to have in their homes? Man, people need to be able to protect themselves. Why are all these new Presidents allowing the Constitution to be crapped on? Does the President think an army of secret service agents are going to protect them, when unemployment and discord in this country are leading to anarchy and cold-blooded killing? I mean check out what's on the fuckin' news, now-a-days. Riots. And look at these stupid, wussey, punk, twenty-nothings. All they care about is the price of gas for their Japanese cars and their big screen TVs with remote controls. This stupid country has turned into a bunch of whining soccer moms and pretty boys. Most of them didn't even know about Pearl Harbor Day last week. Hell, half of those assholes don't even know what Memorial Day or Veteran's Day is. They think it's a fuckin' holiday created by the banks. All these worthless fuckin' liberals. Where are the Patriots?" Dewey huffed, getting some shots of Jack Daniels from the bartender. He let out a big, old burp and passed shots over to Fielding and Joey's table.

"Thank you kindly, Brother Dewey, for that beautiful sermon." Fielding raised his shot tapping Joey and Dewey's glasses. Joey sipped down half the shot, Dewey and Fielding gave the young secret service sharp shooter a looking-over.

"You're defending your country now, son. You're allowed to get shit-faced. Just think. We get to go out to a strange country to die, so that a bunch of whining liberals can go around blowing up abortion clinics and preaching about being 'the Soldiers of God'. Fuck. Even getting paid the big cash for this crap ain't worth it anymore." Dewey protested.

"So you think the abortion protesters might have killed the President?" Joey asked, before finishing his shot of whiskey.

"Hell yes. Now-a-days any American can blow people up in the United States and can get a fair trial that last two years, sells a million dollars worth of books and have their story sold to three or four major motion picture companies for movie rights. And the taxpayers pay for all of it. Shit, yeah. That's the New American Way." Fielding and Joey stared at each other and laughed at Dewey's hostile comments.

"Good night, ladies." Joey kindly waved, as the blondes sitting at the next table, cautiously and quietly snuck away.

"Ah, Dewey. See what you did. You scared the ladies away with all that John Birch and wild preacher talk. There's only one thing to do, gentlemen. Order more shots." Joey said with beer drooling down his chin. Dewey gave a nasty glare; his eyes, black dots in the sockets centered by those wrinkled and weathered crows feet. His beeper went off. Joey and Feilding's laughter stopped. They unclipped their black pagers from their belts and checked the message. Jason and Trench rushed across the dance floor with stunned expressions and smiles on their faces.

"This is the big one, fellas. Next stop, Iran." Jason said grabbing up his black leather jacket. Trench twitched, gazing around the bar. He stepped up to the bartender and handed the man an envelope, stuffed with hundred dollar bills.

"Hey, Theo. Leave this for Marla. Okay?" Trench said with a sad smile.

"Sure, Trench." The huge bartender folded the envelope and slid it into a cigar box on a shelf, underneath the cash register. He shook out his washcloth and returned to rinsing some beer mugs, glancing up at the five soldiers, as they ran out the front door of the bar.

SIXTEEN

T HE CARRIER JET SHIFTED to it's side, avoiding Libyan air space, as it rocketed through the clear blue skies over Egypt, escorted by two F-22s, barely visible against the blinding sun. Jason yawned and squinted his eyes as he took a good look down at the flat, brown earth of the morning. He grabbed his head with both hands and twisted his neck from side to side, until it cracked and he let out a giggle of relief. Trench massaged his eyes and forehead, licked his lips and cringed his face, at the disgusting taste in his mouth. Fielding just sat there, on the floor of the jet, in the aisle, scratching his thick mustache; a perverted smile on his face, reading his little black Bible.

Dewey sat up, adjusting his pants and jacket. "What? Have you been sitting their staring at me all night?" Dewey scolded, in protest.

"Yes. Yes, I've been watching you all night. I sleep with my eyes open. Remember?"

Fielding turned his wrist over, to check the time on his watch. He took another drink from the bottle of mineral water. Trench pulled his duffel bag close to him and started taking inventory of his belongings, pulling out a magazine to look at the centerfold. "Trench." Fielding said with a musical voice. "You can't take that Playboy magazine with you where we're going. You know the rules. If one of those Saudi Arabian officers sees you, you'll be sorry."

"We're landing on the Nimitz first. If that's the latest issue, I'd be more concerned about fighting off those sailors." Jason said stretching.

Dewey's watch beeped. "Well. Time for those lovely fuckin'

shots, fellas. Gotta put it right up the vein." Dewey patted his crotch. "The Big Brass can put it right up this vein."

Trench and Fielding laughed, until Jason pulled out the medical kit, took out a needle and began passing the kit around. Trench turned white at the sight of the needles, cushioned tightly in the box. "Ah, shit. Goddamn needles. It's the twenty-first century. Can't they do that Star Trek stuff yet? The stuff without needles."

Fielding giggled, pulled the green plastic sheath off the needle and flicked the cap back onto the seat of the plane. He slapped his bicep a few times to swell the vein to the surface of his skin. Each of the agents eased the point into their flesh, injecting the anthrax cure. The cryptographer became dizzy and stared away from the burn of the needle. "If this stuff's supposed to make me feel good when I get to Iran, why do I feel like such crap now?" Trench said, shaking his head and puckering his lips as they turned blue. He was breathing hard and heavy. Dewey laid his head back over the top of his lumpy, uncomfortable duffel bag, feeling the turbulence of the jet, rising up from the cool, morning waters of the Red Sea, up from the storm.

Fielding just chuckled, as he finished reading the pamphlet he found in his locker. He grinned and sighed as he whispered the written words: "God, commandeth all men everywhere to repent. Ye must be born again. For all have sinned and come short of the glory of God. For the life of the flesh is in the blood.

So without the shedding of blood, there is no remission."

A long moment of silence, interrupted the thoughts of the soldiers and reminded them of what they must do on their mission.

"How come Joey wasn't sent in with us?" Dewey asked, pulling the needle from his arm, letting a small stream of his blood creep down his forearm; placing a piece of gauze on the hole, as he reflected on the beauty of the blood.

"It's because I'm the better shooter and I've seen more action. And my little brother is just the runt of the litter. He's so green behind the ears, he'd freakin' end up shooting off his own foot. Besides, that chick President thinks he can lead another SEAL team in if we need some back-up." Jason pulled the needle from his arm, laughing as the stream of blood rolled around to his elbow. He licked the blood to sample the salty taste, and then bent his arm, thinking about the suicide mission his team was being sent on.

Trench wobbled from the turbulence and the shaking of the jet. He gripped his stomach and gave a burp of relief. He blinked his eyes and tried to focus from the shot and his hangover. Fielding scooted to the window and commented on the view, to make certain Trench would experience every nauseating second.

"Whoa. Feel that turn, it's just like being on the Raptor. You can feel every roller coaster shift and move. Cripe. We must be ready to start diving down like and elevator on a free fall. We've got at least a few more hours of this swoopin' and turnin' until we reach the aircraft carrier. We're just going to be up here spinning and turning. Oh. Did you feel that? Just lay back and think of that bonus check, Trench. And enjoy the ride. All you have to do is go in an figure out that alphabet shit." Fielding wickedly laughed, tugging at the cryptologist's Chicago Cubs baseball cap.

"Here." Jason said handing Trench a can of V-8 and a bottle of Tabasco sauce.

"Drink some juice and then pour a little bit of sauce, to chase it down. I'm telling you. You'll sweat that alcohol right out of you."

Trench still shuffled through his duffel bag, checking his gear, trying to find his aspirins. "Man, guys. That tequila from last night, is still kickin' my ass. I just need something to get me motivated." Trench got up and held his face, walking through the plane. Jason gave the medical kit a second looking-over and tossed his back-pack over to Trench. "Grab a can of chili from my pack and scarf it down. That'll absorb that booze." Jason said with a grin. Trench searched around inside the pack and noticed the pair of sniper rifles. "Geez, Jason. A Remington 40x and your Arctic Warfare? These are your best rifles. What if you mess them up out here?"

"Shit, buddy. Naughton said that bonus check is going to be twelve grand for each of us. I want to make sure none of them Afghans or Iranians can get within a quarter mile of that factory. When we get back to the states, I'll just buy me a-couple-a new rifles."

"The only reason the FBI is giving us that bonus is 'cause the Pentagon knows if that anthrax gets us, we'll become old men quick. And they get to keep all our pensions." Dewey announced, cynically adding to the conversation, leaning his head back, with his eyes closed.

The jet shifted slightly, causing Jason to look out the window. "The governments always fucking with the people. Always trying to control or take away the rights of the people. That's why we gotta stop them with these new laws on gun control and those Grandfather Clauses." Jason sighed and eased his chair back, closing his eyes. "You better catch a nap, Trench. It's two hours to the Nimitz and it's no fun napping on one of those Apaches. You think you're tummy's rockin' and rollin' now, that chopper is gonna spin you like a frog in a blender and make your eyes bug-out." Jason said, listening to Dewey grunting on about the government, while Fielding snored away with his brown and green hunters cap pulled down, shading his eyes.

SEVENTEEN

BODIES LIE COLLAPSED and twisted on the sides of the roads and in ditches laden with stones. Their decayed remains, toppled on top of baskets from the markets filled with fruits and bread; shriveled and gray from rot. The Apache helicopter scattered the salty, Iranian desert sand against their tattered bones, as she slowly lowered to the ground with the SEAL team. Two Comanche helicopters hoovered quietly; ominous flat black creatures, stealthed and ready, barely making a sound, searching the hillsides and the roads. Exhaust from the turbo-shafts flowed straight back through the tail boom as the black wasp-like killers showed their Stingers and Hellfires; hung from the bay doors, six on each side.

The pilot checked the computer avionics and studied the tanks on the maps off in the horizon. The gunner peered out of the bay window, across the dry, barren tundra, confused and distressed by the carnage. Some bodies laid smoldering in piles, attempts by the living to cremate the dead, adding a putrid green glow to the low clouds in the morning sunlight. Everywhere was the gagging smell of burnt hair and burnt flesh. Extremities were split open, with whole families dead in each others arms, their organs spilled and dried on the desert dirt.

There was no sound outside the city of Esfahan, a city once populated with three million people. There was only the wind and the howling of ghosts, echoing from the markets, mosques, schools and streets.

Jason, Dewey, Trench and Fielding slid off the platform of the Apache helicopter, dressed in dark protective suits and masks.

"Oh, God. The bodies smell so strong. I can smell them through my suit." Jason complained, putting on his backpack and shouldering one of his rifles. Dewey strapped a computer DVD transmitter to the front of his chest and checked his M-16. Fielding patted his holsters to make certain his Glocks weren't left on board the Apache. Trench picked up his rifle and gear and stood for a few seconds, in shock at the sight of all the dead bodies.

"Come on, fellas. It won't stink as bad out near the factory." Jason said walking away down the slope in the direction of the factory. Dewey followed him aiming his digital camera, videotaping and transferring information to the computers on the Nimitz. Trench waved for the Apache pilot to leave. He turned with his M-16, waiting for one of the corpses to move, sensing that this must be some kind of trap.

Fielding and Dewey adjusted their headsets underneath their masks and began narrating what they saw, back to the admirals in CIC on board the aircraft carrier. Fielding raised his leg and tapped what was left of a boy's body with his boot. The boy's ribs crackled in pieces out of his chest.

"CIC. This is Fielding. Do you read me." The strikingly tall lieutenant said, adjusting his supply pack and rifle.

"Yes, lieutenant. We read you loud and clear. We will continue monitoring your audio and cameras. Remember. If you see any enemy troops, you must sign off. We can't take a chance that someone will know your team is in there. Also, remember the pick-up time." The officer at CIC sounded-off.

"So far, it looks like how the Bible explained Armageddon. Nothing but the dead. I'm about five hundred feet from the factory. The rest of the team is about to enter a fenced in parking area outside of . . ." Fielding checked his wrist compass, ". . . the southeast entrance. As you can probably see from Dewey's camera. The parking lot is filled with cars and trucks. A few bodies have collapsed in the parking lot."

Fielding leaned over the body of a man, who was slumped over with his upper body facing his lap; his fingers dug into his ribs. "I have a deceased gentlemen here, who appears to have died while eating his lunch. Now you fellas back at CIC are gonna have to figure, if an explosion happened in this factory would this guy have been calmly sitting here eating his lunch? I also know these people have a special time of day they pray. I have another guy who looks like he died while he was on his knees. Judging from the way this guy's eyes are bugged out and he's grabbing at his chest, he probably went into cardiac arrest within a few minutes of the accident." Fielding grabbed one of the men's petrified faces.

"Eyes quite fixed and dilated. The whites of the eyes; jaundice yellow." He clicked open a small metal, glass lined box and fumbled with a hypodermic needle. He inserted the needle into the man's stomach, extracting a small amount of fluid. He inserted another longer needle, deeper into the chest cavity, drawing fluid from the man's liver. Fielding took a deep breath, his hands trembled, as he capped off the needles, clipping them back into the metal case. He stepped away, trying not to think of the man, and stood back to take ten deep breaths, to calm his racing heart. His attention focused on the truck in the parking lot, next to the dead man. Inside, a pair of flies frantically bounced off the windshield and then rested on the top of the dashboard.

"Well, well. I've got a couple of live flies over in a truck. Just about four hundred feet from the factory. Either the anthrax didn't kill them or these two just recently hatched. Trench? Can you hear me?" Fielding talked softly into his microphone. A figure stepped out from the doorway of the factory.

"Yes, sir. I read you loud and clear. I've already taken tests inside the factory. It looks like the chemicals from the explosion have dissipated." Trench said waving to his partner. Fielding stood for a moment, staring up at the lone Comanche helicopter, circling the perimeter of the factory and the countryside, videotaping evidence for the Pentagon and the Chiefs of Staff.

"This is Fielding. I think the air cleared up. I'm taking off my mask." The lieutenant ignored the protest of his team.

"Negative, lieutenant. Do not take off your mask, that's an order. You know if you get sick or die, Lieutenant Fielding, we'll take away your benefits." CIC protested, paused and then retransmitted, curious to know. "How do you feel, lieutenant?" CIC asked, inquiring about his condition for the record. Lt. Devin Fielding tilted his head back, feeling the breeze play with his blond brush cut. His solid green eyes blinked as he smiled at the clear, blue Iranian sky. He half-laughed and half-cried.

"Allah was right. The skies are magic blue and clear, and perfect. Just like Oklahoma. I guess his daddy was an artist." Fielding folded up his mask and stuffed it in his pack.

"Fielding, buddy. How ya doing?" Trench called across the headset, standing there, studying the soldier walking around the parking lot, with his arms reaching out to the sky.

Fielding paused, his eyes blinking, focusing on the bodies. His thoughts mesmerized by the magnificent sunshine of the December day. "The air out here ain't that bad. Amen, brothers. It's our salvation. I think the wind and the rain diluted the chemicals. Hell, the air is fresh. It's kinda like New Mexico. Shit, fellas. I wish I had my golf clubs. I could drive some of them balls on the screws with my 3 iron, up to our friends on that highway." Fielding chuckled, taking another deep breath, kicking up the dirt from his boots, doing a little shuffle.

"The air's fine." Trench said, looking around at the wonderful skies over Iran.

"He's just crazy and stupid as usual." Still, Trench raised his hygrometer, letting the air outside of the factory into the vacuum, examining the digital display register 'negative' for dangerous chemicals in the air.

"Fielding. Jason's coming out to take some video. So don't shoot him." Trench said, stepping over a stack of bodies in the hallway on the first floor of the factory, near the parking lot entrance.

The captain cautiously moved out of the entrance to the factory and studied his partner, sitting on the bumper of the truck, narrating into the microphone of his headset, while taking snapshots with his CD 500.

"Fielding. Did you take your last injection?" Jason shouted, through his mask, very concerned, loud enough for CIC and the FBI to know what danger they were experiencing. The lieutenant smiled and continued securing the exterior of factory, opening doors, checking for booby-traps. CIC listened closely to every detail of every sound, often having to imagine the surroundings in and around the factory; as they studied aerial and satellite surveillance.

"Hey, Jason. Yeah, I took my shot. I ain't stupid." Fielding waved at Jason.

"I just feel so different being out here. It's a new world. These Muslim people get blamed every time a bomb goes off somewhere in the world.

Jason tapped the lieutenant on the shoulder. "I just want to check you out." Jason touched Fielding's face, studying his eyes, ears and nose for any immediate affects from the anthrax, or any other evidence of chemical reactions. "No unusual distortion of the mucous. No reddening or irritation."

"So, you gonna give me a complete physical, Dr. Jason? You want I should bend over and cough?" Fielding pulled away with that wicked smile.

"Tomorrow, honey. Tomorrow." Jason said, removing his mask. He closed his eyes and took a few short breaths, and then laughed, smiling as he breathed deeper.

"Jason? Fielding? This is Dewey. Are you guys okay out there?" Dewey pulled four wires down through a cold air return, extending down from the roof.

Jason pulled out a pair of hypodermic needles and handed one to Fielding. "Yes, mother. We're fine. In fact, we're taking another injection right now, just in case. Just find that computer and start transferring whatever you can find back to the brass at the Big P." Jason said.

"Well. Make sure our friend out there doesn't start peeing green. You know those Irishman." Dewey joked, pushing a door open to an office on the second floor.

A desk was pulled away from the wall. A uniformed soldier was dead, laying flat on his back on the floor; his dead stare facing the ceiling, his skin shriveled up against his bones. His face and eyes mummified by the chemicals and death. Dewey reached out to the computer on the dead man's desk, prying the drawer open from one of the hard-drives.

"Trench. I need you to get up here to the second floor. I've got a bunch of CD's with names and numbers. I need you to translate some squiggly writing."

"Hold on. I'm kinda busy." Trench replied through the headset.

Dewey studied the office, always taking deep breathes, feeling dizzy, hyperventilating as he stared at the dead soldier. He saw pictures of the man's family and his children; photographs taped to the walls of the small room. He noticed a set of TV monitors attached to the wall behind the desk.

"Jason? Fielding? Let me know if there are cameras positioned outside the factory anywhere." Dewey said, pulling out his knife, prying open the computer tray, picking up the computer CD. He studied the CD and inserted it into the DVD transmitter.

"Okay, CIC. I think I've got the CD that recorded what happened in the factory. It should be the disc that records for all the security cameras inside and outside of the factory. If the power was still on after the accident, the cameras outside of the factory might have recorded the first SEAL team, if they were ever in here."

"I'm down in a big room. It looks like a laboratory." Trench said, trying not to step on the bodies, slowly taking readings with a hand held mass spectrometer.

"The way these guys died. The way they're positioned on the floor. I can't tell if this was an accident, or an explosion, or even a mass suicide. In fact. It might have been someone sabotaging the factory. And CIC, I've got positive readings of nitrates."

Trench raised his camera and made certain his DVD was recording and transmitting the images back to the Pentagon. One of the bodies' arms crackled under the soldiers boot, as he stepped over to one of the laboratory tables. He pulled a note pad away from the hand of one of the victims, reading notes from a ledger.

"CIC. I've got something. There are some letters on these notes that are Cyrillic. I think one of these workers was making a shopping list for our friends up north. From what it says here, a trade might have gone bad. It looks like Russia got double-crossed when Iran received a shipment of plutonium but didn't make the payment. I've got a list of crytonyms. These notes are computer print-outs. Probably from one of the CD files Dewey is transmitting to you." Trench picked up the notes and folded them into his duffel bag.

The humidity was uncomfortable under the protective suits. A thick, clear liquid ran down the walls of the room. Trench opened a test tube and twirled it through the condensated chemicals on the wall, collecting a sample, always careful to get it inside the glass container. He took a deep sigh of relief, snapping the seal shut and inserting the sample into a baggy, and then into a protective metal box labeled: DANGER - BIOLOGICAL HAZARD - PROPERTY OF THE UNITED STATES GOVERNMENT. The next set of walls, in a locker room, were thick with a clear green gel. Trench looked at the dead man, collapsed on the shower floor, fully clothed, water dripping from the shower head above him.

"CIC. This is Trench. I'm down in a locker room. I'm collecting a second sample of the chemical." He studied the body of the dead soldier as he scraped the gel into the test tube. He placed his hand on the body. "Something odd about these last two dead soldiers down here. They're not decomposed like the rest of the bodies in the laboratory. In fact, I think they're Chinese soldiers. My guess, is they showed up to loot the factory and ended up dying from this shit." A crash in the corridor caused Trench to raise and aim his M-16. Dewey walked in with his hands held up.

"Easy, old man. It's just your friendly welcome wagon from Iran. I got tired of waiting for you." Dewey inserted another CD into the DVD transmitter and began videotaping the room and the bodies.

"Are you reading my CDs alright there, Big Brass?" Dewey asked, talking into his headset and checking the clock's LEDs flashing the red numbers on the side.

"We read your signal perfect, captain. Satellite shows artillery moving south on the highway." The voice from CIC replied without emotion.

Jason and Fielding stopped in the corridor, to adjust their masks, looking down at the body of an Iranian worker, lying dead in a closet. "Most of these guys look like they died without knowing what the hell was going on. Like they died instantly in their tracks."

Jason pulled out his camera and flashed off two pictures. Fielding squatted down and removed a gold, jewel-hilted dagger from the dead worker's belt. Jason wandered further down the hallway, noticing how clean and organized the factory was, with shelves lined with plastic trays, supplies meticulously labeled and straightened. Dewey rescrambled a code number inside the DVD case and continued to monitor the transmission of the CD. Trench took a stainless steel pointer and pulled up a layer of mold floating on top of a cup of coffee, sitting on a table with a stack of binders. One was open with a list.

"Okay, Jason. Take a picture of this for the brass. Dewey make sure we transmit this on video." Trench said, as he walked over and opened a window to add more light to the room.

"Well, Doctor Trench. Is that mold a good sign?" Jason snickered, looking out of the window at a sandstorm in the distance.

The lieutenant turned and straightened his shoulders. "Hell, yes it's a good sign. Things are coming back to life around here. That tells me Iran got lucky with this explosion and we'll be going back to collect our pensions."

"We've got a nice little shopping list here." Dewey said, flipping through the pages of the binders. "I recognize three of the names of these cities. One of these suppliers is Russian. These names, dates and locations are written in Russian." Dewey pried open a filing cabinet drawer and found another stack of computer discs. He slid the CDs in between his gloved fingers, trying to interpret the markings on the labels.

"CIC. This is Dewey. I found about twenty more discs here. There's too many to transmit. I think I'm going to have to bring these in. Can we count on that chopper for breakfast?" Dewey asked, stuffing the CDs in his backpack.

"Negative for now. Satellites are showing heavy armament heading your way from the north. You're team will have to sit tight. They might be just passing by. We advise radio silence. Keep your channels open and we'll keep a watch on you." CIC signed off.

Fielding stood with his binoculars, snapping his chewing gum as he watched the road from the factory window. "We've got soldiers heading off the highway. I don't think they know we're in here. They're taking their time and keep yelling back at other soldiers, distancing themselves from the factory."

Dewey checked to make sure that the CD in the computer was still transmitting. "It looks like about nine or ten of them. They seem really hesitant to get very close to the factory. I think they're arguing about going any further into the parking lot.

They keep looking at the ground. I think they're talking about our footprints."

Trench watched the sand blast across the Iranian cliffs, down the slopes across the road, forcing the soldiers to stand and abandon the investigation of the footprints. They moved back to the cliffs, screaming at their comrades.

Jason waved the rest of his team out into the corridor and called out into his headset. "CIC, we're heading to the roof to hunker down! They've got tanks positioned on the highway, aiming their guns at us! Goddamnit, I think they're gonna bomb the shit out of this place! I repeat, those tanks are gonna blast this factory to hell!"

EIGHTEEN

SENATOR TREVOR THOMAS lightly tapped his pencil on his leather covered note pad, daydreaming as he tried to figure out what the crests were called, woven into the blue carpet on the floor of the U.S. Senate Chamber. He stared up at the ceiling and wondered about his upcoming vacation in February and how nice it would be to relax at his condo on Long Key.

"The gentleman from Alabama is recognized. Five minutes please." The President Pro Tempore stated.

"Mr. President. As you can see almost every senator is present here today and ready to begin to straighten out this matter. I wish for more time and wish for any Quorum Calls to be omitted from this very important meeting." Senator Green said with a sarcastic chuckle. Other senators grumbled at the arrogance of the senator, the President intervened.

"That's a difficult request, senator."

"I understand, Mr. President. But, we are talking about sending our troops into Iran. Every second this Senate meets is another click toward a sick and insane, deadly war with chemical and biological weapons of mass destruction. There is a commitment of this Senate to be responsible for our actions, and we must protect the sons and daughters of our country, at this very delicate moment in our history. I am concerned that Iran, as well as Iraq, Pakistan and Afghanistan, and China, and India would see this as being an excuse for the United States to occupy and upset the balance of many countries in that region of the world." Senator Green smiled, confident with his words, turning around to gleam at the senators, as they all waited for their chance to speak.

"Two minutes, senator." The President intervened.

"I will not approve any decision to commit U.S. troops to be deployed to the Persian Gulf or to Iran to be caught up in some international game. And I urge all of you senators to vote 'no' to sending any of our sons and daughters."

A small group of senators applauded as Senator Green stepped away from the podium. A woman senator rushed up and pulled the microphone closer to her.

"The Senate recognizes the lady from Connecticut." The President Pro Tempore said.

"It has already been three weeks since the accident in Iran. Already hundreds of allies in Kuwait and Saudi Arabia have become permanently affected by the chemicals from that factory. We all know the great illnesses our troops suffered after Desert Storm. I do not see why we would need to deploy troops from the U.S. Army, Navy or Marines. Or any other branch of the armed forces. The information from Defense Secretary Rawlings confirms Iran has a strong, healthy, powerful military. I do not believe this incident will in any way weaken Iran as a major power in the Middle East. And I do believe it is not our concern with this matter. But I do urge all of us here who have fought in Iraq, Kuwait or Bosnia. That we remember and that we enforce and maintain sanctions on Iran. It is obvious, with this catastrophe, that the men or women responsible for creating those chemical and biological weapons have evil intentions and they do not care for human life. Thank you, Mr. President."

"Thank you Senator Harding." The President Pro Tempore said, checking the time. Senator Trevor Thomas stood up and handed Lauren his leather covered note pad. The Senate mumbled and one of the senators stretched back in his chair and said out loud, 'here we go.' Senator Thomas raised his hand, and mockingly saluted the senator. "Hey, Shawn. Check my back for any threads. We're on CNN, you know." Senator Thomas paused as his campaign manager brushed at the back of his dark brown wool-crepe Vestimenta. Now the Republican Party Majority Leader placed his hands on the podium. His hanging brows of silver and brown, sloped over his big brown eyes as he turned to command the room and intimidate the Senate.

"I realize we are all very tired from worry and the thoughts of the danger that this incident in Iran brings to the world. The weakened condition of Iran's country has been confirmed. Evidence has been gathered by our U.S. Special Forces teams, show every indication, without a doubt, that the factory south of Esfahan was in fact, producing chemical and biological weapons. The evidence also proves Iran was the victim of a very, sad and tragic accident, resulting in the deaths of nearly a hundred thousand Iranian men, women and children. But this tragedy is not over. Satellite reconnaissance experts have confirmed hostile troops and garrisons with tanks, missiles and heavy armament, moving into southern Iran, threatening to take over, threatening Kuwait and Saudi Arabia."

Other senators yelled out. "How can you tell they are hostile!?"

"It's not our problem!" Another senator bellowed.

The President slammed his gavel to the bench. "Order! You'll have time to speak. Please respect the gentlemen from Indiana. Please continue, Senator Thomas."

"Thank you, Mr. President. I know many of you have seen major wars. Fortunately, times have changed in the world. But the danger is still real. Terrorism is very real and rogue states have acquired chemical weapons, biological weapons and nuclear weapons. And these rogue states will use those weapons to taunt us and then destroy us. These rogue terrorists will kill us. Need I remind you. Our own President George Johnson was killed, not far from here, on American soil. Killed in cold blood by terrorists. And I don't need to remind you that President Arcola lost her entire family when that terrorist bomb began stabbing at the heart of our country. Her husband David, a wonderful, generous businessman. Shelley and Francis. Two young children. All of you remember what happened in Oklahoma City, many, many years ago. The bombings in Cairo and Egypt over this past summer. Flight 191 last year, when a hand-held stinger missile, blew up a plane with a group of exchange students leaving Seattle. The Atlanta Serial Bomber and those planned parenthood clinics. Ladies and gentlemen. They're coming after us and we are just going to let them force us to live in fear for our lives? What happens if another country starts a war with Iran? Already Kuwait and Saudi Arabia have become concerned of Saddam Hussein's legacy, building up troops on Iran's borders. With his newly developed Republican Guards. There are already reports from Abadan that Iran has sustained devastating casualties. All I can say, is that all of us are fortunate that the former Secretary of Defense William Cohen did not let President Clinton veto the bill to expand our naval program back in 1998. Especially now all of you realize how important the SEA Ferret program was to secure balance in the Persian Gulf and the attack three years ago on the Panama Canal."

"One minute please, senator." The President announced.

"And to finalize my concerns at this time! We have no other choice then to commit our troops into the Gulf region to secure our allies in Kuwait, in Saudi Arabia and if need be, we may have to defend Iran because of this incident!" Senator Thomas stood firm, raising his arms out as if he was the preacher delivering the dark sermon to his congregation. Senators booed, hissed and screamed out protest over the applause. The doors flew open, as pages and reporters raced out into the halls to the sound of the President's gavel, trying to call the chaos to order.

"They're coming after us! Do you understand! We are all next! We must send in our troops to secure that region of the world!" Senator Trevor Thomas shouted over the disturbance of the Senate, instigating the arguments. He turned to speak directly into the microphone and said it with that cool, infamous smile. "That is what I have to say for now, ladies and gentlemen."

"Order! Order! This is not the type of behavior to be tolerated in this room!" The President yelled in disgust, at the uproar of the Senate chamber; smacking the gavel to the pad. "Any of you reporters that leave this room, you stay out! This is a very grave matter! This is not a circus! And you will not disrespect these senators!"

Some reporters stopped and returned to their seats while others yelled out in the hall. "We're going to war!" A female reporter shouted, flustered, bouncing up and down with a big smile, trying to sensationalize her story to her newspaper, while she spoke into her cell phone, as the big doors shut her out in the hall. A woman reporter took a seat next to Senator Thomas. "Hi. I like your perfume.' Senator Thomas whispered, with his low, gravely voice, closing his eyes and leaning over the woman as she smiled. Lauren pretended not to notice.

"Thank you, Senator Thomas. It's called 'Believe.'"

"Believe? I like that. Very optimistic."

A tall burly man adjusted his old, wool suit, placing his note cards on the podium. He pulled his shoulder, to crunch his stiff back; his face and body, squared, from his forehead to his waist. He talked softly, pleading with the Senate with his silver, blue eyes.

"It is very difficult to summarize the incidents that are unfolding in Iran. Incidents which are now affecting our country because of the deaths of President Johnson, Mr. David Arcola and his children; the family of the now, President Marie Arcola. It is difficult, in only a few minutes on this Senate floor, to decide the fate of our nation and how we will be seen in the international theatre. But we must decide. Iran, with it's propaganda, will use this incident to persuade other nations to relax sanctions, even though it was their biological-chemical weapons that caused this atrocity. We are not barbarians. Yet, we must think and fight, and kill like barbarians; if need be, to oppose our enemies. In my opinion, we are the most intelligent, powerful, God-loving, God-fearing creatures on this earth. We need to respect everything that involves our lives. We need to preserve our interest in the world economy. Check your statistics. Check and see how many people of Iran, Iraq, Libya, Sudan or other countries in the Middle East have fled their countries, to find peace in this country; the United States of America. To be free of fear and torture. To be free of mutilation, experimentation and oppression.

These chemical and biological weapons exist and are real! They have been confirmed in the rainwater gathered in Kuwait and Saudi Arabia! Another accident could be larger. And that next accident could kill us all. Imagine the country of Iran, on purpose or accidentally, sending clouds of these deadly anthrax poisons into Europe; destroying France, England, Germany and Italy. Contaminating the food, water, seas, air and soil. I believe our time has come. I say we send troops into Iran and capture that factory with it's chemical weapons. Use it as evidence and let the World

Court decide! For decades, the United States has enforced the dismantling of nuclear weapons. Now. It is time for us to dismantle these countries that produce biological and chemical weapons. Chemical weapons are not like smart bombs or cruise missiles, seeking out a specific, military target. Oh no, ladies and gentlemen. Chemical and biological weapons destroy everything! Everything and everyone is the target! We must go into Iran and stop this madness now!" Senator Hayden stepped away from the podium to mumbling and quiet applause. The salt and pepper haired man bowed his head and patted his neutral gray suit.

"Ah, shit. That's Tom's signal for help on the vote." Senator Thomas looked around the room at the slight nods of other senators, giving Senator Hayden the 'thumbs-up'. "Well. I think he'll get it." Senator Thomas checked his Rolex. "Damn. We're going to be done for the day soon. Shawn, did you get that reply out to Mrs. Griffin from USA Today that we have no 'soft money' in our campaign? That it is I, and only I, with my millions of dollars, using every cent that I earned to pay for my campaign."

"Yes sir. And I think I used those exact words." Shawn replied. The woman reporter sitting next to Senator Thomas jotted down some notes; her smile pushed her dimples to the sides of her red lips.

"Ladies and gentlemen of the Senate." The President Pro Tempore began. "As you can tell, this Senate is out of time for today. We will recess until nine o'clock tomorrow morning. At that time we will take care of morning business and proceed with the eight conditions involving the occupation of American troops in the Persian Gulf. Please understand that your presence here tomorrow is very valuable to our nation. Please, also be available in case this incident turns into a international emergency. Adjourned." The President Pro Tempore said, smacking the gavel to the bench in close of the Senate meeting. Senators and pages rushed up the aisles to the big doors, followed by staff and secretaries. Senator Thomas held his hand out, waving for everyone to go ahead of him. He brushed his jacket and waited for Shawn to open the doors for him.

A flock of reporters huddled around Senator Trevor Thomas as he took center stage in the corridor. A tall, red haired woman bumped up next to the senator.

"Hello, there. Mrs.?" Senator Thomas flirted looking at the woman's name tag and her long, muscular legs, through her sheer, black nylons.

"Tanya. I like that name. How can I help you, Tanya?"

"Well, senator. First of all, it's miss. Miss Golding. But I like the way you say 'Tanya'. I work for the International, can I ask you a few questions?"

"Oh, the International. Mr. Redford's new newspaper. A very powerful merger with Murdock's company. A lot of people call your newspaper 'Neo-Nazistic and compulsively paranoid bordering on the fringes of kindergarten journalism, fueled by disgruntled old billionaires.'" Senator Thomas said with his usual grin.

"Oh, you quoted Turner's article very well. Wasn't that in the Times?" Tanya flashed a pretty smile and pulled the senator by the arm through the crowd of reporters, senators and pages, leading him out of the doorway.

NINETEEN

ENATOR THOMAS CUT his medium, rare steak into
meticulous, equal thin slices; Tanya sipped her white Zin-
fandel, shifting her eyes to look around Chadwicks.

"So, did you buy out the restaurant? There's hardly anyone
here." Tanya asked.

"Everyone's probably glued to CNN with all those reports about
Iran and the new lady president. You remember how it was with
Desert Storm. People were addicted to watching those minute to
minute reports of the smart bomb attacks." Trevor said, swirling
his piece of meat around and around in the juice, taking it to his
mouth, joyfully moaning with each bite. Tanya cut up her Lin-
guine Alba, to make certain the bits of pasta would not fall, and
splash as she ate.

"So why did you join the army? You could have gone into the
NBA." Tanya picked up and cracked the shell of one of the crab
legs on her plate.

"Isn't it obvious? I just wanted more power. I would always be at
the dinners and banquets for the coaches and parents. I'd always
listen to them talk about money and taxes. About business. That's
what I wanted to understand. How all that big money worked. It
became my passion and obsession to find out. I had this ability or
gift, for talking to people, but also having the insight to stick
everything out until the end. When Coach Knight pushed us, I
understood why. Besides that. All those millionaires at those dinners, the way they brushed us off, The NCAA Champions, I wanted
to be better than them. Sometimes they'd make a remark because
I was just some 'punk white boy' skimming through Indiana University on a basketball scholarship. They'd say 'shit. How hard is

it for some six foot plus kid to throw a basketball through a little net?'" Trevor reached over and picked up one of Tanya's crab legs.

"A lot of people say you're the most popular Republican since Dole, Bush or Reagan. So how did you get to be so rich and famous?" Tanya asked, sipping her wine.

"Not only am I rich and famous. I'm also good-looking and smart. I got rich because I wanted revenge. And then I got richer because I was terrified of ever being poor." The senator continued again, to brag about himself, swallowing down some steak. "I learned the power of doing favors. Lending money, passing along resumes, advising people, buying businesses when the owners had problems and needed the money. When I was a junior in college, I wasn't getting any NBA offers, so I joined the army, mostly for a change. I guess I was looking for my niche in life. The next thing I know, I'm a captain in the middle of Desert Storm. Now I've got to send boys out to clear booby-traps and land mines. As a promotion, they sent me to Bosnia to lead the shittiest, most secretive team in that battle. But the service gave me a chance to travel and see how international businesses prospered and cut deals. Then my parents were killed by a drunk driver." Senator Thomas paused and sniffed, taking a good drink of his beer.

"Your parents must have been quite dear to you?" Tanya said, studying Trevor's eyes.

"Oh yeah. Even my mom would be out in the backyard with my dad and my brother, Eric, playing basketball. They would always read us books, my dad would read us the sports section or the stock reports. They were really special. When they died, they left my brother and I close to five million dollars in property, investments, stocks, bonds and life insurance policies. That only made me miss and love my parents even more, knowing that they were always looking out for us kids. Well. After I got out of the service I completed my liberal arts degree and I barely passed the LSAT. I was very surprised and pleased to be accepted into the John Marshall School of Law. So, I headed up to Chicago. I wasn't that good at studying, it just wasn't challenging enough. I loved the debates, I was always good on my feet. But, all I cared about was beer, basketball and being popular. I had good times and great times. I made so many friends; other law students with wonderful ideas for this country. Some of them had to work shit jobs to stay in school. I had one friend who was a stripper. I saw one of her shows, she was great. So I said, 'hell, I'll lend you the money. Quit that crappy job and concentrate on law, cause someday I'm going to be the President of the United States and I'll want you to work for me.'" Trevor smiled as the waiter set down another beer.

"It sounds like you were some kind of loan shark."

"Yes but no. Out of eight of those friends, two of them still work with me. One in securities and the other is in international law."

"What about your ex-wife and your two sons?"

"Samantha and her family were very wealthy when we met. From the start we had an agreement and a contract about our money. I guess it's just one of those woman things. She needed a man to help her experience child birth, so after we had Kelly and Evan, she just didn't want to have sex anymore. So we talked, we agreed, we walked through the divorce and we're still friends. In fact, Sam and the kids visit and stay with me on Long Key five or six times a year."

"Any regrets?" Tanya said, wanting to reach across the table to touch this enchanting wise man. Senator Thomas cracked open another crab leg and savored the taste, as he thought about her question.

"No. Not really. I've been a very lucky man. My only concern at this point, is that I am so close to reaching my goal of becoming President. I guess you could call it obsession."

"Do you want to be President because it would make you feel like you are the king?"

"Yes. I want that power. I can shape up America. I am the greatest! I am the king." Senator Thomas tried imitating Muhammad Ali, waving his fists in the air. Tanya couldn't hold back her laughter.

"But I also know, I can make life better for Americans. My kids are growing up in this country too. I'm tired of random violence in the streets and in the schools. It's been twenty-eight years since television and Hollywood started toning down what children were exposed to, with V-chips and parental warnings for programs. The violence in this country has gone up since then. Now these knuckle-dragging liberals are calling for books to be labeled or burned.

They want to burn books like 'All Quiet on the Western Front', 'War and Peace', 'A Tale of Two Cities', 'The Great Gatsby', all the classics because they contain violent acts. Hell, most of the killers that have been executed or locked-up for life can't even read. Half of them never went to school. And now this crap that medical books in bookstores that show naked bodies should be sealed in shrink-wrap and need to have 'sexually explicit material' warning labels placed on them, and that recipes on the internet using the word 'breast' or 'leg' are being labeled as pornographic. Do you know how many lobbyist of chicken farmers have been literally camping at my office?"

"Yes, I remember you threatening to start having bibles burned." Tanya smiled.

"Of course. Look at all the violence and sex in that book. All those people dying and killing in the name of God. That's why I fight so hard to stop these laws that try to take away our first and second amendment rights. We've still got these stupid gun control laws trying to be passed to take away the rights from good law-abiding American citizens. People have the right to protect their homes and their families. Most of these illegal weapons that were given to gang members came off of ships on Long Beach back in 1995 and illegal AK-47's are still the illegal weapon of choice. Did you happen to read the front page of The Times? There's the story about the bomb that killed President Johnson and the article right next to it had the headline 'Could Gun Control Have Saved The President?' The President wasn't even killed by a gun." Trevor shook his head. "I'm sorry. I get all worked-up by this crap."

"Well, you're supposed to. That's what makes you the lovable character you are." Tanya said. Trevor nodded in agreement to her comment and smiled.

"So why did you get a divorce, Tanya?" Trevor asked, finishing his steak. She was quiet for a moment; thinking and trying not to remember her ex-husband.

"My job is very demanding. I have to travel all the time. I didn't want to give up my work. So one day I showed up and the divorce papers were there on the kitchen table and I signed them. We never fought or yelled at each other. It just ended."

"No. It sounds like it began. That is what the journey is all about. Seeking. Finding. Asking. Longing. Fulfilling. It's the human spirit."

For some reason, the senator's words made her feel weak, but also inspired her to ask the next question. "Do you want to sleep with me tonight?" She breathed deep after her question, realizing how awkward it sounded. The wise, old senator smiled.

"No. But I'd be honored to make love to you."

"So, making love, is that different?" Miss Golding asked, chills running over her skin, as he reached out and touched her hand.

"Sex is spontaneous, blatant and costly. Making-love is between two friends and can lead us through the distortion of emotions that blind our needs."

Tanya blushed, always holding onto his fingers, feeling the callused hands; touching them again to find their warmth and their security. Senator Thomas's eyes could tell stories, dark and magical to the flicker of the candlelight.

Senator Thomas waved for the waiter. "Will you need anything else, Mr. Thomas?" The waiter asked.

"No thank you, Ollie. Can you pack up these extras in a doggie-bag for us and also add a six pack and a bottle of the lady's wine to my bill to go."

"Of course." The tall, young waiter replied, removing plates off of the table, walking them away across to the kitchen.

"So are you saying, I'm going to enjoy making love to you as opposed to just having sex with you?" Tanya asked, as soon as the waiter was out of hearing range.

"No. I'm saying I'm going to enjoy making love to you."

"But you have a reputation of being a womanizer. All those other women, what would make me so special?"

"All women are special. All beautiful in all different ways. Like different foods are all delicious in their own special way."

"So, us middle-aged women are your main meal, but the younger women are your dessert?"

"I would describe you more as a feast at my finger tips. That I would want to savor your taste for hours and hours. Over and over again."

"Oh, and then you go out for dessert?" Tanya cooed, and rubbed her hands over his.

"Actually, I'd most likely want seconds."

His words were sincere with that little boy smile. His eyes and expression, were fatherly, enchanting and calm. It was difficult to think this is the same ferocious monster who rattles the dust out of the constitutional concrete of Washington, D.C.

TWENTY

SENATOR THOMAS PACED from the hallway to the bedroom, always taking a peek at Tanya. Her long red hair brushed back across the pillow. Her beautiful breasts slowing moving, as she softly slept. Her sweet lips, curved slightly up, in a peaceful smile. He clicked the alarm 'off' on the clock radio, a few minutes before the alarm would sound at five a.m. A flop outside the apartment door drew his attention from his leather note pad, as he continued to write down notes and calculations, walking down the hall. He opened the door and reached down for the Washington Post. A woman across from his apartment, purposely opened her door and took a deep breath. Almost nude in her long, silky white robe, staring with longing at the senator.

"Good morning, Trevor." The slim brunette purred with a little wave of her fingers and perfect red fingernails. Trevor stood for a few seconds in his boxer shorts, looking up from the headlines.

"Hello, Eva. You look very pretty this morning." The senator barely looked at her, trying to be nice. "Have a good day." He said, mimicking her wave, as he closed his door leaving her still waving at him. He finished his egg bagel and cream cheese, washed it down with a Diet Pepsi and skimmed over the second page, reading an update of the casualties in Iran.

"You're an early riser." Tanya said, sliding her fingers up and down the senator's sides, down to his thighs, nibbling at his naked shoulder. Trevor grinned and turned, with her kiss against his neck. He reached up in fascination, rolling her erect nipples between his fingers.

"You're right. I 'am an early riser.'" Trevor continued his journey, allowing his hands to slide down the small of her back, warming her skin against his belly.

"Are you reading about your stocks?" Tanya asked, with her fingers playing underneath the elastic of his shorts.

"Oh, yes. Everything is up and doing fine."

"So what kind of stocks do you invest in?" Tanya moaned at the feel of the senator's warm, soft hands and his tongue against her breast.

"Robotics. Blue chips. I have a lot of money riding on this one pharmaceutical company that just had a drug approved by the FDA as the cure for HIV. And I like to keep an eye on the companies that I own." Trevor playfully backed away, still holding her in his arms.

"Say. You might be an informant trying to seduce me for all my trade secrets. Well, now I've caught you. You know what this means?" He said with a smile, and those dark brown eyes.

"Oh please, say you'll have to torture me." Tanya giggled with a kiss, as she broke free from their embrace and ran to the bedroom, diving naked into the bed. Trevor came rushing after her, tickling her feet. She began laughing and screeching, squirming in the soft quilts, panting as he smiled down at her. "Stop it! I should never have told you that I was ticklish!" Trevor strategically and slowly placed his tongue on Tanya's moles and freckles, across her belly to her thighs.

"Remember, you had no choice but to give in to my powers, my dear."

"Are you going to start nibbling on my toes again?" She giggled.

"Of course. I love your feet. I just want to . . ." The telephone began to ring and then Senator Thomas's pager beeped. He checked the phone number on his caller ID and reluctantly picked up the receiver.

"Trevor. This is Lauren. There's been a confirmation of the evidence from the explosion. The FBI has confirmed who killed the President. President Arcola is planning to talk to some of the generals from Iran." The voice over the telephone quietly stated. "But there's another problem. You were right about the Chinese supplying weapons to Afghanistan. The FBI has confirmed the reports from sources in Ghazni and Herat."

"Did you get this information from Fred?" The senator asked, gravely concerned.

"Yes sir. He stopped by the office personally with satellite photographs, computer disc's and FBI files."

"Good old Fred. Are we the first one's to get this information?"

"No. Fred told me Agent Naughton called President Arcola two hours ago. He said they're planning to convince the President to start organizing an air-strike. The satellite photographs also confirmed three major Afghanistan tank divisions fighting their way across Northern Iran heading toward Tehran. So far, they've been successful and reports from the Ayatollah to Beijing are calling for help. Satellites confirm jets are on their way."

"Damn it! I should have been called in to discuss this." Senator Thomas huffed. Tanya rubbed her feet up his thighs, giving him goose bumps as she laid back on the bed.

"Thanks, Lauren. I've got to be in the Senate this afternoon. I'll meet with you and the rest of our campaign team this evening." Trevor grinned with Tanya licking his toes.

"You should be in the Senate for morning business, if you expect to win next year's election." Lauren said, in a cold, spiteful tone, listening in on Senator Thomas whispering and giggling with Tanya.

"So who's there with you?"

"Good-bye, Lauren." The senator finished in a cold voice, hanging up the phone, by dropping it to the receiver on the nightstand.

TWENTY-ONE

THE WOMAN WITH the dyed-red hair reached into the crystal dish, taking a hand full of Godiva chocolates. She checked her plum-purple suit dress, eagerly chewing the candies with an overwhelmingly loud, annoying moan.

"My goodness, Marie. Do you understand how wonderful of an opportunity this is for us?" Senator Michelle Harding said, with that shrill, mousy voice, shaking her face with her frigid smile and thick red lipstick.

"We've been friends for many years now, Michelle. I hope now that I've become President, our friendship is not going to be challenged." President Marie Arcola said as she poured herself some orange juice and frowned at the senator sneaking another chocolate candy.

"Friends are very important, dear. Especially at this stage of your career. Votes also become very important from your fellow Congress people. Just because President Johnson's death provided you with this lucky opportunity, it doesn't guarantee you'll still be in this office for another term." Senator Harding eased back into the lounge chair, her hands folded with arrogant confidence. President Arcola rocked in the leather chair, tapping a pencil on the top of the President's desk, smirking back at this greedy witch.

"It's difficult for me to back you up on many of these issues; especially the one's you keep faxing to my office. Last year you were pro-choice, now you're anti-abortion. First, you're opposing the Grandfather Clauses for gun owners, now you want to have anyone convicted of a misdemeanor or a revoked driver's license, be denied their second amendment rights to purchase guns legally. And these changes in the taxes, you and your associates are proposing on people's personnel investments. Can you explain these things to me?" President Arcola said, flipping through a manila file, thick with documents. Senator Harding had a worried expression on her face, wondering what was in that file.

"Well. After reading the changes in the wording of those documents, everything became very confusing. The changes were not thoroughly explained."

"Not thoroughly explained? I really think you should go home tonight and read the Constitution. You are a United States Senator. Your duty to Americans is to preserve their rights under the Constitution. Article one, section nine states 'No bill of Attainder or ex post facto Law shall be passed.' Do you understand what that means, Michelle Harding? And I've heard that you've been receiving contributions from questionable sources."

"I don't think my contributors are questionable. You should understand how concerned many of these small communities have become, now that a woman has become the President of the United States. A lot of these small towns with families have struggled to make their dreams come true. To provide decent educations and safe schools for their children? Do you know how many children have been killed in schools by handguns since the turn of the century?"

"So, that's why the Catholic Church is flooding you with large contributions, to try and influence votes in Congress?"

"You can't prove any of this." Senator Harding laughed.

President Marie Arcola opened a file on her desk and handed several xeroxed letters to the senator. "I made copies of letters for you and hope I do not need to show the originals to the Senate committee; letters I've received at this office over the last few days. These letters were sent to me personally, with contributions in the hundreds of thousands of dollars. These contributors are convinced that because you are a 'close, personal friend of mine' and that we saw issues 'eye-to-eye' they have already won my support. Most of these letters imply that you can persuade my decisions on the abortion issues and have some kind of connection with me to challenge new laws." President Arcola took a deep breath, holding in her disgust for the senator.

"I sincerely believe you should check the list of your campaign contributors. As my 'close personal friend', I'd hate to have to come and visit you once a month in a federal prison." Senator Harding was calculating, as she squinted that spoiled, rich little girl face with those loud, red-lips.

"My goodness. You used to be an attorney. You must remember that xeroxed copies can be very poor means of evidence. Anyone planning to defamate someone's character could easily forge documents like these. If you give me the originals, I can have copies made up at my office for my attorney to examine. Lies like these might distort my reputation."

"Your reputation?" President Arcola laughed. "Have another chocolate, Michelle. The only reputation you have around Washington, is as a gold-digging, daddy's girl, who suckers senior citizens and minorities in this country, out of their life savings. No wonder your husband left you."

"So." Michelle said with her mousy voice. "Remember us 'little-people', as you play out your fantasy to be President. The whole country will be laughing when you fall on your ass." Senator Harding took the last chocolate from the tray and waved 'ta-ta', gliding toward the Oval Office door.

"Michelle. You're such a disturbed, little bitch. Next time, you make an appointment, bring you're own damn candy!" The President said with a snarl. Benny had the door pulled out of his hand, as Senator Harding tripped over him, while she pushed her way out into the corridor. President Arcola picked up her tennis racquet and threw it across the Oval Office at the door.

"I don't need to be pissed off right now, Benny. Are there anymore assholes meeting with me today?"

"Nope." Benny replied with a big smile. "She was the last asshole for the day."

"Damn, that bitch. She doesn't even care about what happened to my family." President Arcola spat, fuming, clenching her fists and gritting her teeth, ready to scream as she gathered up her notes.

Benny set a stack of files and photographs down on her desk. He backed away, stood up straight and smiled as he refilled the candy dish with Hershey kisses wrapped in green and red foil wrappers.

"I called James at the State Department, in regards to the International Rewards Program; if we need to use it to catch the people who set off the bomb at Dulles. And, Agent Naughton is here. Will you nccd a minute?" Benny said, quickly unwrapping a handful of chocolates and squirreling them in his mouth.

"Yeah, sure. And, Benny. Order a tuna fish sandwich on wheat bread up from the kitchen for me, please." Benny playfully saluted and stepped out into the corridor, waving for the FBI agent to enter the Oval Office. The stocky man gave Benny a questioning look; his beady eyes staring up from behind his gold, wire-rimmed glasses.

"What's that all about?" Jeri whispered to Benny, as he scribbled down the President's lunch request and then his own.

"Oh, that's just secret agent, eye-contact crap the FBI's gotta do to intimidate you. This meeting's going to be closed door. So when lunch arrives, call into the office first." Benny said dropping a Hershey kiss on her desk.

"Do you think she's going to send the United States into Iran?" Jeri asked.

"It looks like we might have no other choice." Benny said, scooting back to the Oval Office, holding his finger to his lips, to hush the secretary. Agent Naughton glanced up from his notes, as Benny shut the door with a wave from the President.

"These transcripts show the FBI has confirmed all the evidence from the bomb that killed President Johnson." President Arcola said.

"Yes, ma'am." Agent Naughton cleared his throat and blinked his eyes as President Arcola began examining the photographs from forensics.

"Madame President. I need to warn you . . ."

"What? You need to warn me that some of these photographs are of my dead children and my dead husband? I hope you remember, I was a captain in the army. I've seen soldiers split in half on the battlefield. And right now I don't sleep very well knowing that some bastards think they might have gotten away with this. I'm certain you, as a professional of the Department of Justice, are also having trouble sleeping since the assassination of President Johnson."

The FBI agent's neck trembled, as he gathered his thoughts to reply. "Yes, Madame President. Our job is to collect and preserve all the evidence and to allow the prosecutors to handle any and all judgments based on the evidence. In fact, I've reviewed many of the textbook cases, especially historical incidents relating to terrorism, to make certain that the FBI is one hundred and ten percent sure about these conclusions."

President Marie Arcola paused at the next set of photographs; the autopsy pictures of her son, Francis. Her eyes welled with tears at the dreadful sight of her five year old baby boy. She rolled her fingers and hands across the photographs, struggling to identify her son's face. Another picture, another angle with tags, but still she couldn't remember how he looked or felt in her arms. She pushed a button and Benny was at the door, knocking lightly at first and then he stepped into the Oval Office. The FBI agent had a puzzled look on his face.

"This is a high-profile incident, Agent Naughton. I need to make certain the person or persons that did this do not get away or acquitted." In her mind, she quietly wished for the day that these would be the photographs and reports of the terrorists that killed her family. Benny sat in his chair, taking notes, looking into Marie's eyes with empathy as she continued to study the autopsy photographs. It was obvious she was hurting as she read the notes as to how her daughter's face was seared from the assassin's bomb.

"The bomb signatures have identified nitrates but no urea. Similar metals have also been identified on the victims. No PETN. The explosives ordinance technicians have identified the carpeting in the tunnel as being the detonator."

"How could the carpet be a detonator?" Benny asked.

"Carpeting is a great conductor of static electricity. Thin copper filaments can be used; woven into or inserted into the carpet. The latest detonator of choice by terrorists are the same small electronics used for arming car alarms. Something as simple as a cellular phone could set off the explosives with a combination of tones."

President Arcola glanced up from the examiner's transcripts about her dead husband David. "A cellular phone?"

"Yes. It's a very simple, new way that terrorists set off area explosives. In fact, the FBI has arrested two factions that have begun using this new way of setting-off bombs in airports, subways and crowded, public facilities. One in Egypt and one in France. Wc know how they do it. We just can't figure out where they got the technology. The explosion is so clean and hot. The blast is so traumatic, that most of the evidence is blown away from the point of detonation for several hundred feet. And even then, the evidence is so contaminated, there is rarely ever enough of a sample retrieved to be analyzed in a lab."

President Arcola braced herself with one hand to the Presidents desk, to keep from falling. She closed the file containing the autopsy photographs. "So, what you've told us, Agent Naughton. Is that you don't know how this bomb or explosion caused the damage it did, but you have an idea of how the detonator might have been created. Do you have any suspects?" President Arcola asked. Agent Naughton scooted up in his chair, hiding his beady little eyes into another file that he pulled from his briefcase.

"Yes. We've detained a couple from Iraq at the University of Virginia. They are both from families that have been linked to an extremist group which is being investigated for the bombing of two nuclear reactors that were being built by Germany for Iran, at Bushehr. FBI agents have already raided their apartments and confiscated anti-American literature. We are currently investigating their telephone records."

President Marie Arcola's desk phone rang. "Yes, Jeri. Have those reports been confirmed to General Millings? Thank you."

President Arcola placed her hands over her face, closing her eyes in prayer. "Kuwait has reported two hundred of their people are dead from the accident at the factory. Seventy-four of them are children. Saudi Arabia confirms twenty dead and have begun air force war exercises into Southern Iran's airspace without resistance. Most of their dead are children. Why does it have to always be the children?" President Arcola said.

"We need to be one hundred percent sure about this evidence, Agent Naughton. The FBI labs have had problems with contaminated and mishandled evidence since the nineteen-eightys. I'd hate to have to order operations in the Persian Gulf over a mistake."

Agent Naughton raised his nose upwards, slightly offended. "Well. We haven't made any mistakes since I've worked with the FBI chemistry and toxicology unit."

"Good, Agent Naughton. But if I choose to punish Iran for the deaths from the Dulles Airport bombing, I can't risk making my administration vulnerable to foreign propaganda. NATO has finally started to stabilize and we can't have the United States make a mistake."

Benny scribbled down some notes, while President Arcola began reading the autopsy report for her husband, David. Most of the notes were difficult to read.

"Excessive trauma to the anterior of Mr. David Arcola. Questionable amounts of nitrates have been collected from the mouth, the nasal region, the esophagus into the bronchi of the lungs. I can't read most of this report. Why are these notes so encrypted?" Benny questioned.

Agent Naughton examined his copies. "Oh, I wouldn't say they're encrpyted. It's just the way the lab technicians write. I'm afraid most of them have terrible handwriting. I'll have their typed transcripts delivered to you as soon as they're on the computer."

"Most of this evidence indicates that the victims at the airport were burned to death. Even their insides." Benny mumbled, turning the reports, trying to read the notes from the technicians. "What kind of bomb kills like this?"

"The FBI technicians have set up a simulator in a warehouse, down in Georgia, to re-create the same explosion, under the same conditions. I'll know more when we run those test. But we do know this type of bomb is so unique and new, the people who set this bomb off, will more than likely, use another bomb just like it." Agent Naughton said.

"Has any of the evidence transmitted from the factory near Esfahan helped?"

"So far, the Pentagon has received numerous locations in Iran that are storing biological and chemical weapons, as well as inventories, dates and locations for many weapons to other countries. But nothing similar to the bomb used to kill the President. At least nothing yet."

Something caught the President's attention, as she went through the files a third time. "If your lab has these victims numbered in a specific order. David was the first one to die." President Arcola continued through the photographs, trying to solve this problem in her head.

"Your FBI theory states David was killed first. Francis was killed next, the blast burned his face, setting his clothes on fire; the explosion throwing him from the tunnel, head first, twenty feet to the tarmac below. President Johnson was the third to die. Shelley was the last."

"Yes. Your husband was the one closest to the bomb. In fact, his cellular phone is probably what set off the explosion. The boarding tunnel was the bomb or the catalyst for the bomb. The main incendiary of the bomb was acetylene or oxygen. Maybe even natural gas with the mercaptan filtered out some how."

"A bomb like that would take sometime to set up. Have all the pilots and employees been questioned by the FAA?"

"Yes, Madame President. Everyone in that area for the last month has been questioned and every worker that has ever filed a complaint, been suspended, anything. But all the evidence points to the students we arrested." Agent Naughton's pager began to beep. "I'm sorry, I have to deliver these reports to the Pentagon." The FBI agent stood, buttoned his suit jacket and clicked his briefcase shut. He extended his hand out and shook the President's hand.

"Don't worry, Madame President. I really believe we have the right suspects." Agent Naughton thought President Arcola's handshake was especially strong for a woman.

"Yes. Thank you, Agent Naughton. I really appreciate having you stop by with this information." She replied

The FBI agent didn't know how to take what she said, it showed in his beady eyes, as they rolled before he rushed out of the Oval Office. Jeri walked in carrying a lunch tray with fruits, vegetables, juices and tuna fish sandwiches. President Arcola eagerly took a bite from one of the sandwiches, sighing from hunger.

"So, why's this guy lying to us?" Benny asked, picking up his sandwich. President Arcola opened the lower desk drawer and pulled out a bag of Lays Potato Chips and a bag of Chips Ahoy cookies.

"Agent Naughton is one of those prodigies of our Justice Department who doesn't adjust well to a female boss."

"Are you going to tell him Fred doesn't think the Iranian's or some college students set off the bomb at Dulles?" Benny asked.

President Arcola quickly ate another handful of potato chips. "I've know Fred since the Oklahoma City bombing. I like the way he thinks. I don't like the way Naughton is rushing and jumping to conclusions. We all know how nervous American businesses get when Middle East oil is at stake."

Benny was very concerned, catching a glimpse of Marie tapping her fingers on top of the FBI files. He could feel the hurt she was suffering, seeing her husband and children in those photographs, reduced to measurements, tags and forensic terms.

"My parents are coming into town for the Lighting of the National Christmas tree. We really appreciate the use of your house to stay in. I just know we'd drive each other nuts with them staying in my efficiency for the next three weeks." Benny ran out of things to say and began to devour his sandwich.

"It's alright, Benny. It's going to just take some time." The telephone rang out in the corridor at Jeri's desk.

"Madame President!" Jeri shouted from her desk into the Oval Office. "It's the Pentagon. Iran agreed to a video-conference at midnight our time. The Chiefs of Staff have cleared Mr. Kenny to be present."

Benny raised his eyebrows and quickly swallowed, so he could speak. "Mr. Kenny? Mr. Michael Kenny, The professor of Iranian Studies? I thought you didn't like him because he used to be closely associated with Professor Berger?"

"I like him because he is serious and unbiased. He also has a brilliant passion for the Islamic people and their religion. I just need to know if the Interior Ministry and the Islamic government are sincere. It's gonna be rough waters all the way, Benny. But that's just part of the job."

"It's just so odd to imagine an Irishman being so educated in Middle East affairs."

"It's not that unusual when you look at Ireland's history. Michael Collins's letters and journals dealing with the Black and Tan's and the Troubles. In fact, the earlier years of the Irish

Republican Army and their terrorists tactic's are highly regarded in most factions of the Hezbullah and Hamas."

The telephone rang again at the secretary's desk out in the corridor. "Madame President. It's Senator Thomas again. He wonders why you haven't returned any of his calls?"

"Tell Senator Thomas I'd be happy to meet with him. Have him set up an appointment for the middle of next week." President Arcola said, pacing by the doorway of the Oval Office. Jeri gave the receiver a funny look. "He just started swearing and hung up."

TWENTY-TWO

SENATOR TREVOR THOMAS poured himself a full glass of Bushmills and paced across the living room with a stack of CIA reports in his hands concerning Afghanistan; taking a quick sip of the drink. "Damnit, this crap pisses me off! Why doesn't President Arcola put an end to this and get our SEAL team out of Iran!? Get in there and show them the United States means business! Goddamnit! How can she let this end up like Iran-Contra!? Those soldiers don't deserve to be treated like shit! That whole area is turning into a powder keg! Are you writing all of this down, my children!?"

Two men loosened their ties and opened up bottles of beer, starting to take down notes. "Yes, sir. But we'll have to change a few of those words." Shawn said.

A television talk show host went on and on about the assassination of the President, talking to some professor from Minnesota; promoting his new book on the pros and cons of having a lady President. The senator half listened, staring out of his Watergate apartment at a boat, slowly drifting down the Potomac. The December night called him out onto the patio, to take a breath of the cool, crisp air. His campaign managers heckled and protested the comments on CSPAN, as the interview continued with the political science and history scholar, eagerly promoted his book.

"Jesus, What a bunch of shit! Hey, Trevor, come in here and listen to this guy. He actually thinks he's been sleeping with the President!" Charlie called out.

The senator stood, leaning on the railing. He took a deep breath, closing his eyes, trying to remember how the evenings sitting on his parents back porch felt. The view looking over the golf course, as the twilight changed the shadows of the players into dark. Now, he's thought about the cardinals and their songs. How his mother and father would walk him through the course, explaining the importance of the trees. The way his dad could imitate the calls and whistles of the blue jays and the cardinals.

Today would have been his mother and fathers sixty-second wedding anniversary. For some reason, it was difficult for Trevor to remember what it is like to relax and not compete. The thought only frustrated him more, making him angry at himself for not working harder or faster.

"Now, children. Let's go through this again. And this time, make sure you understand the notes you take. This country is not going to approve a female President. We need to concentrate on the fact that America is only tolerating her at this point, because they feel sorry for her; because her children and her husband were killed a few days ago. What ideas does that give you Lauren?" Senator Thomas swished his drink, and stared down at the delicate, young woman, as if she were a meal.

"The public will soon forget the deaths of President Marie Arcola's family and begin to be more concerned with her stand on certain issues that are affecting our country." Lauren said, giving a quirky smile as she sipped some of her whiskey. A black man raised his hand, bumping his tie in the air.

"Yes, Charlie? What do you think about that statement from Lauren?" Senator Thomas asked, checking his Rolex.

"I think we should begin breaking down the Democrats by quoting the media, using the quotes from journalist from most of the foreign newspapers. You know what I mean. Just change a few words here and there." Charlie explained, using his hands to illustrate and also to hide his nervousness.

Senator Thomas handed the CIA reports to Shawn and passed the bottle of Bushmills to a raven haired woman who poured herself a bit of the whiskey into her glass. She raised a small toast as she took a drink, always keeping the senator in the sights of her dark green eyes. Trevor loosened his red patterned necktie and unbuttoned the top buttons of his shirt. Lauren changed a CD on the stereo.

"Shawn. Have you been monitoring the foreign reaction to our new lady President?" Senator Thomas said, easing himself onto the couch next to the woman.

"Yes, sir." Shawn replied, as if he was addressing a general in the army.

"Over the last few days, since the death of President Johnson, the newspapers and television news broadcasts from France, Italy, Japan, Russia, Mexico, Australia and Spain seem to have changed from concern and sympathy for President Arcola. Since they've been receiving correspondence in regard to the explosion in Iran. They're in a state of panic and are concerned about more bombings. They say, 'if it can happen to the President of the United States, on American soil, it can happen anywhere.' So far, Finland, Britain, Canada and China have unchanged views, at least that's what it shows in the poles. I think they want to wait and see how President Arcola handles this situation in Iran. To see how she solves the problem."

Senator Thomas sat up on the couch shaking his head. "Have any of you ever been in the service?" He gave his usual vulture-stare around the room, already knowing the answer. "Better yet. Have any of your parents ever been in the service, National Guard or in any field of government that endangers their lives to protect America?"

None of the campaign managers responded. They looked back at their note pads and to the television. The senator stared, ferocious, into the eyes of his flock. Their young innocent faces, gazed from the corner of their eyes, pausing in shock.

"I'm sorry. Just fuck what I said." Senator Thomas said, rubbing his forehead. "Okay Lilley, whatcha got?"

The raven haired woman caught the senator's attention, when she slid her emerald green high heels off her feet and stretched her long legs onto the couch.

"I have the final list of the people who sent donations, gifts, flowers, etc., for President Johnson and President Arcola. I've found some weak points." Lilley said, taking a sip of her whiskey, teasing the senator by rubbing her feet against her legs.

"Weak points. See. I like that. That is why I hired all of you to be my campaign managers. Can you imagine the importance of your jobs next year, running the White House?"

"Senator Thomas. The incident in Iran is still the hottest topic on President Arcola's agenda. In fact, the reports by the Chiefs of Staff indicate other neighboring countries have begun to move into Iran to take advantage of the problem near Esfahan. There have already been reports of fighting in the north near Tabas and Kashmar. With heavy casualties to the people of Iran."

"What time is it in Iran, Lilley?" Senator Thomas asked, trying to figure out the time on his Rolex.

"About two a.m." Lilley smiled, stirring her finger in her glass of whiskey, licking her lips and sucking her finger.

"Then that means the Presidents second Bozo SEAL team is already there. Now, I know none of you are going to understand, but when I was in Desert Storm and Bosnia, you learn a few things. Like why a handful of soldiers are sent into a dangerous, hostile country that raises their sons to carry bombs into restaurants in Tel-Aviv or to drive trucks filled with explosives into marine barracks. Blowing themselves to death, being honored by their family and country forever, as martyrs. Can you imagine how that feels? That rush of adrenalin surging through your veins at the few final seconds of your life. Imitating the power of God. Your eyes fixed on those peoples faces, when that blast of white light cinders your eyes and mind, sending you to paradise." The senator paused to take a gulp of Bushmills, staring at the plaque with his ribbons and metals, hanging on the wall, above a picture of his friends who died in the warehouse during a scud attack in Desert Storm.

"These guys are not going to make it out of Iran alive. You see, we are their enemy. Iran is simply trying to defend it's country. They will parade our soldiers through their streets. Starve them. Torture them. And then take a knife and gut them open in the middle of one of their celebrations against democratic countries. Over the last part of your lifetimes; those of you who remain in this political arena, you'll find out many times, nothing works exactly as you planned. Sometimes you're going to have to cut some deals. It's like a big poker game out there in that big, old world. A lot of these world leaders will not leave the table, unless the other players are penniless and left humiliated. Do you see what's going on out there in Iran? President Arcola's administration doesn't see it or doesn't care. But I do. And soon, you will too. There are variables with desperate countries, wanting to strike right now at the heart of Iran. All that land. All that oil. The strategic location of Iran's land on the Strait of Hormuz, the Gulf of Oman and the integrity of the Persian Gulf Nations." Senator Thomas noticed he was rambling, yet none of his campaign managers had stopped scribbling down notes, so he continued.

"Well, responsibility of great magnitude is part of being the President. And this is the big one that is going to make the Democratic Party put the United States into a very weak position internationally. Lauren. Take note. I need you to find a way to introduce us in the media as the one's that can stop America from going to war."

"But, if you want to commit U.S. troops, how does that stop a war?" Lauren scolded, rolling her jealous eyes at Lilley.

"It's simple. Most of these terrorist countries breed cowardly little bullies. Once they see the build up of aircraft carriers and hear the sounds of jets flying over their houses things will change very quickly. They'll be headin' for the hills." Senator Thomas replied.

"Maybe we can slip something into one of those tabloids that says something like 'Plastic and rubber manufacturers praise President Arcola's plan to let Iran be invaded by hostile countries. The body bags and cemetery plots are selling like hot cakes.'" Ryan said.

Senator Thomas took a drink of whiskey, while his audience laughed at his campaign manager's joke. Senator Thomas raised his arms out and smiled. "Ryan. That's a great idea. See. This is what we have to do. Loosen up and hit this thing head on. Shawn, your release to USA was brilliant. I need another article like that next Monday for the L.A. papers."

The young Afro-American man grinned ear to ear, from the compliment. Senator Thomas went into his pep-talk. The senator stood center stage in his apartment living room, loosening up from the whiskey and the beat of the music; and his unyielding hunger.

"Lauren. Any big deals with women's magazines wanting to interview our wonderful lady President?" The senator asked.

"Yes. In fact she's been asked to be interviewed on a number of talk shows on NBC, FOX and ABC. One of the biggest audiences that could damage our campaign is ABC. It looks like Oprah Winfrey's show has promoters begging the President to be on her show."

"Good. Keep me updated and if she makes it on the show, make a copy. We've only got a year to make this thing happen. So let's be mean but clean."

Ryan stood up and weaved, bumping into the coffee table, rattling the empty beer bottles. "Wa. Sorry. I think I need to leave. I think I drank too much." Shawn also stood up stretching, glancing at the clock in the senator's kitchen.

"Sir. It's time I got going too. Ryan can share my cab ride. Tomorrow's the big day. The Senate and the House start to vote whether or not to build up troops in the Persian Gulf. Just so we sleep better tonight, senator. How fast and how much can the United States commit to the Middle East, if or when President Arcola declares war in Iran?"

Senator Trevor Thomas gave his wicked smile and stretched his neck, sipping some whiskey, calculating the possibilities. "First, the Nimitz and the battleships in the area would launch their Joint Strike Fighters. They've got enough Smart bombs and Toma-hawks to last a year. Our subs would back the area by keeping the waters clean. The railroads and bridges would be the next targets. Then the power plants and the waterways. We have enough air strike power in that region, on our own, to destroy anything seen as a military threat, for the next twenty years. Even without the help of any of our allies. The whole region would be a wasteland for at least half a century." Senator Thomas said, with his special little laugh.

TWENTY-THREE

IT WAS FIVE a.m. by the digital red numbers of the clock on the television. Senator Trevor Thomas nibbled on a piece of cold almond chicken and sipped his glass of tomato juice, quietly standing naked, watching the latest news reports from Iran. Some news footage came on with President Marie Arcola speaking during the Lighting of the National Christmas Tree.

"She's gorgeous." Trevor mumbled, feeling Lilley's arms, pulling her naked body against his back.

"So you think President Arcola's gorgeous? Do you want to jump her bones, too?" Lilley purred her hot breath into his ear, running her nails down his back. Trevor pondered the thought of him and the lady President, making him smile.

"No. Actually, I want to be with her. I am deeply intrigued by her. I want to feel her thoughts. I want to savor her weaknesses. I want to find her weaknesses."

"Is that so you can find your weaknesses?"

The senator gave Lilley a flat stare. "Be serious. I have no weaknesses. Well, maybe one. Maybe two. But I don't think of them as weaknesses. I think of them as rewards that I treat myself with."

"But every time you talk about her, it's about you stopping her from being elected. Or how to take advantage of her administration so that you can win next year's election. How could you possibly feel for her?"

"I just do. And I feel for her because of the loss of her husband and children, too." The senator said, as he caught a glimpse of himself in the full length mirror, on the back of the hallway door. He pulled away from Lilley and began to pose for himself.

"Do you like standing in front of the mirror, ogling yourself?" Lilley said.

"Yes. Yes, I do. I'm admiring how a man of my age can be in such great shape." Lilley massaged her body close to his and slid her hands around his stomach. He grinned, feeling her hard nipples against his back.

"So, having wild sex with younger women is one of your treats?" Lilley sighed, pulling Trevor between her legs.

"Anything dealing with sex and power is a treat to me. Remember, I have to be in the Senate in an hour and a half."

"Oh, that's plenty of time." Lilley moaned, wrapping her legs around his back, lowering them onto the couch.

TWENTY-FOUR

SENATOR THOMAS STOPPED at his secretary's desk and gave a curious look into the open door of his office at a silver haired woman seated on the armchair, in front of his desk, typing away on a laptop computer.

"Pam? Do I have an appointment today?"

The thin faced secretary barely glanced up from her desk, taking one of the white lunch bags from the senator, pulling out a Greek salad and an orange. "Yes, you do have an appointment." Pam said, tapping a few keys on her computer and pulling up the senator's agenda for the day on the screen. "And, you also missed her birthday."

Trevor shifted the box of flowers on top of Pam's desk and removed the card addressed to Brenda. Quickly he sauntered into his office and closed the door.

"Mady. How are you?"

Her blue eyes lit up as she set her glasses down on the coffee table. The wrinkles on her face, curved into a wide smile, in soulful wisdom that was apparent in a hug she gave Trevor; an honor that could not be denied. "Hello, Trevor dear."

"Mady. You're trembling." The senator said, setting the box and his lunch bag down on the table by the computer. She gave him another squeeze and pulled herself away; she caught a tear as it rolled down her cheek.

"Did you read the reports of the evidence from the factory?" Mady asked.

"Some of it." He replied, looking at the top of his desk, where a stack of photographs sat with a set of manila envelopes. He reached over and picked up a computer printout labeled: OPER-

ATION INTERCEPT. The senator shook his head at Agent Naughton's corny choice for the file title.

"These are some real bad chemicals. The dates on these inventory sheets go back thirty years. I'm surprised the Iranians aren't giving birth to deformed children. Biological Weapons: Ricin. Botulinum. Anthrax. Chemical: Tabun. Sarin. Hydrogen Cyanide. Xylidine. Phosgene. Butolin X. Saxitoxin TZ. Enterotoxin B. This is quite a grocery list. Some of the customers could probably buy four items or less in the black market express lane."

"One of the formulas from the factory is for Zyclon-B." Mady said with a sigh and a look of hopelessness.

"Zyclon-B. I'm just trying to learn about that one. I guess the Iranian's use it as a paint thinner." Trevor said, remembering Rachel's story about the United States bombing a paint factory.

"It's a nerve gas that was used by the Nazi's to kill the Jews in the concentration camps."

Senator Thomas shook his head and quickly looked away, slightly ashamed.

"It's difficult to find a way to forgive. Or a way to forget." She bowed her head in sadness, the thoughts of a childhood that was changed by the ghastly atrocity of war.

"I'm sorry. I'm so stupid for saying that. I didn't mean to be so thoughtless."

"Oh, Trevor. Stop. It's sometimes difficult for the Jewish. Some of us want to forget and others never want to forget. But facts are facts. Those biological and chemical weapons are there. Those weapons are only designed to kill people. I believe it's time someone ended this once and for all. Your administration can prevent a disaster like this from ever happening again. I believe you and your administration can accomplish that goal. It's important this disaster in Iran becomes an example to the world, before someone decides to use these weapons in a real war." Mady scooted the armchair closer to Trevor's desk and was handed a stack of surveillance photographs from Esfahan.

"Those are the early photographs from a month ago. The first set of photographs were taken from our satellites four hours after the explosion."

The pictures showed hundreds of women carrying bodies of

dead children down from the sandstone cliffs. Their cringing faces were tear filled and showed expressions of shock. A group of women had their hands raised to the sky crying out in hysteria, dressed in their black robes. The Red Crescent Army and volunteers stood by with hundreds of Iranian soldiers, watching the women setting the bodies into the water. "It's good to see the strength of the Islamic women. Even during this horrifying disaster, they practice the rite of washing the dead before they are buried."

Trevor handed her another set of photographs. "These pictures were taken five hours after the explosion."

The women lay dead, collapsed on top of the bodies of the naked children. The brown, muddy water from the small creeks flowed over their faces; their hands clutching at their throats. Their screams frozen in time. On the cliffs near by, most of the soldiers had collapsed and lay dead while members of the Red Crescent stumbled away, suffering from the exposure to the chemicals; even though they were wearing protective suits and masks. The next set of surveillance photographs, showed they had fallen to the rocks and died.

"The women probably had the most exposure. The Pentagons guess is that the water in and around Esfahan is saturated with Anthrax. Now here's the latest reports from the soldiers, President Arcola sent in." The senator said, his chin stuck out as he huffed. "I guess I owe her an apology for that one."

"An apology? For what?"

"For having the guts to send soldiers into the factory. Basically, I told her that no good would come out of it, but it looks like this evidence is going to help us out in the long run."

Mady smiled and shook her head at the senator. "Are you saying your colorful rhetoric is challenging our new President's decision making?"

"Well. Maybe. I just don't like being wrong and I definitely don't like the other person being right. Especially if it's her."

"Why? Because she's a woman or because she's a Democrat?" Mady said. Trevor stood up quickly from his desk and shuffled through another file, still a little angry at himself for being wrong about President Arcola. "No. None of that. I just don't like losing to anybody. You know that, Mady. I'm the one who should be in the White House. I'm the one with more experience than her."

Mady smiled at Trevor, until she continued to read Dewey's reconnaissance reports from the last few days. She typed in notes on her laptop computer of the quantities of biological and chemical weapons CIC estimated might have been in the factory before, during and after the explosion. Senator Thomas began laughing at Agent Naughton's FBI report.

"This guy is a nut case. And I thought I was the guy that was power hungry." Trevor walked over next to Mady so they could both look at the FBI agents report.

"Look at this junk. Naughton has most of these notes encrypted. Half this crap is illegible. And what's this cock-a-mamie story about some college students that blew up President Johnson because of the abortion clinic issues?"

"Isn't Agent Naughton the one that was put in charge of overhauling the FBI evidence storage department ten years ago?" Mady asked.

"Yeah, he's the one. An over-zealous, hot-dogging, brown-nosing pinhead. I bet if you search his family tree, you'll find out his family was probably involved in one of those McCarthyite witch hunts back in the 1950's."

Mady began looking through the photographs of the victims from the Dulles Airport explosion. Tears in her eyes were a sign she was deeply disturbed when she saw the smiling portraits of Francis and Shelley. And then the remains of their bodies on the medical examiner's gurneys.

"My God, Trevor. This is so wrong. I have worked all my life to try to change this. I feel like I have failed. Why do these terrorist go on? The blowing up and the killing. Randomly destroying the lives of so many innocent people. Where do these monsters come from?"

"Well. Our newly, ordained President Arcola has been working around the clock with anti-terrorist specialists from around the world. Some of her cronies are even talking to Mandela's council, the Sinn Fein, the RCU and the Israeli Secret Service. She even got a call from one of the leaders from Hamas, who said it wasn't any of his people and that he was sorry for what happened to her family. I guess I feel sorry for her, too."

"Why would you feel sorry for President Arcola?" Mady said.

"Because, once all this desperate grabbing-of-straws is over, she's going to end up with nothing. All these terrorist bomb experts trying to piece together and link this attack to their own particular causes and religious beliefs is a waste of time. When the dust clears, she'd be lucky to get a tour on daytime talk shows."

Mady rubbed her ear and gave Senator Trevor Thomas that same look he gives everyone else; only with her crystal blue eyes.

"I see you have to learn more about the vision of certain leaders and their use of the design for ethnic cleansing. Trevor. When you were stationed in Bosnia, did you really understand the total agenda the Serb leaders were trying to achieve? Racism and the genocide of the nearest target that is available. All those people turning on their neighbors. Killing children and raping women, people they've known all their lives. All those excuses and reasons were so convenient."

"It's true, I was just a soldier in the middle of the Bosnian conflict. I still feel little came out of the presence of U.S. troops. For instance, look what happened last year in Macedonia and Kosovo. The peacemakers predicted back in nineteen-ninety nine that the ethnic cleansing would begin again. President Johnson was already considering sending troops in again to try to bring order."

"Get use to it, Trevor. Hong Kong is still having tremendous human rights and legal problems with China. And now it looks as though China may plan to attack Taiwan after all. That's going to really be a moral and strategic dilemma for you and your administration."

"Yes. That's one of the reasons I feel we should commit U.S. troops now and take advantage of this opportunity in Iran. It would show China we mean business and that we are not going to tolerate anymore of these violations of international law." Mady held her hand to her chest and then held her wrist to check her pulse.

"Have you seen the latest newspapers? The newspapers have allowed themselves to take great liberties with the pictures of the people killed last week in the riots. I think the Chicago Tribune and the Detroit Free Press got a little too explicit." Trevor said as he set the newspapers at the edge of his desk.

Mady was reluctant to look them over, not wanting to leave the computer disc inventory sheets from the factory. She paused, breathing deep a few times, sad and tired. Trevor blinked his deep brown eyes and poured her a glass of water. He tried to change the subject, hoping to break her from the depressing train of thought. "So. How does it feel to finally be retired?" Trevor playfully asked with a grin.

Mady chuckled and gave him a stare. "Boring as hell. The only thing great about it, is that I get to spend lots of time with my grandchildren. Your new office looks nice."

"Thanks. It's alot better than that closet I used to live in, down the hall from Ralph Nader." Trevor said watching Mady smile.

"I've been reading your latest book on the expansion of NATO in the twenty-first century. I especially like your theory about North Korea and China. It's very distressing about the situation in Hong Kong since their independence from Britain. I really wish the vocabulary between the United States and Europe would have been clearer. I sense a civil war in that region. And I also think it's going to be very messy and cost the U.S. billions of dollars."

The retired Secretary of State grinned when she noticed the book she wrote, sitting on the senator's filing cabinet with yellow and blue pieces of paper as bookmarks.

"Things are going to get a lot worse. China is becoming desperate for land. In the next twenty years, one third of the population of the earth will be Chinese. They still haven't stopped their human rights violations and they still practice their war games to intimidate their neighboring countries, even with the protest from Hong Kong. Are you very familiar with Hong Kong's history?"

"The Opium Wars. The humiliation of British control. Leased in 1898 for ninety-nine years to Victorian Britain. It used to make a hundred and sixty billion dollars a year, until China started controlling a percentage of their trade to subsidize the over-population of Communist China, five years after Hong Kong's independence from British colonization. Sending hundreds of businesses heading for Taiwan and the Phillipines. But also bringing new businesses in. Beautiful mountains, shrouded by magical spirits in the sheathe of her fog. A city filled with mystery and money. Great food, beautiful women. Always bringing in millions of tourist each year. I've been there at least ten times. I love the place."

"Always be vigilant, Trevor. Especially now. The United States needs you to become the next President. This country is coming undone and a true leader is needed to get the American dream back on track."

"The assassination of President Johnson didn't help. All of a sudden I'm getting letters and phone calls with concerns about the safety of public buildings and offices. Hell. This is the tightest security has been in our country since the bombing of flight 191."

"I was so happy when those shits were caught. Punk scum spineless pigs. How can those type of people justify coming to this country with their hatred towards this country, and then go out and blow up innocent people and children."

Senator Thomas reached behind his neck and began massaging his shoulders. He took a long, cool drink of water and peeked at the grandfather clock, on the west wall. Mady caught his eyes, as he checked the time. "You've got to be in the Senate in less than an hour. It's going to be a tough session." Mady put her glasses back on and clicked the keyboard of her laptop computer as she talked to Trevor.

"The darkest part of politics, is having to take the responsibility for the final decision. To do the dirty work."

"Yes. I'm already next in line to be the next Satan. That's a lovely metaphor for someone as charming and sophisticated as myself." Trevor picked up his putter from the corner of the love seat and twirled the titanium club between his palms as he scooted the golf balls to his putting green in front of the desk.

"Nothing is guaranteed, Trevor."

"That's true, Mady. But lately a President being killed on American soil, in a public place. In broad daylight. And the killers still at large. I'm starting to think twice about a thicker bulletproof jacket and a heck-of-a-lot more bodyguards."

Mady closed the FBI file labeled: OPERATION INTERCEPT. She took a drink of water and let it trickle down her throat, finding it difficult to breath. Trevor putted the golf ball down the green and broke into a cheerful smile.

"Oh, yes. Another hole in one."

"The road ahead is going to be very challenging to you Trevor. Over the next year, inspection teams are going to be needed to respond to the non-proliferation of many of these rogue nations. An accident like this one near Esfahan was predicted back in the twentieth century. I was always just hoping this predicttion would never come true."

The senator putted another ball across the floor and raised his arms in a silent cheer, with another hole-in-one. "Well, I knew this job wasn't going to be easy. But at least my administration has some wonderful problems to look forward to."

"Have you talked to the Secretary of Defense about the latest civil wars in North Africa?" Trevor paused, leaning on his golf club, paying startled attention to Mady.

"Doug Rawlings? No. I haven't heard much. Except the British government is in an uproar about losing more territory and having whole villages go on strike, refusing to work for their mining companies."

"The increased ethnic violence is on the rise and Britain doesn't want to be involved. That means the prime minister is going to throw the problem in Iran into our arena."

"Britain doesn't want to be involved? Hell. They can't afford to be involved. Besides that, they can't find anyone to fight for them."

"You realize, North Africa will become an important part of your agenda." Mady said, sitting back in the armchair. Senator Thomas leaned his putter up against one of the filing cabinets and rubbed his tired eyes. He stretched into a big yawn and slid his chair away from the desk, pulling a stack of photographs from a manila envelope, handing them to Mady.

"These are last night's reports from General Tyler at the Pentagon." Trevor said, while she studied the notes from the general.

"The next satellite photographs you'll see are of great concern to the U.S. military presence in the Gulf."

Mady glanced at the pictures of massive tank regiments rolling across roads and the desert. A note attached to the side listed the latitude and longitude of the tanks. "T-72's. There must be a hundred of them."

Trevor handed Mady a picture of women soldiers, dressed in fatigues and green scarves, marching forward with their rifles shouldered and their fist pointing out. A squadron of helicopters rushed overhead and softened the only resistance Iran had left, on the Iraq-Iran border. "These reports from Saudi Arabia indicate more than fifty-thousand soldiers of The National Liberation Army have begun a massive occupation into the Zagro Mountains. It looks like Rajavi's N.C.R. is going to get a little piece of Iran after all."

"Has Iran's military collapsed in that region of their country?" Mady said, with a shocked expression on her face.

"Our satellites can't tell. Some of the generals have theories that Iran is leading the N.C.R. into a trap. Earlier in the week, twelve Scud missiles were launched from the mountains near Sonqor. Now it's all quiet. The Pentagon has already begun listing the possibilities; if Saddam's troops follow the N.C.R. into Iran. Jesus Christ, this thing is turning into one helluva mess."

Trevor picked up the box of flowers and handed it to Mady. "I got these flowers for your birthday. I didn't know what to give the woman that has everything."

"Trevor. You sweetheart." Mady said, her smile and face glowed as she picked up and cradled the dozen red roses. She raised them to her nose, closed her eyes and breathed deep the sweet aroma of the flowers. Trevor tucked his hands into his pockets and shuffled his feet watching his friend, gingerly setting the flowers back in their box. He ran his fingers over the card, making certain it was still there.

"Senator!" Pam called from the other room. "There's a fax coming in from General Kolzalski!"

"Okay. Thanks, Pam." The senator stood and watched the fax machine whistle and begin to print the message from one of the general's from the Pentagon

"By the way, Mady. Happy Hanukkah." Senator Thomas said.

"Thank you, dear Trevor. Have a Merry Christmas."

The senator put his arm around his friend's shoulder and helped her walk out into the hallway by the secretary's desk. The senator tilted his head and glanced at the faxed document, as he held it in his hand. He cleared his throat.

"My God, Mady. Half a million people are confirmed dead in Iran."

TWENTY-FIVE

T HE BIG DOORS were held open for Senator Thomas, as he shuffled past the pages and a smiling Senator Harding. One of the official officers pushed by, instructing a director from the CNBC camera crew; making certain their camera was turned off.

"Hi, Trevor." Senator Harding cooed, reaching out to touch his arm.

"Good morning, Michelle." Senator Thomas replied, not interested, but still being his usual, charming self. He scooted down the crowded row and flopped into one of the brown leather chairs and began pushing back the cuticles on his fingernails with his car key, trying to listen in on one of the senator's conversations. Lauren flipped her long blond hair back and stuck her nose in the air.

"So. Was my ex-girlfriend any good last night?" Lauren said, with a huff, glaring at the happy senator, who only looked away with that proverbial Cheshire cat smile.

"Yes, She was good. But I was much better."

The Reverend Joyce stepped up to the President Pro Tempore's podium. The Senate hushed and the reverend began.

"Almighty God. Who calls us to seek peace and not war. Who has blessed us in victory, in just wars fought for the righteous cause of justice and freedom. We seek your guidance for the crucial decisions at this time as we decide on the fate of our great nation. Our hearts and minds are united with you in the abhorrence in judgment to committing our sons and daughters in the armed forces, to a land foreign to them, such as Iran. But thank you for the diligence for which the Senate has debated the issue of sending our troops into Iran, to defend their freedom and rights, as well as preserving the neighboring countries and our friends and allies in that region of the world.

The research and clear communication on both sides of these issues, have brought illuminating discussions. Sharp differences remain on this issue, to begin operations in the Persian Gulf to help the country of Iran, during a dangerous and unpredictable catastrophe that involves biological and chemical weapons of mass destruction. Now the hour of decision approaches.

Father, fill with your presence and glory, this chamber and then the Old Senate Chamber during the executive session. May the senators seek your guidance, clarify their convictions and then cast their votes, with the sense that they have done their very best. When the votes are counted and the result is declared, unite the senators in an unbreakable bond of unity, rooted in a mutual commitment to patriotic leadership of our nation. Dear God, guide this Senate and bless America. In the name of our Lord and Savior. Amen."

Reverend Joyce turned and shook the hand of the President Pro Tempore, who quickly seated himself, scooting the big leather chair up to the desk, pulling the microphone close to him to begin the session.

"The able Majority Leader from Indiana is recognized." The President Pro Tempore said, in his thick Texas accent. The Parliamentarian passed a small stack of files up to his desk and motioned to one of the pages. Senator Trevor Thomas stepped up to the podium.

"Mr. President, thank you for that recognition and I want to thank the chaplain, as always, for his thoughtful and helpful prayers. For the information of all senators, today at eight p.m., the Senate will begin a closed, executive session in the Old Senate Chamber, to continue debate on the possibility of sending United States troops into the Persian Gulf to aid in case any other emergencies arise in that region of the world, to aid our allies in Kuwait and Saudi Arabia and to send troops into Iran, if necessary. This meeting is so that members can be briefed on certain classified information. This is the first time in several years that we have had such a briefing. I urge all senators to attend, I think they will find it very interesting and they need to know what will come out of this briefing before the next final decision. The closed session is expected to continue until ten p.m. and then the Senate will resume debate and discussion, here in this chamber, until all time is expired or yielded back, by the time agreement. At the end of the closed session, voting will begin immediately, on the subject of committing our troops to the Persian Gulf, to begin operations in Iran.

By previous consent, the Senate will resume debate and discussion until all the votes have been counted. If all votes are not in by twelve a.m., this Senate will meet again at ten a.m. tomorrow and continue until a decision is made. Obviously, the difficult issue of a possible tie vote may occur, and as we all know, there is no Vice-President. So the vote may be decided by the Speaker of the House.

I believe there is four hours of general time left, somewhere thereabouts. In addition, by consent, the eight motions to strike will be in order anytime after the closed session. Separate votes on each of the motions are expected, therefore senators can expect votes throughout these debates and throughout the evening, so that senators can collectively discuss this issue and take action, so that a decision can be reached and presented to the President, President Marie Joanna Arcola.

Especially since the situation in Iran is escalating and the concerns of our allies in the Middle East are in need of our guidance and thoughts. Once again, I encourage all the senators to participate in this issue, this is a very serious, dangerous, delicate situation. I wish to remind all the senators that decisions in the past, that concerned the commitment of United States troops, such as World War I, World War II, the Korean War, the Vietnam War, Grenada, Panama, Somalia, Desert Storm, Bosnia, Cuba, and now Iran, have always been consistent.

The American people have always depended on the House and the Senate to guide and lead with wisdom, in the direction that is true and right. Again, I encourage all of us here to begin debating this matter in the Old Senate Chamber, as well as fulfilling the duties and obligations in this Senate chamber over the next few hours. Mr. President, I now ask that you consent the following individuals, in addition to those officers and employees referred to in Standing Rule Number 29 be granted privileges for today's closed session, and I send a list to the desk."

Senator Trevor Thomas handed a sheet of paper to one of the Official reporters.

"Without objection, so ordered." The President Pro Tempore responded. Senator Thomas turned his notes over on the podium and continued.

"Mr. President, I'd like to call attention to all senators and staff, that Rule 29, of standing rules of the Senate, which addresses the confidentiality of Executive Sessions. Paragraph five of Standing Rule Number 29, reads as follows: Any senator, officer or employee of the Senate, who shall disclose the secret, or confidential business or proceedings of the Senate, shall be liable, if a senator, to suffer expulsion from the body, and if an officer or an employee, to dismissal from the service of the Senate and to punishment for contempt.

I urge my colleagues to keep this in mind when approached by the media, for comments on these proceedings. Mr. President, I also ask, that in accordance with the agreement, that I ask in unanimous consent, that the Senate now begin debate and discussion until eight p.m., when we should all proceed to the Old Senate Chamber."

"Granted."

"First I would like to yield the stand to Senator Graebul and Senator Hollis. And at this time I would like to . . ."

"Objection." Senator James said, interrupting Senator Thomas as she shuffled her notes, standing at the next podium.

"Objection so ordered." The President Pro Tempore said.

"Does the senator seek recognition?" Senator Thomas said, glaring at Senator James.

Senator James, the Minority Leader, raised her hand in the air.

"I would like to allow Senator Parker ten minutes. I believe we have three hours and twenty minutes remaining on our time. If necessary, I would like to grant more time to Senator Parker, if necessary."

"Any objection?" The President called out.

Senator Trevor Thomas gazed around the Senate, stopping his glance at all the opposing senators, taking inventory with his eyes.

"No objections Mr. President." Trevor growled, straighten his notes and peered over his shoulder at one of his fellow senators.

"The senator from Massachusetts is recognized for ten minutes."

"Mr. President, I thank you and I thank the Senate. Next Friday is the anniversary of the death of my father, who served in the Marines and was involved in several small military encounters, around the world." Senator Parker slid her thick rimmed glasses back onto her nose and continued to speak.

"Among some of his services to this country, he was a border guard for South Korea and as an infantryman in Somalia, Sierra Leone and Macedonia. I do not like the idea of war and feel, along with my colleagues, that war is not the solution. It is the biggest tax burden on the government, allowing millions of tax-payer dollars to be scrambled and buried in paperwork, and even-tually is so lost in accounting that the average citizen can not comprehend the result. It has taken the average family decades to adjust and control their own finances, employment and to secure their destinies towards providing for their children, their retire-ments and to finally give them a sense of control in the decision making of this country.

I have, right here, several reports and documents, that show how many billions of dollars have gone unpaid by other countries, around the world, that has become the cross-to-bare for the tax-payers of this country. I have the figures right here, ladies and gentlemen." Senator Parker set a stack of papers to the side of the podium.

"It has taken twenty years for the United States to finally reduce the national debt to the low which it is at today. My colleagues and I do not feel it is necessary to commit the United States into an unclear predicament in the Persian Gulf at this time. I also believe that questionable information from that region of the world should be re-evaluated for validity and clarification to determine whether or not it is even safe for the United States to have troops occupy any land near Iran. For fear of contamination of air and water, as well as the risk of over-exposure to the biological and chemical weapons that were being manufactured with the intent to be used or certainly being manufactured for the sale to other rogue countries that planned to use these chemical weapons in place of nuclear weapons as a threat to provoke and enslave their neighboring countries.

This Senate knows and understands the concerns of the American people from the documentation over the last twenty-six years, that the Biological and Chemical Weapons Treaty violations from several countries around the world have increased into a frightening and deadly concern for all nations. I can look around this chamber and point out fifty senators who have served in the United States armed forces! Of, almost a hundred percent of them, I can assure this Senate, Mr. President! That the nightmare of sending this nations sons and daughters, into an uncharted, unpredictable country, is a risk that America should not take! With these rogue nations who accept the manufacturing and use of biological and chemical materials to be used for weapons of mass destruction, we should always take our time and not rush in to try to be the ones that dictate or police the world!"

"One minute Senator Parker." The President announced.

"At this time, I urge my colleagues in the Senate to vote against sending our army, navy, marines or air force personnel to the Persian Gulf, to occupy Iran, until we have more time to analyze this situation. I do not see this as a time to panic, Thank you. I yield the remainder of my time to Senator James."

Senator Trevor Thomas studied the Senate Chamber with those voracious, dark brown wolf eyes. His logic was impeccable; his mannerisms, always planned. He intimidated his opponents with a face; glistening with his tight-lipped smile, waving for Senator Graebul to join him on the Senate floor.

"Mr. President, I'd like to allow seven minutes of my time to Senator Daly." Senator James said, shaking her head at the Majority Leaders antics.

"Objection, Mr. President. Time is an important factor at this point, since all the senators present need ample amount of time to meet in the Old Senate Chamber!" Senator Graebul called out.

"Objection noted. Continue Senator James."

"Thank you Mr. President." Senator Daly said, stepping to the podium. Senator Thomas held his hands out, palms up, whispering to one of the senators to 'come on' down to the floor.

"Many of the views that will be introduced to this Senate, to decide the issue of committing our American soldiers into the Persian Gulf, may be based on opinions of old soldiers who feel threatened in one way, or another." The large, gray-haired Senator Daly tugged at his silver, walrus mustache.

"It is sad that the newspapers and television talk shows have blown this minor incident out of proportion. I'm certain bookies are taking bets in Las Vegas that this will be one of the most heated and questionable meetings of the Senate, in the history of the United States of America, to date so far. The world is watching us and waiting for us to make the ultimate mistake.

I look around at this Senate gathered this afternoon and see a mixture of many great minds. I see retired officers of all branches of the military. I see ex-attorneys. I see business men and women. And I also see the fiber of the United States of America that has woven us as leaders within the international community. I see the faces of concerned mothers and fathers who do not want to see their children have to be bombarded and traumatized with the nightmare of war. With their dreams diminished to the silent thoughts across the dinner table, as all of us sit and imagine the thousands and thousands of American women and men, having their bodies flown back here to the United States to be buried and cremated, wasted on an accident that this Senate should never have rushed our country into."

A light applause loomed up from behind the senator, in agreement from his colleagues.

"This is not the way a civilized administration behaves. America has become the most powerful country in the world. And we became that way by developing our character and bringing any issue or conflict to the table, to discuss what can be done to solve the problem! Not by gathering up our troops and going to war. I look over at many of my colleagues and know that some of their children are in the military, are ready to defend this country and the freedom of other countries. Biological and chemical weapons have not been a concern in war since Desert Storm. When Iraq threatened many countries with the possible use of SCUD missiles, loaded with chemical weapons. And during those times, Iraq used chemical weapons against the Kurds. Need I remind this Senate, how many thousands of those people were killed or eventually died? I don't think we want that to happen to our soldiers. All of us here really have to think about this. Biological and chemical weapons are not like bullets. You don't have to aim them at someone. Terrorists use them like bombs. They explode them in a certain place and get lucky by killing hundreds or thousands of innocent people."

"One minute, senator." The President said.

"Let's think about this. I, for the record, plan to vote 'no'. We don't belong in Iran. This incident will go away. Thank you, Mr. President. I yield any remainder of my time to Senator James."

"Mr. President! I yield the floor to Senator Yueng for seven minutes!" Senator Thomas called out.

"The senator from Montana is recognized for ten minutes."

The Asian man was greeted at the podium with a handshake from Senator Thomas. He set down his notes and turned to speak to the Senate.

"I realize the dramatic and enlightening speeches of our colleagues across the aisle, are meant to give America a brief history of the East, while skimming over the long list of human rights violations that have risen in China and Hong Kong for several years. Need I remind the Senate here this afternoon, that I was raised under the control of the Communist regime that is now considering the fate of Iran, as it has with Hong Kong, Afghanistan, Pakistan, North Korea and Taiwan. I was a student in Hong Kong. I have witnessed first-hand how a country can dispose of it's people. Namely, the historical significance of my friends who were slaughtered in Tianamen Square. As a boy, I saw the tanks become a constant presence, as the Chinese became desperate to expand their military war machine. Iran will be the next opportunity for the Red Army.

Since the turn of the century, China has continued to practice war games; violating airspace, violating forbidden territory. All these issues we have to be concerned with and treat with the utmost serious consideration. Over the last five years, China's demand for large sums of money, while their threats to the south and their activity with North Korea, must be observed closely. The recent reports are that China plans to send military aid to Iran, to defend them while they rebuild, after this biological and chemical weapons accident.

As I have said to this Senate in the past, during my twelve years in this Senate, we had better never, ever let our guard down when China involves themselves in military affairs. My fellow senators, we all know where China stands on the issues of weapons of mass destruction. They are hard, tough bargainers and they are ruthless people that have constantly put the issue of non-proliferation out of their agenda, ignoring the world's concerns about their secret trade with countries that do not honor the Chemical Weapons Convention and continue to exploit their neighboring countries. Infractions and public humiliations are not the answer at this point. We must all realize, that we are beyond that stage and must consider the horrifying alternative.

If China does not take advantage of Iran during this crisis, some other country will. For decades now, much of China has attempted to move towards democracy with NPC, Rule of Law and Village Elections. But the military refuses to sway from their intentions to dominate that region and has constantly turned the tables on international policy for the last fifty years. Now I know many of us here think these words might be off the wall and might threaten the free trade agreements in the East. But I assure you that if the United States does not get in there and make itself present to keep order, during this situation, later on we will pay!"

The President Pro Tempore pounded the gavel while the Senate broke into applause for Senator Yeung. "The gentleman's time has expired." The President announced.

"I say we must vote 'yes' to send our troops into the Persian Gulf to aid our allies and to make certain that these biological and chemical weapons do not threaten the world again. I thank you, Mr. President. I yield the floor to Senator Thomas." Senator Yueng was met at the podium by one of the official reporters.

"Mr. President. I yield seven minutes of my time to Senator Mallory." Senator James said, checking her watch and her notes as she stood at the podium.

"The senator from Tennessee is recognized for seven minutes." The President replied.

"Thank you, Mr. President. Thank you Senator James." Senator Mallory said, as she placed her eyeglasses on her face.

"I wish to bring to the attention of the Senate, that under the War Powers Act of 1973, we are not the ones who are allowed to control the possibility of military intervention in Iran; if this incident escalates. The power to make that decision has been granted, by our constitution, to the President of the United States. President Marie Arcola. I think we all have to remember, Iran is a signatory of the Chemical Weapons Convention. And under the CWC they have certain rights."

Senator Blasby scolded a pair of senators yelling at each other from their seats. The President Pro Tempore smacked the gavel to the wooden pad.

"Order! Please continue, Senator Mallory."

"As I was saying. All of us present here, in today's Senate, should be concentrating on the alternatives to sending U.S. Troops into Iran. I realize there are dozens of violations involving the storing of biological and chemical weapons because of this incident. But many of my colleagues and I feel that Iran has been punished enough. After all, tens of thousands of their people have died as a result of that chemical factory explosion. Our efforts should be focused on aiding the Red Crescent and allowing their people to receive limited food, water, clothing and medical supplies. As well as monetary support until this catastrophe is passed on to United Nations Inspectors.

I feel that having the army and navy charge into a volatile situation would be a waste of millions and millions of taxpayers dollars. We all know how that would affect our Balanced Budget, especially when America is experiencing the strongest economy in it's history. We all know how costly Agent Orange and Desert Storm Syndrome was to the men and women, who participated in those operations. Going off and exploding targets in a country where more biological and chemical weapons may be stored might have the opposite effect. Causing greater loss of life and countless tragedies that we can not possibly imagine.

Do we all understand the impact a war in Iran would mean for the environment of that part of the world? Remember the oil well fires in Desert Storm? Imagine the oil wells of Iran burning and then combine that with factories filled with chemicals burning.

Already the wells and waterways of Iran are contaminated, what would happen if our air force were to accidentally hit a storage facility or warehouse containing larger amounts of biological or chemical weapons? Are we willing to take that chance? Should we take that risk? Are we the Senate, that will go down in history, as the Senate that started a Third World War?"

"The senators time has expired."

"We must vote 'no'! Do not send U.S. troops into Iran to die. At this time, it is not our responsibility. Thank you, Mr. President."

Senator James raised her hands and applauded the woman Senator from Tennessee, their colleagues also lightly gave praise from the audience.

"Mr. President. I yield the floor to Senator Howard for ten minutes." Senator Thomas called out from the podium, patting the seven foot tall, Afro-American senator on the back.

"Mr. President, I'd like to point out to the Senate the important significance of the events that have occurred between China, North Korea, and now, Iran. All of us know how the different beliefs between China and the Islamic nations affect not only the international trade, but also the security of the world. Profit for China is a major concern for their economic and social control over their people.

Billions of dollars over the last ten years has allowed China to launch and position two new global satellites. One of those satellites is in a strategic location just outside of our country, south of Cuba. Now, China has offered military support to Iran. Because they too, are supporting this ridiculous lie, that the United States sent in secret troops to blow-up a biological and chemical weapons factory. I don't think it is fair to the American people for us to stand here and argue about how many human rights violations, most of these countries have committed. More of this classified information will be revealed in the closed session in the Old Senate Chamber, immediately afterwards.

Since the death of Deung, all of us here know that China has begun closing the doors of negotiation by refusing summitry of President Johnson's Administration on many occasions. Deung's successors have attempted to follow his legacy and dream of a one country, two party system, ruled by a democratic society with the people becoming more aggressively involved with the politics of China, but has been constantly shutdown by the leaders of China's military.

Nuclear weapons are still in the hands of China. China's secret talks with North Korea, a known manufacturer of biological and chemical weapons, has to be questioned. And we all know the horrendous behavior of the North Koreans. Over the last twenty or so years, the people and children of South Korea have sent food, money and clothes to North Korea, because they cared. Because they saw the pictures of the dazed, confused starving children. The pictures of the men and women eating tree bark and roots, just to stay alive another day. All the food and money went to feed North Korea's army and not to the people. Three million men, women and children were left to starve to death. Their bodies simply tossed into huge holes and bulldozed over.

We all know that North Korea's military has become stronger since the turn of the century and that they do not respect the Chemical Weapons Convention. These are the new landlords of Iran, if we do not intervene. I don't think we can allow ourselves to be naive and passive under these conditions. After all, our friends across the aisle have stated that 'The United States is the most powerful country in the world.' That is true. And the reason we are powerful, is because we learn from our history. We think. We plan. We stand vigilant. That is why we must commit our troops now! Or later, millions of innocent people will die! Thank you, Mr. President. I yield the remainder of my time to Senator Thomas."

"Mr. President. I yield the floor to my friend and colleague from Arizona, Senator Madry for ten minutes." Senator Thomas said.

"This chair recognizes the distinguished gentlemen from Arizona." The stocky, white haired man tugged at his sleeves and solemnly stood at the podium.

"I thank the chair and Senator Thomas for allowing me this opportunity to speak. Biological and chemical weapons are a clear and present danger. A danger that threatens the security of our country and the countries of our allies around the world. These weapons have not earned the name 'Poor man's noose' for nothing. They are cheap to make, easy to conceal and can have ghastly, devastating affects.

Since 1995, fifteen hearings have been conducted in regards to weapons of mass destruction. For seven of those hearings, I stood as chairman and advisor for conditions to be made, especially in a case such as this, where an accident could occur, involving biological and chemical weapons. The concern of this Senate should be, that criminal activity does exist. And all of us that attend the closed session in the Old Senate chamber later, will see the atrocious, heinous evidence in regards to this explosion. I honestly believe all of us here, will agree that we have to be the country that steps in and put an end to this living hell that will, without a doubt, show up again in our future, if we do not agree to stop this insanity now. So far, the reports from Iran's Islamic Republic News Agency are confusing and misleading, as are other reports from China, Russia and North Korea. The most disturbing evidence, is what we have attained from intelligence reports, focusing on the offer of military aid to Iran from China.

Now, ladies and gentlemen, doesn't it seem odd, that a country in need of medical supplies and food, would be offered tanks and bomber jets instead? China has already agreed to send up to one hundred thousand troops into Iran, to secure their country, from possible invading factions."

"Objection! There has been no hard-evidence submitted to this Senate." Senator James called out.

"Objection noted, Senator James. Please allow the senator from Arizona to continue." The President Pro Tempore said. Senator Madry let out a slight chuckle and reached out to adjust the microphone.

"As many of us here can see, this incident in the Middle East has struck a very, sensitive nerve, in the minds of some of the delicate and naive thoughts of our American citizens. Theoretically speaking, we will have hell to pay, if we sit by and watch a country with nuclear power, rockets, jets, human rights violations and massive armies, simply move into Iran. Now come on! We are not little boys and girls here. We are the one's that must help out the world. The United States of America is depending on us to make this tough decision. All eyes are on us and will be on us throughout these debates. I wonder what must be going on in the minds of the women of the Senate, present here today. The torture that will be induced on women in that region of the world, if Iran is taken over by a rogue nation.

What will happen to the children? What would a large scale, military occupation of a country, foreign to Iran's culture, heritage and way of life do to the Mullahs and the Interior Ministry?

Yes. This accident that brought on this plague of death and disease, from biological and chemical weapons has weakened the people of Iran temporarily. But, only temporarily. The people of Iran are strong. They have survived against numerous catastrophic events in their history. They will learn from this accident. They will rebuild and become strong. They do not need outsiders, especially countries that offer to send large scale armies into their borders, promising peace by bringing in tanks and rockets.

Ladies and gentlemen, these actions have to be questioned at this time. All of the countries racing to aid Iran, must be held in question. Especially China, Russia and North Korea. This is why history is so important to us and our children. We study the mistakes that were made in previous wars and battles, and do not make the same mistakes again. We learn to solve problems and battles by thinking and working together. If the United States acts know, by sending troops into Iran, there will be no opportunity for any rogue nation to take advantage of this disturbing accident. But once a rogue nation gets into Iran and is dug in, we may never be able to help the Iranian people again. Unless, later on, we declare a full scale war, involving troops from France, Britain, Canada, Saudi Arabia and many other countries. Troops numbering into the hundreds of thousands.

My friend's across the aisle. We, today, have the opportunity to prevent this country and many other great nations of the world from going into a war of unthinkable magnitude. A war that may call millions of troops, from countries around the world, to fight an unnecessary conflict, only to die, in the specter of biological and chemical weapons. A war that will cripple and drag America into despair, as mothers and fathers bury our precious soldiers, over the next nine or ten years, because we did not have the courage to put a stop to this holocaust, right here and now.

I will vote 'yes' to commit our troops, because I have full confidence in the decisions of our Chiefs of Staff and that of President Arcola. I urge all of you senators to also vote 'yes', so that we may save our world from a future hell. I know from experience, the unforeseen death that awaits us if we do not act now and leave the world hanging in the balance. When this Senate sees the pictures of the victims of this explosion, I believe they will be most enlightened. The pictures of blood and babies, splattered dead in the streets. Twisted and rotting, where they fell a month ago. Their organs scattered out, rotting in the hillsides of their country. Their hands grabbing at their throats, gasping for air, frozen in time, murdered, from biological and chemical weapons. Is this what my colleagues across the aisle, want the children of America to look like? China has been making some suspicious moves, into Iran at this time. Are their actions approved of by our friends across the aisle?"

"I object, Mr. President! These comments against China are shrewd and uncalled for, and have little or nothing to do with the situation that is to be voted on." Senator James called out.

"Objection noted. Continue, Senator Madry."

"We have hard evidence! And we must PNG China! If there is a flow of weapons of mass destruction heading into the neighboring countries of Iran! We can not sit here and watch the people of Iran slaughtered!"

"The time of the gentleman has expired." The President Pro Tempore smacked the gavel to the desk.

"Mr. President. I have something to add. I request three minutes."

"The chair recognizes the gentleman from California."

"Mr. President, I must disagree with my friends across the aisle. And I most certainly disagree with Senator Thomas. It is wrong! Wrong! Wrong! This problem in Iran may or may not allow rogue terrorist factions to mobilize within Iran's borders and threaten the integrity of their nation, their way of life and their ability to function in the world! But for us, sitting here in America, to say that China is building up weapons on Iran's borders, is absurd! There is no so called 'hard evidence!' The human rights issues that are pending in Hong Kong are not part of this agenda. And therefore we must exclude these comments and conduct ourselves as professional, mature, intelligent thinking servants of our nation. We must do the right thing. I believe the people of Iran, can and will be able to overcome this unfortunate incident on their own, without the assistance or the aid of the United States. Or any other nation."

The President Pro Tempore began to hit the gavel to the pad with the light applause, in support of the Democratic senator. "Please Senator, watch your time."

"I urge all of you to vote 'no'!" The senator shouted into the microphone.

"This Senate will come to order and conduct itself in a civilized manner! Please treat this matter with grave importance! The senator from Michigan is recognized." The tall black woman stepped proud, up to the podium. She turned and gave a shrewd stare out at the Senate, pushing up her thick, black rimmed glasses, tugging to straightened out her dark blue blazer.

"Thank you, Mr. President. It is very disturbing for me, to look across the aisle at my colleagues and imagine what must be going on in their minds. Going to war is a very serious issue. Going to war kills soldiers, destroys cities and poisons the land around the war, for the ones that live; to suffer and die. Going to war kills mothers and fathers who serve the United States of America. And when those soldiers die, their children become orphans. Their wives become widows. Their mothers and fathers become pallbearers. If we send in troops. Dropping their smart bombs. Exploding Tomahawk missiles. Unstabilizing the country of Iran.

We will commit America into a grave situation that all of us present in this room, must take responsibility for. Let's just use our imaginations for a moment. What if one of those smart bombs, is not so smart. What if that smart bomb hits another factory, storing biological and chemical weapons? What do we do then? How do we deal with an explosion, a hundred or a thousand times worst than this small, incident that occurred near Esfahan, nearly a month ago?

Then we will be to blame for the deaths of the people of Iran. Yes. And the whole, wide world would see that we are the guilty ones. That we are the barbarians who have unleashed our weapons of mass destruction. Against the people of Iran. This is why we study history and need to remember, forever, the atomic bombs dropped on Nagasaki and Hiroshima! We need to remember because we are the one's who began destroying the world, with our hasty use of military force. Look. I have pictures from Nagasaki and Hiroshima." Senator James said, opening up a large book of photographs, raising it in the air for the Senators to see.

"A professor friend of mine from the University of Michigan found this magnificently, terrifying book at the Hatcher Graduate Library on her campus. She cried for days and is still shaken by the thought of these events of mass destruction. You see, her grandparents were killed during the holocaust. So you see, it is indeed disturbing that the members of the Senate majority, revel in the idea of building up weapons in the Persian Gulf to flex their military muscle to help businesses use up weapons that they have in stock, so that they may swindle more taxpayer dollars to manufacturer newer, cleaner weapons . . ."

"Objection! Objection, Mr. President! Can the senator from Michigan, please stick to the issue to be voted on!" Senator Hollis cried out.

"Order! Objection noted. This Senate will respect the lady from Michigan's time. Please continue Senator James. You have one minute." The President Pro Tempore acknowledged Senator James, with a tilt of his hand, as he presided over the Senate.

"As I was saying. We must vote 'no'. We must not commit our troops. We should allow the Middle East nations to address the complexity of this incident at their own pace and have any further matters be directed to the attention of NATO and the World Court; if there is any international concerns. I don't believe China, Afghanistan, Pakistan or any other country is planning to attack Iran. We can not be the one's to rush in every time the world has some small, incident such as this. Our role should not be as dictator. Our role should be a humanitarian one. To help Iran, in their time of need. Thank you." Senator James said, picking up her papers, to the subtle applause of the other Democrats. A tall, skinny, stick-of-a-man laughed and shuffled his index cards, shaking his head as he positioned himself at the podium, in his light gray suit and bright green tie. He adjusted his thin brown hair and smiled.

"I'm sorry, but I have to laugh at the ridiculous fallacies being presented by some of the senators, in this Senate this afternoon, attempting to downplay a dangerous, catastrophic event that has taken so many thousands of lives. We all must understand. This was only a small amount of biological and chemical weapons involved in this accident. This is hardly the tip of the iceberg, ladies and gentlemen. If this little bit of chemical weaponry can wipe out thousands and thousands of people, imagine what the remaining chemical and biological weapons in that country can do? I must admit, I wasn't very good at arithmetic when I was a young boy, but I really think we all have to do a little bit of math here.

This incident, that killed so many, was maybe only one half-of-a-percent of the total amount of biological and chemical weapons being manufactured and stored in Iran and other countries. This is our chance. This is our opportunity to stop this madness. I'm certain, that with the deaths of dozens of women and children in Kuwait and Saudi Arabia, our allies would agree. It is time for this insanity to stop. We can't go on living like this; with our heads stuck in the sand. Living in fear, living in denial, waiting for the next explosion. Just waiting for that next major disaster to take all of our lives. Living in fear from terrorist, should not become a new way of life to Americans. What are the parents of this country telling their children right now about what happened to President George Johnson and President Arcola's daughter and son? All these families trying to keep from breaking down, having to hold their children and saying to them 'oh, don't worry, honey. Everything is going to be fine. That can't happen here. No one is going to hurt us.' These mothers and fathers must lie to protect their sons and daughters, feeling the fear and insecurity in their own hearts. Wondering if maybe, they will be next.

Now let's take out our pens and notebooks and take down

some notes. President Johnson was killed near the Capitol of our country. Years ago, the New York City Trade Center was bombed. Flight 697 two years ago near France blown out of the sky. One hundred and eleven people killed, by a terrorist stinger missile. Over the last year, three U.S. installations in Saudi Arabia were hit by a new cruise missile developed by the Iranians. Another Marine base destroyed this past March, outside of Seoul. One hundred and nineteen American soldiers killed by terrorist bombs."

"One minute, please senator." The President announced.

"We must show our protest to these biological and chemical weapons and show our support to our allies. We must send our troops into the Persian Gulf to ward off any possible act of aggression toward our friends in the Arab nations. And we must do it now. I thank you all. And thank you, Mr. President."

Applause echoed throughout the Senate in praise of Senator Hollis.

"My goodness." Senator Randolph began in a musical Southern accent, looking at his watch, to check the time, as he stepped up to the podium with Senator James.

"I yield myself three minutes." Senator Randolph said.

"The chair recognizes the gentleman from Oklahoma."

"Thank you, Mr. President. Ladies and gentlemen of the Senate, I think we need to understand how strong our country has become, within our family structure.

I have seen some 'independent polls' from many grocery-store-tabloid headlines. All belching out, about how the assassination of President Johnson has destroyed the spirit of this country forever. These are sensationalized articles, only designed to sell newspaper trash. I have spoken to President Arcola, and reminded her personally, how, historically, these incidents can cause the American people to react to a crisis, instead of act. There is no need to send a lynch-mob to Iran, to seek revenge for the explosion at Dulles Airport. Of course, all of our nerves are on edge. We're all ready to jump out of our skins; at the end of our ropes.

But let's keep our composure and not be so judgmental. Let's not be quick to blame for these mishaps. Need I remind all of you, how quick America was to seeking out Iranian or Libyan terrorist in our communities, for the disaster at the Alfred P. Murrah Federal Building. I should know. I was there back, in nineteen ninety-five. My aunt was killed in that building. That's why I became an attorney, and eventually, a senator for my home state.

Many wrong things await us, if we decide to rush our soldiers into a dangerously, unstable part of the world, such as Iran. This is very obvious, from the reports and photographs obsessing this nations televisions and newspapers for the last month. Our economy has recently become stable and we are on the verge of making history by eliminating our national deficit. Another World War may cost us hundreds of billions of dollars."

"One minute, senator."

"After the war with Japan, there were many issues concerning trade with the East. After the war with Germany there were many issues of trade. The concern of trade and political campaign fund donations from foreign sources has been an ongoing issue for many, many years. Our trade with the East and other great nations is proof that there is no concern at this time, with China becoming the leader of a Third World War confrontation. Please. All of you here must vote with wisdom and not from panic.

Voting 'yes' will be very unwise and will make the United States look foolish in the eyes of the world. So please vote 'no'. Do not send our sons and daughters into a strange land to die in a war that never should have been. Thank you, Mr. President. And I yield the floor."

The Senate quietly applauded the comments of Senator Randolph. The big, pudgy-round Santa Claus man frowned with doubt, scratching his beard and taking a deep breath, as he walked away from the podium, to the applause and cheers of his fellow Democrats. The President Pro Tempore began smacking the gavel to quiet the noise.

"Order! This chamber will come to order! Ladies and gentlemen! Please. We have been working on this issue for days now and must soon come to a vote! Please respect each other's time by not wasting time on these outbursts!"

Reporters' cameras flashed and the Sergeant at Arms shook his finger saying 'no, don't do that'. Senator Thomas switched and crossed his other leg, desperately checking the time on his gold Rolex.

"Mr. President." Senator Yeung began speaking at the podium. "The senator from Montana is recognized."

"Mr. President. Just to explain to colleagues what is going to happen next. We are going to conclude debate and then meet in the Old Senate Chamber, for approximately three hours, and thereafter resume debate, if there is time this evening, or begin again tomorrow and at any of those times, resume debate including the motions to strike.

I have a unanimous consent request that has been cleared with both sides. I ask through unanimous consent that one hour of the three hours devoted to the closed session, which will be a three hour session in the Old Senate Chamber, not be counted against the ten hour debate time agreed upon in the consent agreement."

"Without objection, so ordered." The President Pro Tempore said.

"I ask unanimous consent, that after this evening's debate here in and after the closed session in the Old Senate Chamber, that there may be a conclusion with a two-thirds majority vote, and at that time this Senate may continue debate and voting into the morning hours, if their is no objection. That anytime during the closed session and these open debates, an agreement for the Declaration of War and the remaining seven conditions, may be ratified. That if a tie of votes is continuous, the Senate may stand in adjournment, but not fully recess and must stand in honor of Article 29. But, for the information of all senators. If there is a tie of votes, debates will continue at ten a.m. tomorrow morning and that at anytime, since information is continuing to be revealed to this Senate, debate and voting may be called to an emergency order of votes, if the crisis in Iran escalates and becomes an obvious threat to neighboring countries in the Middle East and to the interest of the United States."

"Without objection, so ordered."

"I ask unanimous consent, that a call to meet in closed session, may again be necessary in the Old Senate Chamber, due to the delicate nature of the sensitive, classified, intelligence information being revealed to this Senate. Without objection, a vote may occur at anytime, as each of the eight conditions are voted on."

"Without objection, so ordered."

"I urge all senators to arrive promptly, as debates will begin immediately at ten a.m. and continue through the day and into the evening, with these very important debates. Thank you, Mr. President. I now yield back the remainder of my time."

"So ordered." The President replied.

Senator James waved another senator up to the podium as she requested time for the Democratic senator to speak. Senator Thomas flopped down into the brown leather seat and fidgeted around, huffing and staring at his watch.

"Jesus Christ. This crap is gonna go on into tomorrow. Hey, Charlie. I need you to be around this Saturday and Sunday to help with the press releases. Can you do it?"

"Ah. yes, sir. I just have to get some gifts for my parents for Christmas." Charlie replied, opening his black leather date book, scribbling down a reminder.

"Well, shoot. Come in to work on Saturday. You can take a break and head up to Georgetown Park. Just mention my name at any of the shops, you'll get a good discount. So, Shawn. How does this vote look?" Senator Thomas asked, sitting up in his seat, watching three more senators entering the room.

"It's gonna be a tight vote, senator. All but four senators are here to vote on this Declaration of War issue. I think every senator here is going to have to speak." Shawn said, wrinkling his forehead, raising his eyebrows to the senator.

Lauren shifted her legs and slightly pulled up her skirt, making certain Trevor focused on her white silk stockings, as she played with the snap from her white garter belt. The senator tilted his head, trying to get a closer look. Lauren lowered her skirt, brushed the pleats out and let out a 'tsk'. "Sorry, Trevor. You had your chance."

Senator Trevor Thomas nodded his head in agreement to his campaign manager's comment, crossed his arms, and eased back in his seat, to study his opponents. He noticed one of the republican senators walking down the aisle, trying to make sense of a pile of notes, looking back to his secretary; shrugging his shoulders.

"What is this?' The senator said.

Senator Thomas stood up quickly and scooted toward the main aisle. He felt Senator Harding's leg, brush against the back of his thigh, as he hurried to meet Senator Bush. Another senator rambled on about the affect the occupation of U.S. troops would have on the United Nations. Senator Thomas adjusted his suit coat with a quick tug and strolled down to the podium. His hands and body language were masterful. He tilted his head and licked his lips, placing his palms flat to the wood of the podium, knowing and absorbing the attention of every being in the room, his arms relaxed yet firm, as he imagined himself at the free throw line. The words flowed unrestricted; commanding, gruff and reassuring, his dark eyes, glancing from senator to senator, as he spoke.

"Who yields the time?" The chair asked.

"I yield time to myself. No matter how much time it might take." Senator Trevor Thomas said and eyed his audience, taking mental inventory of the senators strolling into the Senate Chamber from the hallway, giving their 'thumbs up' and nodding 'yes', as they took their seats. Trevor counted eight new senators that indicated that they were ready to approve.

"Let me first read a quote from the Chemical Weapons Treaty debate from April of 1997 in regards to foreign policy and what the concerns were at that time. One of those concerns was 'what is the amount of chemical weapons that could be considered a threatening factor?'

Now, let me quote one of the generals from the Chiefs of Staff. The general stated 'One ton of chemical weapons, is militarily significant, and we cannot effectively guarantee we can uncover, one ton. That a militarily significant quantity of chemical weapons is situationally dependent, but that thousands'. Let me repeat and emphasize that point. 'Thousands of tons of chemical agents, would be required to significantly impact a large scale military engagement. While, a mere ton of nerve agent could be used as a mechanism of terrorism.' The general went on to say, 'in certain, limited circumstances. Even, one ton, of chemical agent may have a military impact. For example. If chemical weapons are used as a weapon of terror, against an unprotected population, in a regional conflict.' End of quote.

Let me go back over the simple math from this very important quote, from a general from Poland, whose family grew up in the midst of World War One and World War Two. What the general has implied, is, any country storing in excess of one ton of chemical weapon agents, is a likely indication, that country may be planning to use those chemicals for non-peaceful actions. And any country that exceeds the 'one ton' limit, may be, in fact, considering the use of those chemicals for offensive, military purposes. Now I realize many of my colleagues across the aisle have strong social and political concerns in regard to this matter. Especially with the looming rumor that the United States would be placed into a long, Third World War, causing several years of death and mass destruction. I assure this Senate, I personally have been in the dirtiest foxholes and trenches of many a battle, and know the minutes that turn into hours, and the days that turn into weeks. The bad food, mixed with water from a mud puddle or a passing rainstorm. The cries of women and children from bombed villages, running up to me, begging me to help them. The sight of blood flowing from bodies into the sewers. The smell of the innocent, lying dead and rotting only a few feet away, outside of the front doors of their own homes. As we all well know, the International Chemical Weapons Convention has given all those countries, that were in agreement, the power to bring criminal charges against foreign countries, as well as enforce additional sanctions against any of those countries that sold, transported, provided, stored or manufactured biological or chemical weapons. That is why it is urgent for all senators to be present in the Old Senate Chamber to discuss this matter further, as well as going over the additional conditions that concern this declaration.

This meeting is not about who, in this Senate, is right or wrong! This meeting is about the United States starting a war or preventing a war! And we and our allies have the knowledge that those chemicals, mentioned in the CWC, were present in that factory, during the time of that explosion. We are committed and we must be responsible, to finding out the truth. Just as the bombs in Hiroshima and Nagasaki showed the world the horror of the use of weapons of mass destruction, this incident in Iran is about to replenish a new nightmare, showing the world what weapons of mass destruction, mainly biological and chemical weapons, will and can do. Over five hundred thousand people have died since this accident near Esfahan. Many more will die from disease and lack of food or water. The United States is not trying to occupy Iran and take over their country. We want our SEAL team back, and we want them back alive and unharmed. We want this incident to go away, without any major confrontation. We have hard evidence now. The explosion at the factory near Esfahan was an accident. Important classified information will be disclosed to all of the senators who meet later in the Old Senate Chamber. We can forgive the earlier reports out of Iran, and excuse the ridiculous rumor that the United States was plotting to overthrow Iran.

Now, we know the U.S. was not responsible. We can forgive the leaders of Iran for something they may have overlooked. An incident that, even we in the United States, would be very concerned with, and might be quick to accuse, to find an answer in the confusion. The leaders and people of Iran are honorable. And they will apologize to you and I, because we did nothing wrong. But. If we do not go to intervene now, we will go to war later. Quite possibly against a stronger, more deadly enemy, who will not be concerned with the consequences of their actions. An enemy with no honorable leaders.

China is making some questionable moves without allowing the United Nations the chance to make a collective decision. China has given us no other choice. They have violated countless treaties and remain an adversary and a threat. Are we ready to have biological and chemical weapons, fall into the hands of international gangster factions? Are we ready to gamble the economic stability of America, by allowing biological and chemical weapons of mass destruction to fall into the hands of terrorist, like the one's that killed President Johnson?

Are we ready to accept terrorism into our lives, as if it were just a natural, normal everyday event? We can't just change the channel on the remote control or put 'parental guidance warnings' on the events that affect this country. History has warned us that an incident like this was inevitable. We know where Iran is, and we know where the biological and chemical weapons are. But if Iran loses! Those weapons might end up closer to home! Maybe Canada! Maybe Mexico! Maybe Long Beach, California!"

"Objection!" A woman senator from California stood up yelling, and is booed and hushed by the Senate.

"The Senate will be in order!" The President called out, to the tapping of his gavel.

"The gentleman from Indiana, please continue." The President Pro Tempore called out.

"Thank you, Mr. President. Ladies and gentlemen. China has already offered to aid Iran by supplying them with jets, tanks and armies. China has extorted hundreds of billions of dollars ever since they took over Hong Kong. Now they want to do the same thing to Taiwan. If you compare twentieth century Hong Kong to what she's become now, Hong Kong is a ghost town. Most of the people from Hong Kong have exiled to Canada. I have to laugh at what the Prime Minister of Canada said back in 1997 when China took over Hong Kong. He said 'China will make Hong Kong work more effectively.' Work more effectively? Hong Kong was making a hundred and sixty billion dollars a year, back in the nineteen nineties. Hong Kong was doing fine on their own. And what did China do with all those billions of dollars? They bought battleships. They bought submarines and cruise missiles. They bought tanks and jets. And now they want to move into Iran.

We must vote now on this stand-off in Iran. At this time I say we have a vote, for the first condition, before all of us recess to the Old Senate Chamber. And compare those votes after all of us have had a chance to review classified information. Then, we will see how overwhelmingly real and terrifying this situation is! We must commit our troops now! Ladies and gentlemen, vote to save this world from another war!"

Cheers and applause echoed throughout the Senate Chamber while senators and pages gave Senator Thomas a standing ovation.

"The first condition is for the United States to send five thousand troops to aid our allies in the Persian Gulf! I will vote 'yes'!"

The President smacked the gavel down three times and called out. "The Senate will be in order! The Senate will be in order!"

The President continued smacking the gavel, to the mayhem of the Senate Chamber.

"Mr. President! Mr. President! I request the issue that we are to vote on, be repeated so my friends across the aisle are clear on this matter."

"Objection!" Senator James yelled out.

"Mr. President, this is a very important issue. It is necessary for the issue to be totally understood." Senator Thomas countered in reponse.

The President Pro Tempore turned to the Secretary of the Senate and the Parliamentarian and smiled, as he was handed the list of minutes.

"The vote this afternoon, which has now become this evening, is whether or not U.S. Troops should be commited to the Persian Gulf in case Kuwait and Saudi Arabia need assistance." The President smacked the gavel to the booing and applause.

"The issue is put forth to the Senate. I feel that we are ready, now to take a vote." Senator Thomas said glaring across at his opponent standing at the opposite podium.

"I object on the grounds that a quorum is not present. Any vote in this Senate without the classified information from the Old Senate Chamber meeting would not apply!" Senator James yelled.

"Several of the senators and I believe we are ready to vote on the issue. Each minute we waste, will mean more and more soldiers may be killed later! We are ready to vote on the first five conditions of this issue, on the Declaration of War, with the remaining three conditions to be discussed in the Old Senate Chamber!"

Senator Thomas smiled at the sight of his fellow Republicans, lining up behind him in support. Democratic senators stood and objected.

"I object! A quorum is not present!" Senator Mallory protested.

"Yes. It is obvious that a quorum is not present . Let the senator's concern be noted for the record." The President said, still standing, smacking the gavel to quiet the Senate.

"All those in favor say 'aye'." The senators yelled out "Aye!!"

"All those opposed say 'no.' Some of the senators yelled out "No!!"

"At this time the President ProTempore and the Senate request a vote by electronic device. This will be a ten minute vote. All in favor will vote 'Aye'. All those opposed will vote 'no'." Most of the senators shuffled through the rows of brown leather seats, grabbing at their fellow senators, to encourage their votes. The clock showed nine minutes.

"Here we go, Art. The Republican tag-team." Trevor said and turned to the microphone, holding his hands out to quiet the Senate.

"We feel the people and persons responsible for this outlandish display of lies against my country and our country, should, if they are men and women of honor, apologize, unconditionally to all of us, the people of this country, because we did nothing wrong!" Senator Thomas filled his lungs with a deep sigh, to the applause from the Senate. Some of his associates gave a small standing ovation.

"The Senate will be in order!" The chairman called out, smacking the gavel down.

"Please respect the gentleman from Indiana. Any members talking amongst themselves, will please remove themselves from the Chamber. Continue Senator Thomas."

"I request a vote of support on the previous question." Senator Thomas said. The Speaker of the House stepped up to the podium meeting with the Majority Leader and the Minority Leader; a small group of senators huddled around and watched as the votes were being electronically counted.

"Mr. President! Please. Mr. President, I move the previous question." Senator Parker said as she leaned to speak into the microphone.

"The previous question. Without objection the previous question is ordered. The question to be voted on is whether or not United States Armed Forces should be sent into the Persian Gulf to aid United States allied forces in that region. All those in favor will vote 'aye' or 'no'." The Senate calls out 'Aye!'

"Thank you, Mr. President." Senator Parker said as she turned and trembled as she felt the arms of her friend, the Minority Leader, Senator James hold her as the Senate chamber roared in response.

"All those opposed record 'no'."

Senator Thomas and a large number of senators watched as the votes were final. The President Pro Tempore responded. "The 'ayes' have it."

Cheers and screams rang through the applause, while Senator Thomas and Sentaor Graebul exchanged handshakes and pats on the back. The room seemed lighter than before. Dreamlike and cold to Senator James as she quietly fumbled with her note cards, in the mayhem of the Senate Chamber.

"Mr. President! Mr. President! I object." Senator Parker shouted out.

"Yes. Senator." The President responded.

"I object to the vote on the grounds that a quorum is not present! Please make and order, that a quorum is not present!" Senator Parker called out.

"Yes. Noted. It's obvious a quorum is not present."

The Journal Clerk set a piece of paper on the desk.

"The resolution is agreed to! A motion to reconsider, is laid upon the table!" The noise increased, filling the Senate Chamber with cheers and applause for the vote to send American soldiers into the Persian Gulf.

"This Senate will be in order! This Senate will be in order!" The President called out, to the pounding of his gavel. Senator Graebul stepped up to the microphone.

"We should all adjourn to the Old Senate Chamber to look at the additional conditions to be voted on! We must commit our troops now! We must stop this madness, now! We must vote now to support our allies, if they need to enter Iran.

Because I swear, if we do not take action right this instant! America will become a landscape of millions and millions of bodies, of dead men, women and children, from the biological and chemical weapons that we allowed some rogue terrorist faction to have!"

Cheers and applause echoed throughout the Chamber, while senators and pages stood to the words of Senator Arthur Graebul. The President smacked the gavel down three times and called out.

"Order! This Senate will conduct itself in a professional manner, biding by the rules and fairness to all senators present!" The President continued smacking the gavel.

"All members will record their votes by electronic device on the second condition, which is to agree whether or not to occupy United States troops in Iran. All in favor record 'Aye.' All those opposing record 'No.'

To the rising roar of applause and cheers, the senator raised his hands, as the camera crews for CNN and NBC zoomed in to his antics, as they began to televise the Senate's decision. Senator Brenda James silently stood, holding her folder and swayed, feeling light-headed with the echoes of the senators, applauding, shouting and cheering. The electronic votes were coming in and being counted.

The Speaker called out over the uproar, held up the printed tally and waved it up in the air. "The vote is in! The 'Nays' are forty-two! The 'Yeas' are forty-five! On the first and second conditions, the 'Yeas' have it!" Senator James hung her head and cried. "Oh my God. We're going to war."

PART TWO

TWENTY-SIX

PRESIDENT ARCOLA PAUSED watching an old woman dressed in a tattered biege dress and a round sun hat with pink ribbons, place a bouquet of wild flowers on the grave. The tiny American flags slowly swayed in the December breeze, quietly flapping across the rolling rye and Kentucky bluegrass, in rows by the hundreds, up the hillside; mixed in the silence of the headstones. President Arcola knelt down to place the small wooden pole for the America flag into the soil. She took her brown leather gloves off and gently ran her fingers over the headstone that read: Francis Andrew Arcola. Beloved for all eternity.

She turned and looked at the other flags, brightly flowing in the fading evening sky, the flags she placed on the grave of her husband David and her daughter Shelley. A secret service agent whispered into his headset and waved for three officers to question two women, who had stepped out of a dark blue Cadillac. An FBI sharp shooter stood near a tree, two yards away; his Remington loaded and aimed. President Arcola stumbled into the arms of one of the woman; her chest heaving from each breath she cried out. "Momma. Oh, momma. Frankie would have been six years old today."

The tall, gray haired woman wrapped her arms around her daughter and slowly began to rock her from side to side, caressing her, soft blonde hair. "I'm here now, Marie. It'll be okay. Everything will be okay."

"It should have been me, momma. Why did I have to live? Why did they have to die? Why, momma? I shouldn't have let them go."

Marie's mother stood quietly holding her daughter in her arms and glanced over at the widowed First Lady, Catherine Johnson, placing the dozen white roses on her husband's grave.

A female secret service agent stepped up to Benny and whispered something into his ear. She pointed at her watch and toward the sky. The press secretary shook his head in agreement and walked quickly toward the women.

"Hello, mom." Benny said, planting a friendly kiss on the cheek of the Presidents mother, wrapping his arms around her and President Arcola.

"Benny. It's so nice to see you. You look skinny. You're not eating right. I will be in Washington over the holidays. I will feed you." The woman patted the blushing advisor's face. "Agent Pryce said it's getting too dark for the security officers. Besides, we have another meeting in an hour." Benny said, handing a hankerchief to the President and another hankercief to her mother.

"Thank you, Benny. You're a dear."

"You're welcome Mrs. Haris." Benny said as he blushed.

"Oh stop. I've known you for twenty years. And now you start treating me like royalty? All those times you would visit with Marie when you two were in law school and you would stop over for dinner on the weekends and take all my daughters out golfing. You have been very good to my family."

"Is she going to be alright?" Benny asked.

"Yes, Benny. But it will take some time. I remember when her father died. Out of all three of my daughters, Marie took it the hardest. In fact, she was more broken hearted than I was."

Benny paused, looking at Marie standing over the graves of her children and husband, her head hung down, as she softly wept, quietly mumbling a prayer. Benny and Mrs. Haris stepped up to her, made the sign of the cross and bowed their heads. "Happy birthday, Frankie." President Arcola whispered.

President Arcola hunched forward in the big leather chair, reading the eight conditions involving the occupation of U.S. troops in Iran. Benny stuck his fork into the near empty bowl of salad, saving the last piece of grilled chicken, rubbing it around with a piece of zucchini and leaf lettuce in the last drops of Romano dressing.

"Oh, lord. Your mother's going to make me fat again." Benny said with a sigh, holding his stomach. President Arcola gave a small, quick smile.

"You know how she loves to cook spaghetti for you. Every weekend you stayed with us when we were in law school, my sisters and I knew we'd be eating spaghetti." Benny read through the faxes that were sent from the Pentagon.

"How bad are land mines?" Benny asked.

President Arcola leaned back in her chair and stretched her arms up over her head, trying to crack her neck. "The Pentagon and the Red Cross have worked together since 1995 on the land mine crisis. About thirty-two thousand people have been killed by them and another forty-five thousand have had their limbs blown off. Most of the victims are civilians. Farmers plowing their fields or curious children. They only cost about three dollars to make and many times after a battle or a skirmish, soldiers leave them for the sake of revenge. Sometimes the soldiers that lay them are killed or don't remember where they were laid out. When I was in the army, one of the pilots in my squadron landed his chopper on a land mine in Kuwait during Desert Storm and lost some of his toes. A lot of countries wont stop using them."

"How many anti-personnel land mines do you think were set outside of that factory near Esfahan?" Benny asked. President Arcola stirred the ice cube around in her orange juice and took a drink to wash down her dinner.

"The photo analyst from the Pentagon estimated close to three hundred. Most of them alongside the main roads and the hillsides. Soon, they'll have the factory contained. The only way in or out, will be from the rooftop. I remember when Princess Diana died. She was working so hard to convince countries around the world to stop using land mines. I always admired her. I was heartbroken when I knew I would never get the chance to meet her."

President Arcola tilted her reading glasses down her nose to get a look at the grandfather clock.

"Damn. Still no response from the Chinese Crown counsel." President Arcola said with a huff. Benny studied another fax from the Pentagon.

"The Chiefs of Staff are still not getting a straight answer from the Chinese Foriegn Minister. The only response the Pentagon has heard, is their disapproval of the United States decision to stop all visas for college students to be allowed into our country."

"Well. The Chinese Military was warned not to start occupying troops in Taiwan. Their students have no right starting anti-American demonstrations on the campuses of our universities." Benny continued to read the faxes. "Fourteen members of Chinese gangs have been arrested for murdering a group of American college students in the riots in San Francisco. All of those gang members were in the United States illegally. And another incident last night in Ann Arbor. A Chinese exchange student was beat to death during a bar fight. The idea of detainment camps in New York, New Jersey and Los Angeles has become a topic. If this keeps up with China, will you give that order?" Benny questioned as he poured himself a cup of coffee.

"The anti-Chinese sentiments have increased ever since the Chinese Military began confiscating money from the Hong Kong banks to increase their stockpile of nuclear weapons. The governors and mayors have already linked hundreds of hate crimes against East Asian and Oriental families during the riots.

Secretary Rawlings is checking into every incident through the police reports from each state. But can you imagine what will happen if China is planning to move it's military into Iran? China would be unstoppable." The President said.

"Wouldn't the Iranian people fight back?"

"Oh, yes. Definately. But China would overpower them easily within a few years. The world has seen how China lied about Hong Kong. The people of Iran will not be so submissive. Can you imagine the promises the Chinese military might be making to Iran? Can you imagine Iran, finally siding with China to begin controlling the East? Iran has played up this chemical weapons accident in their favor. Even Amnesty International is willing to

temporarily overlook Iran's past history of human rights violations. And besides, the so-called invasion of America's cultural
and diabolical intentions doesn't give us a chance to get to the
real people of Iran. I remember when the year 2000 rolled over,
I thought the world was going to be sucked in by this gigantic,
holistic explosion, kinda like what Nostradamus predicted. Instead, it's the daily game of matching wits. Instead of all the
countries of the world pulling together, all the countries are growing more powerful and pulling the world apart." President Arcola
said, pouring herself a cup of hot green tea.

"Some of our greatest scholars from the Hudson Institute said
this would happen. Even though his advocacy for the devil is
questionable, let me read you a passage from one of Professor
Berger's books. '. . . It is inevitable, that the new children of China
and their children would be slowly weaned into the military ide-
ology of Communist China. They will need purpose, in their dawn
of confusion. They will feel the apprehension of the world's reli-
gions and will be breed that it is their design to serve their country, without questions. Their tiny minds will not be trained in
democracy, but will be grasped by the reigns of the Dynasty. They
will never know differently. They will never question their function as they are ordered by the Chinese Military Machine. They
will gladly serve and die for the Dynasty and the beliefs of the
Dynasty Machine. The need to be part of that machine. All those
billions and billions of dollars that were borrowed from the World
Bank at the turn of the century will be used to fortify the oppression and desire to blame and target a particular culture and society of people, and that target will be the United States of America.
If some event in their life, that can not be explained; like in the
ways of Christian, Islamic, Jewish or any other religion, the strength
of their soul and spirit can produce acceptance of events, as dic-
tated by the Dynasty.

The billions of dollars is still a concern by the Chiefs of Staff
and Congress and is still a mystery but all agree, that the money
was spent on weapons. Scholars also agreed that millions of dollars were spent on the Dynasty's plan to revolutionize their new
society and prepare them for a new dimension of thought. All
cultures of this world need to have a threat to their existence, in

order to give them something to blame for their failures, and to give them purpose in life. Even if that purpose is racism, revenge or hatred.'"

A chill ran up Benny's spine, causing him to shiver. "Jesus Christ. Proffesor Berger wrote those thoughts in his latest book on the relationship between the Combat 8, the IRA and the Sinn Fein."

"Yes. He does have that wonderful, skies-of-blue outlook at life. It's enough to give you nightmares and make you pull all your hair out."

"So. Will we ever be able to put this all together?"

President Arcola thought about Benny's question and took a sip of her tea. "I don't know. But I do know we have to keep thinking forward and keep trying to put it all together. Because there is always someone willing to take it apart. At least, that's what I've learned from the death of David. And Shelley and Francis. All of them were always running around and laughing. Always touching each other and hugging. I miss all those times that the kids would talk their father into playing basketball late at night, or watching those zany Three Stooges reruns."

Marie hung her head and rubbed her hands around the warm cup of tea. "But David was always a good father and husband. Always there. Always overjoyed with life and what he and I had accomplished."

Her tired eyes were closed, briefly, as she changed her thoughts and feelings. She took the last drink of tea, letting the green leaves settle to the bottom of her cup. Her neck cracked as she stood and stretched. "Oh, great. Now my bones are making cracking noises. Benny. Do you have the updated reports from the Pentagon from the second SEAL team?"

"No, I don't. The Pentagon wanted to decipher more of the information from the factory. A lot of the names and destinations from the inventories weren't clear."

President Arcola stood at the window, staring at the peaceful gentle rain, as it fell onto the East lawn, causing the remaining leaves of one of the trees, to fall to the ground. She fussed with the drapes, looking out, hoping to see the Christmas lights across the street. Hoping to see her Francis and Shelley laughing and playing in the family room down the hall. There was a rumble of thunder but no lightning.

She closed her eyes and meditated, relaxing into her thoughts; giving her mind and spirit time to rest. "It's times like this, I wish and pray more than ever, that heaven does exist. The times that I know I am helpless and cannot keep death from showing up. Do you ever feel that way Benny?" President Arcola asked while the raindrops rolled down the outside of the window.

"Of course. But we keep fumbling on. Trying to make it through this world. I remember when my father died of cancer. He was seventy-seven. After that I stopped barbqueing my dinners and started eating oatmeal everyday for breakfast. You remember back in law school. All I ate was cold pizza and anything you could mix with hamburger. I haven't had a hamburger in years. Death makes us think differently about life."

There was a flash of lightning, it caused Marie's eyes to blink. And for her to wonder. "So am I doing all of this out of revenge?" President Arcola pondered.

"No. Definitely not. I've seen you in the worst situations when you were in Congress, fighting to have the Senate urge the National Cancer Institute to aid with cancer examinations for women. And the way you helped to pass the Medical Leave Act for women and single parents. You've always been a diamond in the rough. But remember, you have to keep reminding yourself how strong a diamond is."

She held her arms around her belly and turned to smile at her friend. "Thanks Benny. I just don't know about sending our troops into the Persian Gulf. It's difficult to think of death right now. When I was in the service, I remember being ordered into so many shitty battles I thought were risky and insane. I always thought it was just to scare me or piss me off, just because I was a woman."

"Maybe, to piss you off to make you stronger, so you were fighting mad and wanted to survive to prove yourself. I bet in all those cases, you had a strong, competent leader guiding you. From all the war stories you've told me. From Fort Lee to Desert Storm, and all those letters of recommendation; you have always been a leader who could confront any challenge. That's what you are now. That's why you are here, standing in the Oval Office, as the President of the United States of America, giving me all sorts of orders, while your mother tries to make me explode from eating so much spaghetti, that my clothes don't fit."

President Arcola smiled as she watched Benny stick his stomach out from underneath his suit, pulling the sides of his coat, making it look as if his suit couldn't be buttoned. Her smile quickly faded when she opened a file on her desk. The top sheet of paper showed the possible cost of U.S. jets, helicopters, tanks and armament for an operation to encounter Iran and China. She turned to the next page showing the possible, probable and likely amount of American soldiers that would become casualties, if the U.S. Air Force and Chiefs of Staff waited for a possible ground war.

"Is the possible death of twenty thousand soldiers worth this confrontation?" She asked.

"I know it may sound cold and arrogant. But if we do not show our commitment to preserve democracy, we will suffer more than just the loss of soldiers."

"Twenty thousand soldiers, Benny. How did the Chiefs of Staff come up with twenty thousand soldiers dying? Do they think the factory is a lure? Do they think that it might be a trap?"

"That possibility always existed. Even you told me, this whole thing looks too easy and too planned out. But it might really have been an accident. And it could have been an easy excuse for China and Iran to make a partnership."

The grandfather clock chimed once and drew the attention of the President and her press secretary. President Arcola sat up in her chair and looked at a list of addresses the FBI was investigating in regards to the Dulles Airport bombing.

"So. Do I get used to fatwa's and terrorist threats?" She said sarcastically.

"Yes. You were even threatened before, when you were Vice-President." Benny replied as he checked his Casio watch against the time on the Oval Office clock.

"But why are the children always killed?"

"I don't think there is an answer for that. I think that is a question which will go on and on as long as there is a need for a democratic society in a very violent world."

"Benny. You're starting to sound more and more like a candidate. Are you planning to run for office?"

Benny gave her a blank stare and crossed his eyes, shaking his head. "I was glad just to sell my law practice, so I could have more free time to golf. I really don't want to go back to those twenty hour days."

"Oh. So you prefer working with me twenty-four hours a day instead." The President said with a smile. Another fax rolled off of the Oval Office machine. Benny stretched over and snatched up the rolled piece of paper.

President Arcola stopped her pacing and waited for Benny's reaction to the messege. "It's from the Chiefs of Staff. There are reports coming in from Taiwan that China has postioned an armada of warships off the coast of Tainan and Kaohsiung. The Chiefs of Staff also say Taiwan is requesting a response from the United States. Why would China start behaving like this?"

President Arcola reached out as Benny handed her the fax sheet.

"I don't know? Something just doesn't feel right."

There was a knock at the Oval Office door, startling President Arcola and Benny from their thoughts. Jeri slowly opened the door and peeked her head in. "Madame President. The House has voted and recessed for the evening. They voted two hundred and ninety-eight to a hundred and thirty-seven, approving the use of American troops in the Persian Gulf and in Iran. The Senate has just begun their closed session in the Old Senate Chamber. They still may have a final vote by midnight."

TWENTY-SEVEN

T HE AUTOMATIC DOORS to the secondary entrance opened and President Marie Arcola stepped quickly into the hallway with secret service agents at her side. Curious security guards took a glimpse of the lady President. Standing at attention from their posts, their stoic eyes looked forward, as they whispered and mumbled into headsets.

Additional agents scattered through the corridor, all dressed alike in their black blue, gray blue suits; their shoes clicked and echoed as they frantically rushed to the elevators, tapped in codes on the numberpad and placed their hands on identification grids, while cameras scanned their faces and eyes, confirming entrance codes into the Pentagon.

A thin, dark haired man was shuffled into the elevator, pulling his ramshackle brown leather briefcase close to his frontside, intimidated by the agents. His eyes fluttered nervously under the vigilant predator gazes from the secret service. He adjusted his grip on his briefcase and wiped the creases out of the front of his old black suit. President Arcola half-looked at her FBI reports. She whispered something to Benny.

"Hello, Mr. Kenny. You remember Benny Gruer." President Arcola gave a small smile, as her press secretary and the Professor of Iranian Affairs, shook hands. She gazed at the back of the elevator and glanced to check the time on her watch. She cleared the thoughts from her head, that her children were fast asleep in their beds at home. There was only the cold, quiet hum of the elevator as it descended.

"How's your wife and children, Mr. Kenny?" The President asked.

Mr. Michael Kenny hesitated at first because of the deaths of David Arcola, Francis and Shelley. "Oh. Everyone is doing well." Mr. Kenny said, studying her reaction. His head twitched. He continued in a quiet, shy voice. "I'm very sorry about your family, Madame President. And President Johnson too, of course."

The elevator stopped and the doors slid open into the tall, sleek, stainless steel hallway. Mr. Kenny glanced around, cautiously, uncomfortable with the glances from the agents.

"Have you ever been inside the Pentagon before, Michael?" A group of soldiers rushed by with automatic weapons, positioning themselves in various slots of the corridor; guarding the President as she passes.

"I really liked your feature article in the National Geographic about the Nomads of the Middle East." Benny said. "It must have been difficult living in the desert for four months to write that piece?"

"Difficult? Yes. Mainly the sand spiders and ticks. And of course, it's a chore for a Irishman to go without a good Guiness for that long."

A secret service agent pulled the briefcase from Mr. Kenny's hand and placed it into a large metal box on a cart, wheeling it to the side of the hallway.

"I'm sorry, Michael. It's just a precaution. The assassination of President Johnson has made it imparative to not take any chances. Was there anything important in your briefcase?"

The tall, dark haired man rubbed his thin face, sighed deep and watched the pair of agents roll his briefcase down the corridor in the metal, bomb-proof box.

"Ah, my munster cheese sandwich, a bottle of tabasco sauce, a pair of white socks, my toothbrush, dental floss, a copy of the Chemical Weapons Convention, some notes from the Clinton-Gore Administration. Basic things. Oh, and my tension balls."

"Tension balls?" President Arcola asked.

"Yes. Two tennis balls wrapped up in a pair of panty-hose. I put them underneath my neck to relieve stress. About twenty minutes a day. You just lay on the floor with them underneath your neck. It's great."

"Madame President, we're ready in the communications room

for you. Hello, Mr. Kenny." General Stanton said, as he interrupted the President and her assistants as they paused outside the doorway. The heavy metal doors opened.

"Michael, thank you for the flowers you sent my family; and the donation in my childrens name." President Arcola said, as she walked into the video-conference room. Mr. Kenny stood at the entrance, staring back and forth, from one end of the room to the other. "Amazing." He whispered.

"We're two hundred feet below the ground, surrounded by ten layers of one inch steel walls, with five feet of concrete in between each layer. We have enough water, food and supplies to keep us all alive for ten years. We even have a fitness center, a library, a sauna, a swimming pool and a recreation room with a big screen entertainment center with fifteen thousand videos. All the comforts of home, in case of a nuclear war." General Stanton smiled at Mr. Kenny's uneasiness at the thought and watched the static on the huge video screen in the middle of the room.

"We're ready. Ambassador Abbas will be present with the Ayatollah and two generals. The video signal is weak. Irans power plants haven't been working well since the explosion at the factory. They're having a difficult time powering their other utilities. We're having mixed reports about their military systems. CIA tells us their situation is critical." General Millings said, as he led President Arcola over to a stainless steel table, bolted to the floor, in front of the giant screen.

"Things will probably get dicey, Michael. We need to have the cooperation of the Iranian people. And we would like, very much to avoid having to commit our troops. So I need you to tell me everything you can as we talk with the Iranians. As you know. Our cultures are very different. Their newspapers and news broadcast indicate they do not like the idea of dealing with a female President. They can be very high strung." President Arcola said with confidence while she set out her notepad, files and pens; trying not to think about the next great challenge.

A group of technicians sat to each side of the video-screen and adjusted their computers; each one of them took a peek at the first woman President. One of technicians tapped the side of his headset and pointed across the room to a woman who stood at a wall of DVD recorders. Telephones were set in front of each seat, placed around the table. Mr. Kenny and General Millings took a seat.

"Two minutes." A woman called out, waving out from next to the video screen.

"So, you're Irish, Mr. Kenny." Benny asked.

"Yes. My family immigrated into Atlanta during the troubles, back in nineteen-twenty. My grandfather and father actually helped build ten houses on U street, in Georgetown." Mr. Kenny found it difficult to breath and turned to President Arcola.

"Madame President. I just wanted to remind you. I'm just a teacher. This is all a bit overwhelming."

"Michael. You'll do fine." She replied with a pat to his hand.

"Let's get set!" General Stanton called out, placing a headset over his ears.

The screens flashed on and Ambassador Abbas fidgeted with the electronics on the desk, from the video conference room in Iran. He began to speak. "May I first say. Computers have come a long way for us to see and speak with each other this way." Ambassador Abbas began in a kind voice.

"We have a problem with our audio, Mr. Ambassador. One moment please." President Arcola said and signaled a technician out of the view of the screen, by tapping her headset. She adjusted her microphone.

"Can we still talk amongst ourselves without broadcasting to the ambassador?" The President said. The technician nodded 'yes'.

"Michael. First off. These men don't like the idea of having to negogiate with a woman. I really need you to feel into everything they say. Any inflection. Any variation in tone. Our cultures are very different and neither of us trust each other. A lot of their powerplants are down. The video might be a problem, so don't let what you see interpet what you sense or feel." President Arcola nodded to the technician, adjusting the audio equipment.

"Yes. Yes, Madame President. I'll try my best." Michael replied and cleared his throat. The audio and video of the screens to Iran digitalized with miliions of small colored dots, and then an image of a man became clear.

"Ambassador? Ambassador Abbas? Can you hear us?" President

Arcola asked as she pulled her microphone across the top of the stainless steel table, closer to her. The Iranian ambassador frowned at her and turned, waving and calling out to some men behind him. The generals and the Ayatollah slowly seated themselves next to him. All of their faces were weathered with worry and fatigue. The generals made a comment and Mr. Kenny increased the volume on his headset.

"A general has said. I mean, one of the generals has said, 'you look much better than your pictures in the newspapers'." Michael said, trying to interpet the words, studying each one of the generals as they spoke. President Arcola grinned.

"Ambassador. Who are these generals you have with you today?"

"This is General Sala." A balding man dressed in a uniform, with a salt and pepper mustache graciously tipped his head slightly to the introduction.

"And this is General Zameel." The other general huffed in disgust, rolling his black eyes behind his thick rimmed glasses.

"Of course, you know the Ayatollah Faraji-Ali Khaemeni ."

The man with the full, black beard and mustache, slightly tipped his head. His eyeglasses, with thick black rims, blended with his dark brown headress; simple and reminiscent of the late Ayatollah; Imam Khomeini.

General Zameel made a comment.

"General Zameel said 'your make-up covers your eyes and makes it seem like you are hiding something. That most American women have something to hide'."

President Marie Arcola stared cold and rolled her eyes at the general's remark.

"My looks should be the least of your worries, general. Our reports show that almost five hundred thousand of your people have died from the accident near your factory in Esfahan. I expect the next reports to show maybe as many as a million of your people will be dead within the next month."

General Zameel made a comment and laughed.

"They're making a joke about your hair. How a real woman would have it covered." Mr. Kenny interpetted.

"They seem to be in a good mood, for leaders of a country under siege." General Stanton whispered to the President.

"Please refrain from making comments about my looks, General Zameel. I hope all of you are meeting with us to deal with this matter in a mature and diplomatic way. You are supposed to be the leaders of your country. I seriously believe the fate of your people is more important than the fact you have to negogiate the fate of your country with a woman."

The Iranian generals cursed and shouted, as the words from their translator sounded from speakers, into the tribunal halls of their video-conference room.

"The general; General Sala, is arguing that this talking is a waste of time. The Ayatollah is defending you." Mr. Kenny whispered to the President. "My general's want to know why your soldiers have caused this disaster? Why would you want to kill innocent women and children?" Mr. Kenny said, after he translated the words of the Ayatollah. President Arcola studied the mullah's calm, fatherly voice and gazed down her smile.

"Your country has shunned agreement and conditions of the Chemical Weapons Convention for the last two decades. This incident is one of the reasons two-thirds of the nations of the world . . ."

"You make laws to benefit your America! You and the other nations you speak of have designed your CWC to take away our ability to defend ourselves." Ambassador Abbas said, speaking in English, without his translator. "You want us to die so you can have our oil fields. That is why your soldiers chose to kill at this time and now you blame us for killing your President Johnson . . ."

President Arcola interrupted Ambassador Abbas, causing him to throw his arms up, as she stood up and shouted.

"Ambassador! You know those are lies! All this propoganda, you and your country have created, will only cause deeper problems in the future, for you and the Interior Ministry. We know the explosion was an accident. If you let us help, we can send aid to try to stop the meaningless deaths of thousands more of your people. It is time for our countries to work together." President

Arcola's words were sincere. She tried hard to study the eyes and thoughts of the generals. General Zameel stood up and shouted at the ambassador, waving his hands and cursing, pointing toward the screen at President Arcola.

"General Zameel is saying, you are the liar. That they have evidence that a bomb was exploded by the United States. The explosion was no accident. That all American women are liars. Deliverers of Satan. He prefers to talk to a man. Someone who knows what they are talking about. Maybe one of your atheist would do better than you."

General Sala motioned his hands, frantically waving them at the United States President, as he bobbed his head and growled. "For several decades your country has punished Iran. You do not think we are people. You talk about human rights and now, you do this!"

President Arcola stood, pounding her fist to the table, glaring into the general's eyes. "We have evidence that proves the explosion was caused by your people! It was caused by your workers or your soldiers! We also have proof of the anthrax and the other chemical weapons that were stored in that factory. We have retrived the files from that factory!"

General Zameel laughed and made a remark.

"The general has made a comment about your backside." Mr. Kenny was hesitant to repeat what was said. "The ambassador and the Ayatollah are arguing. The Ayatollah seems sad. Disappointed with the generals behavior. He says. He asks you for an explanation." Mr. Kenny said, desperately wanting a drink of water as he looked at the pitcher, sitting in front of him on the stainless steel table.

"An explanation!? This matter will be dealt with in the World Court! Your water and soil are poisoned! Your country needs our help! By the time this is over, half your country will have died! There is no need for me to give you any explanation!" President Arcola shouted from the intercomm table.

There is a great silence. The Ayatollah paused to meditate, to clear his thoughts. The generals whispered something to each other.

"When this disaster occurred, we had a SEAL team sent in to

gather information that our satellites could not gather from a distance. It was necessary for us to know what happened at that factory. It was also important for us to identify those chemicals. Clouds of chemicals were beginning to rain down on other countries. People in other countries are dying because of this incident. If bombs were being created at that factory; we can excuse that for now. But you may even be targeted for sabatoge by your own people." President Arcola tried her best to help the Iranians. One of the generals started yelling at the ambassador.

"General Sala says. Bombs? No. That is very funny. Ah. The SEAL team you speak of, they are in our prison. They must have brought the bomb. We will have them judged and punished for international terrorism and blackmail. The generals agree with each other." Mr. Kenny translated to the President. General Stanton took a deep breath and folded his hands slighlty, thinking this meeting had become a useless disappointment.

"We sent in a second SEAL team a few days ago." President Arcola began.

General Millings slightly shook his head 'no', but couldn't stop the President.

"They've already retrieved enough evidence to convince any country to hold you and your country responsible in the International Court of Justice. If you don't release my SEAL team from your prison, I will do more than recommend sanctions." General Sala shifted in his seat with a puzzled look on his face, shrugged his shoulders and nervously rolled a pen around on the table top. Again he shook his head and whispered to the ambassador.

"The general says, this is not possible. You lie about this evidence. He has troops near the factory. They report no activity. He seems slower. He's not as angry. He's thinking. General Zameel is trying to change the Ayatollah's mind about something. Something to do with another meeting." Mr. Kenny said, trying to understand all the conversations at once.

"I'm transmitting some of the evidence we gathered on video and film that our second SEAL team gathered for us. I'm certain you recognize these scenes from your factory." President Arcola said as she nodded her head once to one of the technicians.

Another set of video screens appeared on the upper corner of the big screen in the Pentagon; and on the video conference screens in Iran. The Iranians stared in amazement at the images outside the factory near Esfahan, showing the dead soldiers and workers bodies, decaying in the parking lot; one of the DVD segments showed the tanks up on the highway, their turrets slowly turned, lining up their targets, computing and logging distances.

"We also have the computer discs and ledgers, we found in the factory. They contain shipment invoices, destinations, buyers, black market arms dealers, and other countries that were suppling your country. Are you and your country ready to explain to the world why biological and chemical weapons being made in your factory exploded and killed people in Saudi Arabia and Kuwait? Killing innocent people? Most of them women and children."

Michael Kenny fussed with his headset and jotted down notes; his eyes looked away to try to understand every truth in the words he was interpretting.

"The generals are whispering. Ah. General Sala says, 'this is something you made up in Hollywood. You made this up to benefit the United States, to further degrade the people of Iran'." Mr. Kenny finished and glanced up as General Zameel stood throwing his notepad and pencils across the table in disgust, quickly leaving the meeting. General Stanton became concerned, tilting his head to signal one of the technicians.

President Arcola continued to intimidate the Iranians. "Our SEAL team also transferred data from computer systems at your factory. We have names, addresses, bank accounts and aliases of terrorist organizations who have made purchases from your factory. Many of them are business people from the United States sending American money from our country to your banks. The world is about to judge you, gentlemen." President Arcola paused, letting her comments soak in. She confirmed data from a computer and nodded to Benny.

"Ambassador. It must be true, that your intelligence reports show what's happening right now at your borders? Those are not U.S. troops crossing into your country, into the Zargo Mountains or building up garrisons in the deserts near Tabas. Those are troops from your neighboring countries. Moving into your country. Taking advantage of this situation. And they are sitting and waiting for more of your people to get weak and die. You and I both know that they will move in and attack you, and your people."

President Marie Arcola's words were stabbing and precise; she wanted to make certain these men understood the deadly situation they had to face. President Arcola now began to understand her duty to her own country. "When you go hide in your underground shelters tonight. Remember. What the anthrax doesn't kill, those armies crossing your borders will. I'm giving you twenty-four hours to accept my offer to help. Or I'll be forced into taking matters into my own hands. I'm also releasing the information from this meeting to the media and the evidence from your chemical weapons factory to the public." President Arcola finished her speech to the Iranians and nodded to General Millings. The Ayatollah and the ambassador turned and began shouting something to General Sala. Their hands waved wildly in the air, as they smacked the backs of their hands.

Mr. Kenny grinned and held tight to his headset. "Whoa. They're really upset. The Ayatollah is begging, pleading for General Sala to stop and think. The ambassador is asking, actually threatening the general, that if he knows about the enemy troops around the Esfahan factory, he should have told the truth to the Interior Ministry." Mr. Kenny was stopped half-way through his translation of the conversation. "Please." The Ayatollah Khamenei said, as he struggled to talk to President Arcola in English. "President Arcola. You must try to understand. This is much confusion. We can not let America help us."

The President studied the man's eyes, trying to think past their tearful, glassyness; she was always cautious of deceit.

"He sounds very sincere. Remorseful. General Sala and the ambassador have backed down. The Ayatollah is reminding the others that the people of Iran are more important right now. That he doesn't want his people to be sick and die. The Ayatollah is threatening them with dishonor to their country." Mr. Kenny said.

"It is very sad our countries must go on not trusting one another. I honestly believe we can put our differences aside just this one time." President Arcola said.

"The ambassador says they have to talk. They would have to

allow a controlled group of medics from the Red Cross into their country. The general is arguing about strategic military locations in the territories of Esfahan and Fars. The medics will be spies. They will affect their religion and give ideas to their women. The Americans will cause many to be undisciplined and disobedient. And they do not need 'civil uprisings' at this moment in their history. That they need to know who is telling the truth." Mr. Kenny said, repeating the Iranians. The Ayatollah's eyes squinted in disapproval of General Sala's remarks. He turned to talk into the video-conference screen.

"I give you my answer in twenty-four hours. Please." He shut down his audio. The screens distorted and bent the images. The monitors went black. The video screen clicked off. There was a brief, dead silence while the President, the generals and the technicians paused, slightly stunned. One of the technicians took a deep breath and stretched, rubbing her eyes. She reached up and checked the time on two of the video recorders and jotted down some notes on her clipboard. President Arcola clicked off her recorder and glanced at Michael while he poured a glass of water; the pitcher clicking at the glass as he shook.

"I still think they're up to something." General Millings grumbled, as he began to dial on his phone.

"I agree. General Zameel didn't care to finish the meeting. I think he's going to check on the second SEAL team out at the factory. I think we better put everyone we've got in that area on alert." General Stanton said as he scribbled down notes on top of his file.

"I think you're right, general. I think we should be ready for the Iranians to take back that factory." President Arcola looked at her watch and grinned at the nervous Professor of Iranian Affairs. "Well, Michael. I think that meeting went quite well. We'll be meeting with them again tomorrow. Do you have any questions at this point?"

The tall, dark Irishman ran his hands around the back of his neck and drank some more water. "No, Madame President. I'm fine. It's just, I tried so hard not to make a mistake. I'm just so used to having college students bullshit me about their term papers or their homework assignments. Even just today, I had this one woman come up to me after class and tell me she just noticed half the pages in her text book were missing and she'd have to find another book to complete her assignment. Now here I am talking to some of the most powerful people in the world. Trying to stop a war."

President Arcola yawned and thought about Mr. Kenny's words. "Well, Michael. If we weren't here doing this, someone else would be."

The technicians swarmed around the room, some were making copies of videotapes, while others compared information from their notes. General Millings picked up a telephone receiver when it began to ring. "Madame President. It's Fred. He says it's important. He says he has an update on his earlier report."

President Arcola quickly picked up her phone. "Yes, Fred. Are we the only one's who know so far? Alright. I'll call and have security allow you in when I get back to the White House. Thanks."

The generals paused hoping to overhear some of the conversation or at least hoping she would mention what the meeting would be about. The President stood for a moment, her face flushed from exhaustion. She held onto the back of the chair and took a few deep breaths. Benny and Michael stared at her; looks of deep concern on their faces.

"Are you going to be okay?" Benny asked as he stepped up and put his arm around her.

"I'll be fine as soon as I get back to the White House. Mr. Kenny, we'll see you again soon." President Arcola grabbed Benny's arm and hurried back to the elevators.

TWENTY-EIGHT

PRESIDENT MARIE ARCOLA slid her eyeglasses back up her nose and took a drink of orange juice. Fred peered around the corner of the den and watched to make certain the White House guard was far away down the hall, standing at the top of the staircase. The President opened up another file, pulling out a packet of photographs. There was a picture of Dewey and Fielding posing with their rifles in a wooded area, with a trailer in the background. A flag was bent from the wind, flying atop a tall handmade, wooden pole. A flag with three bright red, white and blue strips, with a large white star centered to the left. Another photograph of the American soldiers, showed a picnic with men and women dressed in white robes, shouldering AK-47's; burning an American flag. Jason, Dewey and Trench were in the next photograph, posing with seven other men. All of them wore black uniforms and jackboots; their heads shaved, holding up flags with swastika's. President Arcola paused, looking closely at the eyes of the men in the photographs. She tried to equate the moment the picture was taken as she tried to absorb any of their feelings; if they had feelings. The dark, black soulless expressions on their war-game painted faces; devilish grins seemingly laughing at the President.

"Those mountains in the background, where are they?" President Arcola asked. Fred reached across the desk and picked up one of the photographs.

"My team identified those as the Davis Mountains. It's a militia camp outside of Vinlin. I've already talked to Sheriff Martin and the Texas ATF. All we need is your go ahead to move into that trailor camp to check for evidence."

"What do you think you'll find there?"

"I think we'll find detonators similar to the one used on the bomb that killed President Johnson." He said, handing a report to the President.

Marie paused staring at Fred in shocked disbelief. For a few minutes, the room was silent, the words from the ex-FBI agent still didn't seem to make sense. A chill ran through her heart and she found it difficult to breathe. She held her face in her hands, fighting back the feelings of sorrow and anger. She remembered Fielding and Trench smiling at her as they escorted her through the funerals of her family and President Johnson. One of them even touched her arm as they walked through St. Matthew's. These were the agents that killed her family and could kill her next.

"Those are records of grievances filed by some of the officers that trained Captain Dewey Mullin and Lieutenant Devin Fielding. It seems Dewey beat the shit out of a female major and threatened to blow up her house. Lt. Fielding was also thrown in jail in Texas, while on leave, for threatening a judge. They were also at the airport when the bomb went off." Fred gestured with his hand to a stack of typed forms in another pile.

"Agent Naughton said that he interviewed the secret service team and let them go?"

"He did interview them. He just didn't think to check if they were supposed to be at the airport in the first place."

"Damnit! I knew Naughton would fuck this up!" President Arcola cursed, as she leaned back in her chair and slowly cracked her knuckles, holding back the anger from her mistake. "It's one thirty now. How soon can you have that militia camp investigated?"

"I can call Dan in an hour. The ATF can be in that camp by daybreak."

"But what if we're wrong? Do we have any physical evidence?"

"We're not wrong. We found chemicals on Dewey's clothes that can be linked to the explosion."

"But, Captain Mullin works with expolsives all the time. I can't have evidence that was screwed up like Oklahoma City or Atlanta."

"I also took a sample from the bottom of Dewey and Trench's

shoes. I found magnesium and copper particles. I also found hair and blood samples that matched with Francis."

The room was quiet in the darkness. The only sound was the ticking of the grandfather clock, echoing from down the hallway. A tear rolled down Marie's face from the frustration and the pain. She sniffled and pulled some kleenex from the box sitting next to a wedding picture of her and her husband David.

"The FBI labs have been a big problem for along time. It's very critical that all the test in your facility are one hundred percent. I also want all this information to be kept between us. This whole thing could be turned into one hell-of-a-mess. You know that I ordered Dewey, Jason, Trench and Fielding into Iran to investigate that factory?"

"Yes. I know. They're the best." Fred cautiously replied.

"So far they've been sending all the computer information. We have all the evidence we need to prove our first SEAL team didn't cause the explosion and they should be released."

Fred shifted in his chair and gazed into the darkness of the room. He tapped his fingers to his forehead, over and over, one by one, in thought; and then replied with a grin. "We could just strand them there."

"You're starting to remind me of Professor Berger with that nasty smile."

"They think they got away with it. They really think they got away with killing the President of the United States. When this goes down, we'll have to bring them back and try them for murder. Secret service agents murdering the President, they'll all get the death penalty."

"I would just like to know why they wanted to kill President Johnson? And why on that particular day?"

"It's so strange that Marlin Adair's son, Jason could be a part of this?"

"Well, we've had soldiers snap in the past. It happens all the time." President Arcola was obsessed with the photographs of the autopsies of her husband and children. She always took them out to look at them. She tried not to think this wasn't David anymore; that this was the shell and she should not grieve, but should be happy that he is not alive, crippled and suffering in agony from the burns.

"What if we take care of our soldiers in that factory?"

Fred sipped his hot tea, his neck gave a nervous twitch as he swallowed. He gave a loud grunt and answered the President's question. "I think a decision like that is up to you and should be kept as secret as possible."

"We can't let those soldiers know anything. Can you check to see when the Nimitz is sending a chopper to pick them up?"

"Yes, I can. But wasn't their last report to CIC confirmintg tanks had the factory surrounded?"

"General Tyler informed me two hours ago the situation hasn't changed. I really don't want to have to think what will happen if those tanks get orders to destroy that factory or if those soldiers decide to surrender." The President responded.

Fred picked up a file containing copies of the evidence reported from Dewey, at the factory. "This photograph from their DVD shows half the warehouse is filled with anthrax. And the ether and diesel fuel make that building a highly explosive target."

"They have orders not to trust any radio communications at this time. They're just going to sit and wait for their helicopter ride. Besides, those Afghan's would gun them down as soon as they were out of range of that factory."

"So, you don't think the Afghan's will destroy the factory?"

"Afghanistan has waited for an opportunity like this for a long time. Now they get to humiliate Iran and hold the world hostage. I'm concerned they might become desperate and make a terrible mistake. Especially if there is a nuclear bomb out there."

"So, has a nuclear bomb been confirmed?"

"No. But I want the leaders of Iran to think one could be on it's way. I think we'll have a better chance of stopping this thing before China gets involved."

The ex-FBI agent's wrist watch alarm beeped. He checked the time. "Well, I will feel more comfortable with more evidence." He said.

"So will I. If this problem escalates, I want plenty of options. That's why I'm giving you and the ATF orders to seize the trailer down in Texas. I suggest you leave as soon as possible and inform me of any and all the evidence you find."

The old man stood, pulled his wool coat off of the armchair and made certain he hadn't dropped his gloves and scarf. He extended his hand out and shook President Arcola's. "I just wanted to thank you for letting me help with this case. It's been a rough road since the FBI forced me to resign."

"You're quite welcome, Fred. I know that your nephew was one of the secret service agents killed in the explosion at Dulles. I'm sorry."

"Yes. Thank you, Marie. This one means a lot to me."

TWENTY-NINE

FOUR TRUCK LOADS of ATF officers emptied out into a field where the dirt road ended. Sheriff Martin and his deputies followed up a ridge to the edge of a cliff, where a lone Pinyon pine, stood with it's blueish-black silhouette, balanced in the Texas twilight. Fourteen of the agents shuffled down the side of the Davis Mountain ridge, spreading out to position themselves at all corners around the trailers. They laid low in the thistle and weeds and took aim with their rifles. Another pair of ATF agents crept slowly to the entrance of the small compound wearing night vision goggles; they stopped suddenly.

"Okay, sheriff. We've got some booby-traps about twenty feet in front of us. It looks like gas cans with trip wires running about a foot off the ground. I make out four of them, set about fifty feet apart, a hundred feet away from the first trailer."

Dogs started barking and caused the two agents to back away, crawling into the dust. A shotgun blast flashed into the morning sky, echoing down and around the ridge, up against the foothills. The barking of the dogs turned spastic with their snarling and choking on the chain leashes.

"Okay sheriff. It's your ball." One of the ATF agents whispered into his headset and slid backwards behind a boulder.

A skinny, gray haired man pulled the cup of coffee from his gray walrus mustache and waved for one of his deputies to step forward. The sunrise began to quiet the crickets; higher up on the mountainside, an owl became silent. The tall, thin sheriff limped forward toward the entrance to the militia's camp. He unsnapped the holster for his Glock with one hand and leaned the M-16 against his shoulder with the other.

"Hey Jori! Burk! It's Sheriff Martin! I need y'all to come out and speak to me for a moment!" Sheriff Dan Martin yelled out, in between the howling of the rottweillers. The sheriff stood in the dawn, with the colors of the land exposed to the morning beams of sunlight. He shivered and patted his leather parka, checking for his extra set of handcuffs. "Hey Jori! I know you can hear me!"

A bullet crackled, cutting a groove into the dirt and dust, only a foot away from the sheriff's boot. Sheriff Dan Martin yawned and called out again. "I think you fellas know why we're out here! If you try any of that shit again, I'm gonna give these federal agents the go ahead to vaporize your little trailer park!"

A pair of Apache helicopters appeared in the Jeff Davis county skies; one to the far south of the militia encampment and one to the north. Both of them hoovered far out of range of any weapons the militia might fire. An unshavened man emerged from the middle of the trailers, with his shotgun pointed out at the sheriff, making the agents apprehensive. The man stood for a few seconds, dressed in his long johns and fatigues, grinning and shaking his head at Sheriff Martin. "Good lord, you're a stupid ol' buzzard." Jori said with a smile; his two front teeth missing. He lowered his gun.

"I brought some donuts. Ya got any coffee?" The sheriif asked.

"Donuts!? Damnit, Dan. You know my cholesteral went haywire last year. I got rushed to the hospital and they had to suck out my goddamn gallbladder." Jori glanced around at the other twenty militiamen and women postioned under trailers and in the trees. "Well, maybe one donut won't give me the cramps."

"Jori, I'm here with an agent from Washington, D.C. He's trying to help that lady president find the people who killed her husband and children."

The commando-dressed man laughed and shuffled back, kicking up some dust.

"A woman president. Now ain't that some shit. Women is supposed to change diapers and tend to the children. Not run the freakin' country and start wars."

"We think Dewey and Fielding might have set of the bomb at the Dulles Airport. I just need to look through some of their belongings. I'm here to try to convince the FBI you and your militia weren't responsible for killing President Johnson and those women and children. That it was Dewey and Fielding acting on there own." A falcon flew away, up the side of the mountains, casting it's shadow under the morning sunbeams, causing one of the ATF agents to aim his Ruger.

"What? Just like that ya think ya can show up here and threaten my family because you have some hunch? This is the very reason we choose to live this way, to protect our rights as American citizens. All you federal officer-types think you have the right to go onto anybody's land and do whatever the damn-hell you please. Now this is my land, Dan! And you and these secret agents have no right being here!"

"Jori, I've got a search warrant right here in my hand." The sheriff said, holding out an enevelope. "Now, you know that this country has a big problem over there in the Middle East."

"Oh, yeah! Well it's about time this country fucked up! Always going around the world thinking they can take whatever they want! So, is that why you're here, Dan!? Are you and that girlie president thinkin' the goverment can make up any excuse to take away my second ammendment rights? What kinda officers of the law are you, comin' round here, trying to take away our constitutional rights!?"

"Now, now, J. Don't get your butt all worked up. You and I grew up together, remember? Hell, your mom and dad adopted me because I was the only one who could kick your ass. Did you know your momma still calls me twice a week, just to see how you're doin'?"

"Ah, shit, Dan. You know I got all these warrants out for my arrest. I can't just get up and head off to El Paso to see my momma."

"Damnit, Jori. How many times do I have to tell you, the government knows where you are. You've been here for fifteen years. It's the same damn thing as being in prison."

The daylight lit up the camp, revealing a half dozen trailers, a mobile home and a winnebago, with mosquito netting draped over a set of picnic tables, with home-made green and brown camouflage. Another pair of men stepped forward alongside Jori, one dressed in long-Johns, one dressed in pants held up by dark green suspenders; both holding Chinese AK-47's. The dogs continued to bark and Burk kicked some dirt and stones in their direction.

"Shut-up, damnit!" The man with the full beard and mustache yelled, spitting and putting his cigar back in his mouth. "Jesus Christ, Dan. What the hell's all this commotion so fuckin' early in the morning fer!?"

Some of ATF agents stood aiming their rifles, their eyes cautiously looking down at the trip wires for the gasoline bombs. Fred walked up alongside Sheriff Martin followed by another man dressed in a suit, carrying a briefcase. Jori's eyes widened, when he recognized the man in the suit.

"Calvin? Calvin, what the hell you doin' here with these people?" Jori asked, with a suprised smile.

"Hey, Jori. I'm here to represent you as legal counsel. The President of the United States wants to cut you and the rest of your militia a deal. President Arcola has signed papers to release most of the federal charges. She's gonna give all of you a clean slate, as long as you let Sheriff Martin and Fred gather the evidence they need from Dewey's trailer."

"I don't know about this, Jori." Burk said, scooting up alongside his Brother-in-Arms, his AK-47 still aimed out at the agents to the left of the trailer camp.

"All that talk and pieces of paper is a bunch of lies! It's a trick!" Burk yelled out.

"Now, Burk. Just give us a few minutes to talk. These are real official documents, signed by the President. Even the governor of Texas signed the agreements. All of you will be pardoned."

"Bullshit! All of you work together against us! You just want ta get in here and take away our guns!" Burk yelled out. Jori rubbed his stomach, gazing at the militia-man yelling back, into the trailers, calling the other soldiers to side with him.

"Burk! I really don't want to hold you and your people responsible for the deaths of those women and children back in D.C. Now you can help us out or we'll just leave and let those choppers come down and do the business for us."

A third Apache helicopter appeared on top of the mountain ridge, sucking the arrid dust, rocking the smartweeds and ponderosas. It hoovered and adjusted it's position with it's Hellfires dead-aimed down at the trailers. Jori reached back and pulled Burk close to him so he could whisper.

"We are the patriots, Burk. We are the Founders of The New Republic. We need to work together. We have to start somewhere to set an example."

"What? Jori, you can't be serious? These agents are gonna get in here and tear this place apart."

"Just let them in the trailer. We can have them surrounded in there."

"But they'll know all our secrets."

"Burk. We put all our secrets on the internet and send our newsletters out to people with p.o. box numbers. Let's see if we can make this work for us." Jori looked into Burk's eyes, holding him by the shoulders and nodded his head to convince his partner.

"Hey, Dan! We got enough gasoline and dynamite to napalm half this valley! If I let you, Calvin and that Fred-guy in and your Gestapo decide to fuck with us, I'm gonna blow this place to kingdom come!" Jori looked out at the ATF as he yelled out, waving his shotgun. The helicopters backed away at the wave of Sheriff Martin's hand.

"Okay, Dan. Nice and easy." Jori said, as the ATF agents backed away, lowering their rifles as they breathed a sigh of relief. The sheriff, the attorney and ex-FBI agent met up with Jori and five other militia-men and women and were pulled quickly to a trailer in the center of the compound. There was apprehension as the trio walked with Jori, in between the trailers observing the dirt carpet of the compound. Dan looked for more tripwires or booby-traps. Laundry was hung on clotheslines, with an adolescent pit-bull standing vigilant, growling with a large, snare cable around it's neck. A small boy, maybe seven years old, backed away to the shelter of a trailer, patting his holstered 38; accompanied by his ten year old brother lowering his Tech-9 and vested hand-gernades.

Fred was perspiring, even in the cold December morning. He wiped the sweat from his forehead at the squeaking of the trailer door. He crept slowly into the trailer. Sheriff Martin eased over to the shrine of flags and newspaper articles, scotch-taped to the walls. Calvin slowly pushed a set of dumbells with his shoe, rolling them away from the entrance to the trailer. The room was lined with bookshelves filled with historic novels of Jefferson, Mao and great leaders from all around the world. Copies of None Dare Call It Conspiracy, The Turner Diaries, Giddeon's Bible and John Bunyan's -The Pilgrims Progress were laid out on the nightstand.

The smell of Dewey's trailer was damp from the Peco's canal moisture and the Texas dew. The cots were made with the soldiers clothes neatly folded and sitting in a stack at the end. The dishes were all clean and the cans of food and survival rations were set up in the cupboards, in alphabetical order and in chronological order for expiration dates.

"Dewey has his own way with things." Jori said.

A stack of bowie knives and daggers lay on top of the dresser next to a tray of shotgun shells and rifle ammo and a large stuffed owl. A small television set sat on a VCR with a Remington 12 gauge and Browning rifle propped up against the same nightstand by the window. Sheriff Martin tapped the leather holsters hung on the wall by a coat hook, with the two Taurus Model S&W's polished, shined and loaded. Almost everywhere, within hands reach, was a gun and hand gernades. Calvin backed out of the entrance of the trailer and sat down with Jori at a picnic table.

"Let me give you copies of all these documents."

Burk walked away from the attorney, into the trailer, always keeping a distrustful eye on the agent and the sheriff. Fred took an interest in a Springfield M-14 sitting on the bathroom floor, underneath a bath towel and a bag of marbles.

"Now you best be making me a list of anything you take out of here! And don't be taking anything that aint related to your investigation!" Burk said, turning to yell out at the attorney.

"Hey, Calvin! I don't want anything leaving Dewey and Fielding's trailer that aint related to that explosion! We still got rights!"

Sheriff Martin stood in the narrow hallway watching Burk eating the free donuts. Fred was careful as he opened boxes and reached inside dresser drawers, gently running his fingers along the sides, checking for booby-traps. He opened a small insulated, black metal box and picked up one of the detonators. He studied the small watch battery and electronic trigger. He sighed in relief when he confirmed that it matched.

"Now, I don't understand why you gentlemen think Dewey would set a booby-trap in his own trailer, especially around his partners." Burk grunted with a smirk.

Fred gazed up at the militiaman, and stood up with a stack of binders labeled: SCENARIOS: PROPERTY OF THE UNITED STATES SECRET SERVICE.

"Well. Dewey and Fielding would never do anything wrong to us. That's what I mean."

Fred opened the first binder. Maps and photographs were inserted inside a plastic pencil case with photographs of President Johnson. Newspaper clippings were glued to the next pages, with Marie Arcola's name circled with a blue highlighter. There was a table of contents, listing titles, dates and incidents, starting with the assassinations of Abraham Lincoln, John F. Kennedy and Martin Luther King Jr. Each chapter described the way the political leader was killed. Fred whispered, reading the list of words.

"Obstinate. Worldly-wiseman. Interpretor. Sagacity."

Fred held up pictures and articles of President Arcola from newspapers and magazines. Fielding had scribbled small notes next to pictures of the President and her family. Fred began to read the scenarios, whispering some comments, signed by Dewey. "I also heard of the molestations, troubles, wars, captivities, cries, groans, frights, and fears."

Another photograph showed the lady President with a red circle around her legs, as she posed for the cover of a magazine.

"I was coming along, I was musing with myself of what a dangerous road the road this place was, and how many that had come even thus far on pilgrimage had here been stopped, and been destroyed." In bold red letters were the words: CIVIL WAR.

The next page had a xeroxed copy of an article from an Atlanta newspaper about a bombing at a gay nightclub. The words 'It's about time' are scribbled over the article. Blood was smeared on the next page, over the photograph of a smiling President Johnson, shaking hands with the ambassador from Iran. A picture of President Arcola was scotch-taped next to his, with words ground into the paper with black ink.

"Those that die here die of no violent distemper: the death which such die is not grievous to them. For he that goeth away in a sleep, begins that journey with desire and pleasure. Yea, such acquiesce in the will of that disease." Fred turned the next page and began reading one of the scenarios that Dewey and Fielding designed.

"Oh, my God. This is it." The agent bumped his way out of the trailer, to the surprise of Burk and Sheriff Martin, a copy of the Citizen's Rule Book fell to the floor.

The ATF sharp shooters stood, aiming their rifles at the first sight of the trio stepping out of the trailer. A group of libertarions stood vigilant with their M-16's aimed at the agents. The Texas dust whipped up dry into Dan's eyes from the warm December morning. The agent shook his head and craddled the binders to his chest.

"I'm going to have to take those to my office and give you copies, Fred. Ya understand that all of these people are my clients now." Calvin said nudging Jori. Sheriff Martin stuck his finger in his mouth and pried some donut out from in between his gum and molars.

"Sure, Calvin. I bet you feel pretty hot right about now. You're gonna be getting paid millions of taxpayers dollars to defend these people."

Calvin snatched up his notes and flopped them into his brief-case, giving Jori a friendly pat on the back. "Now, you keep these documents in a safe place. I'm going to be meeting with the attorney general and the governor. In a couple of weeks, all of you are gonna have a clean slate." Calvin said, with that used-car-salesman smile. Jori grinned ear to ear and reached for the bag of donuts Sheriff Martin held out.

"And you will let us know 'bout that book deal. Right Cal?" Jori asked.

"Heck yes, Jori. All those contracts are gonna be tricky. But remember, I'll charge a higher commission when someone buys the movie rights. But you are going to make some big money." Calvin said with a smile and a handshake.

ATF agents poised at the entrance to the camp slowly lowered their rifles, realizing there would be no violent stand-off. Sheriff Martin turned and kindly shook Jori and Burk's hands.

"I want to thank you gentlemen, again. I wouldn't be surprised if the President doesn't give you a cash reward for helping us."

"We don't want any damn rewards. We just want this country to erase all the lies they made-up against us and give us back our rights." Burk huffed with his fiery, dark blue eyes. Jori's grin half-faded, as he shook his attorney's hand.

"Hey, Burk. I'll take that reward money." Jori said.

"You all just let me deal with these politicians. I'll make certain you get all your demands fulfilled." Calvin said, letting out a deep sigh as he passed through the fences out of the camp, stepping up to the sheriff's car. He turned and smiled, waving at Jori and Burk, while most of the ATF agents backed away to their jeeps and Hum-Vs. Sheriff Martin fastened his safety belt and twisted the key in the ignition. He glared at Calvin as he handed the binders with the scenarios to Fred in the backseat.

"Were those really pardon's from the President and the governor?" Sheriff Martin asked. Calvin laughed and snapped his briefcase shut.

"Now don't worry about that sheriff. I've been briefed by the governor personally. Washington doesn't need to know what went on out here. Besides. Fred's got the evidence he needs. President Arcola will be happy. Everythings going to be fine."

Fred glared up through his glasses in disgust, watching the scummy little attorney squiggle in his seat, glowing from his major achievement; until he saw the brown metal sign on the side of the road that read: BLACK MOUNTAIN, barely readable through all the bullet holes.

THIRTY

FRED WAS INTRIGUED by the complexity of Dewey and Fielding's notes. He was entranced by the ideas and revelations the secret service agents wrote in prose, all through the FBI scenarios; scenarios taught to them for the protection of the President. The co-pilot walked by the agent, startling the old man from his readings.

"We'll be landing in about twenty minutes. The tower said there's a car waiting to take you to the White House." The flight attendent said.

"Great. Thanks, Mary." Fred nodded his head and paused his pocket tape recorder and gave the lady a tired smile. He lifted the telephone reciever alongside his seat and dialed in a combination of numbers.

"Hello, Jeri. This is Fred. I've got the evidence we need." The ex-FBI agent said.

"One second. President Arcola's been waiting for your call."

"Hello, Fred. How are you feeling?" President Arcola asked; a concerned tone in her voice for the old, agent's health.

"Good, Madame President. Just a bit jet-lagged. I'm afraid I've got some very bad news." There was a long, silence before the agent continued. "I have a strong feeling that Dewey, Trench, Fielding and Jason are planning to start a war. One of the scenarios I found in Dewey and Fielding's trailer refers to John Bunyan's, The Pilgrims Progress."

"I'm not to familiar with Bunyan's work. Can you read what's there?"

"Yes. I saw Heedless ans Too-bold there; and for aught I know, there they will lie till they rot. As I was thus mussing, there was one in very pleasent attire, but old, that presented herself unto me, and offered me three things, to wit, her body, her purse and her bed." Fred turned a page showing a cut out photograph of President Arcola's head glued to the body of a naked woman. The words: 'ABORTION IS MURDER! BABY KILLER!' were written across her body in blood. "Now the truth is, I was both aweary, and sleepy, I am also as poor as a howlet, and that, perhaps, the witch knew. Well, I repulsed her once and twice, but she put by my repulses, and smiled. Then I began to be angry, but she mattered that nothing at all. Then she made offers again and said if I would be ruled by her, she would make me great and happy.

For, said she, I am the mistress of the the world, and men are made happy by me. Then I asked her name, and she told me it was Madam Bubble. This set me further from her, but she still followed me with enticements. Then I betook me, as you see, to my knees, and with hands lift up, and cries, I prayed to him that had said he would help." He turned to the next page and stopped talking.

"What's wrong, Fred?" The President asked.

He ran his fingers over the next set of pages showing apocalyptic visions of angels and heaven, illuminated with flecks of gold and silver, with the continuing of self-imposed images and quotes from the Founders of the New Republic. "I'm looking at pages and pages of beautiful illuminated manuscripts on vellum." He picked up his magnifying glass, to examine the materials. "The works are made with a mixture of gold and silver flecks. Blood and sand."

"What are the illuminations of?" She asked.

"One is a large, dark green demon, with his hands pulling small people apart. Ripping children into pieces. There is writing on the page. It's a license plate and the time. It's the license plate number from the Presidents limousine. And the time the bomb was exploded at the Dulles Airport. There's also a formula for the bomb."

The agent whispered the calculations and remembered the smoldering bodies at the airport; seeing the visions of the dead and the pieces of Francis and David in the boarding tunnel, dangling down to the tarmac. "If this information is correct. Dewey removed the mercaptan from natural gas and filled the tunnel. He used a simple two-part electronic detonator made with a magnesium and copper ignitor. The carpet in the tunnel was wired with copper filaments."

The agent turned the page and stared at a work of art that folded out three pages wide, showing the Madonna, her long robe draped down, painted with blood, trimmed with gold flecks. "I'm looking at another of Dewey's illuminations. It's the Virgin Mary with a cut out photograph of your face where her face should be."

"Please continue." President Arcola whispered.

"The writings are still from the previous pages. 'I verily believe she intended no good, but rather sought to make stop of me in my journey. Without doubt her designs were bad. Doth she not speak smoothly, and give you a smile at the end of a sentence? Doth she not wear a great purse by her side, and is not her hand often in it's fingering her money as if that was her heart's delight? This woman is a witch, and it is by virtue of her sorceries that this Ground is enchanted; whoever doth lay their head down in her lap, had as good lay it down upon that block over which the axe doth hang; and whoever lay their eyes upon her beauty are counted the enemies of God."

The sign for the passengers to put on their safety belts blinked and rang. The pilots voice calmly announced the plane was making the final approach before landing.

"So. What do you make of it?" President Arcola asked, almost whispering. Fred ran his fingers down the silver trim of the gown, marveling at the great detail of the work, his finger stopping at small words scribbled at her feet. "Absolvi. It's latin."

"Yes. It means to finish off. As in absolution. Fred, do me a favor. Don't use your cellphone around that book. I know I sound paranoid, but that book might be a bomb."

"Thank you for your concern, Madame President. I already had it checked out before I brought it on the plane. But I think we have a more serious problem. This likeness of you has a design of a bomb at the base of your feet. It seems our SEAL team believes they are God's soldiers and will rise again like Jesus Christ. I'm looking at a scenario that describes the destruction of the factory in Esfahan, and how important it is the beginning of the end start in Iran. Madame President. I think they're going to blow up the factory."

THIRTY-ONE

SENATOR TREVOR THOMAS set the stack of one hundred dollar bills underneath Jeri's appointment book. He stared, batting his dark brown eyes with a jingling smile. She picked up the phone and rang the other line into the Oval Office.

"Madame President. Senator Trevor Thomas is here to speak with you. Yes, ma'am. He has an appointment." The secretary set down the reciever and waited to pick up her money. President Arcola opened the door and called out. The senator paused at the entrance and looked the lady president over, just as he does most women; giving her a puerile glance, thinking that he was in control.

"Senator Thomas. You have fifteen minutes. What's on your mind?"

"I was just concerned about your health. All the rumors lately about all the stress in your life. I wanted to see if you need any help or advice with anything?" President Arcola leaned back against her desk and noticed the senator staring at her legs. She felt flattered and smiled, folding her arms across her chest.

"I really appreciate your willingness to help. But my staff is very capable of taking care of my matters."

"Yes. Of course they are. I thought you might need a seperate opinion on, maybe the situation unfolding in Iran. I heard that a militia in Texas was linked to your improvised SEAL team near Esfahan."

"You don't miss a thing now, do you? Always worming your way in from any angle." President Arcola grinned and circled Senator Thomas's name on her agenda.

"I know we're on the opposite side of the court, but a hell-of-

a-lot of the businesses who are supporting my Presidential campaign are going to shut down overseas, if the United States goes
to war in the Middle East. You have to understand, I like all of
those rich friends hanging around. It maintains my self-esteem."
Senator Thomas said while he stretched his long tall frame out,
easing back into the armchair.

"Yes. I like the full page ad that you bought in USA Today,
preaching to the world 'they too, can become independantly
wealthty'. That 'you'll show them how, once you become the
President'."

President Arcola laughed at the way she mimiced the senator's
voice. The funny face, the codger Trevor Thomas gave afterwards,
made her blush. "I'm sorry. I don't know where that came from.
It's just you are so entertaining."

Senator Thomas raised his eyebrows and half-grinned, until
the President's secretary walked in and handed the stack of hundred dollar bills back to the senator.

"How much did he try to pay you, Jeri?" President Arcola asked,
still smiling.

"A thousand dollars." Jeri replied.

"Oh, a thousand dollars, just to talk to me for fifteen minutes.
I feel so special, Trevor."

Senator Thomas sat with his mouth open, enchanted by the
way she moved and looked, and teased him. "Well. You're important to me. I just wish we could put this Democratic, Republican
stigma aside and just try to be friends." Senator Thomas said.

President Arcola smiled with those steamy blue eyes which caused
the senator to shake his head, scrambling him back to the reason
for his visit.

"As I was saying." He began, tucking the money back into his
suit pocket.

"There is a tremendous amount of oil still being pulled out of
the wells near Jahrom and Deh Bid. When I'm elected next year
. . ."

"If, you're elected." The President said.

"Madame President, your insurance agent is here and Mr. Su
from Arcola Electronics will be here in an hour with the merger
contracts." Jeri said as she left the room.

President Arcola carried a frown on her china-doll face. She hung her head from the memories of the last meeting with Mr. Su, Arcola Electronics Vice-President; her husband David was alive then. Her expression and feelings changed. She became cold and down-to-business, with an unapproachable demeanor.

"It's time for you to leave senator. I have things to do." She announced.

Trevor follied in his persistence, always trying to get through the ice and the barriers, and the defenses. He pushed himself up out of the armchair and began to study the Oval Office, imagining where he would place his practice putting green. "Okay. But one more question. What's the most difficult thing you have to do as President?" Senator Thomas asked.

President Arcola shook her head, grinned at the senator and gave him a delicate rub on his shoulder. "The most difficult thing, is keeping unwanted intruders out of my office, so I can get some serious work done. I'm meeting here with the Chiefs of Staff in three hours. I'd like you to be here. Don't be late."

He stood stunned for a few seconds, trying to interpret her touch, her voice, the way she used words. As he stepped away, he had the overwhelming feeling she liked him, or maybe she was attracted to him. But, why would there have been any doubt. Trevor thought every woman was attracted to him.

A chubby man played with his briefcase and tried to put papers and documents back in order before shoving them into the manila folders and gave the White House guard an intimidating snarl.

"Barry. Come on in. It's good to see you again." President Arcola said while she shook the insurance agent's hand. Senator Thomas paused down the corridor, and checked the time on his Rolex. He gave a longing look at the lady president, as she walked back into the Oval Office, sneaking a glance at Trevor before she closed the door.

THIRTY-TWO

BENNY YAWNED AND STRETCHED his arms out on the sofa, twisting his neck until it popped and cracked. Telephones were set down in various locations of the Oval Office, on the coffee table, the desk and the end tables. A fax machine and a computer were rolled into the room by a group of technicians. One of them tested the equipment and handed a clipboard to General Tyler.

"Everything checks out fine, general. We're on-line to the Pentagon." One of the pages said as she shifted cables to the far wall. Secret service agents stepped back to position themselves against the flags by the windows, getting cocky glances from the White House Guards. President Arcola finished her sandwich and poured herself a cup of hot tea, studying the Chiefs of Staff as they entered the room. Senator Thomas bumped his way in and succeeded to manipulate one of President Arcola's pages with small talk, so he could have the second best seat in the Oval Office, the armchair closest to the President's desk.

"I thought we agreed this was to be a closed meeting, Madame President. You have to realize influence by parties who have a personnal interest in this matter, could distort the outcome." General Millings said, in an unpleasant tone to the President, while he eyed down Senator Thomas.

Professor Berger poured himself some Jamesons and snatched a sandwich from the tray; as he gloated over his audience in his usual arrogant fashion. "I respect your concerns, general. After listening to Senator Thomas's presentation in the Senate, I believe he can contribute to this meeting and his ideas may help us with the next meeting with the Ayatollah and the Ambassador from Iran." The professor said. Senator Thomas nodded his head and smiled at Professor Berger's compliment.

"The latest evidence from the explosion at Dulles Airport has been confirmed. Agent Naughton's technicians will be calling in a few minutes. He just wants to be certain of the suspects." General Tyler added.

"Of course. But there's evidence that it was some of our own secret service agents." Senator Thomas whispered out loud, so the general overheard him. President Arcola gave the senator a stare and a shake of her head. Senator Thomas raised his hands in the air and mouthed the words 'okay, sorry'.

"Senator. You've been listening to those tabloid reporters. They're always bashing our military training at the Citadel. You of all people should know the military is not some summer camp for the children of soccer-moms. We protect this country. We need strong, obedient fighters." General Millings laughed.

"I agree with you one hundred percent general." The senator replied.

The fax machine beeped and began to run a print out from the Pentagon. A technician quickly handed the sheet to General Tyler. The Oval Office phone rang and President Arcola was quick to pick up the receiver. "Yes. Hello, Agent Naughton. Okay. Send the information to us. Yes. Here he is."

She handed the phone to General Tyler. His eyes flicked as he listened to the FBI agent. He quickly looked away, trying not to make eye contact with her. "I see. I'm going to put you on speaker phone. Just a second." General Tyler nodded for the technician to transfer the call to the Oval Office intercomm.

"Agent Naughton. This is General Stanton. I'm looking at the report you faxed us. Is this information final and without a doubt?"

Senator Thomas eased back into the armchair and glanced out into the corridor, to see if anyone was listening. The computer printer clicked on and the faces and images of soldiers appeared on the monitors.

"My God. This is insane." General Millings cursed, reading the report as he passed it to the President. The lady president bowed her head in silence as she read the report. She massaged her dry eyes; feelings of relief and rage rushed through her blood, as she handed the report to Benny.

"Are you sure of this report, Agent Naughton?" President Arcola questioned as she closely listened to the agent on the other end of the intercom; practicing what Mr. Michael Kenny had taught her about balancing trust, in cases of terrorism.

"Yes, ma'am. We've checked everything four times. All the evidence indicates Captain Ronald "Dewey" Mullin, Lieutenant Terry "Trench" Garby and Lieutenant Devin Fielding planted and detonated the bomb that killed President Johnson and your family at the Dulles Airport."

President Arcola's eyes began to water and she sniffled, taking a quick deep breath. She peered up at the ceiling and studied the Coat of Arms, while she regained her composure; knowing she sent those soldiers into Iran. "Thank you. Agent Naughton. Please continue to update us with any new information."

"Yes, Madame President." The FBI agent replied and signed off.

The tension of the Oval Office could be seen in the body language of the Chiefs of Staff. General Millings fidgeted, rubbing his hands, uncertain with his thoughts and the equations going through his mind. He gave General Stanton an 'I told you she'd screw it up' look. Another fax slid from the printer, showing the face of Lieutenant Devin Fielding.

"I find it difficult and disturbing to believe that officers who have served our nation for twelve and fifteen years are suddenly being accused of such a damned act against God and their country! I don't believe we have the right to be here, convicting those men without proper counsel!" General Millings stood, protesting, too anxious to sit down.

"General, we all know this is a messy situation. But the evidence has been confirmed. I've also had another agent suggest that Dewey and Fielding might be planning to explode a bomb at the factory. What do you make of that idea, professor?" The President asked.

Professor Berger placed his hands together and twiddled his fingers. Then he folded his hands in the shape of a pyramid. "And I thought it was my job to create horror stories. But exploding a bomb in that factory, by the same men who blew up a bomb, killing our President in broad daylight. I need time to think about that one. Suicidal bombings are more about religious belief than of revenge and grievance."

"I am open to any ideas." The President said.

Professor Berger snuck a dill pickle off the deli tray, squinching his face from the tartness. "Yesssz. Actually, I do have an idea. As was with Sirhan Sirhan, or Jack Ruby, or Oswald. Let's send in a lone assassin to do the job. Kill off the entire SEAL team."

"A U.S. soldier killing U.S. soldiers!? No! This is not right! We cannot do this! What do we tell their parents or families!?" General Millings protested.

"What do we tell the families of the people that were killed with President Johnson, General Millings? What do we tell the dead?" Professor Berger replied, sticking his nose in the air.

"Your idea is the most ridiculous piece of crap I've ever heard. Is this what you do, Professor Berger? Make up crazy fantasies in order to sell your books!?" General Stanton scolded.

"We have all the evidence, general." President Arcola began. "These soldiers did kill the President by setting off that bomb. What's to keep them from setting off another bomb? What remorse or feelings, or conscience, do they have for this country, if they did in fact set off that bomb? We can't afford to send in large scale armies, or alert allies in the Gulf, unless we have this situation under control. My sources have already searched and seized all of those soldiers' apartments, cars and lockers."

"Madame President. The consequences could lead to an investigation on your administration. If the public finds out about this . . ." General Stanton said.

"Then I will go to prison. If I'm wrong. The advantage of an assassin being sent in could help us in another way. It's quick and it's quiet. I would rather sacrifice five soldiers than five thousand." President Arcola said, picking up another sandwich.

"Why the hell would they want to blow up a factory full of biological weapons and maybe kill themselves? That's just not realistic." Benny said.

"It is, if you think you're God's soldiers and you will be resurrected." Senator Thomas said, pouring himself a drink." We should seriously consider the professor's idea."

"It is quieter and a helluva lot cheaper. It's better than commiting thousands of troops and risk damaging millions of dollars worth of military equipment. I think we should send in that polish boy, Joey Adair. The FBI said he's the best sniper in the agency. Let him go kill his brother." The professor added.

"If we do have a bunch of soldiers that are anti-American terrorists. Joey might be in on it too. If that factory is rigged to explode, we could be forced into a war between seven of the most powerful nations in the world." General Standon said.

"Need I remind you, gentlemen. The United Nations is crumbling. If those chemicals are exploded, Iran dies. Kuwait dies. And most of Saudi Arabia dies. The water and oil in those areas would be contaminated for decades. Terrorist factions are already taking chances by crossing the borders. Terrorist will get into Iran before we do and they will set up their little armies, and we will be fucked." Senator Thomas huffed, staring the generals down.

"Thank you, senator." President Arcola said with a smile. The Oval Office phone rang and Benny reached to answer it. "No, shit. Thanks." Benny half laughed. "Iran just told CNN that they wish to negotiate terms of surrender to the United States. They said that they don't want the United States to blow up another factory."

The Chiefs of Staff looked puzzled as they jotted down some notes.

"Surrender? Why would an accident at a factory make Iran surrender to us?" The President wondered.

"I'll tell you why. They're playing you, Madame President. They're hoping the rest of the world will turn against America. They think because you're a woman, your maternal instincts can be played upon. If you let them surrender, then people may believe they were right about the first SEAL team. That U.S. soldiers were sent in to destroy Iran. They're trying to get the sanctions lifted." Senator Thomas responded.

"In a few days, most of Iran's cities will be swamped with rogue bands of soldiers, setting up tanks and rockets. We need to think about a possible airstrike instead of just sending a lone sniper in. My God. They'll spot an American soldier in a heartbeat." General Millings said and shook his head in disbelief.

President Arcola pulled the phone from across the desk next to her.

"Any objections?" She asked, watching the stunned faces of the generals; not really waiting for their response. She turned back to talk into the phone.

"Good. Alex. This is President Arcola. We need to ready Sergeant Joseph Adair for his mission to Iran. Once he's on the plane, give me a call and let me talk to him. Thank you." She hung up the phone and slid it to the left side of the desk.

"You realize you've just ordered a soldier to his death?" Professor Berger grinned.

"I know all the scenarios, professor. Going into Iran under these conditions means he might be killed before he kills those other soldiers. And if they kill Joey and those soldiers make it back to America, I'll make certain they are executed." President Arcola coldly responded, softly stirring her tea with her teabag.

"General Millings, what will you do to Joey?" Benny asked.

"Would you care for me to describe what the Pentagon will be doing to aid our lone sniper?" Professor Berger sarcastically asked the President and the generals, as he shifted his shoulders, trying to relieve the stiffness in his back. "The Pentagon. The great symbol of many a tale of witchcraft and design for conjuring up the angels of hell, are shuffling our Sergeant Joseph Adair into a special vehicle, racing him to meet a jet to fly him to the Nimitz; waiting in the middle of the Arabian Sea.

This scenario has been used before, for many of our special forces to aid in the assurance of the Soviet Unions withdrawal from Kabul and Lashar, in Afghanistan during the nineteen eighties. The surgery on Joey will be quick. He'll be on the best pain killers the U.S. government can provide. But from the looks of his record in the U.S. Navy Special Forces; I'd say he's used to pain. They'll have to make him look as Iranian as possible. Hopefully, he'll be lucky and he'll be able to walk right into that factory." The professor's words were arrogant and deliberate.

"Well, professor. Our sources indicate large rogue troops have broken away from the Majahidin. They've crossed the borders with large amounts of heavy artillery. They may actually be able to move nuclear weapons south along the Makran Coast. That means they could aim their weapons at Oman with no problem. Has anyone heard from the Secretary of Defense? Mr. Rawlings should have been back from London by now." General Tyler said while he listened through a set of headphones; to intelligence reports.

Professor Berger snuck another wedge of brick cheese; always watching the lady president, as she scribbled notes, deep in thought. She slowly sipped at her hot tea and picked up photographs of Sergeant Joey Adair. The picture of the dark brown haired soldier with the brilliant smile hardly seemed threatening. It was difficult to believe this sniper and his brother had served three operations against drug smugglers in Burma and War Lords in Central Africa. Both he and his brother Jason had obeyed orders to kill over two hundred enemy soldiers.

"No one in the media is to know about this. No one outside of this office is to ever know those secret service agents killed the President. I don't believe it is wise for us to let anarchist militias in America or anywhere, think they can infiltrate the security of this administration." President Arcola stated.

"But, Madame President. The public has to know. The country is still blaming Iran for the assassination of President Johnson and your family." General Millings said.

"Can Joey actually kill them? One of them is his brother Jason. What if he hesitates? Has anyone from the FBI or ATF checked Joey's belongings for evidence?" Benny asked, a bit upset by the casual talk of the slaughter of all these soldiers.

"Joey Adair is clean. His brother, Jason, didn't have any sign of anti-government problems or incidents on his record, but he does spend an overwhelming amount of time with the other three. I say we don't take that chance. He might have had a change of heart, once he found out how much military equipment was being shuffled out there, around the black market. I think all of us have many concerns, especially because of what the decryption experts found on the PGP software included with Dewey and Fielding's belongings.

Let me read the list. Military weapons, parts and components in scrap piles bought by private agencies, we call DRMO's, show major purchases signed by Fielding and Mullin. Here is a list of parts from F-117 Stealth Bombers. Here is another list of parts for Cobra helicopters. Modified AH-1Qs, Sea Cobras. BGM TOW's, AH-1S parts, and enough components for AH-Ts and W's to assemble five Cobra helicopters. And that's not all. The FBI is trailing the sale of parts of the Comanche Stealth helicopters." General Stanton frowned as he read the information, nervously tapping his fingers to the lists.

"How much damage can a few helicopters do?" Benny chuckled.

"In future theatre conflicts . . ." Professor Berger started and was interrupted by Senator Trevor Thomas.

"In future theatre conflicts? Professor, the Comanche prototype was the hottest creature in the Bosnian arena. I laid in a ditch near Sarajevo, when the U.S. Navy tested the first stealth Comanches. We were pinned down by sniper fire, during one of those random night assaults. We were running out of ammunition and being flooded by rain. We would have been killed, if it wasn't for those Comanches. You can't hear them! Even when they're only a few feet above you. Shit! Most of the time you can't see the damn things. They hug the country and hills at speeds of two hundred knots. But the best thing about the Comanche; is getting to fly one. Once you fly one of those choppers, you are God." Senator Thomas said, smiling and raising his drink to the nervous laughter of the generals.

"All this over a bunch of helicopter parts?" Benny asked. This caused the Chiefs of Staff to laugh and whisper amongst themselves. "What these soldiers have failed to tell you, Benny, is that one of those Cobra or Comanche helicopters in the wrong hands, has the abilitiy to do more damage then one nuclear bomb." President Arcola said, staring at the generals with intent, not really wanting to recall her disappointing days as an Apache pilot during Operation Desert Storm.

Benny paused, watching another sheet of information rolling out of the fax machine from the Pentagon. A set of pages were printed by the technicians computer, showing unidentifiable weapons.

"Well. They know what they're doing. Dewey found a way around the inventory codes escaping the system. My main concern are these encryption devices." General Tyler said as he passed a copy of the report to President Arcola.

"Fred might be right about these assholes trying to start a Holy War. You realize, we are the only ones who will ever know about any of this information? I will make certain we stop this problem from this office." President Arcola stated to the raised eyebrows of the generals.

"Well, Madame President. You have the power to give the order and deal with this incident in any way you choose. Our job is to assist, to help you to make the best choice for our troops. And for the United States." General Millings murmured, catching the glimpses of the other generals in the Oval Office. Professor Berger had to intervene with his next suggestion.

"Why not a full scale airstrike? Why not go ahead and finish this problem of Middle East conflict once and for all? Don't you realize, these rogue garrisons of soldiers will eventually make it to the oil wells in Southern Iran and they will still threaten Saudi Arabia with military instability in the Gulf region? Once they get dug in, all of us here know that they will not stop. Just imagine, Madame President. A group of rogue, fanatic terrorists, with cruise missiles or a nuclear bomb in the oil fields of Iran, holding Saudi Arabia and Kuwait hostage."

The Oval Office grew suddenly cold. A nightmarish chill caused the President to shiver. She was exhausted by the non-stop events of the last several days. General Stanton stretched his arms out, releasing a deep sigh.

"Well, professor. I guess those descriptions are a classic example of your writings, earning you your reputation. I'm beginning to understand why people call you the 'Anti-Christ.'" President Arcola joked to relieve the tension in the room.

The professor gave a deep-bellied laugh. "Madame President. I believe, if and when the Anti-Christ comes, he or she wouldn't just be a simple being, such as myself. But the chain of events are beginning to unfold, and may lead those soldiers to the Gates of Heaven opening up above us. And the Book of Revelations says: 'a huge cloud of God's power, will descend down to earth. The power to raise the dead'. Me. I don't have all those wonderful powers. I'm just a man. Nothing more, nothing less."

Jeri shoved the Oval Office door open, startling the secret service agents. She rushed into the office holding a memo from her fax machine. She stood trembling as she handed the report to President Arcola. "It's from the Secretary of Defense. Israel's airforce has begun flying their jets over Iran."

THIRTY-THREE

JOEY'S EYES WERE RED and swollen. He smelled like sweaty, burnt skin, his arms and chest were still sore from the tanning beds. His face had brown blotches showing around his lips, next to his thin gray and brown mustache. The co-pilot scooted up next to him in the bay and handed Joey a radio headset. "It's the President of the United States, she wants to talk to you personally." The sergeant stopped for a second and gave the co-pilot a surprised look.

"Yes, Madame President." Joey smiled, fumbling to place the headset up to his face.

"Joey. This is President Arcola. I wanted to talk to you about this mission."

"Sure. Thank you. I really appreciate your call."

"Did you know that I used to be a chopper pilot in the Army?"

"Yes, ma'am. The news has been telling your life story ever since President Johnson and your family were killed. I'm sorry. I didn't mean to bring that up."

"It's fine, Joey. I also wanted to thank you for the donation and the gifts for my Frankie and Shelley." The rotors of the Apache thud and clacked. There were many questions that were to go unanswered in the brief conversation. "I know what you want to ask me, ma'am. You want to know about my brother, Jason. And you want to know if I can go out there and kill him."

There was a pause. Long and silent. Only the sounds of the helicopter and the whistling of the engines filled the void. She cleared her throat, feeling awkward and uncomfortable. Joey continued to explain his feelings. "The government made a mistake, nine years ago, when Jason and I were stationed in South Korea.

Someone in the FBI recieved a set of memos stating my family might be part of a hate group linked to the Aryan Nation. It took a year for the FBI and the military to find out it was a bad prank from a soldier that Jason had a fight with during a poker game.

Jason and I were arrested and taken to Seoul. We were locked up and had all of our benefits frozen for four months. At that same time we were not allowed any phone calls, letters from home, nothing. We were treated like shit."

"Joey. I'm so sorry." She replied, sobbing.

"No disrespect, ma'am. I know you have all the files on my brother and myself. I know your reports show my mother and father were also arrested and detained, and that my parents home was ransacked and destroyed, while Jason and I were locked up. Your FBI reports should also show that my father died of apprendicitis while he was in jail. The sheriff and deputies were given orders to ignore his cries, as he died in his cell."

"I don't have all the details from the jail records. Please believe me. I don't know anything about this."

"Shortly afterwards, my momma died. The doctors said it was a heart attack from mixing prescription drugs and whiskey. I know she died from a broken heart."

"If you want. I can assign this mission to someone else?" The President quietly said.

"No, ma'am. I swore an oath to protect and die for my country. I just wanted to let you know what I was thinking and feeling. I still love my brother with all my heart. But I can't let the world go to war. I'm your best bet. Just don't forget what the soldiers do for America. My pappa was a great soldier and died serving the United States." President Arcola sniffled. "I won't forget. Good luck with your mission, Joey."

"Thank you, Marie." Joey replied.

The radio clicked off and Joey sighed, glancing out of the bay window at the white caps swelling and spraying up from the Persian Gulf shore. He opened a small dark gray metal box and removed a hypodermic needle along with a small glass vial. He barely flinched from the dig of the needle into his vein as he depressed the plunger with the inhibitor for the anthrax.

His eyes were watery from his thoughts; daydreaming to the

wonderful times playing underneath the magnolias in his parents backyard down near Brandywine Lake. The soft, warm spring days after school, playing football with Jason, and his mother and father. Always going down to the sandy shoals of the creek, catching polly-wogs in a mason jar. The wonderful hot summers, playing curbball while tasting the vanilla-chocolate of the twin treat, from the Diary Queen. The injection would only last thirty hours. He took a gauze bandage and pulled his tongue out of the way to inject the nerve block in the bottom of his mouth.

"Well, lieutenant. We're in Iran. The town below us used to be Bander-e Deylam." The co-pilot said, re-checking his avionics. Joey scooted closer to the window and smacked his lips as his tongue went numb.

The waves of the Persian Gulf whipped into the rocky shore, underneath the belly of the Apache helicopter. The coastal city was desolate. Bodies by the hundreds lie in the streets of the marketplace. People collapsed while carrying groceries and while deals were being made between merchants and customers. A soft wind blew across the decayed bodies of a group of women. Their black chadors, weathered by the sea-salt air. Military trucks stood still, with the skeletal remains of Iranian soldiers, dead at their posts.

"We've received reports from Jason and Dewey at the factory. The air is clear of any chemicals. CIC has also confirmed that the air is breathable. They're expecting a lift out at fourteen hundred hours. That'll give you five hours to get into the factory and take care of business." The co-pilot said.

The pilot pointed out the cockpit window at a dozen Comanche helicopters spreading out to the east and the west, zooming ahead of their Apache, fading into the northern horizon. "Does?" Joey tried to talk, finding it difficult to move his tongue without using his fingers.

The pilot tried to understand the sergeant as he pointed his finger at the squadron of helicopters. "Does? Oh, those. Those are Rocky's Vampires. One of the best kept secrets in twenty-first century warfare. The commandors at Red Flag cried, pleaded and begged for them not to leave their Hornets for the Comanches. But. What can be said? They're all one hundred percent fighter pilots. Rocky and Loverboy have served for fifteen years. For old hot dogs they can still dish it out."

The flat black Comanches veered low and clear, hugging the rock and vast, sandy terrain. Rocky's pilots looked down at the cadavers of the shepherds, dead with the remains of their sheep. One pilot glanced down at his speed:160 knots. He flicked a switch, arming his defense system with Hellfires and stingers. The co-pilot studied the on-board maps, checking the skies for jets and the ground for tanks.

"Jesus Christ. Everyone's dead." The co-pilot shook his head in disbelief, dumbfounded by the sight of the carnage. He caressed his St. Jude medallion between his thumb and finger.

"Hey, Loverboy. How's it look up at the LZ?" The pilot said into the radio in his helmet. The reply was wonderfully clear over the headsets and bay intercomm.

"Nothing but the dead. We just passed Ardaf. My radars picking up some heavy artillery to our west. They're moving slower than a dying dog with a bad limp." Loverboy answered.

"How's the package, Scotty?" Rocky questioned.

The pilot turned to see Joey, hugging his duffle bag, fast asleep. "He's doing what I wish I was doing. Dreaming away about some-place other than here."

"Remember. Our lady President and the Brass will be calling all the shots from the Pentagon. So stay tuned gentlemen." CIC replied from the Nimitz.

"Does it bug you to be working for a woman, there, Loverboy?" Scotty joked as he checked the fuel gauges for any drastic changes.

"Negative there, Scotty. She used to fly an Apache, like I used to. It must have been rough for her to have to sit out Desert Storm. Besides, she pays us damn good money to play with all these neat toys."

"You boys mess up those million dollar toys, your ass is grass and I'm gonna be the lawnmower. Do you understand me, gen-tlemen?" A voice snapped over the radio from CIC. The pilots all chuckled.

"Admiral, what are you doing up this early?" Rocky chuckled.

"Never you mind. Just stick to business and no hot dogging."

"Yes sir, admiral." Loverboy smiled and was tapped on the shoulder by his co-pilot, pointing out the window at a group of farmers, huddled in the rocks. They began to call and wave up at the helicopters.

"Hello, CIC. We've got live civilians at Shahr-e Kord. It looks like maybe thirty farmers. There are no guns or vehicles present. It looks like they're waving for help. I'm sending you the DVD's and their location."

"That's fine and dandy, Loverboy." CIC replied.

"Hey, Dracula. This is Rocky. I'm running to your flank about twenty miles. I'm picking up radio messeges. And it's not Farsi." The radio clicked. Loverboy listened closely to the radio transmission.

"Hey, Bubba. This is the Bloodsucker. I'm way north of you. I'm picking up walkie-talkies. It sounds Chinese. I'm recording and transmitting to CIC. So tell me fellas, what are the Chinese doing in Iran?"

"Well, CIC. What do you think?" Loverboy replied as he watched through his bay window, admiring five of the Comanches, rocketing across to the north.

"Still thinking." CIC answered and cut-off abruptly.

"This is Rocky. We've picked up fighting near the factory. Radar and satellites confirm anti-aircraft guns. Maybe 107mms."

"This is Torpedo, over to the north of the factory. About five kilometers. I've got a visual confirmation of tanks. I also have trucks filled with soldiers. They're sure in a hurt to set down those anti-personnel mines. I guess AAA is gonna have to mark that road with a detour on their next trip-tik." Rocky joined in with the laughter of the pilots of his Superteam.

Scotty nodded to his co-pilot, for him to wake Joey up. "Sergeant. We're coming to the drop off." The co-pilot said with remorse in his voice, knowing the American soldier was being sent to his death.

"Yet. Tur." Joey responded, struggling to pronounce words, wiping some blood off of his tongue.

"Five minutes to the LZ." The pilot called back from the cockpit.

"Be careful, sergeant. Someone down there is surrounding that factory with land mines. It's not going to be an easy walk for you.

Between those tanks and land mines, the only way we can come back for you, is if you can stay on the roof of the factory." Joey shook his head 'yes' with a thumb's-up.

"Two minutes, sergeant. It'll be prayer time. You'll be within two miles, just north of the factory. There are a few paths in the hillsides and only one highway going directly by the road to the factory entrance. The Pentagon has radioed CIC asking you to check the factory for another bomb. They think the last SEAL team might have rigged the place to explode. Get ready." Scotty called out. "There may be some shooting."

Joey tapped the co-pilots chest, trying to read the name sewn on his jacket. "Ut or ame?" Joey struggled through the words.

"What's my name? My name's Terry. They call me the Tarantula. I'm a sharp shooter, just like you. Someday when this is over, we'll get together and do some target shooting. Everyone tells me you're the best. But I know I'm better and I will be glad to take your money anyday."

Joey smiled and held up his fingers in an 'okay' sign. "Uh Ah u a other?" Joey asked and stretched his arms, looking through swollen eyes.

"Do I have a brother? Yeah. I had a brother. He used to run with a gang in South Chicago, down in the Heights. He thought he could make a living selling cocaine. He was gunned down just before his seventeenth birthday. That's why I got out and joined the service. I just had to get away. I just didn't want to be another black man trapped in a place he didn't belong." Terry was interrupted by the pilot. "This is it."

"Here we go, Joey! Now you be safe out there. I know you make more money then me and when we get together, I plan to win it all."

Scotty yelled as the bay doors were opened to the sputter of the blades. Dust kicked into the face of the sergeant and the co-pilot as they struggled to see the ground. Joey swung his legs over the side of the chopper bay, watching the ground get closer.

"You take care of yourself now, Joey!" Terry yelled.

Joey nodded his head, hugging his gear and rifle. He pushed off out of the helicopter bay, onto the sandstone and rolled against the rocks. His joints ached from the cramped quarters for sleeping along with the pain from the surgery.

Sand and silt blasted up from the Iranian desert, from the chopper blades; the helicopter was suspended in air a foot off of the ground. The soldier stood in this dream, strange in his need to discern; but calmly familiar. He gathered his thoughts, rubbed the dust from his eyes and waved the olive-green dragonfly away. He touched his gloved hand to the Esfahan tundra and raised his head, looking back at the quiet of the city. His heart skipped beats from his apprehension and the anthrax inhibitor.

The crisp December air was refreshing, much cleaner than the Appalachian Mountain spring evenings.

Joey reached down with the barrel of his Ruger and bumped the petrified cadaver of a man laying in the path. He knelt down and pulled the tattered robe off the shepherd, the rotted bones of the man's ribs and arms, crunched and fell to the dirt. The smell was acidy and strong like ammonia. It caused Joey's nostrils to flare, doubling him over to vomit. He crawled away on the ground, shaking the robes and scarf to air out the smell from the dead body. Gunfire crackled, up over the ridge, by the main road to the factory. Joey grabbed a dead sheep and ripped it's belly open, spilling the entrails onto the desert, while he rubbed the animals body back and forth against a rock. He filled it with dirt to clean and dry up the membrane. Quickly, he took apart his rifle and carefully inserted his weapons and gear inside the animal and pulled the wool, tightly together. He cleaned the blood off of his hands, wiping them back and forth into the sand; he remembered the anthrax.

The rocky cliff caused Joey to stumble to his knees, the factory smokestacks could now be seen down in the valley. He pulled the sheep close to him, listening to the rattle of the tank engines up on the highway. Shouting could be heard from behind him. Joey's heart began to race. Then, two voices became clearer; more accented.

A soldier reached out and grabbed Joey's shoulder, tossing him down on his back. A second soldier aimed his rifle at the decreped shepherd; holding one of his dead sheep from his flock.

The soldier lowered his rifle and waved fresh air across his face, squinting with disgust at the sight of this diseased, foul man.

Joey mumbled, raising his hand out to the soldier, recognizing the Pakistani officer's uniform. He crawled toward their feet, begging for them to help. One soldier pulled out his pistol and clicked a bullet into the chamber, aiming it at Joey's head. The U.S. soldier set the sheep to his side and bowed, mumbling and chanting, kissing the dirt at their feet. One of the soldiers used the barrel of his rifle to pull the man's robe open. The soldier cringed at the sight of all the shepherd's bleeding wounds, glistening with fresh blood. The soldier tapped Joey in the crotch, waving for him to pull his pants down. The other soldier's eyes widened, at the sight of Joey's deformed and bleeding penis, showing signs of abuse and torture.

The soldiers made the sign of the cross. There now is curiousity in the soldiers tone, as he asked Joey 'who did this?' in Persian. Joey spoke, making certain the soldiers could see his blistered, swollen tongue. "Saddam! Saddam!" Joey gasped, falling to the ground sobbing.

The one soldier pulled the other, telling him to leave the poor shepherd alone, that he had been through enough torture.

Gunfire echoed up from the highway, drawing the soldiers attention as they hunched down and shuffled low to the ground with their guns drawn, back toward the road. Joey remained on his knees, trembling from the cold, terrified, thinking how close he came to death. He felt anxious and dizzy, taking long, deep breaths; as he tried to regain his wits.

It was dusk. The sun was large in the hazy blue horizon. A bird screeched, flying away in a panic. Joey smiled; it was a good sign that the anthrax and chemical weapons had dissipated. One of the tanks on the highway fired out at something in the east. The blast thundered, causing a group of soldiers to rush away from the factory parking lot, back up the main road to their encampment.

The building was dark. Joey hoped the almanacs from CIC were correct, that the moon would become a wanning gibbous. Any light from the factory might draw the attention of the soldier's tanks positioned on the ridge. Joey opened his duffle bag and wiped the sheep parts off of his Ruger. Bodies were scattered on the floor of the corridor. Factory workers were collapsed everywhere; their skeletal faces and jaws looking as if they were screaming out from the dead.

The emergency lights cast dim yellow ghosts from every room; with the batteries slowly dying. Joey attached the silencer to the barrel of his rifle and fastened his munitions belt around his waist. He took a long, slow drink from his canteen and set it down in his duffle bag next to the dead sheep.

Gunfire crackled again outside of the factory. Trench lay his blanket out on the roof, watching the hot metal bits of bullets and mortar light up the early evening sky, followed by tracers rocketing toward the moon.

"Just like fireflies when ya think about it." Trench chuckled, nibbling on his cheese, crackers and sardines. A gurgling noise started and then abruptly stopped. It came from somewhere down in the garage, causing Fielding to aim his rifle into the stairwell.

"Fielding. I keep tellin' ya. It's the plumbing. The damn pipes freeze at night and thaw during the day." Dewey said as he loaded the last CD into the transmitter. He picked up his night vision goggles and took a peek across the factory parking lot. "It looks like they're just gonna be shooting their guns all night for the fun of it. Like some kinda celebration. I think they're settling in and waiting for something. And more trucks and tanks are goin' by. Fuck. I wish CIC could tell us what the hell's goin' on." Dewey grabbed his duffle bag and rummaged around inside. Jason yawned and rolled his duffle up under his head. "Time to go to sleep."

"How can you sleep during all this shit?" Trench asked.

Jason scratched at his face, feeling the prickly beard and mustache. "Remember guys. If ya gotta go in the middle of the night, take it all the way over to the far side of the roof, behind those air ducts." He said, adjusting his fatigues; craddling his Arctic Warfare. He took a drink from his canteen and rummaged through his vest pocket for his toothbrush.

Trench looked at his watch when it gave a quick beep. Fielding made a pillow out of his protective suit and propped his head up; aiming his rifle into the stairwell, with his finger on the trigger, ready for the enemy.

Dewey pried open a can of sardines in Louisiana Hot Sauce and scooped them out, one by one with his little finger. "So. Who do you think'll get here first? The Afghans? The Irans? Or the USA?" Dewey asked outloud, smacking his lips as he ate.

"Well. If those Afghan soldiers know what's down in this factory, they'll probably figure ain't no one gonna want to start shooting here and accidentally explode those canisters."

The magnificent amount of stars formed thousands of patterns, deep within each other. The stars caught Dewey's eyes, as he leaned back against the edge of the roof and gazed up, focusing further and further out into space. His rough, red beard itched when he took another bite of sardines. "It all makes us seem so insignificant. Yet the Lord has chosen us."

Jason shifted back on his left shoulder, waking up from the dream. The computer transmitter clicked, stopped and shut down. The moon was gone and the twilight stars began to fade with the rising sun in the desert of Iran. His left side tingled, asleep from laying the wrong way on the flat tar roof. The sleep in his eyes irritated his face when he rubbed them. He yawned and focused on the images across the rooftop.

A big star illuminated high above the darkness to the west, twinkling like the Star of Bethlehem. For a few seconds, he wondered about Christmas.

There was the humid smell of rain in the air; damp and dusty. The sound of the wind whistled, playing a song with the pipes and vents on the rooftop and in the factory. Trench lay, backed up and twisted in a deep sleep; his head hunched over to the side of a five gallon bucket of roofing tar. A river of blood, blackish-red and gummy, streamed down from the bullethole in the center of his forehead; barely the color of the tarred roof.

Jason tightened his grip on his rifle and crouched down at the entrance of the stairwell, where Fielding's body lay dead on his side. His skull, split by a series of shots to the head; the bulletholes so close, it was hard to tell which shot was first. Jason backed away, stunned at the sight of his dead comrade; he cocked a bullet into the chamber. He gazed across the rooftop with his weapon aimed.

The dull, dark blues and whites of dawn, made the shadows of the rooftop targets for the United States Secret Service agent. The ridge was becoming visible, showing the Afghan tanks with their barrels aimed and positioned, still holding the factory under siege. Soldiers yelled and banged on the turrets, while other awakened soldiers inspected the rows of anti-aircraft cannons. The engines of the tanks started up with groans and rattling.

Joey sat at the edge of the factory roof with his Ruger aimed at his brother Jason. Dewey's duffle bag filled with the computer discs, sat at Sergeant Adair's feet. He studied the detonator for the bombs planted by the secret service agents and rested his boot on top of Dewey's curled up dead body. Jason stood with his Artic Warfare, aimed at his brother's heart. Joey unraveled the scarf from around his head and glared at his brother with grave discontent. He looked at his brother's rifle and shook his head in disapointment.

"Ason! Une! Ooh!" Joey yelled, holding up one, then two fingers. Jason tipped his head and blinked to focus his eyes, always ready to pull the trigger on his rifle. He gave a curious grin, because the man looked familiar and then realized this man in front of him was not an Afghan or Iranian. "Well, little brother. Look at you. You're a mess." Jason moved closer and sat on a ventilation duct. "So this is the Pentagon's idea of sending in the calvary? Sending a little boy into the middle of a dangerous country on the eve of the Third World War."

"Why!?" Joey said holding up the dentonator he took from Dewey. "Why, ou illed ah esident!?"

Jason studied the cord running from the detonator, down one of the air shafts, into the basement with the room filled with anthrax and sarin gas; just as Dewey left it. Jason grinned and slowly sighed, glancing around at the bodies of Dewey, Trench and Fiedling. He slowly lowered his rifle to his hip; the weapon still aimed at his brother. "You have to try to understand the genius behind this entire opportunity. All our lives we fought to defend America. All those years you and I put into the service. Even dad. We'd always go home to the same shit! All those young gump boys and gump chicks, whining and crying while sitting on their asses! Racing all around Georgetown University in mommy and daddy's expensive sports cars! With their stupid baseball caps on backwards, always bad mouthing and shitting on our country! While the politicians suck up all the money! Hell, you and I both know President Johnson was in the middle of selling out America to a bunch of foreigners! America is on the brink of civil war and he wanted to take away the guns from the American people! That would mean chaos and anarchy, and the only ones with the guns to defend themselves, would be the police forces working for the government. The average citizen would be herded into camps and enslaved. We need this war! We need to wake up America so we can pull together for a common cause before the government sells us all! The world will see how powerful America will become with the proper race in charge!"

Joey sat back on the ledge, rubbing his face, with his thoughts in confusion. He tilted his head. He tried to think of Dewey and Fielding, and his best friend Trench; as the enemy. Jason eyed the detonator that controlled the C4 in the chemical walk-in, three stories below. He set his rifle down to the rooftop by his feet.

"I'm just hungry, bro. I'm just getting some water and a sandwich." Jason motioned slowly, always showing his hands as he took an item out of his duffle bag.

"See. Just food." Jason said, unwrapping the sandwich from the cellophane.

Joey watched his brother eat, always waiting for his tricks.

For years, the secret service agents spent, practicing scenarios to protect the President. Joey took a drink from his canteen, swished the water around in his mouth and spit out the dried blood.

Jason munched on his sandwich, noticing the bright blue color of the sky. "Isn't it nice out here? The helicopters will be here in a few hours. We can both become heros. We can tell the FBI that it was Dewey, Fielding and Trench that killed the President. That we killed them when they tried to attack us. Do you want to be a hero, Joey?" Jason asked, taking a drink from his canteen.

A cool breeze chilled Joey as if it were a warning. He tilted his head, smiled at his brother and set down the detonator. He scooted low over to Trench, carrying the transmitter and duffle bag with the evidence from the factory.

Gunfire crackled out in the distance, drawing Joey and Jason's attention. The high, gray stratus clouds hung, drifting by, making it a dry, cool December morning across the dusty, barren desert.

Joey glanced out at the highway, wondering why the turrets of the tanks were turning to aim their barrels out to the East, standing guard; waiting for something. Joey thought of the bombs down below, in the belly of the factory. In his mind, he began to extinguish feelings of closeness. He removed the feelings of Christmas, family and his brother. Playing jarts and football with Jason in the backyard of their parent's house in West Virginia; of being rebellious, drinking beer under the huge magnolias. They were the most popular guys in high school; always getting the girls. Their father dying in jail. The never answered question; was their mother driven to commit suicide from the torture by the FBI. Joey understood why his brother hated the government. And then the years after their deaths, the government denied the two brothers their fathers military benefits and how they never gave an apology for the mistake. Joey looked at the detonator on the roof and secured the DVDs, computer discs and transmitter inside the duffle bag. Jason charged across the roof and dove, kicking his brother to the ledge. He rolled back and caught the detonator in his hands. "There needs to be new blood to nourish the Tree of Liberty. Innocent blood is the best. Fresh and pure. See Joey. See how the Presidents death is bringing the nation together. This war will give our country purpose. It'll bring everyone back to the proper frame of mind." Jason stood holding the detonator. "We have to go forward. God has chosen us and this moment. Ignoring what God's people have told us, disrespects God. We'll be in the history books for all eternity. We are the one's chosen to bring it all into order. Do you know what anniversary this is?" Jason's eyes spasmed wild as he spoke. Joey raised his Ruger and aimed it at his brother. "Joey. It's too late." Jason pushed the plunger to the detonator, his eyes wide, his arms stretched out in his obsession; trembling with the power. He braced himself for the resurrection. His body quaked with his eyes locked shut. A moment passed. And after no requital; he burst into a fit of rage.

"No, damnit!" Jason yelled in anger. "Why did you disconnect those bombs!? Those were not your bombs!"

The first bullet struck Jason's chest. Joey could feel the sorrow and fought back his tears; watching his brother collapse to his knees, holding his heart. Joey remembered the words of the priest;

the words far away in his mind; the words from the cathedral. He pulled the trigger a second time, sending his brother backwards, down to the rooftop. A pair of Dead Sea sparrows avoided the winds of the building storm, landing on the ridge of the factory roof, looking with small sympathetic eyes, at the dead soldiers.

Joey fell to his knees, feeling his brother's soul rush through his own, out into the desert. He held Jason's hand, sobbing with the pain in his heart. Blood seeped from Joey's wounds; from the surgery performed by the doctors back at the FBI.

Heavy artillery rumbled in the distance, causing shouting from the Afghan soldiers as they began returning fire to enemy targets in the East. An explosion shattered part of the factory parking lot, sending a hail of asphalt and stones, crashing windows on the side of the building. Joey crouched down, crawling across the roof with the duffle bag and his rifle. A stinger missile whistled over the roof, ricochetting against the hillside, setting fire to a bulldozer. Joey struggled to contact CIC. He coded in the numbers on the phone pad of the transmitter. The LED registered the code was recieved but CIC didn't respond. Joey picked up the transmitter and turned it over to check for damage. He tried again. Still no response. A low, thundering boom rumbled from the North skies. Joey clicked on Dewey's DVD and focused the camera to the black dots emerging from the horizon. The three jets rocketed closer, Joey's eyes were opened wide as he stared in shock. He picked up the reciever and began transmitting the information to CIC. Now the Nanchangs slowed in arrogance and defiance overhead, giving the sergeant a clear view of their bellies, with the 23mm cannons, sidewinders and Iron bombs. Joey whispered into the radio headset as he videotaped.

"Oh my God. What have we done."

THIRTY-FOUR

SECRETARY OF DEFENSE Doug Rawlings shook his head again in disbelief of the information received by Joey's transmissions, from the DVD's at the factory near Esfahan. "These are Chinese jets. Why would Iran allow the Chinese to violate their airspace?"

President Marie Arcola yawned and quickly scribbled her signature on a pile of documents, on her secretary's desk. She picked up a coney dog with onions and cheese and quickly took two bites. "Doug. There's a couple more in the bag. Help yourself. Jeri. Add brocolli, asparagus and extra orange juice to my grocery list. The orange juice with the calcium in it."

"Yes, ma'am." The secretary replied, jotting down some notes.

The President glanced at her watch and swallowed down the rest of her coney dog. "Oh, shoot. We're running behind. The video-conference with Iran is in one hour. Come on, Doug. Let's walk and talk." President Arcola said, taking a quick sip of orange juice. She swung the door of the Oval Office open and was handed a report by the Defense Secretary. "Oh, God. How accurate are these reports, Doug?" The President said.

"Those photographs are from the rooftop of that factory. Chinese jets flying over the factory. These early satellite reports show Afghans with Soviet T-72 tanks and Russia heading in with MIGs. We've tried talking and threatening everyone from Hezbellah to Talibon. This is turning into a regular free-for-all."

"Well, either Iran is allowing China and Russia into their No-Fly Zones. Or Iran doesn't have the ability to stop them." The President responded.

"Iraq has positioned nearly a million troops from the highways of Halabjah to Abahan. We've received reports from Mashad, the Iranians have fought off a tank regiment with minimal casualties."

President Arcola's expression changed to shock when she looked at the next photograph from Joey's DVD transmission. "Here's the truck with the cruise missiles or nuclear bomb we were waiting for. Heading down the highway toward Abbas. They could reach the Persian Gulf in two days. Have missiles or a bomb been confirmed?"

"No, but we're dealing with a lot of players out there who love to bluff. I don't think we are in a position to take that chance. If we were to go in and attack, there would be international repercussions due to our involvement." The defense secretary said.

"But Doug. Chinese jets flying over Iran? With this additional evidence, I'm having a difficult time believing the government in Iran is sincere."

"Another problem is the confirmation from reconnaissance that the Afghans have set land mines all through the hills and the roads around the factory. Why would they do that?" President Arcola asked.

"My guess is they plan to hold the factory and eventually use the remaining biological and chemicals. I think they know by now other countries are going to try to take that factory. We can't allow the factory to be taken by the Afghans, the Chinese or anyone." Secretary of Defense Rawlings replied, rubbing his hands against his dry eyes.

"What the Iranians really need to do, is to get behind those tanks and destroy them from behind. They'd almost have to be fighting the Afghans from the rooftop of the factory."

The telephone on the President's desk rang and Doug jumped. "Yes, General Millings. I'm here with Doug right now. Has it been confirmed? Son of a bitch. Okay. We're on our way." President Arcola said. She rushed to gather notes into her briefcase, dropping the phone on the hook. "The Pentagon has confirmed the Taiwanese Advanced Fighter Jet that was shot down by a Chinese cruiser last week, was no accident."

Secretary of Defense Douglas Rawlings slightly bowed his head.

"What's wrong, Doug?" President Arcola asked.

"I'm just sorry about not being here for the funeral. I just wish

I could have done something. And you. Losing your family." President Arcola patted the Defense Secretary's shoulder.

"Doug. You were ordered not to leave London when that plane exploded and killed President Johnson. All the international airports were locked down and searched for more bombs. Now. I need to understand everything I can about this Iranian situation. Remember, I'm new at this. But if I've got to give the order to start shooting down Chinese jets. Goddamnit, I will give that order." President Arcola's eyes squinted intense and glassy. Her face was flushed from the last week of sleepless nights; alone, crying herself to sleep.

"The strategy is to keep the peace. The United States has worked hard since the Reagan Administration to try to eliminate the stockpiling and manufacturing of chemical weapons. The Secretary of the State was right. She told the Clinton Administration that something like this might happen. Whoever dreamt an accident of this magnitude would have so many countries on the brink of a world war." Secretary Rawlings said, helping the President on with her coat, as they rushed down the White House corridor.

"Yes. It's a tight spot. But we can't risk everything we've worked for with NATO. Iran doesn't want us to help. I don't think they know what their neighbors are capable of doing under these circumstances. I don't want to even imagine one of those tanks shooting at a jet or hitting that factory. How are the QDR's for Iran or their neighbors?"

"Most of the Pentagon scenarios and wargames advise us to use force wisely. Iran has reneged before on policies with the United States and other countries. And that's why I'm here; to help you with the tough decisions." Doug said as he stepped into the black sedan, under the careful watch of the sharp shooters and a dozen secret service agents.

President Marie Arcola closed here eyes and took in a deep breath of the Christmas Eve night air before slouching down into the limousene. "Well, Doug." The President began, fastening her safety belt.

"Advising the President on the use of force is the gravest responsibility the Secretary of Defense holds. I'm ready."

Secretary of Defense Doug Rawlings looked into those dark blue eyes and remembered all the strong decisions his friend, President Arcola, had made since their days in the Service and in Congress.

"Given the situation, and what we have at stake. Israel and Saudi Arabia will not just sit around and be held hostage, with the possibility of a nuclear bomb being carted into the Persian Gulf. My advice is that we attack now, before it's too late." The Secretary of Defense said and let out a deep sigh of regret.

President Arcola sat with her head held high. "Then let's straighten this out once and for all."

THIRTY-FIVE

S ECRET SERVICE AGENTS stepped aside to allow the
President's limousene into the entrance of the underground parking area for the Pentagon. Benny and Michael
stood by nervously double checking the time on their watches.
President Arcola emerged from the sedan, cautiously glancing
side to side as she hurried toward the elevator.

"Madame President. We have a new problem. The shelling
near Tehran has damaged one of Iran's nuclear power plants and
the power is out for most of the cities in the providences of
Tehran, Markazi and Zanjan. The Ambassador from Iran's last
phone call informed the Chiefs of Staff they can not have the
video-conference, but they will attempt to call at the original
scheduled time of the meeting. They might have evacuated the
country." Benny said as the elevator doors opened. President Arcola rubbed her eyes and tried to clear her thoughts.

"Someone hit one of their nuclear power plants? Someone out
there definately knows what targets to hit." General Tyler chuckled.

"Excuse me, ma'am." Mr. Kenny said clearing his throat. "The
Iranian Mullahs are very honorable people. They would never
flee their country. It is their homeland. It is sacred to them. I
believe they are still somewhere in or near Tehran and they are in
great danger."

One of the secret service agents flinched when the elevator
rocked. The doors opened ten stories below the ground.

"Damnit! Tehran is under attack! Did you here the news!?"
General Stanton shouted with hysteria, almost dragging the President out of the elevator. President Arcola rushed forward and

met with General Millings and Professor Berger, waiting outside of the huge, anti-radiation doors of the war-room. Twenty technicians and officers of the Pentagon were frantically adjusting and calibrating recording equipment. They kept looking up at the videio-conference screens that would not break interference. Short-wave radios and cellular phones were being used, as well as satellite imaging on computers to check detailed maps of the providences in Iran, frantically trying to gather any information about Iran's condition.

President Marie Arcola excused herself and rushed into the restroom causing the room filled with technicians to momentarily stop at their posts. Benny reached his arm out to stop one of the secret service agents, preventing him from following the President into the bathroom.

Benny cracked the door open and whispered to the lady President. "Are you okay?"

"Yes, Benny. Thanks. I just need a minute to think."

"Ten minutes!" One of the technicians called out from the video-conference room, before the door clicked shut. President Arcola looked at herself in the mirror, mashing her knuckles into the countertop of the bathroom sink. She began to cry from the anger and the frustration, cursing her mistake for not finding out sooner who killed President Johnson and her family. She desperately needed something to punch.

"I can't call you. I can't touch you. I long so much for you. When you show up in my dreams, you are so alive. Always smiling and watching your old Three Stooges reruns. You used to drive me crazy with those old comedies. I hear your voice. It hurts so much to wake up from those dreams. I'm so sorry, David. I'm so sorry. You didn't deserve to die. Honey, I wish you were here. I'm so sorry." President Arcola bowed her head and cried.

An alarm sounded out in the corridor. Yellow and red lights flashed, calling the technicians and generals to be seated. They still hoped for the video-conference and the communique to begin. Benny whispered into the bathroom, just barely sticking his head in. "It's alright to be upset. All of us know you've been under a lot of pressure." Marie sobbed and sniffled, grabbing up a bit of toilet paper to wipe her nose.

"I can't let them see me like this. I need them to respect my desicions."

"They will, Marie. In time. Right now they feel threatened because you're a woman. They're a bunch of stuffy, old farts. Most of those generals are probably catching hell from their own wives. You got to get out there and show them."

The bathroom door opened wider and President Arcola looked deep into Benny's eyes. "Thank you, Benny. Let's go."

All eyes were on President Arcola as she took her place at the large stainless steel table, secured to the floor in front of the giant video screens.

"Could they be dead, General Tyler?" President Arcola asked as she pulled out the photographs and the reports from Rocky's Comanche Helicopter Squadron. The general was hesitant to answer, twiddling his thumbs nervously, as the technicians kept calling in Arabic, Chaldean, Persian, Farsi; any language, as they tried to get an operator on a radio or a telephone in Iran to respond.

"General Millings. Those red triangles on your map up there." Benny began to ask. "They were on the other maps we had in yesterday's reports."

"Yes. That's true. Those are markers for possible storage warehouses where biological and chemical weapons are being stockpiled. Most of them are within striking distance of the troops that are now invading Iran."

"What if one of those warehouses are destroyed?" Benny was interrupted by a shouting technician. "I have a call coming in. He claims to be General Sala." The technician raised his hand and pointed at another agent to begin recording the conversation. Another agent nodded that she was in the process of tracing and confirming the call.

"Three minutes!" The technician yelled as two agents checked the audio and visuals on the computer monitors. The huge video screens flashed with static and then to color bars; going back to static. The technicians desperately tried to stabalize a signal and communicate with someone at the other end.

General Stanton's phone rang. Professor Berger paced about with his hands clenched tighlty as he studied the red triangles where the newly discovered locations of chemical weapons were stored. General Millings took a magnifying glass to one of the reconnaissance photographs of the land mines, set down in the hills and the highways around the factory near Esfahan.

"We've got another call!" One of the agents yelled out.

"Hello. Hello, Madame President. This is the Emam." The transmission was weak and crackling, fading in and out. Explosions and machine gun fire could be heard in the background. President Arcola stood straight up, focusing on the large video screens, hoping to see the gentlemen from Iran. The voice speakers' red lights flashed on. A technician gave a 'thumbs-up', indicating she had traced the telephone call to it's source.

"Yes, Emam. This is the President of the United States. Where are you? I hear explosions and gunfire. We can help you. We can get you and your generals out of the country safely, until this is over." President Arcola watched as Mr. Kenny listened closely to his headset, talking softly up to her.

"I can hear voices in the same room as the Ayatollah. A mixture of voices. One sounds Russian."

"The evil is at our door. These tanks that do not love Allah. We are both great leaders, Madame President. We make decisions for many. For the future of our countries. We must not give up on what we are." Mr. Kenny paused in the translation. "I am sad about this . . . situation. I must go now."

The phone clicked off. The video-conference room fell quiet, with all of the Pentagon translators and surveilence teams gazing up at the video screens and at President Arcola. The Secretary of Defense nodded his head, as he and General Millings picked up the satellite and DVD photographs from Joey.

"Madame President. We have an idea." General Millings said, sliding the satellite and helicopter photographs across the stainless steel table, in front of the President. "These are the changes over the past three days outside of the factory. Notice the straight line going by the factory. Jeeps and tanks." He said and pointed to a line of twenty tanks, in one of the photographs, but missing from the others.

"It looks as if the Afghans, or whoever it is out there, is setting up a relay of tanks to allow more of that heavy artillary to head south towards the gulf. Also anti-aircraft cannons have been set up, a mile east of the factory. That's pretty suicidal. If they had a mishap, they'd have chemicals sprayed all over them." President Arcola said.

A technician called out from his radio monitor. "We've recieved a coded messege relayed from Sergeant Joseph Adair through CIC. Captain Ronald 'Dewey' Mullin, Lieutenant Devin Fielding, Captain John 'Trench' Belner and Captain Jason Adair are confirmed dead. The DVD's to the Nimitz confirm the deaths. CIC says Joey has their dogtags in his pocket. CIC and Rocky's Squadron are waiting for further orders. Joey's requesting a pick-up off the factory roof."

President Marie Arcola glanced at the young eyes of the technicians, as they looked at her. She could almost read their thoughts; 'How could you do this?' 'How can you do this?' She felt slightly awkward giving orders to graduate students and interns; thinking they should be military commanders and legioners.

Another technician eagerly called out. "I have a fix on those tanks outside of Tehran. I also have a fix on the location of the cellphone transmission and phone number where the Ayatollah was transmitting."

Some of the young computer technicians applauded lightly, with big smiles of accomplishment on their faces; turning to each other to shake hands.

"Good work, Juan." The President said.

A new map appeared on one of the large video screens showing the red triangles in and around Iran. A red phone rang and President Arcola quickly grabbed up the reciever. "President Arcola here. Yes, Bernie. I agree. You know what to do. We'll do the best we can to monitor the situation from here. I agree. You have my permission to ready the JSFs to engage the attack. Thank you, Admiral. Stand by for further orders."

President Arcola watched as Professor Berger paced around, placing one foot in front of the other, one hand holding his chin; the other hand behind his back. He was deep in thought, listening to the calls being monitored in the jumble of Middle Eastern languages. President Arcola tilted her head and squinted her eyes at the professor. "Well, professor. You're quieter than usual. This must mean you have something enlightening to add to this moment."

"Oh, yes. Madame President. I was just wondering. Iran has a very powerful airforce. I was just curious as to why General Sala and General Zameel didn't order an airstrike against those Afghan tanks before they reached that factory near Esfahan? They had plenty of time to blow them to hell and back."

"Damn. He's right. We monitored Iran's airfoce flying Fencers and Mirage F1s around the factory days after the accident. They had ample opportunity to stop those tanks. If they were supposed to." General Millings gruffed, clearing his throat.

"I've confirmed the cellular phone number for the Ayatollah and General Sala, in case you need to call them back." A young man said congratulating his partner with a handshake. General Tyler waved for one of the technicians. "Son. Can you place a map on that video screen showing the locations of those other chemical weapons factories with any railways or highways near them? And then can you plot a possible solution in the computer to show where those biological and chemical weapons could be heading if someone decides to move them?" General Tyler asked in his fatherly, old tone. The young technician nodded 'yes' and turned to his keyboard. Within a few commands, the technician raised all the possible ways Iran could move biological and chemical weapons away from their warehouses and stockpiles, using the roads and railroads to transport them. General Tyler was the first one to stand up and take notice, as the entire northern half of Iran lit up with possibilities. Only four were lit up near the chemical weapons factory near Esfahan.

"My God. The explosion in Esfahan was a decoy. Iran's going to move those biological and chemical weapons to all those other countries." General Stanton said, leaning over the stainless steel table in astonishment.

"Madame President. I tested the lines from the video-conference into Iran. There is no indication the equipment in Tehran was damaged." One of the woman agents said.

"Could it be somewhere else along the way?" The President asked.

"I checked it ten times to be sure. There is nothing wrong."

"They had the ability to talk to us all along." Benny muttered to himself.

"What they're doing is hustling those weapons out of the country before we enforce the CWC and send in inspectors." General Millings cursed.

"Doug. Have you had a chance to decipher any of the computer discs transferred from the factory?" President Arcola asked.

"Just bits and pieces. It takes a while to translate some of the information because of the alphabets and codes."

Mr. Kenny leaned over to study some of the writings on the copies of the reports from the CIC and the soldiers that were sent into the factory. "I think I can give you a few of the names of the cities. Just give me a minute." He said, looking at the information with the Defense Secretary.

"Excuse me." President Arcola said, reaching out to stop one of the technicians, and took a deep breath as she read his identification badge. "Frank, that was my son's name." She cleared her throat. "Frank. If we call the Emam's cellular phone number, can we keep the line open only to us?" The President asked.

"No. But we can listen in on any calls from that phone everytime it's used. We can also jam the signal. But then they'd only just get another phone." Frank said, in a hurry to get back to monitoring the massive amount of phone calls going in and coming out of Iran.

President Arcola paced back and forth from the table with the satellite photographs on the table where the technicians scribbled notes, as they eavesdropped on the phone calls in Iran. General Millings set down the reciever from his phone, stood up and talked above the commotion of the room. "Madame President. The Senate has just announced you have more than the necessary two-thirds vote. If you decide to send troops into Iran."

Most of the young technicians paused, now quietly setting down their telephones to the sounds beeping from recorders of the computers printing out reports.

"Well, Doug." President Arcola said, placing her hand on the Defense Secretary's shoulder. "Part of your job is to advise me about giving orders of going to war. Where do you think those chemical weapons are being moved to?"

"CIC spotted jets heading toward Iran from Russia. I say we go in and finish this job right now." Doug replied.

"Damnit, Doug. What are we getting ourselves into?" The President gazed at the blurry video screens and looked at Frank working through the mayhem of technicians, dropping piles of deciphered information on the desk in front of him. General Stanton overheard the President's conversation and stepped closer. "The decision is yours, Madame President. We'll all back you up on this one."

"This could be a mistake. Especially if we hit that factory. Then we will be held responsible for starting a World War." Professor Berger said, leaning in to shed his words of despair.

"Frank. I'm going to need your help." President Arcola said, leaning on the table to make certain she could speak clearly through the noise and confusion of the war-room.

Mr. Kenny, Mr. Rawlings, Benny and the generals also huddled closer to listen in. Some of the technicians passed by to listen, trying to ease their worries about starting a war. Frank turned and waved them away. Defense Secretary Doug Rawlings nodded 'affirmative', as the young technician quickly displayed a program previous Presidents had designed for a biological and chemical weapons disaster. General Millings sighed and gave a troublesome look to General Stanton. Benny jotted down the words President Arcola wanted Mr. Kenny to read, asking to make certain he knew exactly what she had in mind.

The huddle ended and the lady President stood, gazing at the young technicians. "Ladies and gentlemen!" She called out. The room slowly quieted down to only the sounds of the computer printers and mixed conversations, in several foriegn languages. Her dark blue eyes focused on the innocent faces of the technicians, all of them now aware thousands of American soldiers and allied forces would soon go into battle and could be sent to their deaths, if the decisions in this room were the wrong ones. "I know all of you heard the announcement, that the Senate has given me the approval to send our troops into Iran, with the possiblity we might become engaged in a war. That's not what we are trying to do here. From the evidence and reports we have been receiving from several regions in Iran, a handful of countries have begun invading Iran's airspace. At this point, we do not know if those countries pose a threat. At this point, we do not know if those countries intentions are of a hostile nature. All we know is the biological and chemical weapons from that factory are lethal, and they have killed thousands of the people of Iran and they have killed hundreds of men, women and children in Kuwait and Saudi Arabia. Over the next few hours, the events that will unfold are going to require your keenest attention. It's going to be a big gamble. Please be ready for things to change minute by minute. Here we go. General Tyler, get Bernie to start the Joint Strike Fighters into Iran. Frank, contact General Sala. Mr. Kenny, you know what to say."

The young technician dialed in the cellular phone number while a female CIA agent monitored a computer to compare and identify the voices of General Sala and the Ayatollah. Mr. Kenny sipped his water to wet his lips and took a quick breath, adjusting his headset and phone intercomm. A voice on the other line answered 'hello' in Farsi.

Mr. Kenny replied a phrase in Farsi; his voice remarkably clear, requesting to speak with the Ayatollah. General Sala seemed hesitant, but still complied. The female CIA agent confirmed that it was the general by nodding her head. The Ayatollah answered 'hello'.

President Arcola spoke into the video-conference monitors for the technicians and CIC to hear on the Nimitz.

"Ayatollah Khaemeni. This is the President of the United States. I have ordered an air strike into your country to destroy that chemical weapons factory. I will not tolerate your lies any further. I hope you understand that once the factory is destroyed, the affects of those chemicals on your people will be a hundred times more deadly."

Mr. Kenny listened closely to a group of voices in the background. "I think you got to them. It sounds like an argument. The Ayatollah doesn't understand how we contacted them." Mr. Kenny said with a hopeful smile on his face.

"We know where you are in Tehran. We know that you had the ability to talk with us. Now the time has passed. In eleven minutes, I will give orders to bomb the hell out of that factory and end this once and for all. And Iran will be held responsible in the World Court for dozens of violations under the guidelines of the Chemical Weapons Convention." Mr. Kenny interrupted President Arcola. "General Sala is telling the Ayatollah the United States will not get away with this criminal act. That right now, the world is listening to your words and the world will finally see how evil America is. And they will pay for allowing a woman to be disobedient and out of control."

President Arcola folded her arms across her chest, the welling of anger building up in her eyes. Still her grin of confidence showed that she was in control of this situation. She understood the deceptive representatives of Iran.

"We know all about your plot to trade biological and chemical weapons for nuclear weapons and jets from China and Russia. The world will decide from the evidence from the factory whether or not you and the Mullahs set that bomb off, intentionally killing your own people to gain world sympathy, to try to have sanctions lowered against your country. So please do not even think about trying your secret police tactics against my country and my administration. The next sounds you will hear are the sounds of American and Allied jets dropping bombs and destroying those tanks that have been putting on a show, while your terrorist customers use this incident to endanger half the world."

The voice of General Sala was cold and blatant with a hoarse, uncertain laugh. Mr. Kenny continuted to translate. "This is what happens when women take charge. This is only a desperate lie. You have gone mad and your country will pay."

"No, general! This is what happens when you treat people like shit and they have the ability to defend themselves! Prepare to get your ass kicked." The President leaned forward and spoke into the monitor linked to the Nimitz. "Admiral. This is the President. I'm ordering you to drop those bombs."

"Yes, Madame President." The voice replied from the CIC of the Nimitz in the Persian Gulf, through the monitors in the war room.

The technicians quieted down and listened nervously to the communications from the jet bombers; their young minds scrambling to understand their places in the beginning stages of a possible war. Their eyes were fixed on the movement of the United States and the Allied Forces jets being monitored on the large video screen in the Pentagon; swarming onto their targets in Iran.

The Iranian military leaders questioned the booming noises on the horizon, outside of Tehran. Then there was the unmistakable high-pitch whistling of the Wild Weasels, as the BAT 120's ripped apart the T-55 tanks and the radar tower on the outskirts of Tajrish. The phone communications were broken. The cellphone to the Emam went dead.

THIRTY-SIX

T HE SUN ROSE in the cool December sky, giving the pilots a clear, crisp view of the beautiful blue Qezel Owzan river, stretching her way through the snowcapped mountains and scattered woods of the Zanjan territories. The clouds sprinkled snow squalls in splendid patterns against the horizon; the snow crystals reflected rainbows with blue sky above.

"Okay guys. No hot-dogging. This ain't no Pave Penny. Keep your eyes to the skies, if you wanta be old and wise." The pilot of the F-117B joked as the radio clicked on. The pilot manuvered lower, escorting the three JSFs, sweeping downward towards the valley near the Elburz Mountains.

"That's a big ten-four there, Sweet Pea. You keep an eye on the Old Cancer Man and his sidekicks. I know a lot of you rookies are havin' tummy aches over this whole deal, but follow my lead. We're coming up on Karaj and we've got twenty-plus tanks and anti-aircraft cannons targeted on our radar. And they are hot and nasty." The Cancer Man said waving out to the other two JSFs as the fighter planes rolled to their right sides, plowing down toward the outskirts of Tehran.

The lead JSF decreased it's speed to 405nm and leveled off with his team to both flanks. Scud missile launchers and tanks slowly rolled up the highway to meet with a train hauling flatbed cars and hundreds of fifty-five gallon drums. The computer screen beeped, asking the question a second time: DO YOU WANT TO RELEASE MUNITIONS. YES. NO.

There was a loud click and then a whistle. Another tactical screen appeared alongside the console. The bombs were released, with the pilots keen eye focusing his computer radar on the railroad tracks and bridge a mile to the north. The on-board cameras of the F-117B recorded the kills of the Smart bombs, while CIC and the Pentagon watched in on the video. Within half a second, the tanks and missile launchers were barraged by the KMU's smacking and scattering hundreds of bomblets, raking the quarter mile line of weapons that tried to desperately fire at targets they could not find.

The Cancer Man followed a main highway with his escorts at 990 km, dropping the payload into a massive eruption of flames and projectiles, igniting bunkers, destroying a runway tarmac before the Russian soldiers could lauch their jets. The JSFs screeched southward as the jet pilots radioed to CIC.

"The paveways have been delivered. I'm pulling up my new set of targets." The Cancer Man said, leveling off his speed, eight thousand feet above the deserts of Iran, following his lead team to assist near Esfahan.

"Negative for now, Cancer Man. Rocky's Vampires are at the door. It's a hot zone. So come on home. Big Momma's going to assist those Fencers."

"Assist? Excuse me, Homeplate? Did you say assist?" The Cancer Man grunted watching his radar adjust graphs on his naviagational computers while the jets rocketed over Lake Namak.

A truck transport with tanks and Howitzers in jeeps rolled underneath the cover of helicopters heading south from Khomeynishahr. The relentlessly barren Iranian terrain was cold and lifeless, except for the occasional hopeful tribe of shepherds, who shaded their eyes and pointed up at the horsemen riding down from the heavens, fulfilling the revelations, descending upon Qomsheh.

The sleek, black monsters, hugged their blades less than a hundred feet from the compacted silt, whirling sand and dust into small tornadoes; their voices chanting in rhythm, as the Hell made its way across the desert. Salty marshes at the bases of foothills were invaded, scattering stray birds, panicking them out into the mid-morning.

The moment had arrived. The deliverence of God's messengers onto Esfahan was now. Eight Comanches divided outward, beginning their attack pattern, two tight to the center of the road, the remainig choppers randomly prepared to attack from the flanks; their radar graphics blinked with the heart of the factory set and locked in, as the pilots readied their weapons. Two pairs of choppers divided up in their eerie silence, hoovering above the bluffs then down with hummingbird grace, sorting through the hard-edged shapes with infrared scanners.

Signatures appeared digitally detailing out suspicious images along the hills of the highway; the maps updated by the Central Intelligence Command post aboard the Nimitz. The orders were confirmed and delivered within seconds. The gorgeous black creatures jettisoned across the desert launching their Hellfire missiles and then vanished quickly down the ravine. Two more choppers dodged and swerved, positioning themselves between the factory and the tanks. They caught the regiment off guard with their barrels turned away, not prepared for the Comanche assault. The soldiers were sent running and diving into ditches; the stingers pounding into the tanks and cannons, ripping the armory into a pile of shredded, blazing scrap. Four more Comanches split up; two headed north with the other two heading south. There was no chance for resistance as the missiles and rockets from the helicopters continued to mutilate the tanks and trucks along the stretch of highway for miles.

An Apache lowered itself to the roof of the factory, her bay door already swung open to greet Joey as he staggered into the waiting arms of one of the sailors. He shoved the transmitter and duffle bag with the evidence across the floor and collapsed down onto his side. With his mind dizzy and his eyes swollen, he held his curled body tight to the safety strap, yelling for the pilot to go. The chopper quickly lifted up into the sky. He lay there looking down at the bodies of Dewey, Trench, Fielding and his brother, Jason, spread out on the rooftop and he began to cry.

"Rocky, we've got a problem! MIGs from the north!" Loverboy called out, as the alarms on the Comanches sounded.

The helicopters scattered southwest in all directions, spreading out to lead the jets away from the Apache disappearing over the horizon to the south. Heat-seeking missiles were fired at one of the helicopters as it dove behind a berm with the missiles slamming and exploding into the sandstone. Two comanches aided their partner, climbing vertically at twenty feet a second. Their

AIM-92's were launched, driving the MIG straight up, twisting and veering into the sun. One stinger tore out the wing. The second stinger ripped open the cockpit spreading wildfire and debris into the Iranian skies.

"Oh shit! We got the bastard!" Tornado said with a slap on the back from his co-pilot. Alarms sounded again in the cockpits of the Comanches, three sets of aircraft appeared on the radar displays. The MIGs raced down at the Comanches while another set of Q-511s began strafing the choppers with 23mm cannon fire, chasing them further away from the factory into the open desert.

"He's baiting you, Tubby! Hug those hills!" Rocky yelled out, as he watched his partner drawing fire away from the remaining squadron, goose-leading the Chinese fighters miles to the south.

"CIC! We could use a hand!" Wild Bill called out, pulling the cockpit's sidearm sticks, clutching the ground, trying to shake the MIG fighter jet off of his tail.

"Help's on it's way, Rocky. You keep those Vampires moving and watch those guns on those highways to your east. Those MIGs are trying to drive you into a trap." CIC said trying to monitor all the confusing radio calls from the pilots and the Pentagon.

"I've got gunfire down below! Those MIGs are flanking our route! We can't go over those guns!" Loverboy called out, slowing his speed as the cliffs of Eqlid became a better obstacle for the enemy jets. The MIG launched a sidewinder missle, grinding and shattering the sandstone hills, Loverboy throttled upward, away from the ground, drawing his helicopter out in the open. A white light reflected from the afternoon blue sky, bearing down from the heavens, setting off the alarms in the cockpits of the MIGs.

"Oh, yes! Big Momma, thank you!" Loverboy cheered along with CIC and the other Comanche pilots, as the JSFs swarmed down out of nowhere. The MIGs swept sideways, cartwheeling backwards, attempting to evade the triangular fighters streaking out of the sky. The Nanchangs slowed and showed signs they cowarded out, abandoning the Iranian MIGs; retreating from the 20mm gunfire of the American jets, rocketing to the east.

"Hey, fellas. We've got one of those MIGs coming up our tailpipes. He seems kinda desperate. Can you take care of business and I'll buy you a couple of beers later when this is over?"

"I'm right here, Tornado. The Hustler has him locked on radar." The JSF pilot calmly replied, turning his head in the canopy and glanced at the jet pursuing the Comanche helicopter. The MIG pilot panicked, twisting his head frantically with the JSF bearing down with cannon fire only a thousand feet away, shredding the tail and fuselage of the old Russian jet, causing the pilot to eject.

"My, my. I always hate to have to do that to a fine, outstanding young pilot." The Hustler said over the radio, looking out of his cockpit at the MIG pilot, clutching the parachute, with the busted MIG spiraling down, crashing into flames against the slope of a hollow. The second MIG circled in revengeful chase, driving into the trail of after-burner from the JSF. The second JSF rolled out into the east with Thor turning his head quick inside the canopy as he checked his FBW system, locking his target in on the radar. The AIM-7 slid from its mounting under the belly of his jet, spitting its flaming orange heat trail, twisting as it sailed out into the sky. The MIG was struck in the right wing, just as it turned to dive. Shards of burning metal blistered into the sky, while the ball of exploding fuel ignited across the troposphere. Cancer Man watched the remaining MIG race away to the north as fast as it could.

"We're letting this one go, Big Momma. He's running scared." Thor said looking around for more enemy jet fighters. Pecos circled his jet around, flying into formation with the Cancer Man.

"CIC. We're heading in to the death dot to deliver those Christmas gifts. How's the weather look?" The veteran pilot asked in his low, Kentucky droll.

"The winds are calm to five miles an hour from the southwest. The neighbors are heading out on the highways to the north. You are to stand by for the word from the President and the Pentagon. Hold on for that CCIP."

The JSFs leveled out slowing to 400nm over the target area, studying their HUD's and Doppler's to make certain of their waypoints.

"Now, Pecos. I know you're a little green at this, but, in ten years you'll be teachin' the pups to fly too." Cancer Man glanced over at the rookie jet fighter, cautiously checking and re-checking his navigational equipment.

"Now. The first pass is going to be the hardest. Especially if we just piss them off. And then the second pass will be a piece-a-cake. So are you ready?"

"Yes, sir. This is why they pay us the big bucks. Locking on targets." Pecos said, breathing heavy from the tension and excitement. The JSFs veered down, fifty miles from the hills of the factory. Cancer Man scanned his radar, while CIC began displaying multiple targets from the satellite reconnaissance data for the locations where the landmines were set.

"We're ready, Madame President." Cancer Man said in a gentleman's tone. The Cancer Man had to fly low, only a few hundred feet off the ground. He watched the two wounded tanks, their turrets cracked with smoldering hulls, clanking slowly away, distancing themselves as far away from the factory as fast as they could.

"Captain Overbee, this is the President of the United States. It's time to make our messege loud and clear." President Arcola said, as the small blips showed the Joint Strike Fighters on the Pentagon radar.

The CBU-55 was dropped. The canisters slapped and rolled across the road, kicking and blasting the asphalt at the entrance to the factory, setting off the landmines. The highway ignited spraying earth and concrete up into a thunderous ball of fire. Pecos was a thousand feet above the Cancer Man. He studied the guided missile co-ordinates, as the computer calculated the aircraft's speed, the velocity vector, weapon release parameters, the crosswinds at the surface and the range. The target was locked on and confirmed. The Cancer Man flew up alongside his partner. Pecos seemed hesitant to drop the bomb, twitching in the cockpit, waiting to receive his orders.

"Hey Pecos." Cancer Man started in his usual, fatherly manner, both jet fighters leveling off at five thousand feet. "You got any kids back in the states?" Pecos had to think about the question, still not relaxed about his mission.

"Actually. My wife and I are expecting in June." Pecos replied and glanced at his inertial navigation systems after the first-pass over the factory. The Doppler of the JSF rolled off the new wind speeds near ground level and the wind directions. Solutions were updated and plotted into his jets computer from CIC, adjusting his next pass from low to medium altitude. Both pilots gave a sigh of relief.

"That must mean the SAMs are not gonna bug us. That's a good thing, Pecos. About you and your wife. I've got two kids of my own. Two girls, fifteen and sixteen. My sixteen year old just got her driving permit. It scares the hell-out-a-me just thinking about it."

"You're scared of her driving? Aren't your daughters more afraid of you being a fighter pilot?" Pecos chuckled.

"Nah. Not my daughters. But my wife is. But, I retire to a desk job in a year anyhow. You know, I had a friend that retired two years ago from the Air Force. He never got shotdown or hurt through his whole twenty years in the service. He got killed in a car accident just last May by a bunch of teenagers driving too fast. They lost control of their car, crossed the double lines and hit him head on. It kinda makes you wonder."

A small, white light flashed and the computers on the JSFs ran coordinates for the Cancer Man and Pecos. The pilots activated their bombs and checked their fuel gauges. Pecos backed down behind the Cancer Man, both confirming their altitudes at thirty-five hundred feet. Four more JSFs appeared on radar, flying parallel to the jets; keeping a watch, ready to assist.

"We're ready to go, Madame President." The Cancer Man said softly into the headset of his helmet. His cameras began transferring video of the skies above the Esfahan Providence. The bay doors were opened and the bombs were lowered as the jets veered on their final pass toward the factory.

President Arcola spoke into the monitors, warning General Sala and the Ayatollah. Most of the voices of the war-room hushed; the young technicians scrambled through their notes. Most of Iran's surface-to-air missles had been destroyed. No other invading jets were in the vicinity. The surface winds in the desert halted to a hauntingly, unusual dead calm, in the warm December afternoon. General Tyler and General Stanton's eyes were fixed. The agents and the Pentagon technicians tried to make out the televisual displays of the target from the American jets. Mr. Kenny listened intently to the arguing between the Iranian Ambassador and General Sala; as well as other voices from their location. Benny took a quick drink of water and leaned to look over the shoulder of a female technician as she computed and cleared deceptive jamming, transferring her screens to CIC and the JSFs.

"Delivery. Please check and reconfirm my information." The technician said, whispering into her headset. Pecos glanced over his RWR's, comparing his avionics to the satellite updates from the Pentagon.

"Thank you for helping clean up the paint. I've got the target locked in." The Cancer Man and Pecos re-checked their fuel; the volumes entered on the screens at CIC and the Pentagon. General Millings nodded 'yes' to the president.

"I gave you every possible chance to resolve this problem, General Sala. Your ignorance is a plague upon your people." Mr. Kenny listened, barely breathing as he translated.

"Nothing has changed with your ways. This has proved your Satan ways."

"In two minutes I will push the button that will destroy that chemical factory. We already have the remaining locations of your other biological weapons facilities." The head of the Mullah's interrupted, his voice thick with anger; not the earlier, garrulous manipulator from the previous meetings.

"We have confirmation that your American jets and helicopters have killed almost eighty of our soldiers! You will be held responsible for these atrocities!"

"I am ready to take responsibility for any and all of my actions, Ayatollah. Bernie." President Arcola said firm and cold, staring at the video monitors on the JSFs.

"The order is now. Release those bombs."

"You are insane! You are a crazy woman with your power! Millions of people will die from those chemicals and it is your fault! You will pay! The World Court will have you executed! You will all burn in hell for . . ."

"I'm not very concerned with hell right now, your excellency. When you sleep with your conscience tonight, keep in mind. My administration will vow, that this incident never happened. I am impressed as to how you convinced so many of your people to simply lie down on the ground to let our satellites have a half million plus body count. So you could gain sympathy from other countries to lift their sanctions. Just remember. I'll be watching you."

President Arcola shut off the monitors and disconnected the telephone transmission with the leaders of Iran. General Tyler pointed out that the CCIP/IP was correct and the HUD matched, the target was ready and the drop was dead-on. The huge video conference screens lit-up, displaying the bomb drop in Iran; the same screens that were to be used to discuss and change this type of behavior, for the New World Order.

The Cancer Man heard the click and said a silent prayer, as his bombs were released from their cradles. The white SLAMs payloads turned with their nonchalant noses down, their fins slightly adjusting and seeking their target, skimming down through the brisk clear skies. A group of soldiers pointed and yelled on top of the mountain ridge, twenty miles to the north of the factory.

The white flash was first. Burning the late afternoon sky, sucking the winds from the desert with the wrath of God. Rolling the sand and dust. The bodies of the dead shot up from the rooftop and the desert floor. The burning carcasses of tanks were whipped and tossed like little toys, as the flames and chemicals began to flare up and burn into a mushroom cloud.

The second jet delivered the next set of bombs. Their small, black shells raced down into the head of the chemical cloud, above the sands of the vaporized factory, the debris still burned as the explosions began. Hundreds of small, bright flashes ignited inside the mushroom cloud, each desperately burning away at the airborne sarin and anthrax gases. The sun had now become black. The pale deliverers flew back into heaven while the earthquake still rumbled below, shoving heat and dust for several miles into the ghost town of Esfahan.

Doves hid in the darkness of the dormers and gables, too terrified to move. Their small feathers puffed up in bunches, trembling with their eyes closed tight. Lightning flashed followed by the thunder vibrating the Mosques and the streets of the marketplace. Then the rain began to fall, dropping a putrid, gray dust, carpeting the Iranian desert floor.

An old shepherd paused for a moment, feeling the mountain shake beneath his feet. The sound of the distant thunder slowly quieted into a calm winter breeze. He covered his eyes from the beams of fading sunset, mumbling and chanting a soothing hymm, carefully placing the stones on the graves of his wife and children.

EPILOGUE

PRESIDENT MARIE ARCOLA ran her fingers on top of the cottonball beard on Santa Claus; the one Frankie and Shelley glued on the Christmas card they made for her in December. She slowly rocked side to side in the swivel chair behind her desk in the Oval Office. She looked out the window at a little gray rabbit, sitting up, as it cautiously wiggled it's nose and whiskers with big eyes and ears, flinching at the slightest sound. With a few hops, it was in the flower bed chewing away at the tulip tops, always watching with those big, brown eyes. The President took a drink of warm cocoa and felt the warmth from the beams of sunshine, glowing in through the window, from over the White House lawns. The morning rain clouds began to drift away. Benny thoughtfully knocked on the door and stepped in with an armful of envelopes and files.

Marie slowly rubbed her stomach and sang a little song, as she leaned back behind the desk, between the President's Flag and the Flag of the United States of America. "This old man, he had six. He played knick-knack on some sticks. With a knick-knack paddywhack, give a dog a bone. This old man came rolling home. This old man, he had seven . . . Oh. Good morning Benny. Are those the governors reports in regards to the riots?" President Arcola asked with a sniffle. Benny gave her a curious look.

"Yes. It seems Jackson, New Orleans, Detroit and Los Angeles have reported most of the arrest for fires and looting. They're probably going to all need financial assistance."

"How about the reports from Iran?"

"Well. All of a sudden, Iran has stopped blaming the United States for the destruction of the biological and chemical weapons factory near Esafahan. Radio and television from the Middle East, report tanks and captured soldiers from a rogue terrorist group out of Afghanistan were found near the factory. Even the Resalat isn't talking much. The Iranian mullahs have ordered the military to gather any remains of the factory to use as evidence in World Court. So far, it's just a lot of talk. There is still some fighting going on at the Iraq-Iran border." Benny turned the page of the Tehran Times and began reading another article.

"Here's a good lie for you. 'United States Purposely Bombs Textile Facilities in Iran'. The article goes on and says the new American President is a 'devil of Satan' and a 'witch . . . ordering the murders of innocent women and children'."

"That's good. Now I know they like me." President Arcola smiled and took a drink of orange juice. Benny set the files on the Presidents desk and noticed the construction paper Christmas cards from her children; the cards they made in school for her before they were killed.

"Your face is a little flush. Are you going to be okay with all those reporters?"

"Yes. I'll be fine. The morning sickness finally stopped." President Arcola smiled with tired blue eyes, slowly rubbing her belly.

"How's Sergeant Adair?" She asked, not really wanting to know.

Benny hung his head and shuffled the files, straightening each page. "He finally died in his sleep, during the night. The doctors on the aircraft carrier tried everything to save him. But all that quick surgery and those open wounds. They took him off of morphine after a week and switched him to Dilaudid for the pain. And then, after a few hours, he just stopped breathing." He set an open file in the middle of her desk. "This is all the information about Joey and his brother, Jason. Both their parents are deceased. It's just a matter of his funeral arrangements."

"For Joey. Definitely Arlington Cemetary." President Arcola replied.

"What about the other soldiers? If their bodies are ever recovered? They did help us get the evidence we needed from the factory."

"Yes. Yes, they did. But Joey's report to CIC said he dismantled a bomb those soldiers had set to explode in the factory. If that would have happened, where would we be now?" President Arcola stood up slowly, rubbing the small of her back.

"I'll have to think about that one. Just write me a note for next weeks agenda." She looked at her watch and took a deep breath, stretching her neck and her arms.

"You seem kinda sad." Benny said.

"It's so odd, that's all." She said.

"Odd?" Benny asked.

"Yes. That in the middle of all this killing. All these people dying. I'm going to bring a new life into this world. It's the best thing that could happen to me in my life right now." President Arcola stared at the small Christmas tree, in the corner on the floor with the presents for Frankie, Shelley and her husband.

"Well. We've got to get ready to meet the press." She took the last two bites of her onion bagel and picked up her notes. She noticed Benny giving her a quirky smile.

"What? Do my clothes look to tight?"

"No, it's not that. I just wondered if you had a name picked out for your baby." Benny said.

"Yes, I do. His name is going to be David."

Benny bowed his head, knowing that was the name of her late husband. "David? How do you know it's going to be a boy?"

"Believe me, Benny. I know what a boy feels like."

President Arcola picked up the the home-made Christmas cards again and tried to remember the big smiles from her excited daughter and son when they ran into the house to give her the Christmas cards they made in school. Marie whispered the words with glassy eyes. 'Merry Christmas, mommy. Love hugs and kisses. Shelley and Frankie.' She ran her fingers over the little bits of sparkling glitter, used as garland wrapped around to the top of the green pine tree. At the top a big yellow star was glued. A pair of stick figured reindeer stood waiting with a sleigh filled with multi-colored gifts; one of the reindeer had a bright red nose. President Arcola folded the card and placed it back into an envelope with her husband's life insurance policy. A knock at the door startled her from her daydream.

"Madame President. The reporters have just arrived in the East Room." Jeri said, as she peeked her head into the Oval office.

"Oh, and don't forget. You changed your doctors appointment to one p.m. tomorrow for your ultrasound." The secretary said with a giggle.

Benny held out his arm to greet the lady President, waving his hand, as he genuflected. "Madame President. I am here to serve you. Your kingdom awaits you." A delightful smile forced a squealed laugh from the President , as she gracefully stepped forward across the Coat of Arms, woven into the carpet in front of her desk, where her babies once played with their toys.

"Benjamin. It's really happening." President Arcola sighed. She stood in the middle of the Oval Office and turned, to take in the atmosphere; remembering all the ghosts and memories still in the room.

The White House guards tipped their heads up, standing at attention as she walked toward the East Room. Senator Trevor Thomas mingled by the side door to the stage, near where the podium stood and where the President was to speak for her press conference. The divorced multi-millionaire gleefully smiled, petting his new, two thousand dollar, custom, black, silk Hugo Boss suit. He brushed out the sleeves and checked his tie for the tenth time, in case the reporters wanted to ask him any questions. The secret service agents tightened-up, as the President and her advisor walked up.

"Hello, senator." President Arcola said musically with a smile, catching him in the middle of his ritual of self-lovemaking.

"Yes. Hello, Marie. I'm looking forward to hearing your upcoming news conferences. I was really surprised to see you on yesterdays Meet the Press. I'm even more surprised about the candidate you chose for Vice-President. A blackman for Vice-President." The senator said as he held her hand just a little bit longer to intimidate her with their handshake.

"I didn't choose Senator Williams because he was an Afro-American. I chose him because of his outstanding record and his contributions to the State of Alabama."

"You know the offer I made still stands. I think you'd make a great Vice-President." The senator said.

Benny covered his mouth and tried not to be rude by laughing. "Have a good evening, Madame President. I'll call you with those updates on Cuba." Benny said with a quick hug for the President. "Good night, Benny." The President said with a slight touch to her best friend's hand before he turned to walk away. Senator Thomas stood there with his boyish grin and his dark, wolf eyes.

"I find it very funny you could even think I could be Vice-President. As you know the wheels are already turning and some-day I'll even invite you to my White House for dinner." President Arcola smiled and took a deep breath, glancing down at the notes she was just handed by one of her speech writers. A secret service agent pulled the door open for her while she fidgeted with her ebony blazer, listening to the mumbling of the reporters and the Speaker of the House's voice over the intercomm. Trevor stared at the beautiful President and shook his head at his own thoughts. "By the way," he said. "You handled the Iranian situation quite well. It took alot of guts for you to keep it all together. Oh. And Happy New Year." He stopped for a second with his hands in his pockets, always with that dangerously innocent, schoolboy stare.

"Trevor." She called out, trying to cool her feelings and trying not to sound so friendly, telling herself it was only a fleeting moment of loneliness. "Thank you. Happy New Year." She paused as the senator playfully, moseyed down the corridor.

The lights illuminated warm and blinding, she rubbed her belly with one hand and set her speech cards down on the po-dium with the other. The clattering and mumbling of the report-ers, quieted to a hush. She lifted her head up and looked into the cameras with her wonderful smile and dark blue eyes.

"Ladies and gentlemen." President Arcola began; clearing her throat and turning away from the teleprompter and the speech cards. "As all of you know. The situation in Iran is under control and the ambassador of Iran has begun an investigation of the factory. We still haven't received a formal apology for this misun-derstanding in regards to the accident at the chemical weapons factory near Esfahan.

Because the chemicals in the factory may have caused the deaths of civilians in neighboring countries, such as Kuwait and Saudi Arabia, Iran will comply with the international guidelines of the CWC and Chemicals Weapons Treaty Inspection Team. Iran's mil-itary and government is already working with Pentagon officials to release any necessary evidence or information, to reassure neighboring countries in the Middle East, precautions have been taken to make certain an incident such as this will not happen again. As all of you know, the FBI has confirmed we do have the terrorists who exploded the bomb that killed President George Johnson . . . "President Arcola stopped to regain her composure." . . . airport personnel, secret service agents and my family."

In the back of the room, the tall wooden doors opened and Senator Trevor Thomas leaned himself up against the wall, waiting to catch her eyes, always working his devilish ways, provoking and weakening his opponents . He crossed his arms, and took a romantic interest in the feel of the material of his new suit, imagining what it will be like, having to stand up there and answer these questions. President Arcola noticed him across the room, behind the CNN, ABC and UPN cameras, causing her to cover her smile.

"I know our country is facing a great deal of changes. I have received the updated reports from ten of America's largest cities, regarding the recent rioting. My administration has begun meetings with the governors of each state in an attempt to understand how these riots began. As you all know, we are very concerned with the situation in Cuba. I will be meeting later with one of the spokesmen for Cuba. I will now try to answer your questions as briefly as possible. Yes, Rudy? "President Arcola responded, pointing to one of the reporters, who had called and raised his pen in the air.

"Madame President. With all the closed meetings with the Senate and the rumors of secret voting, how close was the United States to going to war with Iran?" The husky, balding man questioned.

"Not close enough to be a concern. Right now, I have alerted our U.S. troops to only take humanitarian measures to help with aid and supplies for the people of Iran. My administration and the Chiefs of Staff hope this accident from several weeks ago, will convince the Iranian military to stop manufacturing biological and chemical weapons. Yes, Molly?" The President pointed to a woman reporter in the middle row.

"You released a statement to the press yesterday, stating the FBI had gathered evidence and is questioning a group of American soldiers about the bomb that killed President Johnson. Do the soldiers have any link to Iranian or Middle Eastern terrorist organizations?"

President Arcola leaned her elbows on the podium, knowing eventually she had to answer these questions.

"The FBI is still in the process of their investigation of the suspects. I am sad to say these individuals are Americans, they are reported missing and they had a hatred toward our President and our country. The evidence, so far, shows they acted alone and were not part of any Iranian, Middle Eastern or any other terrorist organization."

A man half-stood, raising his hand to be seen. President Arcola pointed to him, nodding her head with a 'yes'.

"Madame President, will the individuals you speak of get a fair trial and if found guilty will they receive the death penalty?" The British reporter asked.

"These individuals will be tried and punished by their peers. The punishment for treason warrants the death penalty. And my adminstration will be passing a new law stating any person or persons, involved with manufacturing, transporting, aiding or setting off a bomb relating to any type of terrorist act, which harms or kills any individual, in this country or abroad, against any American citizen, will automatically receive the death penalty. Detonating bombs to randomly or intentionally harm or kill innocent people is the most disgusting form of cowardice. And those people who participate in these terrorist antics are dishonorable, filth and should be exempt from the human race."

The reporters whispered and shuffled in their seats, surprised with the amount of strength in the tone of the President's voice. Some of them lightly applauded.

"Madame President. Is the recent resignation of one of the senators from California linked to the recent reports the Chinese black markets have been selling sensitive military equipment to foreign countries and that Bin Lodin might be a major financier?" The woman reporter asked.

President Arcola smiled and flipped her speech cards over. "So far, a lot of rumors are floating around the media in regards to the senator from California's sudden resignation. An investigation is still going on to find out if the Long Beach Area has allowed Chinese sources an opportunity to smuggle U.S. military parts and equipment. Yes?" She said, pointing to another reporter.

"How will the Arcola Administration differ from the Johnson Administration? And previous administrations?"

"I can't lie to you. I like being in this position to enforce America's Constitutional Rights. But I also realize what I do, as your President, with the knowledge I have as an ex-Congresswoman, an ex-attorney and as a woman, must benefit and protect the rights of all Americans. And that one of the ways to preserve the rights of all of us, is for government to abide by the Bill of Rights and to stop trying to take away Americans rights under the Constitution. I believe the recent riots in this country are a signal that the pressure of unemployment, racism and distrust in this country, is at a peak. My administration will gain the trust of the people, by giving the people more power over their own lives, and by reducing governmet control. One more question."

"With all the pain and suffering, with the loss of your family, and the death of President Johnson, and now, you being an expectant mother, have you thought about your next steps and where your career will go from here?"

"Yes, I have. I plan on running in this year's Presidential Election."

The East Room became mayhem, as reporters clicked off pictures of President Marie Arcola. Some reporters rushed from their chairs out into the lobby to call their editors and news stations. The White House Guards and Secret Service Agents held out their arms, in a nervous reaction. Many of the reporters stood and applauded the lady President. Her eyes watery, because she knew in her heart the overwhelming and often thankless responsibility she was about to bring upon herself. But she felt a calling in her soul and a need to follow this road on her journey. She wondered why her husband David and her children, Francis and Shelley, were taken away from her. She thought it would make her weak and revengeful. She thought it would distort her and destroy every part of her being. But through the darkness and the storm, often comes the light, and eventually the answer. Even Senator Trevor Thomas stood at the back of the room; clapping his hands with a smile. He shook his head in disbelief, whispering to himself, "Oh, boy. Here we go."